The Secret to a Southern Wedding

SYNITHIA WILLIAMS

CANARY STREET PRESS

CANARY
STREET
PRESS™

Recycling programs
for this product may
not exist in your area.

ISBN-13: 978-1-335-43053-3

The Secret to a Southern Wedding
Copyright © 2023 by Synithia R. Williams

About Last Night
Copyright © 2023 by Synithia R. Williams

For questions and comments about the quality of this book, please contact us
at CustomerService@Harlequin.com.

Canary Street Press
22 Adelaide St. West, 41st Floor
Toronto, Ontario M5H 4E3, Canada
CanaryStPress.com

Printed in U.S.A.

CONTENTS

To mothers and daughters

The
Secret
to a
Southern
Wedding

one

Imani licked her lips and reached out, flexing her fingers open and closed in a "gimme" fashion toward her lunchtime savior. Loretta worked behind the counter in the hospital's busy lunch line. Her black hair was covered by a hairnet and laugh lines creased the dark brown skin around her nose and mouth.

Loretta shook her head and smiled, but Imani didn't care. She was starving and Loretta had exactly what she needed.

"I made sure to put one to the side for you today," Loretta said handing over the red-and-white-checkered food boat with a golden brown fried corn dog in the middle.

"I owe you big-time, Loretta." Imani grinned as she snagged the corn dog and placed it on her tray. "I just knew I was going to miss getting one."

"You're the only person I know who gets so excited when we have corn dogs for lunch," Loretta said. "Most of the doctors prefer the fancy stuff."

Imani shook her head. "Give me a corn dog and mustard any day over fancy. How's your daughter and the baby?"

Loretta's smile broadened, revealing one gold tooth. "They're doing great. I'm so glad I told her to come see you instead of that other doctor. Thanks again for fitting her into your schedule. I don't know if she would have made it without you."

Imani's cheeks warmed and so did her heart. "Of course, I'm going to fit her in. You always save the best corn dogs for me." They both laughed before Imani sobered. "Seriously, I'm glad they're okay. Tell her to call the office if she needs anything."

"Will do, Dr. Kemp," Loretta said with a bright, grateful smile.

The man next to Imani in line cleared his throat. Loretta threw him an annoyed look. Imani shrugged and waved a hand. "I'll see you tomorrow."

She moved on down the line and grabbed a handful of mustard packets and a bag of baked potato chips before scanning the crowded seating area for her lunch partner. She spotted Towanda Brown, a doctor from the hospital's orthopedic practice sitting in a corner near one of the windows.

Maneuvering through the filled tables, Imani kept her eyes down to avoid eye contact as she made her way through the maze of bodies, seats and chairs toward her friend. Still, she received several points and stares with whispered "yeah, that's her—the hospital's chosen one" along with a few waves from some of the less cynical doctors and nurses for her to sit with them at their table. She gave the people who caught her eye a polite nod before pointing toward Towanda.

She sat with her friend and sighed. "Sorry I'm late."

Towanda shrugged. Despite having not run track in over ten years, Towanda still had the tall, muscular figure that once had her on the fast track for the Olympics before an injury ended her career. Her sienna skin was as line-free as it had been when Imani first met her, and she wore her hair in braids that were pulled back in a ponytail at the base of her neck. She looked closer to thirty-three than her actual forty-three.

"It's so busy today, but I knew you'd make it for corn dog day." Her friend grinned and pointed to Imani's tray.

"Loretta never lets this day go by without saving me one," Imani said.

"That was before you helped her daughter. I'd be surprised if she doesn't make extra just to pack up and deliver to your office."

Imani chuckled while opening a package of mustard to put on the corn dog. "I would've helped her daughter despite her support of my corn dog addiction. She was seeing a doctor who ignored all her fears. I was just happy to let her know that her concerns were valid and that I wasn't going to gas her up with fancy talk."

"And that's why you're the hospital's doctor of the year," Towanda said pointing behind Imani.

Imani didn't look over her shoulder. She knew what was there. Her face was plastered all over the hospital right now on signs, cardboard cutouts and television screens. Was she proud of being named the hospital's doctor of the year? Kind of. She'd spent so much of her life trying to become an obstetrician patients could rely on and trust. Did that translate to being comfortable as the "face" of the hospital system for a year? Not one bit.

"Can we not talk about that right now?" Imani squirted mustard down the length of her corn dog.

"Why not? It's something to be proud of."

"And I am proud. I just don't want that to become all I am. Especially when we know the hospital administration's guilt about the last few doctors of the year may have had something to do with it." She raised a brow.

The last four years hadn't included a female doctor of the year at all and only two women were nominated. Ever since Guardian Heath merged with Mid-State Health to become one of Florida's largest health care systems, the struggle to diversify prior to the merger was lost as profits and popularity became a thing. When she learned of her nomination, Imani hadn't believed she'd had a chance of winning against a heart surgeon and oncologist.

"You won because you're the best and that's all we're going by," Towanda said.

Imani shrugged. "Fine, I'm the best. Now can we talk about something else?"

Talking about being the hospital's doctor of the year meant thinking about how the obstetrics unit now pushed her in front of every camera they could find to draw more clients to the practice. Imani, who'd previously been a liked and well-respected member of the practice, but never thrust forward as the only Black doctor for diversity points, was suddenly a double commodity. She didn't like that.

Imani took a bite of her lunch. The savory mixture of the mustard with the hot dog wrapped in cornmeal batter made her groan with pleasure. "This is soooo good."

Towanda's brows rose and she eyed Imani curiously. "Can we talk about how after watching you go in on that corn dog and moan like a porn star, I don't know why you haven't caught a man, yet?"

Imani tried to glare at her friend but could only cover her full mouth and suppress a laugh. She chewed and swallowed hard. "Corn dogs, unlike a lot of men, don't disappoint."

"Chile, please. Everything disappoints eventually."

"Corn dogs never disappoint." Imani took another bite.

"Even microwaved ones?" Towanda asked.

Imani scrunched her nose and shivered. "Touché. Thanks for reminding me nothing in life is perfect."

She'd once believed in perfection. That she'd had the best life ever. That reality had been shattered harshly and abruptly one fall afternoon.

Her cell phone vibrated in the pocket of her white lab coat. She pulled it out and smiled when she saw the text icon from her mom.

"Who is it?" Towanda asked.

"My mom. She only texts with town news or a funny video she found online."

Towanda grinned. "You still care about town news?"

Imani nodded and clicked on the text. "I mean, I don't live in Peachtree Cove anymore, but that doesn't mean I don't like hearing what's going on with all the judgmental people in town."

"The people couldn't be that bad."

Imani grunted and didn't answer. The same people who'd loved her parents together had been quick to talk about all their faults after her dad's girlfriend decided to put a deadly plan in place to separate Imani's parents for good. So, maybe it was petty, but Imani indulged in her mom's texts about the trials and tribulations of the people so eager to cast judgment on her family all those years ago.

Imani opened the text, preparing for the funny video or latest update, but frowned at what looked like an invitation instead.

"Everything alright?"

Imani zoomed in on the invitation and nearly dropped her phone. She had to read the words out loud to be sure her eyes weren't deceiving her. "You're invited to the wedding of Linda Kemp and Preston Dash. What the hell is this?"

Towanda leaned forward and tried to see Imani's cell. "Your mom's getting married?"

"No. She couldn't be. My mom isn't even dating."

At least, her mom never talked about dating. Her mom hadn't dated since the disaster that ended her last marriage. She hadn't been able to trust anyone since. Not that Imani blamed her. Almost getting killed by your husband's mistress tended to do that to a person.

"Who in the world is Preston Dash?" Imani muttered and why was her mom marrying him? In a month! This didn't make sense. It had to be a prank. She called her mom immediately. The phone went straight to voice mail.

Imani stared at her cell phone. "Seriously?"

"She didn't answer?"

"This has to be a joke," Imani said. The watch on her arm vibrated. "Damn." She pressed the button to stop the alarm reminding her that she needed to be back upstairs in the practice in time for her next patient appointment.

"You're probably right," Towanda said. "Your mom wouldn't get married without telling you, would she?" The question in Towanda's voice was the same question in Imani's heart.

"My mom wouldn't get married, period," Imani said. She shoved the rest of the corn dog into her mouth and jumped up. She pointed toward the exit.

Towanda nodded. "I know. Go ahead. We'll talk later. Let me know what your mom says."

With her mouth full, Imani nodded and hurried out of the cafeteria. She shoved the bag of chips into the pocket of her lab coat and chewed the rest of the food in her mouth after dumping her trash into the can. On the way to the elevator, she texted her mom back.

This is a joke, right?

She watched her phone and waited for her mother's response. There was nothing as she waited for the elevator. Nothing as she boarded with a group of people. Still nothing as she tried to avoid eye contact with the others as they slowly realized the face smiling back at them from the picture plastered on the elevator doors was her. In the background the throwback song "How Bizarre" by OMC, played from the speakers. Imani hummed along and watched her phone. The doors opened, thankfully, before everyone connected the dots between her and the life-size photo, and Imani quickly got off. Her phone finally buzzed as she approached the door to the practice.

No joke. Come home. We'll talk.

What kind of response was that? Her mom wouldn't answer her call, but she'd text back telling her to come home. She'd just talked to her mom a few days ago. She hadn't mentioned anything about getting married or even given a hint of there being a special person in her life. A few months ago, her mom mentioned Imani's cousin Halle said something about getting on a dating app for seniors, but Imani had immediately shot that down. No way was her mom about to be played by some random guy online after all she'd been through. Now she was talking about marriage after she'd vowed to never trust another man again? Something wasn't right.

She was preparing to dial her mom's number when she walked through the door of her office.

"Oh, thank goodness, Imani, you're here!" Karen, the receptionist behind the desk, exclaimed.

Imani looked up from her phone to Karen. The receptionist had a bright smile on her face as she pointed to a man holding a camera next to the desk. The white guy wore a blue polo shirt with the logo from a local news station on the breast pocket and khaki's. His dark hair was stylishly cut, and he grinned a hundred-watt smile at her.

"Dr. Imani Kemp, it's great to meet you. I'm here for your interview at one," the man said.

Imani looked from him to Karen behind the desk. "I have a patient at one."

The door behind the reception desk opened and Dr. Andrea Jaillet came out. Tall, red hair with bright blue eyes and a supersweet personality that wasn't manufactured, Andrea was someone who was nearly impossible to dislike.

Andrea beamed. "Imani, you're here, great. We've moved your patients around to other doctors so you can do this interview. Isn't it wonderful? The news wants to feature our doctor of the year."

Imani's phone buzzed again. She glanced down.

Dinner Friday afternoon. You'll meet your stepfather then.

Friday! It was Tuesday. She looked from the text to Andrea's smiling face, to the reporter and his camera. The chorus of "How Bizarre" played on loop in her head. All she'd wanted was a corn dog. What in the world had happened to her perfectly normal day?

two

Cyril Dash stared at the digital wedding invitation on his phone and scratched his chin. The rough hairs of his beard were longer than usual. He'd need to get it trimmed soon, but the brief thought of a future trim immediately faded as he read the words again.

"Are you for real?" He looked up from the invitation to his father sitting on a stool across from him at the bar.

It was just before ten in the morning and Cyril's bar, A Couple of Beers, wouldn't open until noon. His dad usually came over on his days off from the hardware store where he worked part-time. Typically, Cyril enjoyed listening to his dad give an update on the latest happenings at the hardware store or his plans to go fishing with some of the other retirees in the area over the weekend. His dad hadn't had much opportunity to enjoy life in the past decade and any sign of him relaxing and being happy made Cyril happy. He just wasn't prepared for his dad to jump headfirst into marriage after dating for only a month.

Preston Dash grinned from ear to ear. His brown eyes sparkled with a joy Cyril hadn't seen in years. The lines in his golden brown skin deepened and he rubbed his hands together as if anticipating the upcoming conversation. Dressed in a blue linen shorts set with the gold chain he always wore glinting around his neck, his dad looked like the confident, laid-back version of himself Cyril worried he'd never see again.

"I'm for real," Preston said in his deep, scratchy voice. "Linda Kemp and I are getting married in November."

Cyril tapped the thick paper invitation on the bar. "You two just started dating. How are you already getting married?"

"When you know, you know," Preston said with a shrug.

"Okay, I get that, but isn't this kind of sudden?" His dad and Ms. Kemp had only been dating for a few weeks.

His dad waved a hand. The lights over the bar glinted off the gold signet ring with the letter *P* engraved on the surface he wore on his right ring finger. He'd stopped wearing a wedding ring after Cyril's mom died. "You and I know more than anyone else that life is short. I'm not taking anything for granted, including believing I've got a lot of time on my hands."

Cyril grabbed the clean towel draped over his shoulder and went back to wiping down the bar. "But still…" Cyril tried to balance the shock of his dad's announcement with the worry easing into his chest. Marriage? Seriously?

"But still what? When we moved here, we agreed we weren't looking back and would start over." His dad slapped his chest. "This is me starting over. You did the same thing when you opened this bar."

Cyril stopped wiping the bar and cocked a brow. "Come on now, we both know opening a bar isn't the same thing as getting married."

"Why not? They're both a big commitment. You had to put a lot of time and money into this place and look at what you've accomplished. You've turned it into a success."

"I just had my first year out of the red, and that was barely out of the red and you know it."

Yes, he'd worked hard to open a bar. A dream he'd had but never pursued before they'd left Baltimore three years ago to move to Peachtree Cove, Georgia. Back in Baltimore the idea of running his own business, much less opening a bar, had seemed as likely as hopping a taxi to Mars. Something that would be cool, but never going to happen. The struggles of getting his dad's name cleared and finding out the truth about what happened to his mother made dreams seem wasteful.

Yet, here they were. His dad was free. They'd started over in a small but vibrant town. Cyril had not only opened a bar, but he'd survived his first two years. Still.

"Have you told her about Mom?" He tried to keep his words light despite the heavy burden they held.

The smile on his dad's face dimmed and his gaze slid away from Cyril's. "I told her enough."

Cyril's brows drew together. He glanced around the bar even though he knew they were alone. He could count his staff on two hands and have plenty of fingers left over. A Couple of Beers employed a few locals as bartenders and served several craft and traditional beers on tap along with whatever seasonal beer Cyril brewed up in the back. He didn't have to worry about a bunch of people overhearing, but his business partner and friend, Joshua, would arrive any minute. Joshua knew their story, but Cyril still wasn't comfortable talking about their past with an audience.

He leaned closer to his dad. "What does 'told her enough' mean?"

"It means that I told her your mom died and we moved to Peachtree Cove a few years afterward for a fresh start."

Cyril waited for more. When he got nothing, he scratched his head, tipping back the camel-colored fedora he wore over his short, faded hair. "Dad, there's a lot more to that story."

Preston grunted and waved off Cyril's words. "I know that, but the rest of that story only causes problems. I don't want her to look at me with the same suspicion that our family and friends gave me. That part of the story is over. We've finally got closure and I don't want to bring it up anymore."

"You can't just brush aside everything else."

Preston shook his head and scowled. "Why can't you just be happy for me? I never thought I'd find a woman who would make me feel the way I felt with your mom. I've finally found someone and I'm finally ready to look forward to the future."

Guilt arm wrestled with the worry in his heart. "I am happy for you."

"Then act like it," Preston said in a stern voice.

Cyril held up his hands defensively. Guilt won every time. "I'm acting like it."

"No, you're not. You're questioning me."

"I just want to make sure you're good. You know I'm here for you. I've always had your back. I'm being cautious."

"Don't worry. I'm good. Besides, Linda's got demons of her own in her past that she doesn't want to talk about. I understand that more than anyone. We both agreed that we're starting over and not looking back. Trust me, son. I know what I'm doing. I just want you to be happy for me."

Cyril looked into his dad's eyes and sighed. He hadn't seen his dad this excited about anything in years. If he were being honest, he'd opened the bar hoping it would make his dad remember the good ole days. Back when Cyril's uncles and Preston would sit in the backyard of their home and talk late into the night about any and everything. Cyril and his cousins would hover in their periphery, soaking up the advice of the coolest men they knew. He'd learned a lot about life, relationships and family watching his dad interact with his brothers-in-law.

Relationships that were violently broken with the unexpected death of Cyril's mother. Sides were chosen, ties severed and damaged almost beyond repair. A Couple of Beers was a nod back to that happy time. But even that hadn't made his dad smile the way he had since meeting Ms. Linda Kemp.

"I'm happy for you, Dad," Cyril said honestly.

"For real?"

Cyril nodded. "For real. Whatever you need just let me know."

"Will you be my best man?" his dad asked with a hopeful smile on his face.

Cyril placed a hand over his heart. He never thought he'd hear those words from his dad. Never thought his dad would ever get married or love again. To see the joy and excitement on his face after years of pain and heartbreak brought a swell of emotion through Cyril's chest. "Of course, I will."

He reached out a hand and his dad slapped it. They clasped hands and his dad rose so Cyril could hug him over the bar. When they pulled back his dad looked away and quickly wiped his eyes. Cyril smiled and grabbed one of the glasses from behind the bar.

"How about a drink to celebrate."

Preston waved a hand. "You know it's too early for me."

"That's why I'm only giving you a taste."

Preston narrowed his eyes and pointed at Cyril. He tried to glare but ended up laughing. "What you put together now?"

"It's the last of my winter blend. I'm going to put it on sale so I can make room for the spring blend I'm working on." He went to the tap and poured a small amount of the cinnamon-infused lager he'd brewed for the winter.

"Look at us. You've got the bar. I'm getting married. Who would have seen this seven years ago?"

Cyril shook his head. "I always believed things would work out."

"You never doubted me once?"

Cyril handed his dad the glass. He held on when his dad would have taken it and met his eye. "Never once."

When his mother was murdered and the cops immediately

tried to pin it on Preston, Cyril refused to believe it. His dad had loved his mom and Cyril had witnessed that love every day. Was their marriage perfect? No. Something that had come to light during the investigation, but despite being witness to his parents' flaws Cyril never believed his dad would hurt his mother. It had taken way too long to prove that, but they had. Now they were here and happy. He'd do anything in his power to protect his dad's happiness. He deserved it after losing so much.

The sheen returned to his dad's eyes, and he blinked several times. "You gonna give me this beer."

Cyril chuckled and let go. "Take it."

There was noise from the back of the bar. Cyril looked that way as Joshua came into the main area. Joshua was about five years younger than Cyril's thirty-eight years, with his hair cut short on the sides with dreads at the top that he wore in a ponytail. His circle wire—rimmed glasses enhanced his expressive eyes, and he wore a black Couple of Beers T-shirt with a pair of distressed jeans.

Shortly after opening A Couple of Beers Cyril realized that while he loved beer, he did not love managing the books. He'd immediately looked to hire a business manager and Joshua, who'd grown up in Peachtree Cove and had left for college in Atlanta before returning home, was the first person he'd interviewed. They'd immediately clicked; he liked Joshua's laid-back vibe and his thoughts on ways to market as well as manage the business. Three years later and they were not just partners but friends.

"What's up, Mr. Dash," Joshua said coming over to shake Preston's hand. "What are you doing here so early?"

Preston raised his glass. "I'm just here to give my son the good news."

Joshua's brows rose and he glanced at Cyril. "Good news?"

Cyril nodded his head in his dad's direction. "That's his news to tell."

Joshua turned back to Preston. "Don't leave me out. What's going on?"

Preston grinned from ear to ear. A sight Cyril would pay to see over and over again. "I'm getting married."

Joshua's eyes nearly bugged out of his head. "For real? To Ms. Kemp?"

Preston nodded. "The one and only. You know since we moved here I think I figured out the secret to why so many people move south."

Joshua raised a brow. "What? Lower taxes?"

Preston laughed but waved a hand. "Nah, all the sweet Southern women. Find one, and marry her quick." He pointed to both of them.

Joshua shook his head. "I'll leave that to you."

Cyril waved a hand. "I've got to get you through this wedding first before I even think about getting married."

Preston grinned. "You've got to not only get me through the wedding, but since you've agreed to be my best man, I need you to convince Linda's daughter to go along with the wedding."

Cyril's smile dropped and he frowned at his dad. "Say what now?"

three

"Who is this guy? Have you met him?" Imani glanced at the green road sign that read *Peachtree Cove 10 miles* before focusing on the two-lane highway in front of her.

Her cousin Halle's voice, sounding every bit the school administrator that she was, came through the Bluetooth speakers in the car. "Yeah, I know him. Everyone knows Mr. Preston. He works part-time at the hardware store and cuts the grass for us here at the middle school. He's a really sweet guy."

"Well, this sweet guy is trying to marry my mom. When did this happen?" Imani asked squeezing the wheel.

"Mmmm…about a month ago or so," Halle said as if she had to think back. "I remember talking to your mom and some of the other ladies at Joanne's beauty salon about getting on dating apps. I think that's how she and Mr. Preston met."

"Dating app! My mom is on a dating app? Since when?" Hadn't she shut down the idea of dating apps? Imani had tried them and so had some of her friends. There was nothing but frustration and disappointment on the dating apps.

Halle chuckled. "Since Joanne showed her how to sign up for one. Are you really on the way here?"

"Yeah, I just got off the interstate. I'm about ten miles out."

Imani wished she could feel a tenth of the excitement coating her cousin's voice. She wasn't in Peachtree Cove for a fun family visit. Her visit was twofold. One to escape the frenzy surrounding her doctor of the year announcement. The practice and the hospital had not been pleased when she'd asked for time off right at the peak of her popularity, but when she'd told them it was an emergency with her mom they'd readily agreed. Her patients had been shuffled to other doctors for the next few weeks while Imani went home. She'd told no one the emergency was finding a way to stop her mom from making a colossal mistake.

That was the second reason for her trip and why she'd called her cousin. She needed to find out about this man who thought he could marry her mom. Getting to the bottom of this mystery and preventing a rushed, and shady, wedding was her main goal.

"You're here! Dang it, Imani, why didn't you tell me? I would have tried to meet you." The sound of a bell ringing came through the background.

"Tell you for what, Madam Assistant Principal? You can't leave the school and come meet me. Not in the middle of a school day."

Halle sighed. "I know and things won't settle down here for a while. We have benchmark testing, it's the middle of soccer season and we're planning eighth grade graduation."

"Please don't tell me Shania graduates this year?" Imani squeezed the steering wheel. Her little cousin was still a snaggle-toothed six-year-old in Imani's eyes.

"Not quite. We've got another year before she moves to high school. I wish that were the only thing I had going with that girl." Voices sounded in the background. "Okay, I'll be right there." Halle switched to the professional, clipped tone of voice she used at work which meant she wasn't talking to Imani. When she spoke again, she was back to her regular voice. "Imani, I've got to go handle something. Call me later after you see your mom. Let's hang out."

"Where we gonna hang out in Peachtree Cove?"

"Girl, quit hating. Peachtree Cove has got a lot going on for it now. Just wait and see after you get here. And don't give Aunt Linda a hard time. Let her be happy, okay?"

"I'll let her be happy as long as he's not a creep." Or worse.

Halle laughed. "He's not a creep. Bye, girl."

Imani ended the call and sat back in the leather seat. She was tempted to let the top down on the convertible rental car she'd been stuck with after landing at Augusta Airport, but with no hat or scarf her hair would be a mess by the time she reached her mom's house. Her heart leaped at the thought of seeing her mom, who'd effectively avoided all of Imani's calls since sending the text with a picture of the wedding invitation. She had no problem texting Imani back to say, yes, she was getting married, and no, she hadn't lost her mind. Imani assumed the refusal to answer the phone was her mom's way of getting her daughter back in town.

Well, it worked.

The two-lane state highway that led from Interstate 20 into the east side of Peachtree Cove, Georgia, was lined on both sides by fields filled with rows of peach trees. All of them with empty branches that would soon flower as spring came in, before overflowing with leaves and fruit. Imani smiled despite her problems as she glanced at those trees. Every summer during high school, her cousin Halle and their mutual friend, Tracey, would make extra money harvesting peaches with the other seasonal workers.

It had been a fun and profitable part of the summer. Spending the mornings getting peaches or working at the peach stand on the side of the road for Mr. Shubert—the man who owned the peach field where they worked. Followed by afternoons swimming at the lake or hanging out at the skating rink. Back then life had seemed so simple and wonderful.

Simple and wonderful until everything shattered.

She crossed the line into Peachtree Cove. The familiar *Welcome to Peachtree Cove, Home of the World's Best Peaches* sign greeted her. Imani shook her head and laughed. So that was still going on? The town of Peachtree Cove had a friendlyish rivalry with the City of Peach Valley located across the river in South Carolina. Peach Valley also claimed the "world's best peaches" much to the citizens of Peachtree Cove's dismay.

Crossing the border also meant she'd soon come across the Peachtree Cove Dairy Bar. The small restaurant located on the outskirts of town, but close enough to the interstate to advertise to travelers passing by, first opened in the seventies and had the best soft-serve ice cream and fried chicken in the area. That wasn't what made her excited about stopping, though. They also had the best corn dogs outside of the state fair.

She shouldn't stop. She really needed to get to her mom's and get to the bottom of this. Her stomach growled just as the sign for the Dairy Bar came into view. Well, eating before getting there was a good idea. She didn't need to be hangry when she confronted her mom about this impromptu wedding.

She pulled into the gravel parking lot. The Dairy Bar consisted of a one-room peach-and-blue building. Inside, the employees made the food customers ordered at the windows spanning the front of the building. A huge hand-painted sign hung over the windows with the variety of offerings. Covered picnic tables were lined in two rows on the side for those who wanted to eat at the location.

The Dairy Bar wasn't too crowded for a Friday afternoon. Imani stood in line behind two other people after parking. She scanned the menu for any updates even though she knew what she was going to order and smiled. Halle may have said things changed, but this place hadn't. Except for a few new ice cream flavors, the menu was the same.

"Next customer," the young woman behind the window called out.

Imani stepped forward. "Yes, let me get a corn dog—"

"Regular or foot-long?"

Her eyes perked up and her stomach growled in approval. Imani shook her head. "Um…regular." She'd tackle the foot-long when she had more time. "Add a Diet Dr Pepper with that, please."

"Anything else?"

Imani shook her head and stepped to the side to wait the five to ten minutes the girl promised. She pulled her cell phone out of her pocket to text her mom that she'd be there in a little bit.

"Hey, I'd like a chocolate-dipped cone, please."

The sound of a man's smooth baritone with a northern accent that said he was not from Peachtree Cove made her look up from her phone. Her head tilted to the side, and she took in a long breath. He couldn't be from around here. Halle would have told her if there was new hotness like him in Peachtree Cove.

He was taller than her, but she wasn't sure if he was much over six feet or right at it. He had golden brown skin, and a full beard with a sprinkle of gray surrounding thick lips. Tattoos on his biceps peaked out from the short sleeves of his cream-colored button-up shirt, and wine-colored shorts fit just well enough to draw her eye to his round ass. She liked a guy with an ass.

He turned her way. Dark brown eyes collided with hers and Imani blinked and looked down at her phone. Heat filled her face. Had she said that aloud? She bit the corner of her lip and kept her eyes trained on the phone.

The guy slid to the side after his order. Closer to her. She looked up and was surprised to see him watching her. The corner of his mouth lifted in a slight smile, and he raised his chin in hello. His dark eyes narrowed slightly as if he appreciated what he saw.

Imani smiled back as she stepped out of the way. Oh, he was

cute, confident by the way his direct gaze followed her, and if she wasn't in town to deal with her mom's stuff, she might consider flirting. She was woefully single with no prospects. Not by choice, but due to lack of contact with a man she could tolerate for more than a half hour.

"Order number forty-two," the girl behind the glass called.

That was Imani's number. She gave the guy one last glance. He watched her. His sexy lips curved in a grin that made her stomach flip. She returned his smile before going to get her food.

Imani grabbed her stuff and slid to the end of the bar where the ketchup and mustard sat. She tried to squirt mustard on her corn dog but nothing came out. Sighing, she shook the container and squeezed harder.

"Excuse me."

His voice. He was behind her. He'd spoken to her. He was going to make the first move. She spun toward him, a flirty grin prepped.

"Yes...oh no!" Her eyes widened as a line of mustard shot across his shirt.

"Shit," he muttered and stepped back.

"I'm so sorry." Imani rushed to put her food on the counter and snatched a bunch of napkins. "Here."

He took the napkins and dabbed at the mustard on his shirt, but the stain only spread. "Damn," he said under his breath.

"I'll pay for it. Just let me know how much."

He shook his head and when he met her gaze, the flirty look from before was replaced with annoyance. "It's all good."

"Did you want anything?"

"I was going to ask for napkins." He held up the ones in his hand. "I'll just use these."

"Order number forty-three," the girl behind the window called.

He gave her one last irritated look before turning and getting his ice cream. He then walked away without a backward glance.

Imani watched him walk to his car and drive away. She let out a long breath and looked up at the fluffy white clouds in the blue sky. If this was how her time in Peachtree Cove was starting, she did not have high hopes for the rest of the trip.

four

Cyril brushed at the bright yellow stain in the middle of his shirt and frowned. Just like the last fifty times the stain didn't shrink, fade or magically disappear. He shifted from one foot to the next before ringing the doorbell. Visiting his future stepmother for the first time while wearing a stained shirt wasn't how he would have liked for this to go. Although he knew who Ms. Kemp was and had met her through the Peachtree Cove Business Guild, he didn't know her well. Their previous interactions were mostly exchanging pleasantries at a guild meeting. This visit would give him the chance to get to know more about her and, hopefully, make a good impression. For his father's sake. If his dad was happy enough to try his hand at marriage again, then Cyril was going to do his best to support him.

The door opened and Ms. Kemp stood on the other side. She was average height, with a curvy figure and short, stylish hair. A welcoming smile brought out the dimples in her cheeks and the same nervousness churning in his midsection reflected in her tawny brown eyes. Eyes that reminded him of the woman who'd squirted him earlier. For a moment he'd believed in the stories his dad had talked about, of seeing his mom and knowing immediately she was *the* woman for him. Cyril's eyes had met the mystery woman's and his pulse raced, he couldn't tear his gaze away from her and all he'd wanted was to get to know everything about her. Then she'd squirted mustard on him.

His dad shifted from where he stood a few feet behind Ms. Kemp. Cyril pulled his thoughts away from fated love fantasies and focused on the reason he was here. Preston rubbed his hands together, one of his nervous gestures, and nodded at Cyril.

"Hello, Cyril, come on in," Ms. Kemp said in a cheerful voice. She pushed open the glass screen door.

Cyril crossed the threshold. "Sorry I'm late."

"You're right on time. Imani hasn't gotten here yet. She should arrive soon." Ms. Kemp's eyes dropped to the stain on his shirt then jumped back up to his face.

Cyril's cheeks burned with embarrassment. He brushed at the stain again. "Unfortunate mustard incident. I would have gone home to change, but I didn't want to be too late."

His dad frowned at the stain. "Mustard incident? You don't eat mustard. How did it get on your shirt?"

"I stopped at the Dairy Bar. There was a woman there getting a corn dog and she accidentally squirted me."

Before the mustard attack he had considered the best way to initiate contact. The woman had snatched his breath away. Those eyes, not hazel but a bright, golden brown that seemed to pierce right to his soul. She'd been slender, with slight curves that made his hands curious to explore and a smile that made him think having his soul pierced was a good thing. He hadn't reacted to a woman like that ever. The jolt of attraction so strong he'd been willing to be late for this dinner if it meant getting her number. He shouldn't have been rude after she squirted him, but the accident meant he would show up here looking a mess. That quickly broke lust's hold on his brain.

"Oh no!" Ms. Kemp exclaimed. She placed a hand on his shoulder. "Well, that sucks. I hope she at least apologized."

Cyril smiled at the affront on her face. She looked like he imagined his mom would have. She too would have been upset that someone dared hurt her "baby" as she used to call him and would've immediately asked if the person apologized. Though the gesture was small, the tiny resemblance to his mom helped him understand why his dad had fallen for her so quickly.

"She did. It's over now, and the mustard will come out in the wash."

She led him from the entryway into the living area of the home as he spoke. His dad brought up the rear behind them. "Your dad has a few shirts here. Go put your shirt in the wash and put on one of his."

Cyril's brows raised as he looked at his dad. "He does?"

His dad grinned but lowered his eyes. He cleared his throat and waved his hand. "I messed up one of my shirts when I helped Linda clean up the other day."

"Uh-huh," Cyril said not believing his dad for a minute. He wasn't going to press. This explained the few nights his dad came home late or not at all. "You don't have to worry about washing my shirt, Ms. Kemp. I'll get rid of the mustard stain later. Let's not make a big deal out of it."

The sound of the front door opening was preceded by a woman's voice. "Mom! You here? The door was open."

Ms. Kemp's face lit up. "Yeah, baby, in the living room." She hurried toward the foyer as she spoke.

No sooner had Linda made it to the hallway did a woman enter. Linda squealed in delight and held open her arms. The woman did the same and the two were wrapped up in a huge hug. Cyril looked at his dad, who grinned at him, and nodded before looking back at both women. Cyril couldn't suppress his own smile. His dad was not just happy. He was giddy. An emotion he never thought he'd see again on his dad's face after his mom died. He may not have understood why his dad suddenly decided he wanted to get married, but he couldn't say he was against the decision. Not when faced with the excitement and joy on Preston's face.

Cyril looked back at Ms. Kemp and her daughter, preparing to greet her and start the process of getting to know the woman who would become his stepsister. But when his eyes collided with the golden brown gaze that had trapped his heart earlier, he sucked in a breath and pointed.

Her brows drew together, and she pulled back from her mom. She pointed at him, as well. "What are you doing here?"

Imani stared back at the man in her mother's living room with shock and dread. Why was he here? She'd already embarrassed herself by squirting mustard on him in her bad attempt at flirting. Now he stood in her mom's living room looking at her as if *she* were the intruder.

Her mom turned back to him then frowned at Imani. "This is Preston's son, Cyril." Her mom gestured to the other man, an older version of the guy from the Dairy Bar. He gave her a nervous grin and dipped his chin. "Do you two know each other?"

Imani shook her head. "No."

"We met at the Dairy Bar," Cyril spoke at the same time.

Her mom gasped and placed a hand on her mouth. "Imani? You're the mustard girl."

"W-what? Who said I'm the mustard girl?" her cheeks flamed. They'd heard this story already. Did he really come here and immediately go on about the woman who'd *accidentally* squirted him with mustard?

Linda slapped her forehead. "I should have known when he said corn dog. You always stop there for one." She dropped her hand and gave Imani a disappointed look. "Why did you mess up his shirt like that?"

She glared at Cyril. "You told my mom?"

"I explained what happened to my shirt," he replied in a

voice that was way too calm for a snitch. "And in all fairness, I didn't know she was your mom."

"But you couldn't wait to tell someone about the klutz who *accidentally* squirted you with mustard."

He held up a finger. "I also didn't call you a klutz." He shrugged. "I just said you attacked me with mustard."

She stood there stunned for a second, then the guy had the nerve to smirk. Her hand went to her hip. "You're laughing at me."

His smirk broke out into a full-fledged smile. "I'm making light of an awkward situation."

"I told him I'd wash his shirt. Now, we really need to," her mom said. "Cyril, go get one of your dad's shirts and leave that here. Imani will wash it."

She turned to her mom. "I'm not washing his shirt."

"It's really not necessary," Cyril spoke simultaneously.

She spun back toward him. "I know it's not."

He blinked and the edges of his smile stiffened. "If the stain doesn't come out then you can just buy me a new shirt."

Imani sucked in a breath and glared. "I already offered to buy you a new shirt."

His dad stepped forward. "Now, kids, let's not get overly excited. It's no big deal."

Cyril pointed to the stain on his shirt. "This is one of my favorite shirts."

"And she apologized," his dad said. "Now let's move on."

Imani crossed her arms. "Exactly. I'm glad to see that your dad is being reasonable. I was worried."

Cyril frowned at her. "Worried about what?"

She lifted her shoulder in a half shrug. "That someone who's trying to rush my mother into a wedding wouldn't be reasonable at all."

"Why would you worry about that?"

He put his hands on his hips and cocked his head to the side.

The defensive stance made him look bigger, sexier. Instead of being intimidated she was thrown off guard by the flutter through her midsection.

Flutters for this guy were not good. Especially now that she knew who he was. She hadn't planned to go into her reasons why she was against this wedding as soon as she met them, but now that the conversation had gone this way there was no reason to hold back.

"Because if he were unreasonable then he wouldn't listen to why it's clear this wedding cannot happen."

Her mom gasped. "Imani!"

Imani held up her hand. "I'm sorry, Mom, but someone needs to say it. I only came here because you wouldn't answer my calls, and now I can say everything I need to say in person. This wedding is rushed, and I don't even know who this guy is. I don't think you should marry him."

"I can tell you I want nothing but the best for your mom," Preston said. He pressed a hand to his heart and Imani noted the gold signet ring on his finger. Nothing good came from a guy with a gold signet ring.

She shook her head. "I want the best for my mom, too. I can't trust someone who just suddenly pops up and says they're going to marry her. For all I know you're a serial killer or something."

The congenial smile on Preston's face evaporated. A look of pain, stark and raw, flashed in his eyes. Cyril spoke up before Imani could analyze the look.

"My dad is not a killer."

She turned to him. "Of course, you'd say that. You're his son. I don't know you either."

Cyril scowled and pointed. "Look here—"

Preston placed a hand on his shoulder. "Son, not right now. Linda, we'll go. Give you and Imani some time to talk about everything. Let's try this again when everyone has had a chance to cool down."

Linda moved to Preston's side. "We don't have to do that. That was the point of this meeting. To get everything out all at once."

Preston gave her a small smile then kissed her cheek. "It's okay. The kids started off on the wrong foot and you haven't seen your daughter in over a year. You two catch up. We'll come back over for dinner tomorrow. Okay, sweetie?"

Imani snorted. *Sweetie?* This man didn't know her mom at all. If he did, he'd understand she hated pet names and public displays of affection.

Linda's expression melted into one of acquiescence and affection. She nodded demurely and patted his chest. "Okay, baby," Linda said in a sweet voice.

Imani's jaw dropped. Who was this woman and what had she done with Linda Kemp? Linda who ate men's balls for breakfast and claimed to never be a fool for any man ever again. This was not her mom, and this was further proof that she'd come just in time. This guy had brainwashed her mother and Imani was going to do everything she could to reverse the effects and stop this wedding.

five

Cyril and his dad left Ms. Kemp's place shortly after Imani's outburst. Cyril couldn't believe she wanted to call off the wedding. Didn't she understand how happy their parents were? Did she want her mom to be alone for the rest of her life? Yeah, the wedding was sudden, and their parents had planned it quickly, but that didn't mean they didn't care about each other. Their parents were over sixty and smart enough to know their own minds. Yet she didn't trust them to make the right decisions.

Then there was the serial killer comment. He was more sensitive to the offhand comment because of what his family had gone through. He knew his dad wasn't a killer, but after having to deal with the false claims and suspicion from his mother's family after her death, those kinds of accusations struck a chord.

The shaken look on his dad's face had shaken Cyril. He didn't want his dad to sit alone with his feelings. Luckily he'd taken the evening off at the bar to spend time with Ms. Kemp and her daughter, so he followed his dad home.

They lived together in a small brick ranch-style home on the outskirts of Peachtree Cove. Cyril parked his truck next to his dad's old sedan in the driveway and followed him inside. His dad went straight to the fridge and pulled out two cans of the basic beer he preferred no matter what Cyril brewed up. He handed one to Cyril before sinking heavily into one of the seats around the kitchen table.

"Did you have to tell her to replace your shirt?" his dad said after taking a sip of the beer.

Cyril's eyes widened. He pulled out another chair and sat facing his dad. "You're not seriously blaming me for this?"

"You could have been nicer to her," Preston said in a gruff voice.

"I was nice to her. I didn't know she was Ms. Kemp's daughter when she squirted mustard on me. I also didn't make a big deal out of the situation. She was the one who kept it going and then used it to insult you."

His dad sighed and took another swig of his beer. "She doesn't know me."

"But the serial killer comment was out of line."

Preston shrugged. "A lot of people say stuff like that. She didn't mean anything by it."

Cyril frowned, measured his words, then spoke what was on his mind. "She did, if she believes the rumors."

His dad shook his head before sipping his beer. "She was just talking."

Cyril closed his eyes and let out a long breath. When he opened his eyes, his dad was staring off into space. "You don't know that."

His dad sighed and met his eye. "Do you know about Ms. Kemp's ex-husband?"

"Why would I know about her ex-husband?" he asked, surprised by the question.

"Small-town talk. You own a bar. I figured someone must've come in and told you the story."

"I don't get into small-town gossip. You know that." Being

on the end of malicious gossip in his neighborhood after his mom's murder, he didn't find participating in gossip of any kind to be interesting or necessary. He always found a way to change the subject to something else.

"Even if you don't participate that doesn't mean you don't hear snippets here and there."

"I haven't heard snippets. I barely remembered she had a daughter until you decided to marry her." He grunted. "I can't believe it had to be her."

"You really that mad about the mustard?"

"Nah…it's just… I don't know." He glanced at his dad then looked away.

What could he say? That he'd had a weird moment where he'd believed in fate before reality crashed down on him? None of that mattered now. She was against the wedding and he was supporting it. There was nothing he could do with this attraction but push it to the deepest recesses of his mind.

"Alright, I won't push, but I need you to at least be nice to her. I don't want any problems popping up between you two that'll then cause problems with me and Linda."

"You know I'm for this wedding."

"Are you?" his dad asked seriously.

"I haven't seen you this happy in a while. Hell yeah, I support this marriage."

His dad smiled and stood. He slapped Cyril on the shoulder and squeezed. "Good. Then don't worry about what she said and play nice with Imani. If you can win her over, maybe she'll be okay with me."

"Shouldn't you be the one to win her over. You're trying to be her stepdad."

"She's going to take a minute to warm up to me. But maybe, if we're lucky, she'll like you, and when she sees how happy her mom is, she'll be okay. If that's the case, then she'll come around the mountain and support this wedding."

★ ★ ★

"Mom, what was that?" Imani asked as soon as the door closed behind Preston Dash and his son.

Her mom placed her hands on her hips and glared back at Imani. "That's the exact question I was going to ask you. Why were you so rude to Cyril? You were the one who messed up his shirt."

"Forget his shirt. I'm talking about the way you turned into a different person with Preston."

Linda's head jerked back. "What are you talking about?"

Imani relaxed her shoulders and pretended as if she were leaning against someone. She smiled and batted her eyes before saying, "Okay, baby," in a sweet, exaggerated voice while pretending to pat a man's chest.

Her mom scoffed and waved her hand. "I didn't sound like that." Linda spun away and went toward the kitchen.

Imani was hot on her heels. Her mom wouldn't have walked away if there wasn't some truth in Imani's words. "Oh, yes you did. Mom, you practically melted against that guy. And those words, *practically melted*, are not words that I would have ever used to describe you before."

Her mom looked in the pots on the stove. The smell of spaghetti and garlic bread filled the kitchen. A bowl of salad sat on the counter next to a variety of dressings and a pitcher of sweet tea. For a second Imani felt guilty for ruining the dinner, but then the memory of her mom leaning into Preston flashed before her eyes. Breaking things up before they got too far was exactly why she was here.

Linda pursed her lips while frowning at the pot of bubbling sauce. "What's wrong with using those words now? Guess we'll be eating a lot of spaghetti." Linda returned the pot and picked up one of the plates stacked next to the stove.

Imani braced her hands on the counter. "What's wrong is that you always said that you wouldn't be silly over a man again.

You preached to me to never trust men, to always look for an ulterior motive behind their sweet words. *Don't be a fool over a man* has echoed in my head with every guy who's shown interest in me since I turned fourteen. Now I'm seeing you *melting* and just going along with whatever he says? Of course, I'm gonna ask what that was."

Linda sighed as she dished spaghetti noodles onto her plate. "Oh, so your lack of dating is now my fault."

"Mom, that's not what I said, and you know it. I care about you, and when you act completely different…yes, I'm going to worry."

Linda set down the plate and gave Imani a hard look. "When you haven't seen me in over a year and the time before that was a quick weekend for my birthday that you spent mostly on the phone with the hospital, you might not have noticed that the change in me, as you call it, wasn't all of a sudden."

The fight left Imani and guilt dropped like lead on her shoulders. "Mom…"

Linda held up a hand. "I'm not mad about that. I understand you're busy and you live in a completely different state. I'm proud of you and your work as a doctor. The fact that you're doctor of the year is proof of how hard you work. I understand you didn't want to stay in Peachtree Cove—and there's nothing wrong with that. But you have to admit that you don't know everything I've done or how I've changed in the time you've been away."

"We talk almost every other day. You never once mentioned him."

"That's because I knew you'd react like this."

"Like what? Worried?"

"Suspicious," her mom said. She picked up her plate and put sauce on the noodles.

"I'm concerned. And yeah, I'm suspicious about a guy I've

never heard you mention before but now say you're marrying. How do you expect me to be?"

"That's why I asked you to come home. I want you to get to know him and his son. They're both good men. And I'm not just saying that because I'm marrying Preston. Everyone around town likes him and Cyril. They've become a part of the community."

Imani bit her tongue instead of saying what immediately came to mind. What she remembered of the Peachtree Cove community didn't give her a lot of confidence in them. The small towns depicted in books and on television weren't as ideal in real life. In real life gossip, pettiness and stagnation were the rules, not the exceptions.

"How long have they lived in Peachtree Cove?" she asked.

"About five or six years. Moved down from Maryland. Near Baltimore."

Imani's suspicions rose even more. What on earth made a person leave Baltimore to come to Peachtree Cove, Georgia? "Do they have family down here?" Her mom shook her head and Imani frowned. "Does he have a wife up there we don't know about?"

Her mom gave her a side-eye before grabbing a piece of garlic bread. "He's a widower. We both agreed to leave our pasts out of things."

Imani threw up her hands. "What? That means anything could be in his past. Mom, you can't just openly trust people. You know that more than anyone."

"I also know that I'm tired of living in fear. You know what your dad did? He sent me a letter from Puerto Rico. Apparently, he's engaged."

Imani gasped. "What? How?"

After the disaster her dad's mistress had caused, he'd moved out of Peachtree Cove after the divorce at her mom's request. He bounced around from place to place and barely kept in touch, which was how both Imani and her mom liked it. He may not have pulled the trigger, but his claims that her mom was "holding him back" had fueled his girlfriend's delusions that getting rid of Linda would be the key to her happily-ever-after.

Linda rolled her eyes. "Some woman who works at the bar near wherever he's staying. She's thirty. Younger than you! He wrote and asked if I could give him your address so he can invite you down to meet her."

Imani's hands clenched into a fist. "What? I don't want to see him or meet her."

She hadn't visited her dad once since his girlfriend's conviction. She never wanted to see him again. The trial had brought out all of the other women he'd been cheating with. Her dad, the man she'd looked up to and cherished, had turned out to be a master of manipulation and deceit. How could she trust him after what he did?

Her mom shook her head. "I told him that. Don't worry, he knows not to come bothering either of us."

Imani's shoulders relaxed and she let out a breath. "Good."

"I don't like him contacting me, but this time something struck me." She put the plate on the counter and crossed over to Imani. When she spoke, her eyes were sad but determined. "I let what he did stop my life. I lived in fear and mistrust and I closed my heart off to ever being happy while this asshole is dating and getting married again." She grunted and shook her head. "I'm not doing that anymore, Imani."

"So you're going to marry the first man you met after my father contacted you?"

"He's the first man to pique my interest in a long time. And he's a gentleman. He makes me laugh. He's kind and supportive." Her mom's eyes lit up and her smile went dreamy. "Not to mention the way he makes love."

Imani held up a hand. "Mom! Please, stop! Okay, I get it. You're…ready to start over."

Linda laughed and patted Imani's shoulder. "I am. So please, be happy for me and get to know him and Cyril before the wedding."

Imani couldn't believe her father would contact her mom, but then again, if the man was anything it was audacious. He was controlling and knew how to press the buttons of people around him to get what he wanted. As a kid she'd trusted her dad completely. Trusted him to keep her safe and love her for the rest of her life. Now, she could barely trust anyone. How could she, after wicked raised her with a warm hug and a kiss on the forehead before bed each night?

She looked at the happiness on her mother's face. Wary, and a bit hesitant, but it was there. Imani still didn't believe her mom's feelings about men and relationships would change so drastically, but she could see how this news about her ex-husband finding love after everything that happened might make her mom re-evaluate everything.

"I will, if you let me do a background check on him."

Her mom shook her head. "We said we wouldn't pry."

Imani didn't care about any promises he may have coerced out of her mom. Knowing everything was more important. "And I'm saying I want you to be happy, but I don't know him. Let me do the background check. And in the meantime," she sighed. "I'll be nice to him and his son and help you plan this wedding."

Linda's eyes narrowed for a second before she nodded and smiled. "Fine. Do the check, but you won't find anything. Now fix yourself a plate and eat."

Imani didn't argue. For her mom's sake, she hoped she didn't find anything. But if she did, then neither Preston nor his son Cyril would get away with trying to deceive her mother.

six

Imani woke to the smell of coffee and pancakes. She smiled and stretched in the same twin-sized bed she'd slept in as a child. One of the reasons she told her mom she didn't like spending the night was because the twin bed at her mom's house was much smaller than the queen bed she had in her apartment. Despite the size difference she always slept like a baby whenever she came home. Not only was the bed the same but so was the room, from the posters of Destiny's Child, Foxy Brown and Lil' Kim on the pale pink walls to her old diary hidden beneath the mattress.

Her room was like walking through a time capsule to when her world was perfect. Her dad was still the loving husband and father everyone in town assumed him to be. Her mom was still a successful business owner, wife and mother people admired. Imani was the popular and smart captain of the Peachtree Cove high school science club and cheerleading team. She liked that her room was a memory of happier times, before her world was turned upside down and everything changed.

Pushing the unpleasant thoughts out of her mind, Imani slid out of the bed and focused on the delicious breakfast awaiting her. Her mom always cooked when she came home. One much-appreciated bright side of this impromptu trip.

She quickly washed her face and brushed her teeth in the bathroom. Back in her room her cell phone chimed. She checked the messages and immediately wished she hadn't as she read the text from her boss, Dr. Jaillet.

I hope you made it safe. Take your time but let us know if you can remote in for Monday's board meeting.

Imani texted back a quick thanks and I'll try. The hospital agreed to her absence if she continued to try and do as much work as she could remotely. As doctor of the year, she had an ex officio seat on the board to give input from staff in decisions. The seat was something that looked good, but she knew what it was. She may have a seat at the table, but she didn't have a voice in decisions.

Imani threw her phone on the bed before heading down the hall to the kitchen. If she was going to figure out the best way to slow down the plans for this wedding, then she couldn't be distracted by texts and emails from the hospital. The enticing aromas grew stronger, and her stomach rumbled in anticipation as she neared the kitchen.

"Mom, you didn't have to cook but I am so glad you did," she said as she entered the kitchen.

Preston Dash turned away from the stove and grinned at her. Imani froze in her tracks, jaw slack. He wore a light green robe that stopped right above his knees and opened enough at the top to reveal a gold chain nestled in dark chest hair. He appeared completely at ease barely dressed in her mother's kitchen.

Which meant he *was* at ease. Probably because he'd been there before. Multiple times. The reason for him to be so comfortable in her mom's kitchen at…her eyes slid to the clock on the microwave…eight thirty in the morning…meant he either came very early or stayed the night.

"What are you doing here?" she blurted out before the reason why Preston Dash would be spending the night at her mom's house could take hold.

Undeterred by her obvious shock, Preston turned back to the stove. "I'm making breakfast. Your mom doesn't like making breakfast, so I do it for her. Don't worry, I made enough for you, too."

"What? Why?" She was at a loss for words. She didn't want him to make breakfast. She didn't even want to see him this early.

He chuckled and flipped the pancakes. "So, you can eat, too. That's why."

Imani placed a hand to her temple. "I know so I can eat. What I mean is...why are you here. In a bathrobe?"

Her mom came up from behind. "He spent the night, and that's his robe. I told him I'd buy him a new one."

Linda gave Imani a quick hug before hurrying past her into the kitchen. Imani watched, shocked, as her mom leaned up to meet Preston's quick kiss.

"Did you add blueberries?" Linda asked.

"You know I did," was Preston's happy reply.

Imani stared at them, waiting for the scene to change, but it didn't. She pinched herself just to make sure she wasn't dreaming. Pain shot out from the spot she twisted on her arm. Nope. Not a dream. Her mom really was grinning like a love-struck bird fluttering around a man in her kitchen.

Imani hadn't seen a man in this house since her dad packed up his bags and moved out while her mom was still in the hospital. "Mom?"

Linda gave her a curious look. "What, baby?"

What? What did she mean *what*? Imani pointed to Preston, who was now humming as he took the pancakes out of the pan. "This is *not* okay."

"Why not? He's going to be your stepfather. Did you expect him to not be around?" Linda asked in a sweetly innocent voice. As if it shouldn't be an astronomical shock for Imani to find the man flipping pancakes in a tiny-ass robe first thing in the morning.

"Mom!" she said with another pointed look at Preston's back. Were they really going to have this conversation in front of him?

"Don't 'mom' me and quit acting as if you can't talk in front of Preston. Get yourself a plate and eat with us. Then I can tell you about the plans for later today."

"Plans?" Were they going to buy a defibrillator? Because if this was what she'd have to deal with while home, then Imani would need one to shock her heart back to normal.

"We're looking at the wedding venue later. All four of us. It'll be a good way for you and Cyril to start over."

Preston turned around with the plate of freshly made pancakes. "Breakfast is ready. Imani, can you get the syrup out of the cabinet?"

Imani stared first at Preston's grinning face. He stared at her with such eagerness. She doubted puppies at the pound had such hopeful "love me" looks in their eyes. She focused on her mom who also smiled, but where Preston appeared eager her mom was determined. Imani had seen that look before. The "don't back talk and don't give me any problems" look. They really wanted her to sit around the breakfast table like they were some type of family? To not act like the last time three people sat around that table was back when her family was still together.

Frustration, disbelief and more than a pinch of anger twisted her insides. She shook her head and took a step back. "You know what. I'm not hungry."

She turned and hurried back to her room without another word.

"And they both just stared at me like I was the one acting out. So, I left and came over here."

Imani finished her rant and sat back, arms crossed, in the

wooden seat around her cousin Halle's kitchen table. After the scene with her mom and Preston she knew she couldn't stay in the house. Whenever she'd felt like that as a teen she'd escape to Halle's house. As if two decades hadn't passed, Halle was the first person she'd thought of when she left in a rush.

Halle still lived in the small cottage-style house in Peachtree Cove's former mill village with her daughter, Shania. She'd inherited the place after her father died when she was in college. Just three years after Halle's mom passed. Halle had hired a housekeeper to keep the house clean while she finished college, then returned to Peachtree Cove with a master's degree in education and a newborn baby. She didn't talk about Shania's dad, and after hitting numerous brick walls, Imani stopped pushing for the entire story.

Halle leaned against the kitchen counter, a white-and-purple polka-dot robe over her full curves, and a red satin bonnet over her hair. She cradled a mug of coffee between her hands and gave Imani the same, even, *I'm listening despite you being extra* stare she'd adopted when they were kids and perfected over her years working at a middle school.

"That's why you had to run over here and wake me up?" Halle asked before sipping her coffee.

"Yes!"

"You do realize I don't get up before ten on the weekends if I can help it," Halle said in a dry tone.

"No, but this is an emergency. Remember, we always stick together in emergencies."

Halle rolled her eyes. "Imani, this is not an emergency. I told you Mr. Preston is a nice man. Everyone in town knows how much he loves your momma."

"He was in a bathrobe, Halle! All his chest and legs out for anyone to see." She slapped the table and leaned forward. "He spent the night."

Halle smirked. "You saying your momma can't get any?"

Imani waved a hand. "Stop, I don't want to hear anything about that."

Halle laughed and shook her head. "If you don't stop being silly. I'm happy for Aunt Linda and you should be, too. She deserves this after everything she went through, and honestly, I'm glad she's getting some on the regular. If only I could be so lucky," Halle mumbled.

An image of Cyril smiling at her at the Dairy Bar drifted in her head. "Ain't that the truth," she whispered.

Halle's eyes widened. "It's been a while for you, too? I thought you were seeing some guy."

"I went on a couple of dates with a guy last month. The sex was mediocre at best, but that's not the point." Imani swiped a hand through the air. No need to get lost in the disappointment of her last sexual encounter or get sucked into the lingering attraction she had for Cyril. "We're talking about my mom. The same woman who for years told me not to trust what a man said and never, ever be a fool for love. She said she would never, ever get married again, but now she's having some rushed wedding. She gushing over this man, and letting him spend the night? And I'm supposed to just…accept it?"

Halle nodded. "Yes."

Imani cocked her head to the side. "Halle! I'm serious."

"I am, too. Your mom was hurt after your dad. Hurt and angry. No one blames her for that, but do you really want her to be hurt and angry for the rest of her life? To never find someone to make her happy?"

Maybe she did sound like she didn't want her mom to move on, but no one had seen how hurt her mom was after what happened. In public Linda held her head up high; she was strong, and only expressed gratitude for surviving and finding out who he really was. Imani heard her cry out at night from the nightmares of reliving the event. Imani noticed the way her mom stiffened whenever a man so much as said hello to her. Imani had to sit through her mother's lectures about the dangers of falling for a man you couldn't trust.

Imani rubbed her temple. "I just don't want her to rush into anything. I don't want her to get hurt again."

"Your mom is smart and one of the shrewdest women I know. It took Mr. Preston a long time to crack through her defenses, but he did."

Imani pointed and shook her head. "See, that's the thing. I don't know if he really broke her defenses or my dad writing from the sunny beaches of Puerto Rico about marrying some thirty-year-old bartender did it."

Halle straightened. "Your dad did what?"

Imani rolled her eyes. "Yes. I don't even have the whole story, but can you believe it? Even after all these years he's trying to control and manipulate her."

Halle put her coffee mug down then placed a hand on her hip. "I'm going to need this entire story."

Shania shuffled into the kitchen rubbing her eyes and wearing red pajama bottoms with a Peachtree Cove Middle School Panthers T-shirt. "What story? I like stories."

Imani ran a finger over her mouth for Halle to zip it before smiling at her young cousin. "Hey, Shania."

Shania dropped her hand from her eyes and looked at Imani. A second later she beamed and hurried over. "Imani, what are you doing here?"

Imani stood and gave Shania a hug. "Oh my God, you've grown so much."

The last time she'd seen Shania was a year ago. She'd been at least four inches shorter, thin as a rail with a shy smile. Now she was nearly Imani's height, thick with the beginnings of curves and muscle developed from playing sports. She smiled and met Imani's gaze with a confidence that hadn't been there before.

"That's because you don't come home enough," Shania said

pulling back. "Not that I blame you. As soon as I graduate high school, I'm out."

Halle snapped a finger. "Hey, I've got you for five more years. Don't talk about leaving until then."

Shania went over and hugged her mom. "Sure, Halle."

Halle slapped her daughter's behind. "Girl, call me by my first name again."

"Sure, Mommy," Shania said in an exaggerated kid's voice. She pulled away quickly to avoid Halle's second swat at her butt and went to the fridge. "Why are you here so early?"

Halle answered first. "Imani had to come over here and have grown folks' conversation."

Shania pulled out apple juice with one hand. "I'll be thirteen in three months. That's almost grown."

Halle rolled her eyes. "Nowhere near all the way grown. Get dressed, we're going out for breakfast."

Shania grinned. "Eggs and Griddle?"

Imani frowned. "What's eggs and griddle?"

"A new restaurant downtown. At this time on a Saturday… if we hurry we might avoid the rush." Halle looked at Imani. "I'm assuming you're coming with us. Your stomach has been growling since you got here."

Imani pressed a hand to her stomach. "You know it."

Halle put her coffee mug in the sink. "And for waking me up—you're also paying."

seven

Linda texted Imani while she was at breakfast with Halle to say they were meeting at the wedding venue later that day and that Imani better be there or else. Imani had no idea what punishment her mom could really dish out to her thirty-six-year-old daughter, but instead of trying to call her bluff she'd just texted back for the address and time.

She pulled into the side parking lot of The Fresh Place Inn thirty minutes before the scheduled time. A huge grin spread across her face as she took in the yellow two-story colonial-style home. She remembered the place as the Shubert House, where old Mr. Shubert used to live. Some people in town viewed Mr. Shubert as a mean old man, but he always paid well and fair whenever Imani, Halle and their best friend, Tracey, worked in his peach orchard over the summer. He also didn't get mad when Tracey set up a peach stand on the end of his property to sell some of the peaches she'd siphoned off the top. For whatever reason, the old man liked Tracey. As she walked around to the front of the house that was now a bed-and-breakfast, she realized he must have really liked Tracey.

Imani hurried up the stairs and opened the front door. The

smell of potpourri met her, and the sunlight coming through the windows gleamed off the polished wood surfaces. The entry room was converted into a warm and welcoming reception area with thick sofas and upholstered chairs in front of a huge fireplace. A young woman sat behind the reception desk. She wore a yellow polo shirt with The Fresh Place Inn on the front and looked up from her cell phone to smile at Imani.

"Welcome to The Fresh Place Inn, I'm Monique, how can I help you?"

Imani crossed over and placed her hand on the smooth countertop. "Hey, my mom is getting married here and we've got a meeting to look over the venue."

Monique nodded. "Ms. Kemp, yes, her appointment is in thirty minutes."

"I know. I'm early. I was hoping to see Tracey Thompson. Is she available?"

"Mrs. Thompson? Yes, she's in the kitchen going over the menu for the day. I'll buzz her."

Imani thanked her and waited for her to get Mrs. Thompson. Even though Tracey had eloped with Bernard Thompson after high school Imani still was surprised when her friend was referred to as Mrs. Thompson. The elopement had surprised her and Halle. Imani hadn't held back on her opinion that marrying Bernard, no matter how nice he'd been back then, wasn't a good idea. Thankfully, her doubt hadn't ruined her friendship with Tracey, and time had proven Imani wrong. They were still married and apparently were doing well with the opening of the inn.

The sound of footsteps preceded Tracey entering the reception area. "Imani! Girl, it's been forever!" Tracey exclaimed before rushing across the room.

"Tracey!" Imani exclaimed before opening her arms and hugging her old friend.

Tracey's hugs were just as tight as they'd been when they

were younger. She hugged you as if she'd squeeze the life out of you. Tracey was just as stunning as she'd been in high school. Tall and curvy with cinnamon brown skin and the brightest smile Imani had ever seen. She wore her hair in long sienna-colored braids which were pulled up into a high ponytail that made her look ten years younger than thirty-five.

"You look amazing!" Imani said.

Tracey glanced away before pressing a hand to her hip. "Well, Halle convinced me that monthly facials were worth the price, so I guess that's why." She lifted her shoulder in a half shrug.

"Well, I guess I'll have to sign up for that, too." She looked around. "This is you? Like, for real, Old Man Shubert left you his house?"

Tracey sucked her teeth and shook her head. "That man didn't give anything away. He offered to sell it to me a year before he died. I just happened to talk him down to a ridiculously low price. You know what I'm saying?"

"I think it was more than that. That man always liked you better than the rest of us."

"Back in the day I always figured he felt sorry for me. That or he was an old pervert expecting me to be like my momma, but he actually turned out to be okay."

Imani bumped Tracey's shoulder. "Everyone knew you weren't your mom."

Tracey raised a brow. "I appreciate you, but let's be real."

Imani shrugged, deciding to let it go. Tracey's dad was an alcoholic, and her mom hadn't bothered to hide the affairs she'd had with men around town. Tracey had grown up being both embarrassed by her family and quick to defend them, with words or her fists, against anyone who dared say something to her face.

"Forget those people. I'm amazed you talked him down to a good selling price. That man was stingy."

Tracey laughed but nodded. "That's true. When I asked him

why he offered to sell it directly to me instead of putting it on the market, he said I needed a safety net." She sighed and a sad smile crossed her face. "Turns out he might be right."

Imani frowned. "Why, what's going on?"

Tracey waved the words way and grinned. "Don't we all need a safety net? I've only been open a year and I'm still trying to make this place successful. I don't know if you heard, but Peachtree Cove is up for Best Small Town in *Travel Magazine*?"

Imani cocked her head to the side. "Seriously? Peachtree Cove?"

"Yep. I know it seems impossible, but ever since the town voted Miriam Parker into office—you remember Miriam Bryant?"

Imani nodded. "I do. She married one of Halle's cousins on her dad's side a few years back, right?"

"She did," Tracey said. "Well, she was elected mayor seven or eight years ago. Since then she's pushed hard to revitalize the town. Things are so much better and we're taking advantage of being close to Augusta but far enough away to offer quaint small-town life."

"Peachtree Cove is quaint now?" Imani said barely hiding her disbelief.

"Yes and stop scrunching up your nose like that. You just got into town. Get out and about and see what I'm talking about."

"I will. Halle was saying the same thing. I'll admit that Eggs and Griddle place we went to for breakfast was nice."

"They're alright. You want a good breakfast, come here one day. But anyway, if Peachtree Cove is named Best Small Town, then they'll also name the best place to stay in town. I have got to get the inn on that list."

"If anyone can pull off being the best at something then I know it's you. You don't give up on anything you put your mind to. And I feel bad for anyone who tries to get in your way or say you can't. Nobody messes with Tracey and walks away the same."

Tracey laughed. "Lord, girl, I don't fight like that anymore. Not unless I need to," she said with a wink. "Come on, let me give you a tour before your mom gets here. Girl, I can't believe your mom is getting married! I'm so excited for her, and Mr. Dash is *the* nicest man I've ever met. He cuts the grass here for me. Hurry up, let's start in the kitchen."

Imani let Tracey pull her toward the kitchen. "Not you, too. Everyone is telling me how nice Mr. Dash is."

"What's wrong with that?"

"Nothing really. I just don't know him. I'd like to form my own opinion."

Tracey nodded. "That makes sense. We know him, but this is new to you. Just try not to be too much of a man hater with him."

"I'm not a man hater."

Tracey grunted. "Umm, were you not the one who told me I was throwing my life away by marrying Bernard so young and that he was only going to ruin my life?"

Imani flinched. She stopped walking and put a hand on Tracey's arm. "I never should have said all that. Obviously, I was wrong. You two are still together and I was in a bad place back then after my dad."

"I knew all that when you said it. That's why I didn't go off on you like I normally would. Besides, who knows, the man may still ruin my life."

"Don't play like that. You two are the only couple I know still making it work. You're my last hope that love exists."

A shadow flickered across Tracey's face before she grinned and pointed at Imani. "No I'm not. Your mom and Mr. Dash are. Now come on. Let's finish this tour before the lovebirds get here."

"You did a great job with this place, Tracey," Imani said when they finished the tour.

Tracey had shown her first the small dining area located off the kitchen, and the parlor that could serve as a private meeting room or be opened to allow easy flow through the downstairs for other parties. They didn't go out back to the yard with the gazebo where she held outdoor weddings or other events because that was part of what they'd do when her mom arrived with Mr. Dash.

Imani wasn't excited about seeing her mom retie the knot, but she was impressed by what Tracey had accomplished in just over a year.

"Thank you," Tracey said leading Imani down the stairs from where she'd shown her the tastefully decorated suites back to the reception area. "Although business has been pretty good this year, if Peachtree Cove can get the best small town designation and The Fresh Place Inn is highlighted, then that will be even better."

"I've got to ask. You didn't do Fresh Place as a nod to The Get Fresh Crew, did you?"

Tracey grinned and clapped her hands together. "You know it."

Imani's eyes widened and she laughed. "For real? You named it after our silly group name?"

"That name wasn't just a silly group name. You all were my best friends. We had so much fun working here. You were my safe space away from home, so when I thought of a name I had to go there. That, and we do serve fresh food from local vendors, so if anyone officially asks then I'm going with that story versus me and my homegirls called ourselves The Get Fresh Crew."

"I don't know. If you get the best place to stay designation, then that may be worth putting in the story."

They made it to the reception area and walked over to the front desk. "I could imagine Miriam having the committee she put together for this designation adding that to the write-up."

"There's a committee for this?"

"Yes. Miriam is serious. She pulled in the Business Guild,

chamber of commerce and town officials to work on the application, which is due in about a month or so. First *Travel Magazine* has to narrow down the finalists from the list of applications. After that, representatives from the magazine will visit and select the best one. The top fifteen towns will be featured in the magazine, and one will be named the best small town."

"And she really thinks Peachtree Cove will make the final cut?"

Tracey leaned against the reception desk. "If anyone lives and breathes Peachtree Cove it's Miriam Parker."

Imani's eyes widened. "I'm still surprised she's back in town. Didn't she go to Harvard or something?"

Miriam was a year or two ahead of Imani in high school, but she remembered her. Class valedictorian and student body president. She'd been the epitome of the perfect student, and because she was genuinely sweet and wanted to be helpful, everyone loved her. She was the biggest star of their class with her acceptance to Harvard. Everyone in town compared Imani to Miriam and expected her to achieve just as much if not more. The admiration had switched to pity shortly after the scandal with her dad.

"She did. She even got her MBA from Stanford and worked at some large firm in California. Then later, she realized she missed being home. Moved back and made it her mission to revitalize Peachtree Cove. And you know Miriam."

"She never gives up."

"Exactly."

Imani frowned then asked. "What about her sister?"

Tracey grunted and rolled her eyes. "Mattie is still a bougie bitch."

Imani shook her head and lightly hit Tracey's arm. "Still?" Mattie had been a year ahead of Imani in high school. The complete opposite of her sister and exactly the way Tracey described her.

Tracey nodded. "Yep. But because we love her sister, everyone just ignores the negativity she tries to spread."

The door of the inn opened, and Imani turned expecting to see her mom, but Cyril walked in instead. Imani quickly sucked in a breath and straightened. She didn't know why she stood at attention just because he entered the room. Maybe it was his commanding presence that had drawn her interest from the moment she'd first seen him. She was supposed to be digging a hole and burying those feelings. Doing that should stop her breath from hitching and her heart from fluttering when she saw him.

She'd met him, been attracted and discovered he was off-limits in the same day. Obviously getting her body on board with her brain would take a couple more days of training. By then, she'd get her mom to realize this wedding was a bad idea and she'd be on her way back to Florida with Cyril as nothing but a brief spot in her memory.

He met her gaze, looked around the room, then frowned back at her. "My dad isn't here yet?"

He wore a black T-shirt with "err thng blk" printed on the front. The soft material clung to his wide shoulders and thick arms. Dark jeans fitted his hips and thighs just enough to make her imagine the muscles beneath, and a black fedora covered his hair.

"Neither is my mom." She checked the time on her phone. She'd been here forty minutes. "She said she would be here by now."

He walked over to her and Tracey. "Yeah, dad texted he was on the way. What's up, Tracey?" He smiled when he spoke to Tracey, and Imani had a brief moment where she wished he would have smiled at her like that.

"Nothing much, Cyril. Just showing Imani around. How are things at the bar?"

Cyril lifted a shoulder. "Pretty good. I've got a new spring blend debuting this Friday. You and Bernard should come through."

Tracey's lips tightened for the briefest second before she relaxed and grinned. "Sure. I'll make sure he doesn't have any plans and we'll hang out." She pointed at the kitchen. "Let me check something in the kitchen then come back and talk about the wedding. Your parents should be here soon, but if you two want to go ahead and check out the gazebo, do that. I'll meet you out there in a few."

Imani didn't want to be left alone with Cyril. She wanted, no needed, the buffer between them. The thought made her uneasy. If she was going to get over this, then she couldn't run from him.

"Sure thing, Tracey. Thanks for the tour."

"Of course. Now that you're back in town we can hang out again. Maybe we can hit up Cyril's bar instead of me and Bernard. Lord knows I need a night out." With a twist of her lips, she turned and walked away.

Imani turned back to Cyril. His eyes were on her. His gaze direct and potent. Awareness tightened her skin and she took a step back even though they weren't very close to begin with. "You own a bar?" she asked in a rush.

He nodded. "I do. It's downtown. On the corner of Main and Sumter Streets."

"I wouldn't have pegged you as a bar owner."

He raised a brow but grinned. "What would you peg me for?"

Why did he have to look at her like that? With that hint of fun and mischief in his dark eyes. It made her want to have fun and be mischievous right along with him. Made her want to follow him down the yellow brick road on all sorts of adventures. She hadn't had fun or been adventurous in such a long time.

She cleared her throat and crossed her arms over her chest. "I don't know. I figured you worked, but owning a bar isn't something that immediately comes to my mind when I think of anyone working."

"You don't like beer?"

She crinkled her nose. "Not at all. It's disgusting."

He only laughed. A deep, husky laugh that sent delicious prickles across her skin. "What kind of drinks do you like? Sweet? Dry? Fruity? Savory?"

He licked his lips after speaking. Imani wondered if his lips were sweet, dry, fruity or savory. She blinked and forced the thought away.

"Umm… I like things that are sweet and a little fruity. Beer is not sweet or fruity."

He shook his head. "I've got a strawberry ale you may like. Come by on Friday with Tracey and give it a try."

"We'll see." She wanted to hang out with her friend but hanging out with her friend at Cyril's bar? She wasn't about that life. She couldn't mix alcohol with off-limits temptation.

Her cell phone buzzed at the same time his chimed. She pulled her phone out of her back pocket and read the text. Cyril grunted at the same time.

Suppressing a sigh, she looked up at the disbelief on his face. "Let me guess. That's your dad texting he's not coming."

He smirked at her. "I guess your mom sent you the same thing."

Imani read the text aloud. "'Sorry can't make it. Look around with Cyril. You two have fun. Get to know each other.'"

"My dad's is shorter. 'Be nice to Imani. See you later.'"

They met each other's eyes then shook their heads. "I'm betting this was a setup," Cyril said.

"I wouldn't take that bet. I like to win." Imani put her phone back in her pocket.

"I would have pegged you for someone who likes to win," he said with a smile.

"Same for you," she replied.

"Which means, as long as you're against this wedding, we'll be working against each other. That'll make us enemies, and Imani, I don't want to be your enemy."

His voice, soft and rumbling, slid over her and drew her closer. What did he want to be? She had an idea of what she'd like him to be. The same idea she'd had when she'd first met his enthralling gaze the day before. She'd wanted him to be a nice guy. A guy she could flirt with a little who'd flirt back. But their parents were getting married. She didn't trust his dad or him by proxy. There was no flirting with him.

"We aren't enemies, Cyril. I'm surprised by the wedding, and I don't understand why my mom is doing this so suddenly. I do want her to be happy, but I'm going to look out for her and protect her as much as I can."

"That's exactly how I feel about my dad. I'll always fight for him and defend him. I know you don't know us, but I'm hoping that you'll give us a chance before you jump to conclusions."

He held out a hand. "Can you do that?"

How could she explain to him that she couldn't promise that? How could she turn off a lifetime of looking for the worst in people just because he had a nice smile and everyone said his dad was great. She wished she could, but she knew better than anyone that trust had to be earned and even then it could just as easily be snatched away.

Explaining her hesitancy required digging into her past and Imani did not dig into her past. But she could try and get along with them until she found someone to handle the background check or convince her mom to break off this wedding.

She took his hand. "I can try."

His hand was warm and slightly calloused. He gently squeezed as they shook. A jolt of awareness shot up her arm and she quickly pulled back.

"Well… I guess we can either leave or go see the gazebo."

He cleared his throat and nodded. "They want us to play nice. Might as well look at the gazebo for them."

She'd hoped he'd choose the former, but she nodded. She ignored the small spark of pleasure that he wasn't ready to leave already. This was good. It would give her more time to feel him out. That was all.

"Sure. Let's check it out."

eight

The bell on the door chimed as Cyril entered Books and Vibes, the independent bookstore and coffee shop that opened six months ago right off Peachtree Cove's Main Street. The smell of coffee greeted him along with the low hum of voices from the people sitting around the shop as he entered. He spotted the owner, Patricia Norris, standing behind the counter. He lifted the small basket in his hand, then walked further inside after Patricia grinned and waved him over.

"Good morning, Patricia," Cyril said.

"Call me Pat." She handed a paper cup to the customer waiting on the other side of the counter. "Here you go. One black coffee. Did you get your muffin?"

"I did," the man said. He took his coffee and headed to the only empty table in the corner of the shop.

"You're busy," Cyril said when Pat came back over to him. "I'd hoped to miss the rush."

Patricia was in her early forties, with a confident smile, and bubbly personality. A transplant from nearby Augusta who'd decided to move to the small town of Peachtree Cove to open her coffee shop instead of competing with the larger chains.

"We don't get the morning rush like we do on weekdays. On weekends there is a steady stream of people coming in." She pointed to the basket. "What's this?"

Cyril slid the basket toward her. "This is your official Peachtree Cove Business Guild welcome basket."

Patricia's eyes widened and a huge grin broke out over her face. "When you all said I'd get a welcome kit I thought I'd get an email or something. Not an actual welcome basket."

Cyril leaned one arm against the counter. "That's one of the things Emily changed when she became president. This has information about the guild, but also some promotional items from the chamber of commerce and other businesses in the area."

"Do you hand deliver these to everyone?" Patricia asked eyeing the goods through the cellophane wrapper.

"It's one of my duties as secretary. If I can't hand deliver, then I pass them out at the monthly meeting. I needed to stop in here anyway. Van said the novel I ordered arrived."

She nodded. "It did. He's in the back getting more vanilla syrup."

"No, I'm not. I'm right here. Hey, Cyril, you come to pick up your book?" Van Norris, Patricia's husband, walked up to the counter. Van was a few inches taller than Patricia, with a bald head and round frameless glasses.

Cyril pointed to the basket. "That and to make a special delivery."

Patricia poked her husband's shoulder. "It's our welcome basket for joining the guild. See, I told you it was a good idea to join."

"I never said it wasn't." Van looked at Cyril and said, almost apologetically, "I never said that."

Cyril chuckled. "It's okay, Van. I realize joining a business organization might not be the first priority when you're starting a new business. I felt the same after I opened the bar, but the guild is doing a lot to help with the revitalization efforts in Peachtree Cove. Not to mention sponsoring the package with the town officials for Best Small Town."

Van pointed at Cyril. "As long as we get it before Peach Valley across the border then I'm good."

"Peach Valley doesn't stand a chance," Cyril said with a firm nod which was returned by Patricia and Van.

When he'd first moved to Peachtree Cove, he hadn't fully appreciated the rivalry the town had with the neighboring town on the other side of the Savannah River in South Carolina. Over time he'd learned that despite Georgia being known as the Peach State, South Carolina liked to point out that they produced more peaches. The two border towns played up the rivalry, mostly in a good-natured kind of way, but both were equally serious about proving their town's superiority.

The chime at the door rang and the three of them looked to see who entered. Cyril smiled when he caught sight of Halle Parker and her daughter, Shania. His smile immediately stiffened when Imani strolled in behind them.

He'd agreed to be nice to her for his dad's sake. He'd even told himself that the attraction he'd felt for her was something he could forget and get past. But the day before when they'd toured the venue, one side of his brain refused to forget that he was interested in this woman. The other, more logical, side of his brain recognized that although she'd agreed to get to know him and his dad, the suspicion was still written all over her face.

Imani must have felt similarly because the pleasant expression on her face morphed into one of irritation before she adopted a neutral expression. Cyril took a deep breath. He could and would play nice. Getting on her good side was the best way to get through this wedding with no problems. His dad deserved to be happy and if overcoming Imani's suspicions was the way to ensure that happiness then he'd deal.

"Well, look who's here," Halle said with exaggerated surprise. "Imani, it's your soon-to-be brother-in-law. Cyril, what are you doing here?"

"Dropping off a welcome basket and picking up a book."

Halle grinned. "You're still delivering those?"

"The other duties as assigned," he said with a laugh. He glanced at Imani who appeared confused. "I'm the secretary for the Peachtree Cove Business Guild."

"I didn't say anything."

He chuckled. "Your face did." He looked at Van. "I can go with you to get my book."

Van shook his head. "No need! I'll get it and you can stay up here and talk with your family. Nice to meet you, Imani."

"She's not my family."

"We're not family," Imani said at the same time.

Patricia made a clucking noise eyeing them both. "From what I hear you will be in a month or so. Nice to meet you, Imani. We're both so happy for your mom and Mr. Dash. They're so cute when they're out and about around town together. Are you two excited about the wedding?"

Cyril nodded. "I'm thrilled for my dad."

Imani gave a tight smile. "I'm still getting used to the idea."

Halle wrapped an arm around Imani's shoulder. "Which is why you should sit here and get to know Cyril while I order coffee." She gave Imani a quick shake before going to the register. "Patricia, let me get a vanilla latte and a hot chocolate for Shania."

"Thanks, Mom." Shania looked at Patricia. "Any new romances?"

Patricia pointed toward the back of the store. "We've got a few that came in yesterday."

"Cool." Shania hurried off in that direction.

Cyril looked over at Imani. She looked good, again. The dark leggings she wore hugged her hips and ass perfectly, and the fitted, black athletic shirt she'd paired them with did the same thing to her breasts. His body reacted as his instincts went on alert. Imani was the type of woman he typically wouldn't hesitate to try and connect with. But everything about Imani from her distrust of his dad, the fight against the marriage and the fact that if the marriage went through they would, indeed, be family, said to ignore his instincts.

He was searching his mind for something to talk to her about since Halle insisted they get to know each other when she blurted out, "Do you have a second to talk?"

"Yeah, what's up."

She glanced over his shoulder. He turned to find Halle and Patricia watching them with thinly veiled interest. She looked back at him and hesitated.

Cyril pointed toward the door. "Wanna talk outside? Unless you were going to order something?"

She shook her head. "No, I was just hanging out with Halle to avoid being at home." When he frowned, she shook her head. "Outside is good."

Cyril followed her. Books and Vibes wasn't directly on Main Street, but it was close enough that the Sunday afternoon crowd spilled over to the shops lining the side streets. They hung close enough to the front door to avoid being in the way of the few people leisurely walking and browsing the shops.

"Is everything okay?" he asked.

Imani crossed her arms and narrowed her eyes. "Does your dad spend the night at my mom's house all the time?" she asked in an accusatory tone, as if he were responsible for his dad's sleeping habits.

He frowned. "He stayed at your mom's place? I didn't hear him leave last night."

"You two live together?"

The surprise in her voice made him wonder if she had a problem with him living with his dad. Then he pushed that away. They'd only had each other when they'd moved to Peachtree

Cove. The choice to get one place versus two made sense as they started over. One reason the setup worked so well was because they stayed out of each other's business for the most part.

"We moved down from Baltimore together. It was easier to share a place than find something separate. Besides, my dad is all I've got. I don't mind spending time with him."

"Your mom…?" she asked with a raised brow.

"She died. Six years ago." The pain squeezing his heart came through in his voice. No matter how many years passed and how many times he said it the words never became easier. His mom was supposed to still be with them.

"I'm sorry."

He took a deep breath. "Yeah, so am I."

"And you're still okay with him remarrying?"

"Why wouldn't I be? I saw how much my mom's death hurt him. Losing her changed…everything. If he's happy again, then I'm going to do everything I can to keep it that way."

She crossed her arms and looked away. She pulled the corner of her lip between her teeth and frowned. The movement drew his eyes to her mouth. Her lips looked soft. Kissable.

He cleared his throat. "Your dad?"

She blinked and looked back at him. "What about him?"

"Where is he?"

"Puerto Rico apparently," she said without batting an eye. His shock brought out her own surprised expression. "We don't talk to him. You didn't know? I thought half the people in town would be willing to tell you the story."

"I don't listen to gossip. I listen to what people tell me directly and pay attention to what they show me. I'm sorry about your dad."

She looked away and kicked at a pebble on the sidewalk. "Yeah…me too."

Something in her voice made him want to reach out and comfort her. He didn't know why she didn't talk with her dad, but it couldn't be good. No one pushed a parent out of their life without a good reason. The mystery of Imani, who she was, where she came from and what made her tick only deepened. He could ask under the pretense of getting to know her as his potential new family member, but he wasn't interested because her mom was marrying his dad. He was interested because he wanted to know what brought the sadness into her eyes and make that sadness go away.

"I guess we can both agree our parents deserve a little bit of joy and that this may not be the worst thing ever?"

She sighed and crossed her arms again. "I woke up to find your dad in our kitchen, wearing a bathrobe, making breakfast. Not once, but twice. I can't just suddenly get used to that."

He placed a hand over his eyes. "Please tell me he wasn't." He hadn't even heard his dad leave the house the night before, and because he was used to Preston getting up early and leaving the house to do odd jobs around town, he never really questioned his dad's whereabouts.

"The visions are burned into my brain now." She tapped the side of her head.

Cyril placed a hand over his heart. "I'm sorry, but at least he was wearing a robe."

"He doesn't always wear one?"

"He's big on...being free."

Her eyes widened and she pressed a hand to her heart. "Stop it."

"I wish I could. I always ask if he's dressed before entering a room. Honestly, that's the worst part about living with him."

She shook her head and laughed. "Thank god my mom doesn't walk around naked."

"For now. Who knows what she'll do after the wedding?"

She gasped then placed a hand on his arm. "I said stop. I don't need the image of both of them now."

Cyril's laughter caught in his throat. Her touch was light as a feather but branded him like scorching iron. When she pulled back, he had the urge to reach out and hold on to her hand. Pull her closer. See the smile on her face melt into something a lot more decadent and promising.

"Watch out!" a voice yelled a second before three kids on bikes hurried down the sidewalk.

Cyril grabbed Imani by the shoulders and pulled her out of the way. The air stirred as the kids whizzed by with shouts of "my bad." The scent of something spicy with a hint of sweetness beneath filled his senses. Imani and whatever perfume she wore. The softness of her body pressed against his and the heat from her hands which had seared him before from the briefest touch now pressed against his chest and burned straight through him.

Their eyes met. Her lips parted with her quick breaths from the sudden movement. His stomach clenched as the urge to pull her even tighter into his embrace rammed him like a bull. He quickly pushed her away and took a step back.

"You good?"

She nodded. "Um...yeah. Thanks for getting me out of the way?" Her words came out more of a question than a statement.

He didn't have to haul her against him like that. He could have just as easily taken her by the elbow, pulled her aside and kept full-body contact at a minimum. He'd reacted without thinking. That was the problem. He'd reacted to the impulse to hold her instead of remembering to keep his distance.

Embarrassment heated his face, neck and chest. He had to get away before he made even more of a fool of himself. "Yeah. So I'll see you later. I forgot there's something I need to do at the bar."

"Um...sure." She sounded breathless. Damn why did she have to sound like that. As if he'd kissed her, because that only made him want to kiss her and he had no business kissing Imani.

He turned to leave, when she called out, "Weren't you picking up a book?"

He tossed up a hand but didn't turn around. "I'll get it later. I'm running late." He hurried down the street. Ashamed that he'd pulled her against him, that he'd wanted to kiss her, that the press of his growing erection meant his body was reacting as if he had. He was trying to get on Imani's good side. Hiding a growing erection from an innocent encounter was not the way to do that.

nine

Imani sat on a stool behind the register in her mother's store and watched as Linda arranged a bouquet for delivery later that afternoon. It was a scene that had played out so often in her childhood that she'd gone back into the routine almost as if she'd never left. She couldn't count the number of hours she'd spent after school and on weekends watching her mom put together flower arrangements from the elaborate to simple. Weddings, birthdays, anniversaries or just because, her mom's flower shop was the place to go for flower arrangements in Peachtree Cove.

Nowadays, with the ease of sending prepackaged, box arrangements with the click of a button, her mom had managed to keep her shop open. Despite the hardships, Linda had overcome, survived and thrived. Imani was proud of her mom. Part of the reason why she didn't want anyone to come in and threaten all that she'd built.

"I think you've got enough baby's breath on that bouquet," Imani said after watching Linda stuff another sprig of the tiny white flower on the arrangement of pink roses.

Linda sighed and shook her head. "Not when it comes to the flowers for Amanda Jones. Her favorite color is pink, and she adores baby's breath. Says it reminds her of lace. So, her husband always asks for extra for their anniversary arrangement."

"It didn't say that on the order?" Imani knew because she'd gone through and read the orders for delivery that day.

"I've been putting together the arrangement for Mr. and Mrs. Jones for fifteen years. I don't need to see that on the order."

"But shouldn't you account for putting a field of baby's breath in the bouquet?" she asked with a laugh. "I mean, how do you stay in business if you don't charge for the extra."

Linda placed a finger on her chin and studied the arrangement. "It's not about charging extra, especially with a longtime customer. Every year Amanda's husband sends these to her at the hospital, and like clockwork, I get several calls for deliveries to various people who work on her floor. You know seeing one person get flowers often pushes other people to order."

Imani tapped a pen on the counter. "Probably people ordering for themselves so they could pretend to have someone who cares."

She waited on her mom to agree as she usually did. Except, Linda shook her head and gave Imani a half smile. "I used to think the same thing."

"I know. You're the one who used to tell me that."

Linda sighed before putting down the remaining sprigs of baby's breath. "Well, I admit when I'm wrong. There are a lot of people in love in Peachtree Cove. It was easy to overlook that when I focused mostly on the number of orders versus the reasons for them. Flowers aren't just sent when someone has messed up. They're mostly sent to express love."

Imani blinked, surprised to hear the sentimental note in her mother's voice. "Mom, are you serious? When did you become the believe in love type?"

Her mom shrugged. "I've always believed in love."

Imani waved a finger and shook her head. "No, you have not. You said love was a trap."

The look Linda gave Imani was full of regret. "I'm sorry. After your dad...well...after that incident with your dad I'll admit I stopped believing. I never should have taken my pain out where you could see."

"She showed up at the door with a gun and shot you. Kind of hard to hide that pain from me," Imani said with an eye roll.

Since then, Imani had tried not to let the fear and anguish of that day show. Giving into that fear meant her dad still had a hold on them and she refused to give him that. He'd treated her mother as if she were disposable. It didn't matter that his mistress held the gun and pulled the trigger, if he hadn't used her mom as the reason why he couldn't leave then maybe she wouldn't have gone to such an extreme.

"Just because I wasn't happy didn't mean I wanted you to be unhappy. Or alone. It may be easier said than done, but don't take everything I told you after that to heart."

"I'm not just taking what you said to heart. I have been dating for a while, and believe me when I say it's horrible out there."

"That doesn't mean that you won't find the right person."

Hearing those words with that amount of hope from her mom made Imani laugh out loud. "You're kidding me, right? The right person? Even if I think that person is fantastic, they may not actually be who I thought they were. You know just as well as I do that the face people put out to the world can hide a whole lot."

Linda walked over to where Imani sat and placed her hands on the counter. "Learning to trust isn't easy, but it can come with time."

Imani pursed her lips. "Have you known Preston long enough to trust him?"

Her mom lifted her chin. "I trust him and I trust how I feel. He makes me happy, and I've spent a long time being unhappy."

"That doesn't mean—"

"And having you here makes me happy. Having you help me plan my wedding makes me happy. Getting a chance to start over again is exciting. It's the happiest time of my life." Linda's eyes sparked with a light Imani didn't think she'd ever seen before. Not even when her parent's marriage was good.

Guilt glued her lips together. She swallowed the reply that she was being forced to plan this wedding. That she'd barely gotten a chance to be alone with her mom because of Preston being there first thing in the morning. Working at the flower shop was the first time she'd gotten a chance to be alone with her mother since arriving on Friday. And that was only because the shop had been empty for twenty minutes and her mom's other employee, Kathy, was out delivering a bouquet. In those twenty minutes she hadn't been able to successfully divert the conversation to Preston and all the reasons her mom should call off the wedding. Now, seeing the excited light in her mom's eyes, Imani felt guilty for wanting to call everything off.

Maybe her friends were right. Maybe she needed to just go with things and let her mom be happy. She wanted her mom to be happy. She didn't want her alone and sad for the rest of her life. She just didn't want her mom's happiness to come with any unexpected surprises that would hurt her. She might survive another blow, but it wasn't something Imani wanted to chance. Not when the first blow had literally almost killed her.

"I'm glad you're happy."

"You are?"

"I am. I just…you know I'm going to worry."

"Which is why I want you to spend more time with Preston and with Cyril."

Imani didn't want to spend more time with Cyril. Every time he came around, her body reacted to him. She couldn't like the man actively working against her. Because even though she understood why Cyril wanted his dad's happiness, his dad's joy came at the potential expense of Imani's goals of protecting her mother.

The door to the shop opened and a short man walked in. He raised a hand and waved at Linda. "Hey, Linda, do you have any good daisies?"

Linda smiled back. "I do. Got some in this morning. How many do you need?"

"Just a dozen. Ray wants to celebrate getting the promotion. It'll be much needed with the baby coming."

"That will help out." She gestured to Imani. "You remember Imani, don't you?"

The guy looked at her and grinned. "I do! Hey, Imani."

Imani looked back at him and frowned. He did look familiar, but she couldn't quite place where she recognized him from. "Um...hey. Sorry, I've been away for a while and I've forgotten some names."

He laughed and waved a hand. "It's no problem. I didn't expect you to recognize me. I'm Kaden, but you probably remember me as—"

"Oh my God? Kaden!" Imani said with surprise. Kaden Sims had been in several of Imani's classes, but Imani remembered Kaden as a she.

He shrugged. "That's me. I transitioned about two years ago."

"I'm happy for you."

Kaden's brows drew together. "Seriously?"

Imani nodded. "Seriously. I admire people who have the courage to be who they are and go after what they want. Not a lot of people do that."

The tension around Kaden's shoulders eased. "I appreciate that. Everyone around here hasn't been as understanding."

"Everyone should mind their own business."

Linda pointed from Imani to Kaden. "Did you know Imani's an obstetrician."

Imani laughed. "Mom! You don't have to announce it like that. Sorry, she's really proud of me."

Kaden's eyes widened with excitement. "Will you be opening a practice here?"

"No, I'm just in town for the wedding."

Kaden deflated. "Oh, I was hoping for someone more accepting here."

Imani frowned. "Accepting?"

"I'm pregnant and Dr. Baker, the town's only ob-gyn, refuses to see me. I have to drive two hours to Atlanta to find a doctor who'll see me."

"He won't see you? How can he just refuse you care?" Imani said, indignant.

Kaden seemed momentarily surprised by her anger before answering. "Men can't have babies. That's what he told me."

Imani had at least two transgender patients, one of whom she'd helped deliver a baby. After watching Halle lose her mother due to shitty medical care, she refused to be a doctor that sat by and let her patients suffer because of other people's prejudices. To her, the safety of the child and the person carrying the child was more important than anything else. Making sure both lived was her mission.

"I'm sorry he won't treat you. That's unacceptable. Is the Atlanta doctor good?"

Kaden nodded. "She is and I love her, but it's hard to commute. Too bad there aren't more doctors like you around here."

Her mom nodded. "Agreed. We need more doctors of the year around Peachtree Cove."

Kaden's eyes widened. "Doctor of the year?"

Imani waved off the words. "It's just a title. I'm decent."

"More than decent if you're as accepting as you appear to be." Kaden sighed then looked at Linda. "Well, enough of that. Do you have any arrangements already together?"

Linda nodded. "I do. Come over to the display and I'll show you what I got."

He nodded then looked at Imani. "Good to see you again, Imani."

"Same here, Kaden."

She watched her mom and Kaden go over to the display and talk about the prearranged bouquets. She'd like to believe Dr. Baker wouldn't turn Kaden away, but from what she remembered of the man she wasn't surprised. He was old-school all the way. God forbid any teenager got pregnant and had to see him. They'd have to sit through a lecture on respectability and how they were ruining their lives. Not surprising that he'd outright refuse to see a trans man.

Imani shook her head. She'd check out Kaden's doctor just to be sure he got the best care. Even though she didn't plan to stay in town, she could at least do a small part to try and make things better for her old classmate.

ten

A week after being in town Imani called Tracey and Halle and begged them to go out. She was exhausted and needed a break from her mom's great romance with Preston. Imani had completely underestimated how easy it would be to break up this wedding. She'd expected to arrive, talk some sense into her mom, then enjoy a few days relaxing and spending time catching up. Instead, she woke up to Preston either already there or arriving shortly after to make breakfast for her mom, spent the day helping at the flower shop, then going back home, only for Preston to show up again to make dinner or bring the newest superhero movie for them to watch. Imani needed an escape from the "happy family" scenario they were forcing on her.

Now, as she sat at the corner of the bar in A Couple of Beers flanked by Tracey on her right and Halle on her left she wondered if coming here was such a good idea. She was trying to avoid Preston, but she really needed to avoid Cyril. The man had a direct link to her attraction button. Tonight, his deep laugh as he talked to the patrons around the bar sent unexpected shivers down her spine. She couldn't understand how a man could look so desirable in just a cream-colored shirt and dark pants.

She cut her eyes at Halle. "There isn't any other bar in town other than Cyril's?"

Halle scoffed. "Peachtree Cove has a lot to offer, but an abundance of breweries isn't one of them. Besides, his place has a good vibe. You don't like it here?"

"I wanted to escape the Dash men for one night," she mumbled.

Tracey leaned her elbow on the bar and raised an eyebrow as she watched Imani. "Why? Cyril and his dad are cool."

"You try spending every available minute with them. Preston and my mom are joined at the hip. I've barely gotten three seconds alone with her."

Halle rubbed Imani's back. "Ahh, poor baby can't get all the attention."

Imani cut her eyes and wiggled until Halle's hand fell away. Her cousin laughed and Tracey snickered along with her.

"How am I supposed to figure out why she's doing this if he's always around?" Imani said.

Halle pursed her lips. "You know, that may be why she's doing this."

Imani's eyes narrowed. "You think he's pressuring her and not giving her time to rethink things."

Halle closed her eyes and took a deep breath. When she opened her eyes again, she gave Imani an *are you serious* stare. "*Maybe* she's marrying him because she *likes* having him around all the time. *Maybe* your mom loves him and *wants* to spend time with him."

Imani huffed before turning to Tracey. "You hear this?"

Tracey raised a hand. "Don't look to me to back you up. I'm hashtag team Preston."

"What? Why?"

"Not only does he cut the grass for me at the inn, but he's

supersweet and a gentleman. They don't make them like that, if you know what I mean."

Halle chuckled. "Yes, they do."

Imani raised a brow and Halle motioned toward Cyril. He looked their way at the same time and cocked his head to the side in inquiry. The three of them looked away and burst into laughter.

Instead of ignoring them acting silly at the end of the bar as she'd hoped, Cyril came over to them. "Looks like you're having a good time tonight."

"We are," Halle said.

Cyril nodded. "What can I get you?" The tan fedora he wore slightly cast his eyes in a shadow. Imani's fingers twitched with the urge to push it back and get a better look.

Halle answered first. "Let me get that lime pilsner you recommended last time and nachos."

He nodded then looked to Tracey whose brows drew together. "Are you serving the spring blend you told me about?"

"Just put it on tap today."

She snapped then pointed. "Then I'll go with that and nachos, too."

"Got it." He focused on Imani. "No need to order. I've got you." He winked, and Imani never knew she could physically feel the effects of a wink deep in her midsection until that moment.

She shook her head. "I don't like beer, remember."

"And I said I've got something you might enjoy. Try it on the house. If you don't like it, you've lost nothing."

Sighing, she shrugged. She was here to relax and unwind. "Fine. I'll give it a try."

He grinned as if he hadn't expected anything else before moving along. After he walked away, she looked at her two friends. "Since when did you two start drinking beer?"

"Since Cyril opened this place," Halle said as if that made perfect sense.

"Facts," Tracey said with a mischievous grin.

"So you only come here because of him?"

Halle's look said the answer was obvious. "A fine, *single*, Black man opens a bar in downtown Peachtree Cove? Ma'am, half the available women in town started drinking beer."

"And half the thirsty men in this town started coming to hit on the women," Tracey added. "Once people realized Cyril was cool and his beer was good, then everyone else started coming."

She looked at Halle. "That's why you came? Did you two…" Halle was single, and despite not talking about Shania's father, she did date and was on the lookout for her forever romance. Maybe she'd considered Cyril as a possibility.

"What? No." Halle held up a hand and shook her head. "Cyril is cool and all, but he's not my type."

"Why not? He's handsome?"

The minutes the words left her mouth she wished she could pull them back. She wasn't supposed to be attracted to Cyril. *But if you convince your mom not to get married then it wouldn't be weird.* She shoved that thought right out of her head. She wasn't going to break up her mom and Preston just to start something with Cyril.

"He is, but you know Halle loves dark-skinned dudes," Tracey said with a smirk.

Imani nodded slowly. "You know, you're right about that. She does go crazy for a chocolate man."

Halle chuckled and shrugged. "I can't even be mad at you two, because it's true."

The three of them laughed as Cyril came over with their drinks. He raised a brow as he looked between them. "What's so funny?"

Tracey shook her head. "Girl talk. Don't worry about it."

He passed out their beers and food. "Got it." He placed his

hands on the bar and met Imani's eyes. "Let me know what you think."

She eyed the drink before her. "It's pink."

"You don't like pink?"

She did. It was one of her favorite colors. She wasn't giving him the satisfaction of admitting that. "I've never seen pink beer before."

"Ale," he said.

"What?"

He pointed to her class. "It's a strawberry ale. Give it a try."

She pursed her lips before lifting the glass and sniffing. It smelled fruity. He maintained eye contact with her as she took a tentative sip. The sweet taste of strawberries was undercut with a tartness that reminded her of a nice jam. She lowered the glass and licked her lips. Cyril's eyes narrowed in on her mouth. The corner of his lips lifted in a half smile and the confident look in his eye that had attracted her when they first met returned. Heat spread through her body like wildfire.

His eyes returned to hers. "You like it?" he asked in a low, self-assured voice.

She did. More than she'd expected, but she didn't want to admit he'd so easily guessed her tastes. Imani shrugged. "It's tolerable."

Chuckling, Cyril's voice lowered. "Not easy to please. Means I'll have to work harder to find out what you like."

The words were innocent. They referred to her taste in beer. Yet the wildfire in her body increased in temperature, and her breathing hitched. She shouldn't have come here. This man was a threat to her good sense.

Still smiling, Cyril pushed back from the bar. "Ladies, holla if you need something."

He turned and walked away to help the new group of people who'd sat at the other end of the bar. As soon as he was out of earshot, Halle and Tracey leaned closer to Imani.

Halle spoke first. "What was that?"

Imani took another sip of her ale before trying to ask nonchalantly, "What was what?"

"Nah, girl, quit playing," Tracey said in a no-nonsense voice. "There's a vibe between you two. Are mother *and* daughter about to be hooked up?"

Imani scoffed. "What? No! Not at all. I mean…if they get married, we'll be related."

Tracy shook her head. "Y'all ain't related."

Halle raised a finger. "Facts. I can confidently say that man has never been to any of our family reunions and is not kin to you."

Imani held up a hand. "Can you stop. I'm not interested in Cyril. Other than to find out what's up with him and his dad and why my mom is completely different."

"Happiness makes people act differently," Tracey said. "I've known your mom all my life and I don't ever remember seeing her this happy."

"I agree," Halle said. "She wasn't even this happy when Uncle Barry was around."

Imani frowned at her cousin. She remembered the time before. When her parents had been viewed as one of the town's perfect couples. "What do you mean? Before my dad…before that incident, my mom was happy."

Halle raised an eyebrow and shrugged. "Not like this. She's kind of like Tracey was before her wedding back in the day."

Imani shook her head. "Nah, no one can beat Tracey. She was the queen of rainbows, unicorns and happily-ever-afters." Imani chuckled and looked at her friend.

Tracey looked away. "Yeah. I was kind of ridiculous back then." She sipped her beer.

"But you're still together after everyone said you were too young. Myself included," Imani said pressing a hand to her chest. "I've already admitted I was wrong on that."

Tracey lifted a shoulder. "Your mom knows her mind much better than I did back when I decided to marry Bernard. Instead of speculating about the reasons why, talk to her."

Sighing, Imani ran her finger through the condensation on the side of her glass. "I've tried. She's also the queen of deflection. She doesn't care about me understanding her reasons. She just wants me to go along with this and act like it's normal."

Her mom had done the exact same thing after her husband's indiscretions came to light. Linda refused to talk about what happened and acted as if he'd never been in their lives. From the moment she came home from the hospital, every trace of Imani's dad was removed from the house. Pictures, books, clothing right down to a stray sock was tossed out. Even during the trial and subsequent conviction of her dad's mistress she referred to him as "that man." If Imani asked her mom how she felt, she got a clipped "I'm fine" and a change of subject. Linda acted as if the change was nothing more than one less plate to set for dinner every night. Imani wasn't sure if her mom ever truly processed what happened in her efforts to move on. Imani wasn't sure if *she'd* ever truly processed it.

"That's Aunt Linda," Halle said by way of excuse. "My mom was just like her. Act like everything's okay until it's not okay."

Imani patted Halle's back. "Remember when we vowed to not be like that. That we'd always be open and upfront about what we want in life and how we feel?"

Halle laughed and nodded. "I remember."

"Didn't we write that vow down somewhere and bury it?" Tracey asked.

Imani's brows drew together then she gasped. "Oh my God, we did! We buried it in the peach field."

"Lord, I forgot all about that," Halle said chuckling. "Those vows to our future selves. They've probably rotted away now."

"Just like our dreams," Tracey muttered before taking another sip of her beer.

"Our dreams haven't rotted away," Imani protested. "We are thriving and doing great. That's what we vowed, remember? I'm a doctor, Tracey has a beautiful family and business, and Halle is still giving back to the community through her work at the school. We're great."

Halle leaned an elbow on the bar and propped her head on her hand. "Honestly, I don't even remember what I wrote on that thing."

"Me either," Tracey agreed.

Imani shrugged. "I'd forgotten about it until just now, too. Maybe we should try to find it."

Tracey frowned and quickly shook her head. "Girl, there's a whole gazebo in that area of the peach fields. We are not about to go digging for our old vows in the middle of my best wedding spot. Besides, I don't think I want to remember my teenage dreams. Reality might not live up to them." She took a long sip of her beer.

Halle raised her glass. "Amen to that." She took a swig then stood. "I'm going to the bathroom."

"I'll go with you," Tracey said.

"I'll watch your bags until you're back," Imani volunteered. She took another sip of the strawberry ale after they walked away and sighed. Tracey was probably right. She didn't need to see those teenage dreams again. Back then she'd hoped to become a doctor who made a difference and changed the world. In fact, she was just another cog in the corporate hospital wheel. She could only go so far and do so much before the administration pushed back. She was doctor of the year, but felt stifled. Lauded for being a part of the team while also expected to sit quietly and be happy with the title. Was she really thriving or had she just checked the appropriate buttons for a comfortable, boring, life?

Imani shook her head then drained her glass. She was supposed to be here having a good time. Not questioning her path in life. She slammed the empty glass against the bar then cringed at the loud clack. When she looked up, her eyes met Cyril's. He had that delicious smile that made her heart skip a beat.

Feel safe enough to fall in love.

The one vow she'd put on that buried sheet of paper years ago that she'd never forgotten whispered in the back of her head.

She looked away quickly. Tracey was right. Dreams from the past belonged in the past. She was a doctor, and corporate cog or not, she was making a difference in the lives of every patient she helped. Maybe she'd foolishly hoped she could fall in love after what happened between her parents, but she was enough of a realist to understand she never would. Her dad's mistress hadn't succeeded in killing her mom, but she had killed any part of Imani that believed in happily-ever-after. No matter how much her body wanted Cyril, her heart would never trust him. Trust came with vulnerability, and she could never open herself up to the kind of hurt her dad put her mom through. Her goal coming home wasn't to bring back the secret hopes of the girl she once was. Her number one goal was, and would remain to be, to ruin Cyril's plans to see their parents get married.

eleven

As soon as Cyril pulled up at the Sweet Treats bakery and saw Imani standing outside talking on her cell phone he knew he'd been set up. His dad had called and pushed him to hurry up and help him, Ms. Kemp and Imani sample cakes for the wedding.

"I don't know anything about cakes. Just get what Ms. Kemp likes and call it a day," he'd said.

"This isn't just about picking a cake. It's getting to know Imani. Now tell Joshua to handle setup at the bar and get over here," his dad had prodded.

"You do realize Joshua is my business partner and not an employee I can order around, right?"

Preston only grunted. "He also said he'd help with the wedding in any way. This is him helping. Now get your butt over here, son."

Cyril turned off his car and scanned the small parking lot. Not that he needed to. Neither his dad's vehicle nor Ms. Kemp's sat in front of the small blue building that housed one of Peachtree Cove's oldest bakeries. They were being urged to play nice again. Not a problem if he could remember that the only relationship he should have with Imani should focus on convincing her to go along with their parents' wedding and not getting lost in thoughts of what a relationship between them could look like.

She threw up a hand as he approached. Her smile didn't quite reach her eyes before she spoke into the phone. "Hey, Towanda, I've got to go. I'll be sure to remote into the board meeting. Thanks for the heads-up." She listened for a few more seconds before nodding and ending the call.

"Everything okay?" Cyril asked.

She lifted a shoulder and slid her phone into the side pocket of the burgundy hooded dress she wore that reminded him of an oversized T-shirt. Beneath the dress she wore dark leggings and sneakers. "Yeah. Work stuff, but I'm good." She looked at Cyril, disappointment in her eyes.

"Is it one of your patients?" he asked.

She frowned up at him. "Huh?"

"You look upset. Is something wrong with one of your patients? Your mom mentioned you're a doctor."

Her face cleared and she shook her head. "No. The other doctors in the office are seeing my patients while I'm out. That was one of my friends. She said the word is getting around that the hospital administrators aren't happy I took off so quickly. Family emergency or not."

He didn't bother asking why she'd said a wedding was an emergency. He already knew the reason. "Are they usually upset when people have family issues?"

"I'd like to say no, but that would be a lie. They're not as bad as some places, but they're only flexible to an extent. For me, they're very upset because they can't prop me up in front of news cameras to make them look better."

"Why would they do that?"

"I'm their doctor of the year." The way she said the words, in a mocking tone while making air quotes with her fingers, surprised him.

"You aren't happy about that? I would think that's a great thing."

"Maybe, if it wasn't a PR stunt." She crossed her arms before continuing. "The staff has complained about the lack of diversity among the administration after a recent merger. Some of the complaints got out to the media which made some patients at the various medical offices complain about discriminatory practices of some of the staff. Right as that happened, bam, I'm announced the doctor of the year and they're putting my face up everywhere."

He shrugged. "So what's the problem?"

She scowled. "So? I don't want to be anyone's token for diversity points."

"What benefits do you get as doctor of the year?"

She opened her mouth as if she was prepared to snap back but then paused. Her brows knitted together before she answered. "The benefits are all for show. My picture goes up all over the hospital. I play spokesperson during media events, and I'm invited to a board meeting to represent staff. And there's a parking spot."

"Wait a second, you get all of that and you're upset?"

"Because I don't want to just make the hospital look good. I became a doctor to help people."

"Then don't just make the hospital look good. Right now, you've got the spotlight. If there are issues you want to bring up, then do it. Who cares about the reason they selected you? You're already there. Take advantage of the opportunity. Who knows? Maybe you can change some things."

"That's sounds great, but if I go off script it's a surefire way to get fired. The few times I tried to speak up at board meetings they shut me down or talked over me."

"Then keep talking until they hear you. My mom used to say don't be afraid of getting fired."

"Why would she say that? No one wants to be fired," she said in a dry tone.

"My mom used to say that no one always agrees with the decisions their higher-ups make. She told me to never be afraid to speak up when I see something wrong. Smart supervisors aren't afraid to hear differing opinions. If you're afraid to speak up and afraid of getting fired you're more likely to turn into a yes-man."

Imani sighed. "That sounds great, but it doesn't always work in the real world. I'm not trying to rock the boat. I'm trying to do my job, help my patients and go home."

He shrugged. "Then don't complain about being doctor of the year. Show up, smile, say nothing and go home."

She glared. "I wasn't complaining."

"Sounded like complaining to me." The breeze picked up and Imani tightened her crossed arms. He pointed to the door. "Let's go inside."

"Fine." She spun away and went through the door without looking back at him.

Cyril let out a grunt and rubbed his temple. "So much for playing nice," he muttered before following her inside.

The sweet smell of baked goods greeted Imani after she entered Sweet Treats. She hadn't been inside the bakery in years. Her mom used to always get Imani's birthday cakes from there along with cakes for any parties or showers they'd hosted over the years. The memory of those fun times almost pulled her out of her irritation, until Cyril came in behind her.

He was so smug and sensible. Talking as if she could easily go against the hospital's administration without consequences. He didn't know what her job was like. She didn't need his judgment. What really sucked was how much his words made her feel as if she were being ungrateful instead of reasonable.

Behind the counter a brunette white woman who looked

vaguely familiar and a few years older than Imani smiled and greeted them. "What can I help you with today?"

Imani ignored Cyril standing next to her and smiled back. "My mom had an appointment to try different cakes."

The woman's eyes lit up. "Imani, hey, come on over. We've got the cakes ready for you to try."

Taken aback that she knew her name, Imani gave Cyril a look but he was focused on the woman. "They've already picked the cakes?"

The woman nodded. "Sure did. But, Cyril, your dad insisted that you come and try the German chocolate he wants for the groom's cake."

Cyril laughed. "That's because he loves your German chocolate cake." Cyril followed the woman over to a table set up at the side of the shop.

Imani followed them. The woman, who Imani thought she went to high school with but still couldn't remember her name, indicated they sit down at the two chairs.

"Now, I've set out the cakes samples they tried. Imani, your mom said to let you try the different ones and then see what you picked. She doesn't want you to be swayed by her choice. Cyril, your dad didn't care. He said go with the German chocolate."

Cyril laughed and glanced over at Imani. She looked from him to the woman and then back. She felt like the odd person out in this entire conversation.

"I figured as much, Carolyn. But I'll go along and pretend as if I have a say-so." He winked at Imani.

Her heart flipped even though she was still mad at him from earlier. She didn't need him giving his unsolicited advice about her job, but damn if the man didn't have a smile that could push past her irritation. He'd taken off the black fedora he'd worn when they sat down giving her an unblocked view of his eyes and face. He pushed up the sleeves of his dark T-shirt, revealing the edges of the tattoos on his arms. Awareness sparked in her midsection which reignited her irritation. She didn't like how much her body liked Cyril.

Carolyn went through the various types of cake samples she'd put out. There was yellow cake, lemon, angel food, pound, caramel and chocolate. After going through the rundown of cakes and leaving them with their rating cards, Carolyn walked away.

Cyril leaned forward. "You don't remember her, do you?"

Imani blinked. "Who?"

He nodded his head toward the front of the bakery where Carolyn was now talking to a customer who'd walked in. "Carolyn."

"I think we went to high school together or something."

"She grew up here. She spoke as if she knew you, but you looked confused."

She picked up a fork and cut off a piece of the lemon cake sample. "I didn't look confused."

"Yes, you did. You know a lot of people around town remember you."

"A lot of people around town know my mom and like to pretend as if they know me, too. That's all."

"No, a lot of people remember you." He took a bite of the pound cake. He licked a few crumbs from the corner of his mouth and Imani quickly focused on the cakes in front of her.

"And I'm sure they have a lot to say about me," she muttered. She could only imagine the gossip they continued to spread about her and what happened with her family.

"Most aren't surprised that you're a doctor. A lot are proud of what you've done. Your mom will sing your praises to anyone who'll listen. Most of the members of the Business Guild know about your work as a doctor."

"Is that all they say? They're proud of me?"

"What else do you think they'd say?"

He looked so clueless, as if he had no knowledge of the scandal or what her dad did before. She couldn't believe it. Her family had been the talk of the town. But as he continued to look at her as if he were waiting for her to say something else, she wondered if enough time had passed that people no longer talked or cared about what happened to her family.

"They don't talk about my mom and dad?"

"If they do it's not to me. Plus, I don't get involved in town gossip. I run my bar and do what I can through the guild to help the town. If it's not that or related to my dad, I don't care."

She frowned, took a bite of the yellow cake. She liked the lemon better. "You care about the town."

"I do."

"But you're not from here?"

He shook his head. "I'm not. Does that mean I shouldn't care?"

"Why do you care? You're from Baltimore, you can't tell me that Peachtree Cove is more interesting."

He chuckled and shook his head. "Not more interesting. I'll admit I do miss the hustle of the city. I never thought I'd want to stay here forever when me and my dad decided to move. In fact, I kind of hated the idea of starting over here."

"Why did you come to Peachtree Cove versus Charlotte, Atlanta or Augusta?"

"My mom's grandmother was originally from this part of Georgia but moved to Baltimore and stayed. She remembers coming down for vacations as a kid before her great-aunts died off and the rest of the family moved away. After my mom died..." He swallowed hard before continuing, "My dad wanted to go somewhere that had been a happy place for her. So, this is where we ended up."

"And you were okay with that?"

He shook his head. "Not at all. I hated it at first. Too quiet, stores closing at nine, everything moved slow."

"What changed your mind?"

"Honestly, the people here. They were friendly and welcoming. They asked why we were here and as soon as they found out my mom's people originated from this area, they took us in as if we belonged. I met Joshua and told him of my dream to open a bar. He introduced me to Miriam Parker, the mayor, and she told me of her efforts to revitalize the town. One grant later to redo a storefront downtown, and a small business loan, I was opening the bar. Finally living a dream I'd had for years. Before I knew it, I was a member of the guild and a part of the community." He grinned and the wonder in his voice washed away the last remnants of her irritation. "Peachtree Cove became home to us."

"So you're never moving back to the city?"

He shrugged. "I don't know. I thought I'd always be a city boy, but I spent a weekend in Atlanta with Joshua a few months back and couldn't wait to get back to Peachtree Cove." He shook his head and laughed.

"Don't tell me you're a true country boy now?"

"Not all the way, but I'm halfway there."

"I can't imagine coming back to live here forever," she said. "I'll admit, the town has grown and the revitalization efforts are great, but it's still a small town."

The door to the bakery opened and Imani glanced that way. She saw the person entering and grunted softly. She had no problem recognizing Mattie Bryant, the mayor's bougie sister. Imani shifted in her seat so her back was to the door and tried to hide her face with her hand.

"Cyril, what are you doing here?"

Cyril groaned before pasting on a tight smile. Imani guessed he also wasn't a fan. "Hey, Mattie," he said dryly. "I'm just tasting cakes."

Mattie walked closer to the table. "Oh, that sounds like fun. And who's this with you?"

Imani dropped her hand and looked up. Mattie was average height with curly auburn-colored hair that brought out the sienna tone to her complexion. Her dark eyes widened, and her manicured brows rose nearly to her hairline. "Oh, my goodness, it's Imani Kemp."

"Hello, Mattie," Imani said with a tight smile.

Mattie looked from Imani to Cyril and then back. "Are you two tasting cakes for the wedding?"

Imani nodded. "We are, and we just got started so—"

"It's so nice that your mom is getting married again. I swear I never would have imagined that she'd *ever* be ready to do that. Not after what happened." Mattie tilted her head to the side and eyed Imani expectantly.

The words hit, but because Imani was always on guard in Peachtree Cove, she didn't give the desired reaction. Mattie used to love pretending to give comfort through sly remarks and barely concealed insults.

"Mattie," Carolyn called from the front of the store.

Irritation flashed across Mattie's face before she turned to Carolyn. "What?"

Carolyn held up a cake box. "The cake you ordered is ready."

"I'll be there in a second." She turned back to Imani.

Cyril pointed to the cakes in front of them. "We'll get back to what we were doing. You have a good day, Mattie." Cyril's firm voice quickly dismissed her.

Mattie looked at Imani. "I was hoping to catch up."

"Maybe some other time," Imani said, not bothering to sound sincere. "Which one do you want to try next?" She looked at Cyril.

Mattie huffed before turning and walking away. Cyril and Imani tasted cake until she was out of the bakery. Imani looked at the door then at Carolyn, who gave her a smile before focusing on the register again.

"Mattie is a character," Cyril said.

"That's putting it nicely." Imani sighed and speared a piece of cake with her fork. "She's why I like the anonymity that comes with living in the city. No one in my business or trying to bring up my past."

Cyril swallowed his cake before speaking. "When you have a community in the city, anonymity goes away. Those people can hurt you just as much as people in a small town can."

She looked back at him. Their eyes met. There was pain in his eyes. A pain that resonated with the hurt in her heart. Had his community back home turned on him the same way Peachtree Cove had turned on Imani and her family before?

"What happened?"

His eyes shuttered and he looked back at the cakes. "Things just weren't the same after Mom passed. What do you think of the cakes? I'm good with whatever they choose. Besides, I need to get back to the bar."

She wanted to push. The fact that she was looking for a reason to call off the wedding urged her to push. The hurt in his voice as he talked about his mom stopped her questions. Just like she hadn't wanted to go there with Mattie, she wouldn't be the person who pushed him to delve into the pain in his heart reflected in his eyes. She felt a moment of solidarity with Cyril that she couldn't explain. As if he also felt the same loss she'd felt. She nodded and pushed the plate away. "I'm done. Let's go with whatever they choose."

twelve

Cyril had to do a double take to believe what his eyes saw as he left his house the next day. Even though he initially passed by, a glance in his rearview mirror confirmed what he saw. That was Imani, kneeling on the side of the road, working on a bicycle. The unexpected sight caused a multitude of questions to pop into his mind.

Why was she out there? It wasn't quite ten in the morning, and he was on his way to the bar to get ready to open later. What was she doing with a bike? Her mom's place was at least five miles away and he couldn't imagine she'd ridden the bike all this way. Was she okay? If she hadn't ridden out here, then had she been dropped off or her car broken down nearby?

He stopped his truck, confirmed no one was behind his vehicle, then backed up to her. She frowned up from where she crouched next to the bike. Cyril popped off his seat belt and slid over to lean out the passenger side window. When she noticed him, her eyes widened with surprise before her frown returned.

"I can't escape you two," she said with a toss of the hand.

"Are you in trouble?"

She stood, winced and rubbed her hip, before shaking her head. "No. Why do you ask?"

"Because you're on the side of the road squatting next to a bike. If you're good, I can leave." He moved to go back to the driver's side, though he had no intention of leaving her there.

She held up a hand. "Sorry. I guess I do look like I'm in trouble. No, I'm okay. I'm just..." She sighed. "Just tired."

He studied her more closely. Sweat beaded across her forehead, several strands of hair escaped from her ponytail and stuck to the side of her face. Her long-sleeved thermal T-shirt and black workout leggings were covered in dust. She looked tired, and beautiful.

"Did you ride that bike all the way out here?"

She cringed and scratched the back of her head. "I did."

"What for?"

She shrugged. "I used to do this ride all the time. Right up there—" she pointed in the direction he'd been driving "—is a trail over to Ridgeview Lake. I used to hang out with Halle and Tracey there all the time. I was going there to see how much it changed."

"And you couldn't drive there?"

"Again, I used to bike out here all the time." She frowned and rubbed her hip again. "I guess spin class is *not* the same as riding my old bike out to Ridgeview Lake."

Cyril tried and failed to suppress a chuckle. "Nah, it's not." He got out of the truck and walked around to her. "Give me the bike."

She clutched the handlebars. "Why?"

"I'll put it on the back of the truck and drive you the rest of the way."

Her stance relaxed. "The trail is literally right up the road."

"And you literally look as if you're about to pass out. Come on. Besides, in all the time I've lived here I didn't know there was a trail to the lake off this road. I've only been to the public access side and that was once."

"Really?"

"Yep."

She bit her lower lip to consider. Cyril took the bike from her instead of focusing on the way seeing her bite her lip twisted his insides. She didn't argue as he put the bike on the back of the truck.

"You know, everyone really should see the lake from this side," she said. "I'll let you drive me, only because I feel like I should show you the way."

"That's the only reason?" he said raising a brow.

She gave him an innocent look. "What other reason could there be?"

"Not that you're tired."

She opened the passenger door. "Not at all."

Cyril chuckled and shook his head. Her lips twitched with her own amusement, and he had the strongest urge to brush the hair back that clung to her cheeks. The attraction he was trying to pretend he didn't feel picked the worst times to show up. He'd been worried she would still be upset with him from the cake tasting the day before. Ignoring his attraction was easier when she scowled at him, but when she smiled...her smile left him dumbstruck and wanting.

He looked away quickly and hurried to his side of the truck. He was being romantic, and except for the out of character moment when he first met her, he was not a romantic. He was a realist. Realistically, anything between him and Imani wouldn't turn out well.

He put the truck in gear and started down the road. "Tell me when to stop. I've driven down this road every day since moving out here and I've never seen a tra—"

"Stop." She pointed out the front windshield. "That's the spot."

He pulled to the side of the road. "What spot."

"Right there." She continued to point then looked at him. His confusion must have been clear because she shook her head. "Just come on and I'll show you."

She was out of the truck before he could respond. Sighing, because he did not see anything and wasn't excited about walking through the woods, he opened the door. If it were anyone but Imani, he would let her go on her way. That wasn't quite true either. He wouldn't have left anyone alone on the side of the road and waved them off down a barely visible trail in the woods, but he knew he couldn't leave her. Not only would his dad and her mom skewer him, but something inside him rebelled against any thought of leaving her alone in the middle of nowhere.

He followed her to the edge of the brush line. She turned back to him and gave a triumphant grin. "See. The trail is still here."

He looked over her shoulder and cocked his head to the side. "I'll be damned. There is a trail."

A small path through the woods. Not so clear that a vehicle could get down, but also not so overgrown that he couldn't tell people used it. If he walked down the road or even biked the way she had, he may have noticed, but not driving past in his car.

"Told you," she said smugly.

"And this leads to the lake?"

"It does." She glanced at his truck. "I would ride my bike, but I don't want to leave you behind."

"Who says I'm coming?"

"I haven't been down here in years and since you're here you might as well come with me. Two people are better than one."

"You weren't worried about that when you biked your happy ass over here," he muttered but softened the words with a half smile.

She laughed and shrugged. "Maybe not, but that's why fate

put you here. My momma always says God looks after fools and babies. And I was most definitely a fool for biking over here alone."

"Does that mean you're not going to do this alone again."

She turned away and headed toward the trail. "We'll see."

He shook his head but followed her. "I may not be here to save you next time."

"I'll drag Halle or Tracey with me next time," she said.

The light of the late morning sun faded as they entered the shade of the trees. Away from the road it was much cooler. Though late February in Georgia wasn't as cold as it used to be back home, it still wasn't walk through woods without cover weather. He pulled off his jacket and slid it around Imani's shoulders. She stopped and her hand lifted to her shoulder. Their fingers brushed. Cyril quickly pulled his hand from the electric zap of her touch.

Imani turned toward him. "You don't have to give me this."

"You were sweating and it's cold. Put the jacket on." He looked past her down the trail that didn't seem close to ending. "How far are we going?"

"It's not that far." She thankfully slid her arms through the sleeves of his jacket.

"That's not an answer," he said.

"You can see the lake through the trees since the leaves are down." She pointed down the trail. "Come on, we're almost there." She started walking and he followed.

"I've never noticed the lake through the trees."

She glanced at him over her shoulder. "How long have you lived out here?"

"Almost six years. Why?"

"Are you always this unobservant?"

"I'm not unobservant. I go to work, I go home and I help around town. I don't *do* nature like that."

She chuckled and turned away. "This isn't *doing* nature. This is a shortcut to the lake."

"Last I heard, the lake is also part of nature."

Her laugh echoed in the quiet of the woods. He smiled, too. Despite being cold, in the damn woods, going who knew how far toward a lake, instead of making his way to the bar to get ready for the day.

"What brought you out here anyway? I thought you were working the flower shop with your mom today."

"I am, but after I got up for breakfast your dad was there and—"

Cyril waited for her to continue. She glanced at him quickly then looked away. "I just decided to take a quick ride before going there."

"Is he being a nuisance?" His dad was spending more time at Ms. Kemp's house.

She shook her head. "Actually, he's being very helpful. He cooks meals and cleans up afterward."

He skipped ahead until he walked next to her. "Hold up. Is that…something positive about my dad?"

She bumped him with her elbow. "I just said he cooks and cleans up after. That's stating a fact."

"But you still don't want him there?"

She was quiet for a few seconds before speaking slowly, as if being careful with her words. "I think it's more of the setup they planned. I can't help but get to know him if he's around. It's just that I'm not used to having a man around the house like that. Not after my dad. It's kind of awkward."

"I can ask him to back off. If you want."

Considering how Preston and Ms. Kemp had already set up for him and Imani to spend time together he wouldn't put it past them to consider forcing Preston's presence on Imani as a way to make her go along with the wedding. He understood they wanted Imani to feel more comfortable with the idea of her mom getting remarried, but Preston would stop if he thought he was making Imani too uncomfortable.

"As much as I want to do that, I won't."

"Why not? You're home after not being here for a while. You shouldn't be uncomfortable."

"I appreciate that, but I know that if I ask him to leave then my mom will be upset. I told her I'd try, so I'm trying."

"And leaving every chance you get. Like on Friday night when you came to the bar."

"Hey, I wanted to spend time with Halle and Tracey. That was good." She pointed ahead. "Almost there."

She was right, he could see the sun glimmering off the lake at the end of the trail. "That wasn't too far."

"Told you."

"Whatever."

They were silent for the few minutes it took to walk out into the small clearing. He assumed they were at a cove at the back of the lake because across from them were more trees and to the right was the rest of the lake.

"Whose property are we on?" He'd been so concerned with not leaving her alone that he hadn't thought about the possible trespassing they were doing.

"It's owned by the town. It's part of the trail system."

"Peachtree Cove has a trail system?"

"You really don't do nature," she said with a laugh. She walked over to a large boulder. Spray-painted messages covered the boulder's surface. Claims of who was there, people being in love and high school classes.

"I guess this is a popular spot." He pointed to all the messages.

Imani's answer was to climb up to the top. "It is. Usually at night with the younger crowd. You can also camp here if you get a permit from the town."

Cyril stood back so he could look up at her. "Good to know, but I won't be applying for that permit."

Her light laughter echoed in the quiet. "Not a camper, either?"

"I'm a city boy. I have no reason to go into the woods."

"You're missing out. Halle, Tracey and I know all the trails in Peachtree Cove. We'd ride our bikes from one side of town to the other and go exploring. It was always fun, and it gave us an escape from the real world."

"If my dad is the reason you needed the escape, then I'll talk to him."

She bent her legs and wrapped her arms around them before settling her chin on her knees. "Your dad isn't the only reason I needed an escape. Yesterday, too."

Cyril pushed back his hat so he could see her better. "The thing with Mattie?"

She frowned before shaking her head. "Nah, I don't care about her. I mean what you said yesterday. About me not taking advantage of being doctor of the year."

He'd wondered if that was going to come back and bite him in the ass. "I pissed you off."

"At first."

"But..." He waited.

"But, when I vented to my friend Towanda last night, she said you had a point."

"I don't know Towanda, but I like her," he said with a half smile.

Imani gave him the side-eye but there was no heat in her gaze. "We work together at Mid-State Health. She's been telling me that being doctor of the year isn't all bad. You're both right, I could use my platform to raise awareness while I have it. I became a doctor to help people. Specifically, an obstetrician to try and prevent what happened to Halle's mom from happening again. I can talk about that and use my platform to try and remind people that we're here to help and save lives.

Not preach our personal beliefs or be blinded by our biases. So, you were right."

He tilted his head and stared up at her. "One phone call and you're telling me I'm right? Can I get Towanda's number to call her for future backup?" he teased.

"Not happening," she said with a laugh. "I also thought about Kaden. He came into the flower shop the other day."

Cyril frowned. "You mean about him having to go to Atlanta to see a doctor."

"You know about that?"

"In a small town like this, everyone knows. And most are angry about it, too. Dr. Baker doesn't care. He says he can run his practice how he feels. And, unfortunately, he's got enough patients. Since he's the only ob-gyn in town he doesn't feel the need to change."

"Ugh, this is why I left Peachtree Cove. Such small-town mentality. People here can't see or understand that everyone isn't going to fit their idea of perfection."

"Hey, don't be too harsh on the town. I said there were just enough, but not a majority. His other patients would go somewhere else if they had the ability. Everyone in town can't drive to Augusta or Atlanta. But I do know that since we moved here most of the people we've dealt with have done nothing but make us feel welcome. It takes time to see the results of progress, but the town is progressing. As for Dr. Baker, if we get another ob-gyn here then he wouldn't feel so high-and-mighty."

"That's what my friend Towanda said. Peachtree Cove needs its own doctor of the year."

"Maybe you should move back."

She scoffed then stared out at the lake. "Not hardly. I left for a reason, and I am not moving back."

Her quick answer sent disappointment through him. He wasn't sure why. Imani never gave any indication that she planned to move back. Her disdain for Peachtree Cove was clear in almost every conversation she had with him. Still, he hadn't thrown out the comment as just something to say. Imani was a doctor that cared and wanted to help. As the town continued to grow, they'd need someone like her practicing in Peachtree Cove.

He glanced at his watch and cringed. Joshua would be calling him in a few minutes to ask where he was. He'd left him to prep by himself yesterday because of the cake tasting and promised to be there on time today. "How long are you staying out here? I need to get to the bar." And even though the spot was a part of the trail system, there was no one out here and he wouldn't leave her alone.

"Oh, we can go back. I wanted to make sure the trail was still here."

"I can take you back home?"

She shook her head. "No need. I can take the bike back."

"You barely made it here. Let me give you a ride." He lifted a hand. "Come on down. It won't take long."

"Well, if you insist," she said with a grin.

Cyril's lips twitched with his own laughter. He doubted she really wanted to bike all the way back to her mom's place. Imani took tentative steps down from the boulder until she could reach his hand. He expected her to continue to step down, but instead she jumped at the last second. He reached out to catch her, but the momentum made her bump hard into his chest. The air rushed out of his lungs. Her hands landed on his chest and his arm automatically wrapped around her waist to steady her.

"You're trying to kill me," he said with a breathless laugh.

"I'm so sorry," she said, humor sparkling in her eyes. "I always jump down. I didn't know you would try to catch me."

"I wasn't going to let you fall," he wheezed.

"Instead, you were going to let me crush you?" She raised a brow.

His laughter made it even harder to catch his breath. By the time their laughter settled they stood smiling at each other.

"Are you going to let me go?" she asked softly. But there was nothing in her voice that sounded offended, nor did she make a move to step back.

"A part of me doesn't want to," he admitted.

Imani's eyes widened and her lips parted as the air thickened around them. She felt good in his arms. He'd known from the moment their eyes met that she would fit against him like this. That her soft curves and enchanting eyes would make him forget everything else in the world. The sound of nature, birds chirping, the lapping water of the lake all faded away as the pounding of his pulse in his ears took over.

Her gaze dropped to his mouth. She bit the corner of her lip and he bit back a groan. If she kept looking at him like that he was going to kiss her. If he kissed her, he wouldn't be able to forget kissing her, and if he couldn't forget kissing her they'd never get through this wedding. The wedding his dad wanted. His dad's second chance at happiness. He couldn't mess that up. If kissing her turned into something they later regretted it would ruin everything.

Cyril quickly let her go and stepped back. "My bad. I shouldn't have said that. Let's get back."

Confusion filled her brown eyes. For a second, he thought she would question why. Instead, her eyes cleared, and she nodded and avoided eye contact. "Yes. Let's hurry up and get out of here."

thirteen

When Imani's mom invited her to attend the Peachtree Cove Business Guild meeting with her, Imani hesitated. She wasn't going if it was just another excuse to get Imani to hang out with Preston, but when her mother let her know Preston wasn't attending because he had a deacon board meeting at the church, she'd quickly agreed. Finally, she could get some time alone with her mom. Between working at the shop, wedding preparations and Preston always being around Imani hadn't had much one-on-one time with her mom. In fact, she'd spent more time with Cyril than anyone else. At this rate she'd never get the chance to have a real talk about her mom and Preston.

"I'm glad you decided to come to the guild meeting with me tonight," Linda said as they drove the few minutes to the town hall.

"I wanted to come. We haven't really had time to hang out with each other."

Her mom glanced away from the road to give Imani a half smile. "I know. Things have been so busy with the wedding planning and the shop. But we've still had fun."

"It's been fun seeing you."

"That's the only thing that's been fun?"

"I know the wedding planning is really just a chance to make me hang out with Cyril."

Linda scoffed and tried to look shocked by Imani's words but the twitch in her lips gave her away. "We're not doing that. Preston and I have just gotten caught up in other stuff."

"Okay, Mom, we'll go with that."

Her mom laughed and patted her leg. "You need to get to know him. He's going to be your family."

She did not want to think about Cyril in that way. Not while the attraction she felt for him was still there. Not when she'd thought about the look in his eye that morning by the lake. In her fantasies he'd pulled her into his arms and kissed her instead of being smart and stepping back.

Imani held up a hand. "That's yet to be determined."

Linda sighed. "Don't tell me that you're still against me marrying Preston."

"I'm still not sure if I understand why you're getting married."

Linda shook her head. "Why do people typically get married?"

"I don't know. Money, security, desperation." Imani held up a finger with each word.

"Lord, I did a number on you didn't I?" Linda said sounding regretful.

"No, you only made sure I didn't view life through rose-colored glasses. I will admit, Preston seems nice, and Cyril is…" Insightful, sexy, irresistible. Imani cleared her throat. "He's cool, but this is still sudden. I'd feel better if you were getting married next year or something and really giving me time to get to know him. This feels rushed and forced on me."

"I'm not trying to force anything on *you*, Imani. I'm happy. Finally. Can't that be enough of an answer?"

As much as Imani wanted to say no, she couldn't. Preston did seem to make her mom happy. The ease of her mom's laughter and the sparkle in her eyes were all real and something Imani hadn't witnessed in years. Linda seemed more relaxed now that she wasn't angry at the world. Imani didn't believe a rushed wedding was what needed to happen, but she also couldn't help but feel good seeing her mom shedding the hurt from the past. Which was why even though she'd come to break up the wedding, she was starting to feel guilty for wanting to do so.

"I want you to be happy, Mom. I really do. That doesn't mean I want to make Preston my stepdad without really knowing who he is," she said.

"That's why you're getting to know him now," Linda said in the *that's final* tone of voice that told Imani the discussion was over. "Ooh, I like this song. Have you heard it?" Linda turned up the radio.

The song in question was a new R & B ballad that had played repeatedly on every radio station for the last month. Classic Linda Kemp move. Pretend everything was okay and change the subject. Imani wanted to push, but years of knowing that pushing only caused her mom to retreat had her nodding and listening to the overplayed song about love and joy.

They arrived at the town hall two love songs later. The guild meeting was held in the community room on the second floor. The same place where the group met when Imani was in high school and had to tag along with her mom to the meetings. Back then Linda had been a very active member of the guild, but after the scandal with her husband, she'd pulled back when she discovered most of the people on the guild had either known about her husband's affair and said nothing, or tried to console her in an attempt to get every salacious detail. Imani was surprised Linda had rejoined, but according to her mom, the board and the membership had changed.

Imani walked in behind her mother and expected to find the small group of nine or ten members who'd made up the Business Guild when she'd been a teen. To her surprise, the room was filled almost to capacity.

She stopped at the door and looked around. "Wow."

Linda turned back to her. She looked at the crowded room then back to Imani. "Way more people than you remember."

"A lot more. Before it was like a social club."

Linda shook her head as she waved at a few people in the room. "Not anymore. The new board is focused on promoting the businesses in Peachtree Cove, keeping the economy strong, working with the town on economic development and having fun. It's not a social club, but we do have socials to encourage networking. Come on, let's get an agenda and find a place to sit."

She followed her mom to the front of the room. Cyril sat behind a table set up next to the podium. Several papers were stacked in neat rows in front of him.

Imani frowned. "What are you doing here?"

"I'm the secretary," he said with a brow raise.

Yeah, he'd already told her that. "I know you're the secretary," Imani said in a rush.

Cyril's answering smile made her stomach tighten. His black fedora was tilted back giving her a clear view of his direct gaze. "I know you know."

"I just forgot for a moment. I keep forgetting…" Because if she'd remembered she wouldn't have come. Not when she was fantasizing about the man kissing her when he obviously realized that kissing her was the dumbest thing to do right now.

He grinned that sideways grin that made butterflies take flight in her stomach. "It's fine. We didn't talk about the guild the last few times I saw you."

No, they had not. Just like that the memory of his hands on her waist and the muscles of his chest beneath her palms flashed in her mind. Heat filled her cheeks and her heart rate jacked up twelve notches. Clearing her throat, she looked away.

Cyril took a sheet of paper off each stack and handed it to Linda. "Here you go. Agenda, minutes from last meeting, treasurer's report and a handout from the town on the St. Patrick's Day Festival."

Linda grinned between the two of them. "I was wondering if they were going to do something big this year."

"Where are we going to sit, Mom?" Imani asked.

Linda looked over Imani's shoulders. Her eyes widened and she waved someone over. Imani turned and barely contained her groan. Preston was there and not at the deacon board meeting as her mom had said.

"Linda, I saved us all a seat at the front." Preston pointed to four chairs that had papers in the seats. "I'm hooking up the projector for the mayor and then they'll get started."

Her mom grinned and blushed. "Thank you, baby."

"Anything for my sweetheart."

Imani barely stopped herself from rolling her eyes. "I thought you had church or something?"

Preston beamed at her as he placed a hand on the small of her mom's back. "I did, but I told the pastor that I wanted to be here with my family. He understood. It's important for all of us to spend time together before the wedding."

Linda practically batted her lashes at him. "That's exactly what I was thinking."

Imani did roll her eyes. She looked to Cyril to see if he was just as disgusted, but he just shrugged before handing papers to someone else.

Getting no help from him then. "Let's sit down."

"Imani, hey! I'm glad you came tonight," a woman's voice.

Imani turned and recognized Carolyn from the bakery. "Hey, Carolyn, yeah, I decided to come with my mom."

"That's great. The guild is so much better than it used to be when we were in high school. I'm glad you decided to come. We didn't get to catch up at the bakery. How have you been?"

"I've been good. Just...getting up to speed on everything."

"Sorry about that thing with Mattie the other day. She's still a busybody," Carolyn said with an eye roll.

Imani shrugged. "Thank you for distracting her."

"No problem. You'd think that after all these years she'd learn to be more like her sister. Everyone loves Miriam."

Carolyn pointed at Miriam. The mayor was shaking hands and smiling with a group of people near the podium. She looked like she had in high school. Average height, slim build and a bright, welcoming smile.

Cyril cut into their conversation. "Hey, Carolyn, here's your agenda."

"Thank you, Cyril," she said before looking back at Imani. "Give me a call while you're in town. We can get together for coffee or something."

"Umm... I'll try. It's been busy. Wedding prep and everything."

She liked Carolyn and appreciated what she'd done, but Imani wasn't trying to make more connections here in Peachtree Cove. She wasn't staying long and didn't want to give the impression that she was going to be one of the ones who left but planned to return.

"Oh, I understand. We're all so excited. Well, it was good to see you."

"You too," Imani said with a stiff smile.

After Carolyn walked away Cyril leaned forward at the table and said in a whisper loud enough for her to hear. "Why don't you want to hang with her?"

Imani scoffed and turned away. Was she that obvious? "Mind your business."

"I will next time," he said with a sly grin. Her lips twitched, but she looked away before laughter would bubble up.

She followed her mom to the seats Preston had saved for

them. When they were seated, she asked her mom, "What's up with Carolyn wanting to hang out with me?"

"Who, Carolyn Jones? She used to live around the corner from Halle. Wasn't she in that play with you back in middle school?"

Imani thought back. They had been in a play together. They'd also hung out a lot over the summer after that school year. That was the summer before her life changed forever. "We were," she said. "I'd forgotten about that."

Forgotten about the friends she'd had before that time. Halle hadn't gone away because she was her cousin and Tracey had refused to be pushed out of her life, but Imani hadn't bothered to keep any of the other friendships she'd once had. She'd been too ashamed and afraid that someone would pretend to be her friend only to hurt her later.

Her mom gave her a knowing smile before saying, "It was a long time ago and you've been away for a while. Want me to point out the rest of your classmates I remember?"

"Sure," Imani said.

Linda nodded and gestured to the various people around the room. Some of them Imani remembered. Her mom also pointed out the new faces of people who'd moved into town in the years since she left. A few even came over to speak to Imani and her mom. Bringing back other memories of the people she'd liked before her life was turned upside down.

"Oh, there's—"

"Brian Nelson," Imani said when her mom pointed out the man who walked in. "I remember him."

A knowing smile curved her mom's lips. "Oh yeah, you did have a crush on him once."

Imani glanced around to make sure no one had overheard. "You could call it that," Imani said in a rush. More like she'd been obsessed with him. Her and half the other girls in school. "I thought he moved away from Peachtree Cove."

"He did. Lived in Atlanta for a while and I think Dallas, too. But he came back to town about a year or so ago, opened a nursery, and won't talk about his life away from Peachtree Cove."

Imani's interest was piqued. What had happened to Brian to make him return? She never would have expected him to settle in Peachtree Cove. He'd been handsome in high school. So much so people said he should be a model, and to no one's surprise he'd done some modeling while attending Morehouse College. He was still just as good looking. Dark brown skin, bedroom eyes and a smile that could boil lava.

"I wonder what made him come back?" she murmured.

"Made who come back?" Preston's voice interrupted.

Imani turned away from Brian, who had several of the women swarm his way after he entered the room. Preston and Cyril had walked over and stood next to her mom.

"Imani was asking about her old crush, Brian," Linda said a little too eagerly.

Imani lightly bumped her mom with her elbow. "Mom, will you stop?"

Linda shrugged. "For what? You did have a crush on him. You, Halle and Tracey."

"That was a long time ago." Her face heated. She glanced at Cyril who watched her with a bemused expression. Of course, he'd take pleasure in her embarrassment. The man loved to tease her. If he knew how much her crush on him far outweighed any crush she'd had on Brian she'd really be in trouble.

fourteen

Cyril tried to focus on the guild president's presentation about the upcoming St. Patrick's Day Festival, but he was having a hard time because one: he wasn't a big St. Patrick's Day fan. He was more likely to curse out someone who pinched him for not wearing green than laugh. And two: he couldn't get his mind off Imani sitting next to him.

From the way she kept looking over her shoulder to take in the rest of the people in the room, he doubted she paid much attention either. He wanted to believe she was merely being observant, but her mother's words echoed in his head.

"Imani was asking about her old crush, Brian."

Cyril hadn't felt jealous of another guy since he was fifteen and Pamela Davis said she'd rather go to the homecoming dance with Rodney Watson instead of him. He shouldn't care if Imani once had a crush on Brian. Shouldn't care if she still had a crush on the guy. Who Imani did or did not like wasn't his problem. His only problem was whether she liked his father or not.

"Did you get that, Cyril?" The mayor's voice cut into his musings.

Imani stopped looking around the room and focused on

him. He was caught staring at her. Heat prickled his face as he cleared his throat and looked toward the mayor at the podium. "I'm sorry, what?"

"We just assigned people to the St. Patrick's Day committee," Miriam said. "Are you good with identifying which businesses are participating in the storefront decorations for the St. Patrick's Day Festival and coordinating with the committee for any additional supplies needed?"

Cyril blinked. That's what he got for not paying attention. When he'd been asked to be the secretary of the business guild he'd agreed because the guild supported him as a new business, and he'd wanted to give back. He hadn't considered taking meeting notes and sending out the agenda to be too hard. He should have read the bylaws more carefully. The secretary did a lot more than he'd assumed. Half of his time was spent coordinating many of the projects the guild thought up.

"Umm... I may not be able to handle all of the coordination on this."

"Why not?" Miriam asked with a slight tilt to her head.

"St. Patrick's Day is a big day for the bar. I'll be busy mixing up a new beer for the occasion. If everyone who's participating lets me know if they're going to decorate, I can get that to you."

"But we'd really like to have a list of exactly what they're doing to avoid duplication."

"It's St. Patrick's Day. There are going to be four-leaf clovers and leprechauns all over the place," he said with a shrug. "It's going to be hard not to duplicate."

"Still, I wish we could have a more detailed list, or a way to coordinate two businesses that want to do the same thing."

Ms. Kemp raised her hand. "I have an idea. Imani can help Cyril keep track and coordinate the participants before the festival. That way you can also focus on mixing up your new beer."

Imani spun in her seat toward Linda. "Mom? I'm in town because of the wedding. Not to plan an event."

"The wedding is almost planned, and this will be a good way for you to also help out the town. Don't you think?"

"I think it's a great idea!" Miriam said before Imani could respond. "It's all settled. Cyril and Imani will collect the list of businesses participating to avoid duplication of decorations. This is going to be a great festival. I'm sure the town will be happy to promote it so we can get people from all over to come out and participate. Those folks across the river won't be able to compete."

A round of cheers and claps went up from the crowd. Imani frowned. "Don't tell me we're still beefing with Peach Valley?"

Cyril let out a sigh. "We are. Even harder since they're going for the best small town, too."

Imani groaned. "Good grief."

Cyril's laugh was drowned out by Miriam speaking into the microphone again. "Well, it's been over an hour and I think we can conclude the business. Don't forget we have refreshments set up in the back."

Cyril stood and went straight to Miriam after the meeting ended. "You know you just strong-armed me into doing this festival."

She smiled and patted his shoulder. "I call it strongly encouraged. Come on, Cyril, St. Patrick's Day can be fun."

"I don't know if you can't tell, but I'm not Irish."

"Neither am I, but you don't have to be Irish to enjoy the festivities. Besides, having a great festival with good business participation will result in a stronger application for Best Small Town. It was your idea that Peachtree Cove apply for the designation. You can't back down just because you don't want to wear green."

He sighed but had no better argument. Going for Best Small Town had been his idea. Granted the idea was more of an offhand comment after seeing the call for applications in *Travel Magazine*. He'd asked Miriam if the town ever considered applying, and when she said no, he had to open his big mouth and ask "why not?" Now he was designated as the person who'd come up with the idea and therefore was *strongly encouraged* to participate in every town event that could possibly strengthen their application.

He wanted Peachtree Cove to win the designation. The town had become a haven when he and his father had left Baltimore after his mother was killed. Peachtree Cove, and the people who'd welcomed and accepted them as part of the community, was the best small town in America.

"I'll do what I can, but I can't speak for Imani," he said. "She doesn't live here, and she may not want to help. No matter what her mom says."

"I knew Imani in high school. Back then she was always the first person to volunteer for a cause. And I know her mom. If Linda wants her to participate, then she'll participate."

He grunted instead of answering. The Imani he knew, the one who was against the wedding, wouldn't just roll over and accept whatever her mom ordered her to do, but he wasn't about to put that business in the streets. Several guild members came up to him to give him their plans for the festival. He took note of what they said and thanked each of them for participating. Even if he wasn't a St. Patrick's Day fan, he was a Peachtree Cove fan and wanted the festival to be a success. When he finally got a second to breathe, he looked around the room to see if Imani was still there or if she and her mom had left. He spotted her in the back of the room. Smiling up into Brian's face.

"Imani was asking about her old crush, Brian."

His feet moved before another thought could form. Imani's laughter reached him as he got close to them. Cyril didn't have a problem with Brian. The guy was nice and even though the women in town loved him, Cyril hadn't seen him running through the single ladies in town. He sold the plants at his nursery, paid his dues to the guild and minded his business. But as

Brian smiled down at Imani, Cyril wanted to push him aside and tell him to keep his smiles to himself.

"Hey, Imani." Cyril walked up and stood between the two. "What's up, Brian?"

Brian reached over and dapped Cyril up. "Nothing much. I guess I need to think of a St. Patrick's Day theme for the nursery."

"It should be easy for you," he said. "You own a nursery, so greenery shouldn't be a problem."

Imani's eyes widened. "Mom did say you owned a nursery?"

Brian shrugged. "It's a small one. I reached out to your mom for advice since she has a flower shop."

"I'll have to come by one day."

"Do that." Brian nodded at someone across the room. "Let me go holla at Joe. Nice seeing you, Imani."

"You too, Brian." She grinned after him and gave a little wave.

Cyril barely stopped himself from rolling his eyes. "Crush still there, huh?" He tried to sound teasing even though he felt some type of way.

Imani waved a hand and shook her head. "No, Brian's nice. I'm proud of him. Owning a nursery and all that."

"Yeah, sure."

"Why do you say it like that?"

Admitting to being jealous about her smiling and laughing with Brian went against his *we're not supposed to be pursuing this attraction to Imani* stance. So, instead he said, "No reason. Are you okay with helping me out for this?"

She sighed. "Mom won't let me rest if I don't and it'll give me something else to do besides wedding preparations."

"You do realize I'm not a good excuse to avoid wedding preparations? If we work together on this then they'll find even more reasons for us to hang out together."

"Well, I just view that as more opportunities to get to know you better."

If only her getting to know him wasn't connected to their

parents getting married. There would be fewer complications with that. Still, he couldn't help but meet her eyes and ask, "Do you want to get to know me better?"

Imani hesitated for a second. For a second, the attraction between them pulled taut, before she glanced away and took a step back. "Isn't that the point of this? For me to get to know you so that we're good with the wedding?"

"I'm good with the wedding."

"Well, I'm not quite there yet."

"Then this is good. We can work together on the wedding and the St. Patrick's Day Festival."

"I'm not here forever," she said quickly.

The words hit him like a bullet to the heart. He rubbed his chest and tried to ignore the hurt caused by her words. "I know you're not here forever. That doesn't mean I can't enjoy your company while you're here."

Her eyes met his. Just like the first time, he was lost in her gaze. "Are you enjoying my company?" Her voice was soft and curious.

Cyril tugged on his hat and glanced away before she saw how her words, her voice, affected him. "More than you know."

fifteen

Imani had to circle the block twice before she could snag a parking spot downtown and was still a block away from Cyril's bar. One of the many surprising changes she was starting to notice in the town she'd remembered as slow and sleepy. Downtown Peachtree Cove wasn't exactly bustling, but there was a steady stream of people in the area.

As she walked the block toward Cyril's bar, she noticed how many of the storefronts which were abandoned when she'd left town after high school were now filled with shops. A clothing store, pharmacy, coffee shop, art studio and insurance agency now occupied the once empty stores. She stopped in front of one storefront. The windows were covered with brown paper which prevented her from seeing what has happening inside, but she recognized the woman coming out.

"Joanne? Is that you?"

Joanne Wilson looked up from where she was locking the door. Joanne was a couple of inches shorter than Imani, with caramel skin and blond microlocs that fell to her shoulders. Even though she was several years older than Imani they knew each other well. Joanne had successfully styled Imani's hair for prom, homecoming and every event in between.

Joanne squinted at Imani then grinned. "Imani! Oh, my goodness, girl, your momma did say you were coming home for the wedding."

Imani stopped herself from cringing. No one in town thought the wedding was too sudden. Everyone loved her mom and Mr. Preston together and couldn't wait for them to tie the knot.

She smiled at Joanne. "I am. Let me guess, you're doing the hair of everyone in the wedding?"

Joanne's face lit up. She pointed to the door she'd just locked. "Actually, that's the plan. The grand opening for my new salon is coming up the Saturday after next. I'd give you a flyer if I had one, but it's been a busy day. I've got to go pick up some packages from the post office."

Imani looked from the covered windows back to Joanne. Her cheeks hurt, her smile was so big. "Oh my God! Congratulations! I know you've wanted this for a long time."

"Thank you, it's definitely a dream come true. Come by later and I'll give you a pre-opening tour." She checked her watch. "I've got to go. It's nice seeing you. Tell your mom I said I'm ready to make everyone beautiful for her big day, okay."

Imani nodded; another tug of guilt twisted her insides. If she did figure out how to get her mom to cancel or postpone this wedding it would have a trickle-down effect on the various people her mom had hired to prepare for the wedding. Hopefully, everyone would understand she was only trying to do what was best for her mom and not ruin their business.

"I'll be sure to tell her," she said.

Joanne waved and then hurried across the street to her car. Imani looked back at the paper-covered windows. Joanne was finally achieving her dream and opening her own salon. She was the best stylist in Peachtree Cove. Now, not only was she opening a salon but in one of the nicest buildings downtown.

Imani had to admit that the claims from her mom, friends and Cyril that Peachtree Cove was "coming up" might be true.

She made her way to Cyril's bar, which was located on the corner of Main and Blossom Streets. She pulled on the door, but it didn't budge. Frowning, she tried again but with the same result. Taking out her phone, she texted Cyril. He'd asked her to meet him there at nine and she was there on time. She hoped he hadn't forgotten he planned to meet up with her.

Hey, I'm outside. Where r u?

A few seconds passed before three dots bounced on her phone screen indicating he was responding. The dots stopped with no response. Grunting, Imani narrowed her eyes at the screen. Was he seriously going to ignore her?

The lock on the door clicked. She looked up and spotted Cyril's smiling face on the other side of the glass. He pushed open the door for her. "My bad. I forgot to tell you that I keep the front locked when I'm working in the back. It was easier to just open the door than text back."

"I was worried you'd forgotten about me."

"There's no way I could forget about you, Imani."

The words were innocent enough, but the way he said them... With that look in his eyes that made her bones melt and a smile that made her stomach flip. That made her hear a lot more of a promise in his voice. A promise she wanted to know if he'd keep.

Fearing he'd see the unexpected jolt of yearning in her heart on her face, she slid by him to get inside. He held the door open for her, so she was close enough as she passed to notice the spicy clove scent that clung to him. He wasn't wearing a hat today, which meant the rich chocolate brown of his eyes wasn't partially hidden when their eyes met. Connecting gazes with Cyril was like an electric shock to her system. She sucked in a breath only to once again be hit with how damn delicious he smelled. She quickly moved and put distance between them.

Inside the bar was empty and quiet. Too quiet. She swore her heavy breathing echoed in the spacious interior. "What time do you open?" she asked in a rush to make a sound. Any sound that would cover up her pounding heart and erratic breaths.

"Not until one. Joshua is usually here to have us ready for the afternoon crowd, but he had to visit one of our suppliers today."

"My bad if I'm intruding on you working. We could've met another time."

"It's not a problem. Even if Joshua handles the afternoon crowd it's not unusual for me to get here early, especially if I'm working on a new blend. Come on in the back and I'll finish up what I'm doing while we talk."

Nodding, she followed him to the back of the bar. She tried not to notice the way his thin T-shirt clung to the muscles of his back and shoulders. Tried not to focus on the smooth swagger of his walk and how his hips and ass seemed to beg for her attention.

"It's cold outside. Why are you only wearing a T-shirt?" She sounded irritated when she shouldn't be. He hadn't worn the T-shirt to deliberately entice her.

"I've got a hoodie around here somewhere, but it's not too cold. It's fifty degrees."

"That's freezing." Imani had grown up in Georgia and now lived in Florida. Anything fifty and below felt like blizzard conditions.

He chuckled. "This is nice weather."

"This is turn on the heat weather."

"You sound like my dad. He's already grumbling about it being cold. As if he didn't live his whole life in Baltimore."

In the back large metal bins lined one wall. Along another wall were several large kegs with hoses attached to them. A small table sat in the middle with glass jars filled with what looked like beer. Cyril walked over to the table.

"What's all this?" She pointed to the jars and tubes.

Cyril held up one of the jars and swirled the dark gold liquid inside. "Testing out the lager I'm brewing for St. Patrick's Day. It'll be a special blend. Just while it lasts." He brought the jar to his nose and inhaled.

Imani cocked her head to the side. "Wait, you brew your own beer, too? I thought you just brought in beer."

"Let me guess. I don't look like the kind of guy who would brew his own beer."

She grinned but shrugged. "I mean…can you blame me for assuming you just had a bunch of beers on tap?"

"Honestly, that's mostly what I do. I like beer and I don't mind trying to make my own, but I'm not trying to become a beer maker. I mostly stock beers from local brewers around the state. Some of the larger ones I keep here, too. Then, when I get an urge, I'll make a batch of my own blend to see if people enjoy it. Whatever I make is only on sale for a short time."

"Why beer? I mean, I get that people love it, but what made you want to make and sell beer?"

He leaned his hands on the edge of the table. The muscles in his forearms and biceps flexed, drawing her attention to the edges of the tattoos on his arms. Imani's fingers extended with the urge to push up his sleeve and see what he'd decided was important enough to permanently ink onto his body. She looked away from him to the jars of beer. Studying the items on the table was much safer than studying Cyril's body movements.

"I like beer, and I've got good memories around it."

"What kind of memories? You sneaking a beer from your dad when you were a teenager?"

He laughed. "Nah, my dad would've kicked my ass if he'd caught me stealing beer and my mom would've been right behind him."

"Sounds like my mom."

"I can see that." They both laughed before he sobered. "Nah, my memories are of my dad and uncles sitting out back. Every payday Friday they'd get together at our house. My mom would take off with my aunt and their friends and my dad would hang with the guys. They'd open up a pack of beers and just shoot the breeze. They'd talk about work, politics, relationships, even pop culture. If me and my cousins were in the room, they didn't change the subject or censor what they said. They let us listen in, as long as we didn't interrupt. Said it was their way of giving us life lessons. I loved those times. When I was finally twenty-one and could join in, I felt like I'd arrived. After my mom died… I missed those days. When we moved here, opening a bar was a way to kind of bring back those good times."

The emotion and trace of longing in his voice as he confessed the reason behind his business pulled at her heartstrings. "Sounds like those were good times."

The smile on his face was nostalgic. "They really were."

"You and your dad don't go back home to visit and hang out like that anymore?"

His smile faded and the shutter from before hid the longing in his eyes. "Nah, we don't. After my mom died things changed."

"Was she the one who held you all together?"

"You could say that." He crossed his arms, shutting off further discussion. "Guess we should talk about the St Patrick's Day Festival."

She wanted to know more about him. His story about hanging out with the men in his family had piqued her curiosity. Not because she wanted to dig up more information on him. She was genuinely interested in knowing more about him. She wanted to know what made him smile, laugh, and get that warm and gooey tone in his voice. She liked that tone. It made her want to get warm and gooey in his arms.

Which was exactly why she was going to let him change

the subject. "Yeah. I'm wondering how much work you actually need from me."

"Not much really. Miriam made things seem more involved than they need to be. I'll email all the guild members and ask who's participating and if they'll have a theme. Then if anyone has a similar theme, I'll connect them to each other. They really didn't have to rope you into this."

Imani placed a hand over her heart, relieved. "Oh, good. For a second I thought this was going to be a lot of work on top of all the wedding stuff."

"There's not much left to do for the wedding. We just have to finalize the details. It isn't that far away."

It wasn't that far away. She also wasn't making much progress in getting her mom to consider postponing the wedding. The festival was a way for Imani and Cyril to get to know each other, but as much as she wanted to get to know him she also wasn't there to get distracted from her true goal.

She shrugged. "There's always more things to consider." Like decide if her mom was rushing things and if she should still try and stop the wedding.

"There isn't much work for the wedding, but I wasn't ready to get involved in planning the festival," Cyril said. "St. Patrick's Day isn't a holiday I get excited about."

She laughed. "Really?"

He raised a brow. "You say that as if you're into St. Patrick's Day?"

"I mean, I'm not going to die my hair green or anything, but I do enjoy a good St. Patrick's Day parade."

He shook his head. "I'm glad you didn't say that in the meeting. Otherwise, the guild would do a—"

"Do you think they'll want to have a parade before the festival?" she asked, kind of excited about the idea.

Cyril held up a hand. "Stop it. We've got enough on our

hands with a wedding and promoting the businesses decorating for the festival. Let's not add parade to the list."

Imani sighed but agreed. "I love parades, but I'll admit I'm probably not the best person to organize one. I'm good with helping out with anything you need to coordinate the decorations."

"So, you're big into parades, huh?" he asked.

She grinned. "I am. Seeing the floats, and the way people dress up their vehicles and throw out candy. They're so much fun. And when there's a vendor there, they typically sell fair food, and I am a sucker for a good corn dog."

"Yeah, I know," he deadpanned.

She narrowed her eyes. "If that tone is because of the mustard incident, we both agreed to move past that."

"I may have moved past it, but my shirt hasn't."

Imani moved closer and examined the beer on the table. "Well too bad. The statute of limitations has passed on me replacing your shirt."

Playful laughter danced in his eyes as he drew nearer. "So me and my shirt are just SOL, huh?"

She shrugged and grinned. "Pretty much."

"What if I still want some type of compensation for my loss." He turned to face her.

Imani tilted her head to the side and raised a brow. "What kind of compensation would you want?"

"I don't know." He placed a hand against his chest. "I'll have to think about what it'll take to make me and my shirt feel better."

She rolled her eyes but grinned. "When you think of it don't bother to let me know because I can't help you."

He made a face as if she'd wounded him. "You're a cold-hearted woman."

"I can heat up when I want to." The teasing words were spoken softly with way more innuendo than she'd intended.

Desire flashed in his dark eyes. "And I would love to see you all nice and warm." His voice dipped to levels that were dangerous to her libido.

Goose bumps sprouted across her skin. The air charged between them as the underlying meaning of his words rained over her. They were flirting.

Reason said she should stop it. Attraction made her reply. "I bet you would."

Cyril eased a little closer. "Maybe one day you'll show me."

She wanted to show him. Badly. She would have been on her way to showing him if she hadn't squirted him with mustard. The mustard had been embarrassing, but it had saved her to an extent. Things would have been more awkward if they'd exchanged numbers and planned to meet up later only to later discover their parents were getting married. She should remember that. They both needed to remember that.

"I would…if our parents weren't getting married." She admitted to the only reason she held back from getting warm and gooey in this man's strong arms.

The fire left his eyes, and he took a half step back. "Yeah… they are."

"It would be weird for me to show you just how nice and warm I could be…wouldn't it?"

A tense moment passed before he answered slowly. "But right now, our parents aren't married." He rubbed his chin. "It wouldn't be weird, but it might be awkward later."

Imani shrugged. "It has the *potential* to be awkward. We don't know if it will be awkward. We may be surprisingly mature about the entire thing."

He took another step closer to her. "Which means you should show me before they get married, right?"

She sucked in a breath as excitement exploded in her veins. "Maybe I should."

sixteen

Her good sense had fled. Or maybe, she hadn't wanted to kiss a man as much as she wanted to kiss Cyril right now. Either way, she was making a big mistake, and she was willing to live with the consequences.

She stood still, breathing shallow and body tight with anticipation as Cyril erased the small space between them. His hand slid around her waist slowly. Almost as if he too realized they were crossing a line that would be hard to come back from. The heat of his body seeped into hers, melting her bones and softening the last bits of her resistance. His eyes never looked away as he pulled her body against his.

His head lowered and finally his lips were on hers. First with a soft press before he pulled back. Imani sighed, his body relaxed and then he kissed her deeply. Their tongues slid across each other's as the attraction that had first sparked between them ignited into flames. Her arms wrapped around his shoulders, and she pulled him tighter against her. The hardness of his chest and the hardening length of his erection pressed into her belly, making her want more. To have every inch of his skin against hers while he kissed her just like this. Kissed her until she lost herself in his embrace and forgot everything else in the world.

She felt safe, comforted, precious in his arms. Something she hadn't felt in any other man's embrace. This was more than the desire she expected. This feeling was dangerous, because this feeling could cause her to overlook all warning signs and trust in the emotions and feelings Cyril stirred up in her. Emotions she didn't trust or believe in herself.

She pulled back quickly. Her arms slid from around his neck until her hands pressed against his chest. His heart was a jackhammer beneath her palms.

"Are you okay?" he asked softly. She would have expected him to sound surprised or maybe even a little frustrated that she'd ended the kiss so abruptly. Instead, concern filled his voice.

Her heart twisted. Emotion swelled inside her. This was too much. She wasn't supposed to feel this much. This was supposed to be just desire.

"Imani?" he questioned.

She shook her head and stepped back. He let her go. "I'm good."

"Was that weird?"

"No, it wasn't." It was one of the best kisses she'd ever had. She wanted to kiss him again. Wanted to do a lot more than kiss him. "But we can't do it again. It'll be weird if we keep this up."

"We could always stop after they get married."

The temptation of those words spoken in his rumbling voice made her sex clench. Not only that, it made her heart flip. What was wrong with her? She couldn't fall for him. Sleeping with him was one thing, but catching feelings? Not an option. Their best bet was to stop this now. After one quick, delicious, amazing kiss.

She stepped back. He curled his fingers into a fist as if he was trying to stop himself from reaching for her.

"I should go," she said.

"Yeah, that's probably for the best."

The barely veiled desire in his voice made her heart race. "We'll talk about the festival later."

He nodded. "Later."

She turned and quickly left the bar. She didn't bother to look back. If she did, there was no guarantee that she'd be able to leave without crawling back into his arms.

After kissing Cyril, Imani didn't know where to go. She couldn't imagine facing her mother. Linda would be sure to ask her how things had gone with her meeting with Cyril and the kiss was too fresh in her mind to hide that something happened. She didn't want her mom to know anything about the kiss. She needed to go somewhere to process everything, but she also needed to talk about what was going on. Which had her dialing Tracey to see if she could come by her bed-and-breakfast for coffee. She needed Tracey and Halle, but Halle was working and couldn't come over.

When she arrived, Tracey was on the phone with Monique, the woman who worked at the front desk of her inn. "Don't worry about it, Monique. Whatever you need to do just let me know," Tracey was saying. She looked at Imani and shook her head.

Imani sat down in one of the wingback chairs in the living area and watched Tracey pace back and forth.

"Just be careful and let me know what you find out. Okay. Talk to you later." Tracey pressed the button on her cell phone and sighed. "Well, that sucks."

"What's going on?"

"Monique says she has a family emergency and needs to take her cousin somewhere with her mom. I don't know." Tracey twisted her lips and narrowed her eyes at her cell phone.

"Do you think she's lying?"

"I think she's always got something going on. When I first opened this place she was great and I knew I could count on her. Lately though…she's been distracted and out of it."

"Maybe it really is a family emergency. She could have a lot going on."

"It feels like something else." Tracey shrugged and waved a hand. "Either way, it doesn't matter. We've only got one couple staying today and they're very low-key. Anniversary trip and mostly staying in their room. I'll let Bernard know I'm staying here tonight."

"You spend the night here?"

"Not a lot. Monique lives nearby, so she usually stays here until around ten then she locks up the place and I show up in the morning."

"Then why are you staying? You're not too far from here. You can go home."

Tracey scrunched up her nose as if the idea of going home was distasteful. "I'm not far, but it's still too far if something comes up tonight. It'll be fine. So, what brings you here today? When you asked about meeting up with me you acted like something was wrong."

Imani groaned and put her hand to her forehead. The reminder of why she'd sought out her friend hitting her. "I messed up."

"Chile, please, of everyone I know you're the one least likely to mess up."

"No, for real, I messed up. Like, *really* messed up."

Tracey's eyes widened before she sat in the chair with Imani. They both could barely fit and giggled as Tracey wiggled her hips to push herself between Imani and the edge of the chair. "What happened?"

Imani laughed. "Are you serious?"

"When Imani says she really messed up then I need to hear it. What did you do?"

"I…" The words stuck in her throat. She placed a hand over her eyes and sighed.

Tracey tapped against Imani's leg. "Don't play with me. You're about to make me worry. What's wrong?"

"I kissed Cyril." She said the words in a rush and kept her hand over her eyes.

The silence that fell was deafening. Imani spread her fingers and stared through the slits. Tracey's mouth hung open. She stared at Imani with wide, shocked eyes.

Imani dropped her hand. "Did you hear me?"

Tracey blinked. Then used her knuckle to shake her ear before clearing her throat. "I think I heard you wrong. I thought you said you kissed Cyril."

"I did." She leaned forward and said in a softer voice. "And I liked it. A lot."

"Oh my God!" Tracey exclaimed and tapped Imani's leg again. "I can't believe you did that."

Imani slapped her hands over her face again. "I know. It's messed up, right? I can't be kissing Cyril."

"Why not?"

Imani dropped her hands and gave Tracey a shocked look. "Because our parents are getting married."

"And?" Tracey said as if that were no big deal. "If you would have met him first, kissed and hooked up, and then your parents met, would you break up with him because your parents fell in love?"

Imani frowned. "What?"

"Don't make me repeat what I said when you heard me. Would you?"

"No… I mean. I don't know what I'd do. This isn't a normal situation. He's going to be my stepbrother."

Tracey shook her head. "No. If you two grew up in the same house and were raised together then he's your stepbrother. This is just the son of the dude your mom is marrying."

"Tracey, that's the same thing."

"No, it's not. I think you should go for it. I like Cyril. He's a good guy and you might as well get you some while you're in town."

"Nope I shouldn't. What about after our parents get married? What if we start seeing other people and bring them around? Wouldn't that be weird?"

Tracey huffed and waved away Imani's words. "Worry about that when it happens. Right now, think about what you want."

"I don't know if I even want my mom to marry Mr. Preston. How can I then turn around and hook up with Cyril?"

Tracey settled back in the chair and gave Imani a serious look. "You don't want your mom to marry him because of the stuff with your dad."

"The stuff with my dad is serious."

"I'm not trying to make light of it. What that woman did was horrible. But you have to admit you're holding every man since then accountable for your dad's mistake. You only want to see the bad in people which is why you're seeing the bad in Mr. Preston."

"I didn't come here to be analyzed." She pushed against Tracey and tried to get up.

Tracey pushed back and didn't budge. "Oh no. You came here for me to tell you to go ahead and kiss Cyril again and you know it."

"I did not!" She tried to get up again only for Tracey to press back harder.

"Yes you did. You always come to me when you want someone to tell you to do the thing that you really want to do but know you probably shouldn't do. That's why you ended up doing it with Rodney Turner."

Imani sat up straight, narrowed her eyes and pointed at her friend. "We were not going to talk about Rodney anymore."

Tracey gave her a fake innocent look. "Why not? You enjoyed it. I don't know why you cut it off with him."

"Because…he wasn't the type of guy I should get caught up on." Rodney was the guy she'd dated the summer between high school and college. They'd met at a summer 4-H program and the sparks had been immediate. She'd lost her virginity to him, but at the end of the summer she'd broken things off because college was more important than a summer romance.

"That's what your mom and those people at church said. But you liked him and that's why you came to me to talk about your conflicted feelings. You know I'm going to tell you to go with your gut just like you're doing now."

"Dang. Why you gotta know me so well," Imani said with mock frustration. She had come here because she knew Tracey would tell her the truth even if she didn't want to hear it.

"People don't change very much. I know what you want. You want Cyril."

She shook her head. "I can't have him. I have to focus on my mom and figure out why she suddenly wants to get married after swearing off men for so long. Cyril will distract me from getting to the bottom of what's up with her. I get it. Mr. Preston is a nice guy and everyone loves him. I even admit that he makes my mom happy and seems decent. But my mom has completely changed. I've got to get used to this and figure out if this is what she really wants or if it's just because my dad decided to be an asshole and rub it in her face that *he's* getting married again."

"When you put it that way, I can't really blame you." Tracey's cell rang. She frowned at the screen. "This is Bernard. Let me make sure he's okay."

"Then can you get up while you talk. We can't fit." Imani pushed on Tracey's hip.

"We can fit," Tracey said, but she hopped up and answered. After a few seconds the smile on her face vanished and a frown replaced it. "You have to go tonight?" Tracey said in an irritated voice. "You know I have to stay at the bed-and-breakfast. I thought you would stay here with me—" Tracey stopped talking and pinched the bridge of her nose. "I don't understand why you have to go. I thought we could… Fine, whatever, I'll talk to you later." She ended the call.

"Is everything okay?"

Tracey rolled her eyes. "His cousin is having issues with his girlfriend. He's going to help him move his stuff."

"Really?"

"His cousin and his girl are always fighting. Bernard is always up there trying to play peacemaker." Tracey sighed. "I'm just irritated about his cousin calling him to Augusta tonight."

"He'll be back tomorrow?"

"He will." Tracey nodded but didn't sound exactly sure.

Imani felt there was more to the story, but she could tell by Tracey avoiding eye contact that she didn't want to delve into the full details. Imani didn't want to push. She could barely give herself advice about what to do with Cyril. She would be no help to Tracey in her marriage.

She slapped her hands against her thighs and smiled. "Well, since you're staying here tonight…do you mind if I share one of your rooms with you?"

"Why do you want to stay with me?" Tracey asked, but a light brightened her eyes.

"I don't think I can face my mom or Mr. Preston. Not yet."

Tracey laughed. "Girl, yes. It'll make the night more fun, and you can tell me all about how and why you kissed Cyril."

seventeen

Even though there were several customers in the bar that night to keep Cyril busy, he couldn't get kissing Imani out of his mind. If someone ordered his special blend, he thought about telling her about his love of beer right before they'd kissed. If someone asked about St. Patrick's Day, he thought about her admitting she loved parades and then his kissing her. Just watching his patrons talk and laugh made him think about how relaxed he was in her company and the way they'd teased about compensation for his shirt right before they'd kissed. The woman, her sweet lips and soft body, were imprinted in his brain and he was worried he might not be able to erase her.

"Cyril, I hope that's not my beer because I ordered the lager and not the pilsner," Jay, a customer at the end of the bar, called out.

Cyril blinked and looked down at the glass he was filling. Sure enough, the glass was half full of the pilsner. He stopped the pour and groaned. "Sorry, Jay. I'll get that right order for you."

"Don't pour out the pilsner. I'll give it a try," Jay said with a big grin.

Cyril slid the glass across the bar. "You know what, you can have this on the house."

Jay's eyes lit up. "For real? Thanks, man!"

"No problem." Cyril grabbed another glass and filled it with the lager he'd originally ordered.

Joshua stopped cleaning glasses at the end of the bar and came over. "You need to take a break?" he asked with a raised brow.

Cyril nodded. He wasn't afraid to admit when he was distracted and making mistakes. "Yeah, let me take a minute. Things have calmed down for a while. I'll be right back."

"Cool. Take your time. I'll holla if I need you."

"I appreciate that, man." Cyril walked away from the bar and headed toward the office in the back.

The door to the bar opened and his dad walked in. Preston glanced around the bar, spotted Cyril and grinned. Instead of going to the office Cyril waited at the end of the bar for his dad.

"What brings you in here tonight?" Cyril asked.

"I was waiting on you to call me. How did things go with Imani earlier today?" Preston's voice was filled with anticipation, and he rubbed his hands together. He wore his favorite peach-colored linen suit and his hair looked freshly washed and brushed to a shine. Which meant he was probably going to visit Ms. Kemp after leaving him.

Cyril's stomach clenched. Visions of Imani in his arms, the taste of her lips and her breasts pressed against his chest filled his mind. That's exactly why he hadn't called his dad. How could he pretend as if nothing happened? He could barely remember to pour the right beer for his customer.

"Uhh…it was fine."

The grin fell from his dad's face. "You two didn't get into a fight, did you?"

Cyril quickly shook his head. Thankfully laughter at the back of the bar gave him an excuse to look at something else. "Nah, nothing like that. We talked about the St. Patrick's Day Festival and beer."

"Beer?" his dad asked frowning. "Why were you talking about beer?"

"She asked why I opened a bar."

The confusion on his dad's face cleared up. "Ah, I get it. That's good. You two bonded, huh."

"You could say that." Cyril scratched his jaw. "Anyway, I told her about the good times I used to have sitting around with you, Uncle Tommy, Uncle June and Uncle Otis, listening to you all give us advice while you went through a twelve-pack of beer. That I opened this place to bring back those good feelings."

The concern crept back into his dad's face. "What else did you say?"

Cyril immediately understood his dad's concern. Had he gone so far as to go into the details of why they didn't all get together anymore? Had he gone into the scandal surrounding his mom's death?

He shook his head. "Nah, I didn't get into all that. I figured that story needs to come from you. It's not mine to tell."

His dad glanced away. "Well, I'm glad things worked out." He looked back at Cyril. "What did y'all decide for the festival?"

They hadn't gotten anything finalized. They'd gotten lost with the kiss. "Umm...we talked about getting a list of themes from the businesses. And Imani mentioned wanting a parade."

"Parade!" Sam, the bartender helping them that night, said with a bright smile. "Are you doing a parade?"

Jay looked up from his two beers. "We're having a St. Patrick's Day parade? I used to go to the parade back in my hometown."

Cyril held up a hand to push back the excitement coming his way. "I said we talked about a parade."

"I think that's a great idea," his dad said. "We only have the Christmas parade in town, but having another one would be a good way for businesses to get the word out."

Sam slid a beer to a customer before chiming in. "I agree!

We could even do a truck with a keg on it and pass out flyers with discounts for the bar."

"And advertise it to the surrounding towns that it's not only a parade but also a day-long festival. That'll go a long way toward strengthening our application for Best Small Town."

Cyril spun around at the sound of Emily's voice. When had she, the president of the Business Guild, come in? Had he been that out of it?

"I can't put together a parade. I've got enough going on," Cyril said firmly.

"That's fine. We'll pull together a committee to help. In fact, when I tell the mayor she'll be on board and could probably get some assistance from the people who work for the town," she said, excitement clear in her voice. "This is going to be great. I'm glad you and Imani came up with such a good idea."

"It wasn't my idea. Imani thought this up."

His dad slapped him on the shoulder. "I'm glad you two worked together so well."

He looked from his dad to the rest of the people around the bar. A few patrons who sat at the tables and chairs closer to the bar watched with enthusiasm and others spread the word to those who couldn't hear the conversation. The news that Peachtree Cove would host a St. Patrick's Day parade would be all over town before the sun rose.

"I'm taking my break." He turned away from the excited chatter about parade plans and went to his office.

"I'm coming with you," his dad said.

Cyril would have preferred to be alone, but he wouldn't turn his back on his dad. He stood by the door and let Preston go in before him. Once away from the crowd in the bar he headed to where he'd blended his beer, but a vision of him and Imani there earlier formed. He made an immediate about-face and headed to the desk in the corner.

"I know you probably want to be alone, but I needed to tell you something," his dad said, tuned in to Cyril as usual.

"I'm good. What do you need to tell me? Are you not going to be home tonight?"

His dad grinned sheepishly then shrugged. "I may stay with Ms. Kemp tonight, so I wanted to catch you. I was worried you and Imani wouldn't get along earlier today."

"Nah, we got along pretty good." He shifted his stance and tried to ignore the vision of him and Imani still clear as day in the opposite side of the room.

"Good. Linda and I really want you and her to be like family. Like brother and sister. We haven't had that for a long time, and well, this is our chance to build up our families again. One day you'll get married and so will Imani. There will be grandchildren and we'll all be together. I'm really happy that I'll be able to give Linda that."

The vision across the room evaporated. Guilt kicked Cyril's stomach to his feet. "I don't know if we'll ever be like brother and sister."

"Yes, you can and you will be. If you two keep getting along and become friends. Then we'll be like one big ole happy family. Can you at least try? I know how much it hurt when your cousins turned their backs on us after your mother died. I know they were like siblings to you, and I want you to have something similar in your life again. Maybe Imani can be the start of you getting that. Don't you think?"

His dad was right, the loss of those relationships hurt almost as much as losing his mother had. It tied into the grief he held on to and tried not to show for fear of making his dad worry about him. No matter how much he missed those relationships and had tried to fill the void with the friendships he'd made becoming a part of the Peachtree Cove community, Imani would never fill that spot because he didn't view her as just a friend. He didn't want Imani for a sister figure or as a replacement for his cousins.

But did he view her as something more than that? Could they really make anything work if their parents were getting married? He knew how she made him feel, but was he ready to handle a serious relationship? What would he do if he lost her the way his dad lost his mother? Or worse, they didn't work out and his dad's dream of a rebuilt family was lost forever?

"You're right, Dad. I should try to view her that way. We'll rebuild the family."

eighteen

Imani's eyes popped open the next morning. It took a second for her vision to clear and adjust to the sunlight filtering in from behind the curtains illuminating the smooth white ceiling. She'd spent the day before helping Tracey at the inn, then they'd stayed up late, sitting around the table in the kitchen, talking and laughing about old times, present day concerns and future hopes. Halle even joined them via a quick video chat, but couldn't come because of an event with Shania.

Imani missed having close friends around. In Florida, she had Towanda and some of the other doctors at the hospital, but they were work friends. People she laughed and talked with during the day and occasionally went out to lunch with or got together with after work for drinks, but that was it. They talked about the hospital, patient woes and only touched the surface of the deeper problems they might have at home. Imani hadn't had the chance to open her heart and tell her true feelings to anyone in a long time. Going back to work was going to be hard, not just because of having to navigate the doctor of the year scenario, but because she wouldn't have her mom, Tracey or Halle around.

"Well, it's not like you have a lot to confide when you go back," she mumbled to herself. Work, slim dating prospects and even less time to pursue the few good prospects was what her life was like back in Tampa.

She got out of bed and stretched her arms. Tracey had given her a toothbrush and toothpaste the night before, so Imani went into the adjoining bathroom and freshened up before going downstairs. Instead of finding Tracey in the kitchen, she found a Black woman standing behind the massive island pouring grits into several bowls.

"Oh, hello," Imani said.

The woman looked up at her and grinned. "You must be Imani. Hey, I'm Shirley Cooke. I make breakfast and the pastries here. Tracey said you'd be down for breakfast soon. I hope you like cheese grits, smoked sausage, scrambled eggs and fresh baked biscuits."

Imani's stomach answered for her and grumbled loudly. She pressed a hand to her midsection and returned Shirley's knowing grin. "You're speaking my language."

Shirley chuckled. "Everything will be ready in a few minutes. The couple staying here requested breakfast in their room, but I'll have you and Tracey's food ready in the dining room. She's out back going over the plant delivery for your mom's wedding. You can go out and listen to what they're saying and make sure it's what your mom wants."

"Plant delivery?"

"Tracey has a contract with a local nursery to bring over shrubs or extra greenery if there's a wedding. Your mom ordered some extra items."

"Oh, yeah, okay." She nodded even though she hadn't known about a shrub delivery for the wedding, though it could have been mentioned in one of the various wedding prep discussions she'd tuned out. "I'll go catch up."

"Everything will be ready in about fifteen minutes or so."

"I'll let Tracey know," Imani answered then went out to find her friend.

Tracey and Brian Nelson stood behind a dark blue Blazer with the name Nelson's Nursery in bold white letters on the side. Imani walked up to the two of them. Tracey's back was to the building so Brian noticed her first. He stopped talking and nodded in Imani's direction. Tracey stiffened before spinning around. When she saw Imani, she relaxed and smiled.

"You're finally up?"

"Yeah, I've been up for a while. Everything okay?" She glanced between Tracey and Brian.

"Everything is good. Brian was telling me about his trip to Augusta last night. I don't need all that," Tracey said with a snap of her fingers. "All *I* need is to know is if the decorative plants Imani's mom ordered to go around the gazebo will be here on time for the wedding."

Brian looked as if he wanted to say something, but when Tracey glared, he shrugged as if he no longer cared. "Whatever, Tracey. I'll have the plants here on time. You mentioned a change in what you'll need?"

Tracey nodded. "Yeah, I left the list inside. Let me go grab it." She looked at Imani. "I'll be right back. He can let you know what we're renting for your mom's big day."

Imani watched her walk away. When she was out of earshot she turned back to Brian and pointed over her shoulder. "What's that about?"

He shook his head. "Nothing. You know me and Tracey were always like oil and water. I'm back to minding my business."

He was right. Back in high school Brian used to always rub Tracey the wrong way. Tracey claimed she only tolerated him because Imani and Halle both had crushes on Brian. She never understood why her friend disliked him except for her saying he was too full of himself.

Imani raised a brow. "Were you minding her business?" Tracey hated for people to get into her business.

Brian shook his head. "Not anymore." He pointed toward his vehicle. "So, the plants. I've got some samples in the back. Want to see?"

She was intrigued to know exactly what business of Tracey's he was minding, but she'd get the information directly from Tracey. No way was she going to potentially stoke the wrath of Tracey by talking about her with Brain.

"I guess so. It is my mom's wedding."

"Why you say it like that?"

She cocked her head to the side. "There you go minding my business now."

Brian chuckled and shook his head. "Y'all damn Get Fresh Crew. You three were always hot-tempered."

"Better believe it. Now show me the plants." She softened the words with a smile.

Brian grinned and nodded. "Come on, take a look."

A truck pulled into the drive as they walked to the back of Brian's vehicle. Imani recognized it from the day she'd foolishly thought she could bike from her house to the path out to the lake as if two decades hadn't passed since she'd last been on a bike. Cyril pulled up next to them.

Their gazes met through the windshield. Imani's breath caught in her throat. She'd almost pushed the kiss to the side this morning. Revisiting it repeatedly the night before while talking to Tracey about the reasons why she should or shouldn't go ahead and sleep with Cyril helped her to wake up and think clearly. Last night she'd just about convinced herself that the potential problems that might arise if she slept with Cyril weren't worth her desire.

Today, though. Meeting his eyes, remembering the feel of his lips against hers, and having the need, so sweet and sharp, slice through her like a blade changed her mind. She wanted him. They were adults. They could set boundaries. She could protect herself from becoming too attached.

She was going to sleep with Cyril.

She smiled and waved. Confident and almost giddy about her decision, she pushed down the deeper, scarier, emotion that fueled her excitement. That could be dealt with later. Instead, she concentrated on the possibility of having what she hoped and prayed wasn't mediocre sex. It would be such a waste if Cyril was mediocre in bed.

Cyril got out of the truck and walked over with a sexy swagger and intense look in his eyes that took her breath away.

There is no way in the world this man is terrible in bed.

"What's up, Brian, Imani," he said. He dapped up Brian then looked at Imani. "What are you doing here so early?" He glanced back at Brian then at her.

"I stayed the night here with Tracey," she said quickly, then wanted to cringe. She didn't owe him an explanation.

"I came by to show Tracey the shrub samples for the wedding," Brian said. "She went in to get the updated number list." Brian raised a brow and smirked. "What brought you out here so early? Looking for Imani?"

"Nah," Cyril said with a quick head shake. "My normal trip to try and convince Tracey to join the guild. The president was in the bar last night talking about the parade somebody wants to throw and later brought up having The Fresh Place Inn listed as a place to stay on the guild's website would be easier if she were a member."

"Tracey's not a member?" Imani looked back to the house where Tracey had come out and was heading their way.

"Not yet, but I'm hoping she'll join soon."

Tracey reached them, spotted Cyril and grinned between him and Imani. "You're either here to hunt her down or to convince me to join the guild again."

Cyril's eyes widened and he held up a hand as if to push

back Tracey's teasing. "I'm here about the guild. I wasn't sure she was here."

Tracey's grin widened. "Wasn't sure, huh. I guess that means you guessed she might be here. You usually don't bother me this early."

Cyril shifted his weight from foot to foot. "I've got a busy day. I just came by early to get it out of the way."

"Uh-huh, well, Shirley said breakfast is ready. We've got enough to feed you, too. Come on in and join us." She glanced at Brian and her smile dimmed. "Brian, you're welcome to stay, too."

He shook his head. "I'm good. I'll take the list and then get back to the nursery."

"Suit yourself," Tracey said not sounding the least bit put off by his denial. She handed him the paper. "Call me if you have any questions on the shrubs."

"Will do. Cyril, see you later."

Cyril nodded and they all stepped back to let Brian get to his SUV. Tracey looked at them and brightness returned to her smile. "You two can come in behind me. I'm sure you've got plenty to talk about." Tracey winked before spinning and hurrying away so fast her braids swished from side to side.

Cyril groaned. "You told her about the kiss?"

"Tracey is one of my oldest friends, and I had to tell someone. Would you rather I tell my mom?"

He shook his head. "Hell no. Our parents don't need to know it happened."

"That's what I was thinking," Imani agreed. "Tracey was a sounding board to help me clear my thoughts. She won't go telling anyone."

"I know Tracey doesn't gossip."

"Good." She took a deep fortifying breath. "And my thoughts are clear."

He nodded and straightened. "So are mine. I'm sorry about

pressing up on you yesterday like that. It was out of line, and we shouldn't have gone there."

Imani's giddy confidence deflated like a week-old helium balloon. "That's what you think?"

"I do. I talked to my dad last night." When her eyes widened, he held up a hand. "Just in general. He came and asked how our meeting went. He really is excited about the idea of making us a family. He's starting to view you as a daughter and wants us to be like siblings. I haven't seen my dad this happy or excited since before my mom died. I can't… I won't do anything that'll mess that up. I'm sure you feel the same about your mom."

Imani was struck speechless. She wasn't sure how she'd expected their next conversation to go. He'd been the one to hold on to her tighter when she'd pulled away. He'd said he hoped she would show him her softer side one day in the future. So far, she'd been the one to always pull back and be the voice of reason. Silly her for assuming Cyril would find her so irresistible that he'd risk his dad's happiness for a few rounds of sex. And if he believed that sleeping with her would ruin any future chances of them getting along then what did that mean? That if they were to sleep together things wouldn't end well?

She'd read the signals all wrong. No, it was worse than that. She'd let her guard down with him. Her mom might believe in love now, but Imani knew the truth. She could never let her unguarded feelings guide her when it came to relationships.

"You know what, you're right. I was thinking the same thing."

He visibly relaxed. "Good. I was worried…"

"That I'd throw myself at you and propose that we have a *no strings attached* affair filled with nights of wild sneaky sex?" She laughed, way too loud and way too forced.

He winced. "Do you want me to leave? I can talk to Tracey about the guild another time."

"Why would I want you to leave? We both agreed yesterday

was a mistake. I don't feel awkward or embarrassed. Do you?" When he shook his head, she wanted to disappear. She had completely misread this situation. "Good. It never even happened as far as I'm concerned. Let's move on."

She headed toward the house and waved for him to follow. She put her guard back up, fortified the defenses and Gorilla Glued the seams. She would not let Cyril get to her again.

nineteen

"That I'd throw myself at you and propose that we have a no strings attached *affair filled with nights of wild sneaky sex?"*

Cyril stopped walking dead in his tracks in the middle of the Peachtree Cove Meat Market parking lot. Yes, a small part of him had dreamed of her saying that, or some version of those words. He hadn't really expected her to suggest they sleep together. He'd assumed she'd agree with him and pull back. Her agreement made the decision easier. In fact, the entire conversation had been much less awkward than he'd expected, and they were in a good place now.

So why were her words running through his head like a hamster on a wheel?

Had she thought about having a *no strings attached* affair? Had she also pictured them having nights of sneaky, wild sex? Did a part of her believe they could do this and then part ways later on amicable terms? He'd had similar relationships before with no problems. There were no angry ex-girlfriends or former lovers who wanted to take him down. His track record with ending relationships on a good note and remaining amicable was solid.

But none of those women were Imani. Could he really walk away from her unaffected?

A horn honked. Cyril jumped and looked to his left. Mr. Sheppard threw up his hands behind the wheel of his sedan.

Cyril *was* having a moment in the middle of the parking lot. Nodding and waving, Cyril quickly moved out of the way. Mr. Sheppard continued to glower as he drove past Cyril and out of the parking lot.

Cyril was at the Meat Market for his dad. The butcher's shop was where most people went for good cuts of meat and decent prices. Preston wanted to make a pot roast for the family dinner he insisted on having. Now that he believed Cyril and Imani were ready to act like a family, Preston had decided to go all in on the "we are one family" vibe starting with a dinner for everyone on Thursday night.

Inside he stopped short again. It would be just his luck that he'd run into the one person he'd tried to avoid. Imani's gaze collided with his before she quickly looked away. A second later, her shoulders straightened, and she met his eyes again. Her smile was warm but a little stiff. Maybe she was having just as much trouble as he was with forgetting that kiss and the uncomfortable conversation afterward.

He looked behind the counter, but the owner and butcher, Mr. Crowley, wasn't there. No one else was in the store so that left looking back at Imani.

"What brings you here?"

She readjusted the strap of her purse on her shoulder. She was dressed casually again in black leggings and a fitted dark red thermal shirt and looked beautiful.

"Mom wanted me to pick up some chicken breasts and wings. She said Mr. Crowley was having a sale."

"Is he?"

She nodded. "He is. He's checking in the back for me. What brings you here?"

"My dad wants a roast for dinner on Thursday. You know about Thursday dinner?"

Her smile tightened even more before she nodded. "I do. I guess we really are becoming one big family, huh."

She laughed with the words. He guessed it was supposed to sound light, but it came out tight and forced. He couldn't muster up more than a soft grunt. Yeah, they were doing this for their parents' benefit. The thought make him feel as good as it had two weeks ago.

Stop it. Your dad is happy again. Imani is leaving. This can't work.

Mr. Crowley came from the back. He spotted Cyril and grinned. "Well, hello there! I got both of you in here now. Soon-to-be best man and maid of honor, huh. I bet you're both excited."

"Thrilled," Cyril said.

Imani nodded stiffly. "Yeah."

Mr. Crowley didn't pick up on the sarcasm in their voices and continued talking. "Imani, I've got your three pounds of chicken breast. I get that a lot of people love the breast, but I prefer a juicier cut from the chicken. Give me a nice leg or thigh any day. What about you, Cyril? Breast, leg or thigh?"

Don't think about it. Don't be juvenile. Don't think about it.

The mantra didn't help. Thoughts of Imani's beautiful breasts, lean legs and toned thighs pressed against him filled his head. He was a twelve-year-old trapped in the body of a thirty-eight-year-old man.

"I like all three," he said glancing at Imani. Her eyes darted away from his. He really hoped she hadn't realized he wasn't referring to chicken parts. "Umm… Mr. Crowley, my dad said he called ahead for a shoulder roast?"

Crowley nodded and waved a finger. "He did. Said y'all were having a family dinner. I've got it together for you."

"Thank you." The faster he could get out of there the better.

"Let me ring up your girl Imani here and then I'll get you ready."

Cyril's heart picked up a beat. If only she were his girl. He nodded and scratched his nose. "Thanks."

The door to the market opened and Cyril breathed a sigh of relief that someone else would be in the shop to distract him and make it easier to put thoughts of kissing Imani out of his mind. Kaden came in, breathing heavily and sweat beading along his brow.

Cyril frowned. It wasn't hot enough outside for that much sweat. "Kaden, are you good?"

He waved a hand and nodded. "Yeah, just a little tired." He put a hand on his extended belly and wavered.

Imani pushed past Cyril and hurried over to Kaden. "Are you sure? How are you feeling?"

Kaden grinned and patted Imani's shoulder. "It's nothing, really. I just finished putting something on the back of my truck and it's got me feeling a little dizzy. That's all."

"You shouldn't exert yourself right now," she said. She held a hand near his belly. "Is it okay if I touch you?" After Kaden nodded, Imani placed her hand on his stomach and frowned. "Are you feeling anything else?"

Kaden shrugged. "Nothing too terrible. I've had a headache today and a little pain, but it's nothing I haven't felt before."

Imani's frown deepened. "How long has this been going on?"

"A few weeks, but for real, Imani, I'm good."

"You're also pregnant. You should take notice of things like this. Is anything else feeling off? Have you told your doctor?"

Kaden frowned. "I did call my doctor, but she's in Atlanta and her next appointment isn't available until next week."

Mr. Crowley grunted and shook his head. "You shouldn't have to go to Atlanta. It's ridiculous that Dr. Baker refuses to see you because you're trans. I mean, everyone in this town watched you grow up and knows you. Nothing else should matter."

Kaden tried to smile, but the lines around his mouth proved he was uncomfortable. "Everyone in this town doesn't feel the way you do, Mr. Crowley. It's all good. I'd rather see a doctor who wants to help me than deal with someone who hates my existence."

Imani sighed as she rubbed Kaden's back. "I understand that, but you could still go to the emergency room if something happens and you can't get to Atlanta. Better safe than sorry."

Kaden nodded. "I understand. I'll keep that in mind." He took a step forward and then stumbled.

Cyril quickly moved forward to help Imani hold him up so he wouldn't fall. Kaden's body shook as he placed a hand to his head. He took short, unsteady breaths as they tried to get him stable.

Cyril looked at Imani. "Is he okay?"

She shook her head. "No. Let's get him to the emergency room."

"I'll help you get him there." He looked at Mr. Crowley. "We'll come back for the meat."

Concern masked Mr. Crowley's face as he waved them on. "Don't worry about the meat. I'll get it delivered. Just let me know how Kaden is later."

"Thank you, Mr. Crowley," Cyril said and helped Imani half carry Kaden to his truck.

Imani's neck and shoulders ached as she and Cyril left the hospital later that night. Tension and suppressed rage had tightened her muscles from the moment she'd seen Kaden enter the Meat Market through getting him settled in a hospital room. Kaden had been admitted because his blood pressure was too high. He'd have to stay the night so the doctors could monitor his condition. Imani and Cyril had stayed with him until his partner, Barry, could get off work and come to the hospital.

"I can't believe Dr. Baker refuses to see Kaden," she said the moment they were in the parking lot.

Cyril walked beside her toward his truck; weariness lined his eyes. "I wish I could say I can't believe it, but Dr. Baker has some old-fashioned views. He gave a lecture to one of the teenagers from the high school who visited him about being loose and without morals because she wanted birth control."

Imani stopped in her tracks. "How do you even know that?" Was the doctor going so far as to spread his patient's business around town?

"The girl's parents came into the bar that night. They were upset and complained about how he even went in on them for bringing her there in the first place. Honestly, a lot of people in town are fed up with him and wish they had other options."

They started walking toward his truck again. "I can't believe another obstetrician hasn't come to town," Imani mumbled. She'd hoped after what happened to Halle's mom that there would be someone in town who would try and prevent other women from getting inadequate care. Her hopes had obviously been in vain.

"Small town. Most people here are used to going to the local doctor for help and traveling to Augusta or Atlanta if they need a specialist."

"That sucks. Especially when the reason you can't get care is because the only specialist in town is an asshole."

Cyril grunted. "That's true."

They were silent as they walked up and got into Cyril's truck. He didn't speak again until he maneuvered out of the parking lot. "Have you dealt with this situation before?"

Imani stopped glaring out the window to look at him. She appreciated how he'd stayed with her the entire time. He didn't have to, but his concern for Kaden was just as deep as hers. "What situation?"

"A trans man having a baby? I'm just curious." He paused.

"Having someone who's more accepting in this town would be so much better than the closed-minded person we have now."

She let out a sigh. "I have. I wish I could say the all doctors in Tampa are any different. There are just as many closed-minded OBs there. Patients just have more options. There was a doctor in the practice at my hospital who had a problem with it. I've only wanted to see people get quality care no matter what. When Halle's mother died after childbirth when we were teens that's when I decided I would be an obstetrician. At first, I said I didn't want to see another woman die the way she did. Because the doctor didn't see her as a person and didn't believe her when she said something was wrong. Later, when I had a pregnant trans man come into the office to be seen, I changed my statement to not wanting to see another person die because a doctor refused to see them."

"Sounds like you really are worthy of being called doctor of the year."

"I don't see it as being anything special. At the bare minimum doctors should help people regardless of who they are or where they come from. I was selected for doing the bare minimum."

"It's not the bare minimum. Some Black people have mistrusted doctors for decades and for good reasons. It goes beyond doing the bare minimum to showing compassion, caring about your patients and giving them a place to go where they can be heard. Don't undermine what you do. Kaden is proof that everyone doesn't have what you try to provide."

Imani was silent as she considered his words. She had viewed the way she treated her patients as the way she was supposed to behave. That she was doing what every doctor *should* be doing. Sure, she understood there were doctors out there who didn't treat their patients with respect, but she hadn't considered herself as special. Realizing not everyone had the luxury of being believed or even seen as deserving of care hadn't hit home in years.

"I haven't thought of myself as unique in a long time," she admitted softly.

"Why not?"

"Because when you start to think you're special something happens to prove that you're not."

He glanced at her from the corner of his eye. "Now I don't know about all that."

"It's true. I grew up thinking my family was special. That my dad was perfect. That my parents had the greatest marriage. That I was the smartest and brightest kid in the Peachtree Cove school system only to find out that my family wasn't special, we were just messed up."

"Everyone's family is messed up."

"Not like ours." She considered revealing what happened between her parents. She wasn't sure how much her mom had told him and his father about what happened. They had to have heard from the gossips in town. "You know our story…right?"

He shook his head. "I told you I don't get into town gossip. All I've heard is people say your mom deserves to be happy and they're glad our parents are together."

"Really? That's it?" She couldn't believe that's all he heard.

He nodded. "That's it. Is there more you want me to know?"

"My dad cheated on my mom. A girl at school told me she'd seen my dad with another woman at a hotel over the weekend. I called her a liar. Later that day…we found out she hadn't lied."

Later in the day when that same woman came to their front door with a gun and shot her mom. The ramifications had sent shockwaves not only through Imani's family but the community. In the days and weeks after, as people came to check on her and her mom and make sure they were okay, many let it slip that they'd known about the affair but hadn't said anything because it "wasn't their place." If they'd been as nosey as they'd been before the shooting as they'd been after, then maybe her mom wouldn't have had to deal with what happened.

She'd left town after high school because she couldn't bear being in the same town that hid her father's affair and later relished in their misery. She'd only remembered the pain of living in Peachtree Cove. Prior to this time, all her visits were arranged to get in and out quickly. She'd kept her ties to Halle and Tracey through phone calls, social media and video chats. But being back here, seeing the way the town was trying to progress and being with her friends reminded her of the good things that were in Peachtree Cove.

"My life is in Tampa. It would be hard to relocate." She spoke the words out loud because she needed to hear them. Her life was back home at the hospital. Not here in the small town that turned its back on her.

Cyril didn't reply. She guessed he wouldn't. He and his dad had moved from Baltimore to Peachtree Cove. Not being able to relocate was an excuse. As much as she missed her connections here, she wasn't ready to move back home or start her own practice. Dealing with small-town living, the politics and gossiping. That wasn't something she wanted back in her life. Life in Tampa might be lonely, but it gave her the anonymity she wanted. Until the doctor of the year designation, she hadn't been in the spotlight, people didn't talk about her, no one looked at her to be special or cared about what happened in her house.

It didn't take long for them to arrive back at the Meat Market. Cyril pulled up beside her car. Imani faced him. "Thank you for helping me with Kaden and everything."

"No need to thank me. I like Kaden. He worked part-time at the bar when I first opened. I want him to be okay, too."

"Can I ask you something?"

He leaned against the steering wheel and met her gaze. "Go for it."

"You come from a large city and moved to a small town.

Don't you hate how everyone is in your business and enjoys trying to bring you down?"

He chuckled softly. "Honestly, other than people being curious about us and where we came from, no one has bothered us. My dad and I wanted to be a part of the community. As people got to know us, they also respected the boundaries we put up. We don't fool with the ones who don't want to respect our privacy. Simple as that. Peachtree Cove isn't that bad of a place, and most people want to make things better and see the town grow."

That didn't sound like the town she remembered. "I hated it here. I couldn't wait to get out."

"Honestly, that's how I felt about our neighborhood back in Baltimore. I wanted a new start. Someplace completely different where I could make a name for myself and let go of the pain of the past."

"That's what Tampa did for me."

"I get it, but you have family and friends here who still care about you. I don't have that back in Baltimore."

"If you did, would you go back?"

He thought about it for a few seconds then shook his head. "I like what's happening here. What I've built here. I don't think I'd go back."

"That's kind of how I feel about my life in Tampa."

He let out a long breath. She could have sworn disappointment flashed across his face before he asked, "No chance of you moving back, huh?"

"Not right now."

"That's too bad," he said softly.

"Actually, it's good. If I move back, it makes it easier for us to pretend that kiss didn't happen. Before we know it, I'll come visit and we'll both have forgotten and moved on."

He grunted before nodding. "Maybe." He didn't sound very sure.

"I mean, that is what we both want, right?" she asked. She

held her breath. Waiting, and a small part hoping he'd take back the words he'd said earlier. That he'd admit she wasn't the only one feeling a connection between them.

"It's what we both want," he said slowly. But the look in his eyes. Hot and intense contradicted his words. She wanted to push but she wouldn't. Not tonight at least. Tonight, she was tired and upset and bound to make a rash decision. She wanted to go home, take a shower and clear her mind. She'd love to do that in Cyril's arms, but she wasn't going to be the one to expose herself. She'd wondered if he'd regretted pushing her away. The look in his eyes now confirmed her thoughts. Her emotions were too raw after dealing with Kaden. For now, she would pretend as if she hadn't noticed the longing and regret in his eyes. She was too vulnerable and wasn't ready to open herself to that.

"Thanks again. I'll see you at the dinner later this week," she said before getting out of the car.

twenty

Dinner at Ms. Kemp's house was as awkward as Cyril expected it to be. His dad and Linda were cute and loving with each other, but that wasn't what made things uncomfortable. Awkwardness hit him in the gut every time they mentioned them all being a family or how much they enjoyed knowing Cyril and Imani had gotten over the initial disagreement and were getting along so well before the wedding in two weeks.

Cyril had never wanted his dad to stop talking as much as he did during dinner. Imani wasn't making the situation easier. She seemed content with the entire thing. Laughing at Cyril's dad's jokes and agreeing whenever their parents talked about their hopes for them all getting along in the future. She ate the food as if it were the most delicious roast she'd ever had in her life and gave no indication that they'd kissed or connected in other ways.

"How about we play a game after dinner?" Ms. Kemp asked as everyone finished their meal.

Imani's hand jerked and the forkful of peas she'd held scattered to her plate. She frowned at her mom. "You want to play a game?"

Ms. Kemp nodded and smiled at Cyril and then his father. "No need for the night to end and playing a game is a lot more fun than just watching television. Don't you think so, Preston?"

"Let's do it, baby," Preston readily agreed.

Imani slowly put down her fork. Cyril could sense the tension radiating off her. He wasn't that interested in playing a game, but he wouldn't have expected that particular response. Considering how their parents were trying to make tonight the perfect gathering he wouldn't have been surprised if they'd asked them to do arts and crafts or sing a song after dinner.

"You really want to play games?" Imani asked sounding astonished.

Linda stared back at Imani with a cheerful smile and innocent look. Cyril couldn't tell if she didn't know or didn't care about the sudden change with Imani. "Why wouldn't I?"

Imani was still for a second before her body relaxed and a bright smile covered her face. "You know what. Let's do it. We're working our way to being one big happy family, right? Game night is perfect." She looked over at Cyril. "Don't you think it's perfect?"

No, he did not think this was perfect. The entire dinner felt like he was being forced to put on a sweater two sizes too small. The fit wasn't right. He still was for his dad and Linda getting married. But sitting there acting as if he felt no attraction for Imani and thinking that he had to spend the rest of their lives ignoring that everything in him wanted to reach over and rub the tension out of her shoulders made him want to call the wedding off himself.

"Cyril? You good?" his dad asked. The excitement and joy in his dad's face stopped Cyril from voicing the disagreement in his heart. What was he going to do? Ruin the dinner, his dad's happiness, and shout out that he was what? Infatuated with Imani? Not happening.

"Sure, let's do it," he said in a forced cheerful tone.

His dad nodded enthusiastically. "Good thing I bought a new pack of Uno cards!" He reached into his pocket and pulled out a package of the card game.

"I love playing Uno," Ms. Kemp said.

Imani let out a humorless laugh. "You sure do. I'll clean off the table." She pushed back from the table and stood.

"I'll help," Cyril said. They grabbed their plates and their parents' and took them to the kitchen.

Once in there he gave Imani a sideways look. "What's the deal with Uno?"

She scraped the food off the plates into the trash with stiff, jerky movements. "There's no deal." She nearly slammed the plate on the counter.

"Umm...the way you're trying to kill that plate says differently." Cyril took the remaining plates from her and cleared the food into the trash.

Imani crossed her arms under her breasts. "It's just..." She sighed. "Nothing. It's like you said, we're supporting our parents."

She turned and walked out of the kitchen without another word. Puzzled, Cyril put the plates in the dishwasher and followed her out. Their parents had pushed the rest of the stuff on the table to the side and his dad shuffled the cards.

"Y'all ready?" Preston asked.

Imani sat across from her mother. Her gaze remained focused on her mom. "I'm ready. Mom, you good?"

Her mother raised her brows. "I'm great. Why wouldn't I be?"

Cyril looked at his dad, who gave a quick shake of his head. So, his dad had no clue about the change in the mood either. This was a thing between Imani and her mom. He would stay out of it. He sat down next to Imani. His dad finished shuffling the deck then handed the cards to Linda.

"You can have first deal, baby," he said.

Ms. Kemp gave him a flirty look. "Thank you, sweetie."

Cyril barely stopped himself from rolling his eyes. He glanced at Imani who did roll her eyes. Their gazes locked. He raised his brow and gave her a "you good?" look. The tension around her eyes and shoulders faded and the hard lines around her mouth softened into a smile. Reaching over beneath the table he placed his hand over the one clenched into a fist on her lap and gave a reassuring squeeze. Maybe he shouldn't touch her, but when her hand unclenched, and she returned his squeeze before pulling away, he couldn't regret the move. The moment was over quickly, but the warm imprint of her soft fingers against his lingered.

The first game came down to a back-and-forth between Imani and Preston. Imani eventually snagged the win, hitting his dad with a draw four and changing the color before he could drop his final card. Neither he or her mom had lost as many cards during the second game, and even though Linda tried to change the color to force Imani to draw it didn't matter.

"Uno!" Imani yelled, slapping down another wild card.

A series of good-natured groans went around the table, followed by laughter and complaints about the bad hand Ms. Kemp had dealt. Imani picked up the deck.

"Mom was never good at shuffling. I've got the next hand," Imani said grinning. The tension and frustration from earlier diminished as they played. Cyril couldn't prove it, but he wanted to believe he'd helped bring out the smile on her face.

Ms. Kemp's house phone rang. Imani continued shuffling as Linda got up and answered the cordless phone across the room.

"Hello... Are you kidding me!"

All laughter and talking stopped as everyone looked at Linda. Her body was stiff, and her hand trembled as she brought it to her temple. His dad immediately got up and went to her side.

"Didn't I tell you I don't care about you or what you're doing? Stop calling my house!" She pressed the end call button and tossed the phone down.

Preston placed a hand on her shoulder. "Baby, what's wrong?"

Linda shook his hand away. "Every time I get my life together that man tries to ruin it." She turned and rushed out of the room. Preston was right behind her.

Imani jumped up. She took one step to follow then stopped.

Cyril looked in the direction their parents had gone then back to her. "Was that your dad?"

She nodded stiffly. "No one else would get that kind of reaction out of her. Why does he keep calling her?" She pressed her hands against her temples. "This is why I hate coming home." She hurried toward the kitchen. A second later he heard the back door open and close.

Cyril immediately followed her. He expected to find her getting in her car to leave. But as he headed toward the driveway, he found her hidden in the shadows cast by the house and the setting sun. She leaned against the house with her arms wrapped around her midsection.

Cyril approached her slowly. "Are you going to be okay?"

"I will be," she said in a clipped voice.

He moved and leaned against the house next to her. "When was the last time you spoke to him?"

She sniffed and quickly wiped her eyes. "The day after their divorce was finalized. I told him goodbye, and I never want to see him again. I haven't seen or spoken to him since."

"Are you going to check on your mom?"

"I was, but your dad went to her. She doesn't need my comfort."

"I think she will. It obviously upset her. And you."

"I doubt it. She's starting over." Imani said the last part with a humorless laugh. "Tonight was all about acting like the past never happened. The dinner and game night. Just like we used to do before my dad…" She grunted and shook her head. "Just eject my dad and insert Preston."

Cyril's brows drew together. That explained why her mood shifted when her mom suggested they play a game after dinner. "I'm sure that's not what she was trying to do." He tried to sound reassuring, but discomfort wiggled its way into his thoughts.

Her eyes narrowed. "I can't believe he would call her. His reaching out is part of the reason why I think she agreed to get married. He's found someone, a younger woman at that, and after he told her, my mom suddenly is getting married to your dad."

Cyril straightened. "What?" Had that been the reason she'd agreed to marry his father? He didn't want to believe that. They both seemed to want this, despite it being quick.

"That's what she told me. My dad has always been manipulative. Now he's doing it despite years of them being apart. Why can't he just leave us alone. He already ruined our family." She swiped at her eyes again.

Cyril reached over and wiped the tear that followed with his thumb. "I'm sorry that he hurt you and your mom."

She looked up, anguish and rage bright in her eyes. "It's more than that. His mistress tried to kill my mom, Cyril. He kept telling her that my mom was the reason he couldn't be with her. That he couldn't break his vows and only death would make him leave. That woman came here and shot my mom. I don't know if he realized saying that would make her try to hurt my mom, or worse, that he knew what would happen. He didn't just hurt us by cheating…his actions nearly killed her." Her voice broke and her shoulders shook with a sob.

The sight of her tears and the sound of her crying crushed him. He pulled her into his arms and hugged her tight. Imani's arms wrapped around his waist, and she cried against his chest. He held her as the truth of what happened with her dad ricocheted through his mind. Her father's mistress had tried to murder her mom. Something that took the betrayal of cheating to another devastating level. When Imani found out the entire truth about why he and his dad had left Baltimore there was no way she'd ever want to see him or his dad again.

twenty-one

Imani couldn't sleep, so when her mother finally emerged from her room at one in the morning and went down the hall to the kitchen, Imani stopped pretending as if she'd eventually fall asleep and followed her mom to the kitchen. Linda stood at the fridge, filling a cup with water from the dispenser. She looked over her shoulder when Imani entered the kitchen.

"I thought you were asleep."

"Thought or hoped?" Imani leaned against the wall and watched her mom.

Linda let out a heavy sigh. "Hoped."

"Because you don't want to talk about him calling?"

Linda took a sip of water. "Because I'd hoped you wouldn't worry. I hate the thought of anything to do with your dad keeping you up at night."

Imani moved to the kitchen table, pulled out a chair and sat. "Kind of too late for that. Sometimes I still think about that day and what happened. When I do, I usually can't sleep at night."

Concern clouded her mom's face. "You shouldn't still be thinking about that."

"It's kind of hard to forget, Mom. I was home that day. I... saw you on the ground. I thought she would shoot me next."

She'd never forget being in her room doing homework and hearing the gunshot. When she'd run to the front of the house, she still hadn't believed the shot was real. She'd assumed the television was too loud, or that if it were real then it had to be outside somewhere not at her home. Instead, she'd discovered her mom unconscious on the ground, her dad's mistress standing at the door holding the gun. She'd jerked the gun in Imani's direction when she'd run into the room. Their eyes met and for the longest second Imani thought she was going to die, but the woman turned and ran instead.

"I'm forever grateful she wasn't that heartless," Linda said in a tired voice before sitting across from Imani.

Imani watched her mother warily. After the divorce and subsequent conviction Linda refused to talk about the situation. There was no mention of her dad, the shooting, the trial, nothing. Her mom pretended as if he'd never been there and anytime Imani brought him up, Linda changed the subject to something else. Imani had followed her mom's lead, believing that was the best way to help her move on. This was the longest conversation they'd had about that horrible day in years.

"Is he calling you a lot? You mentioned he contacted you before to say he's seeing someone."

Sighing, Linda tapped a fingernail against the side of the glass. "It's coming up on the anniversary of when we first met. I think that's why he's reaching out more."

Imani slapped her hand on the table. "More? So, he's reached out before now?"

"He would try to call the house every so often. Wrote letters here and there asking about you. He always wants your contact information, but I never pass it along to him."

"I didn't know he reached out to you so often or that he bothered to ask about me." She'd always assumed her dad had listened to her when she said she never wanted to hear from him again. She'd meant the words when she'd said them. All these years later, there were so many things she wasn't sure she wanted to know.

"Do you want to talk to him?"

"I don't know. A part of me wants to talk to him. To ask all the questions I couldn't ask back then. Why did he do this to our family? Did he realize his words made her think killing you was the only answer? Then I realize that no matter what he says I wouldn't believe him. He lied to us and put us in danger. I have nothing to say to him."

"I've thought those same things myself. I also don't know if I want the answers. But, he is your dad and if you ever want me to give him your number… I will."

Imani shook her head. "Not right now. Maybe not ever."

Linda nodded and took another sip of her water. The silence stretched and Imani knew that her mom would easily move on to another topic and let this conversation fade away. But there were other things she wanted to know. Things only her mom could answer.

"Cyril doesn't seem to know the entire story," she said hesitantly. "I thought everyone in town would have told him by now."

"What happened between me and your dad isn't the hot topic in town anymore. Nearly twenty years have gone by. There have been other scandals, other betrayals. When I stopped talking about it and moved on with my life other people stopped talking about it, too. Are there those who have probably brought it up now that I'm getting married to Preston? I'm sure, but for the most part the town doesn't want to focus on the bad things that happened here. Everyone is excited about the best small town designation. Bringing up old scandals and attempted murder cases isn't what's going to help us win."

"It's hard to believe. Back when it happened, I couldn't imagine what he did becoming anything other than what the people in town would talk about."

"I'm not going to pretend everyone here is a pillar of virtue, but a lot of time has passed. You don't have to worry about everyone you meet asking you about your dad."

Imani crossed her arms on the table and rested her chin on her wrists. "I guess that's why Cyril didn't find out. He says he doesn't gossip, and he hasn't asked about our past."

He hadn't pushed when she'd cried either. He'd just held her. Gave her the comfort she needed and let her walk away when she'd stopped crying. He'd been there for her without pressing for anything in return, which only made her wonder if she could always rely on him in that way. A dangerous thought for someone who planned to never open herself up to anyone.

"That's one of the reasons why I like Preston and Cyril. They moved to town and minded their own business. Preston was hurt when his wife died. They came here for a new start. He respected my privacy, so I'm respecting his."

"Do you know what happened to his wife?"

Her mom shook her head. "I only know it was unexpected and tragic, but he doesn't like to get into the details. Her loss took a lot out of him and broke the family apart."

Imani frowned and sat up. "What about her dying would tear the family apart?"

Linda shrugged. "People act stupid around weddings and funerals. It could be several reasons." She reached over and patted Imani's hand. "Which is why I wanted you here for my wedding. You're my baby, Imani. I want you to be here to celebrate with me."

"I'm here and I do want you to be happy."

Linda raised a brow. "But you're still not convinced this is a good idea."

"It's still sudden to me. We used to play games after dinner with dad. Particularly Uno. Then we stopped after everything happened. Now you're acting like everything is okay and we're doing the things you used to do with Dad. It's a lot to get used to."

It's why she'd been so upset at dinner earlier. She'd tried to pretend as if things were good, but they weren't. No matter how much she hated her father and the consequences of his actions, she wasn't ready to insert Preston in his place and pretend as if everything were great.

"I let your father have control over my life for long enough. Just because I didn't talk about what happened didn't mean I wasn't living under the pain of everything he put me through. This is me starting over on my terms. Creating new memories to erase the old ones."

"And Mr. Preston is the man you want to start over with? You really want to get married again?"

Her mom stared down into her glass of water. After a few seconds she took a long breath and gave a determined nod. "This time will be different. I can trust Preston. He's never lied to me. We're both recovering from painful pasts. I think we'll be good for each other."

"I hope you're right."

"You can still do the background check on him if you don't trust him."

Imani hadn't started a background check because she'd expected to easily prove that Preston was some sleazy scam artist who wanted to take advantage of her mother. Nothing he'd shown her so far had set off any alarm bells. Then there was Cyril. He seemed just as sincere and caring not only about her mom but the town and the people in it. She wanted to believe in them. The feeling was new and unnerving. She hadn't believed in any man in so long.

"I think he's okay, but I want to be sure. You understand, right?"

"I do. But believe me when I say that Preston isn't hiding

anything from me. I believe him when he says he only wants to make me happy—make all of us happy. He's missing a piece of him after his wife died. We're filling that piece."

Imani couldn't say anything to that. She finally understood why Cyril had backed away from her after their kiss. Their parents were finally healing after being heartbroken. If she and Cyril did something that ruined that, she'd feel guilty for the rest of her life. The joy of seeing her mom happy again was something she wouldn't trade, but how could she also suppress the disappointment of knowing she could never find out if the spark between her and Cyril could actually turn into a flame?

twenty-two

"You need to tell Ms. Kemp about what happened after Mom died," Cyril said the following morning.

His dad spent the night at home the night before but hadn't given Cyril the time to talk to him about what happened after dinner or what he'd said to Ms. Kemp when he'd followed her out of the room. He'd claimed he was tired and gone straight to his room when they'd gotten home.

Cyril typically didn't like to ambush his dad, but this morning he wasn't giving his dad the opportunity to skip out on this conversation. He'd caught Preston just as he'd poured his first cup of coffee and was slathering the homemade muscadine jelly one his friends at the VFW made on his toast.

"What are you talking about?" his dad asked mid spread.

"Exactly what I just said. You need to tell Ms. Kemp the entire story."

His dad frowned. "She doesn't need to hear all the details about what happened. That's behind us now."

"It's behind us because we moved away, but it's not exactly some trade secret. If she goes looking, she'll find out."

"Why would she go looking?" his dad asked as if Cyril were

making up wild conspiracy theories. "There's no reason for her to go looking for anything. She knows I don't like talking about what happened to Vera. Just like I don't press her to talk about what happened with her ex-husband."

"But you know what happened right? Imani told me last night. His mistress tried to kill her."

His dad scowled before taking a bite of his toast. "I know about that. That situation was terrible."

"And you still didn't tell her about Mom?"

"I told her enough. When she first mentioned what happened with her ex-husband, I wasn't about to tell her that I was originally a suspect in your mom's murder. She would have turned away from me. So much time has passed now, it doesn't even matter."

Cyril couldn't believe his dad would think that. "It does matter, Dad. You saw how she reacted to him calling last night. They don't talk about it, but what happened because of him still affects them."

"You think I don't know that?" Preston snapped back. "That's exactly why I'm keeping the suspicions about me quiet. I don't want to make Linda feel as if she's got to worry about me."

"Telling her everything proves she doesn't have to worry. Keeping everything to yourself only makes things harder on her if she finds out. Keeping quiet makes it look like you're hiding something."

"I'm not hiding anything. You know that."

"I know you never hurt Mom. I never once thought you did, but keeping the entire story a secret won't help you with Ms. Kemp. Don't give her a reason to doubt you."

"Why would she doubt me? I care about Linda, and I want to start the next chapter of my life with her. Why can't you see that I'm doing what's best for both of us. I'm protecting her."

"Are you protecting her or are you protecting yourself? I've always supported you, but right now it seems like you're pretending what happened after Mom died didn't happen to avoid seeing doubt in Linda's eyes."

Preston pointed at Cyril. "You saying she's got reason to doubt me?" His voice was tight.

"If you don't trust her with the truth, then yes."

"Out of everyone I thought you had my back."

Cyril frowned, surprised by the hurt in his dad's voice. "I do have your back. If anyone has supported you through everything it's me. I'm trying to help you out now by telling you that getting this out of the way sooner rather than later is for the best."

"No, you're saying you don't think I know what I'm doing."

"Honestly, I don't. I don't know why you're trying so hard not to say anything."

His dad threw down the toast. "Because I can't take another loss. I lost your mother and it almost killed me. I didn't think I'd be able to start over, but I have. I don't want to bring in the messed-up stuff from the past to ruin what I've got now. If you don't understand that, then you don't want to help me."

Cyril tried to tamp down his frustration. He waited a few seconds to calm himself before responding. "All I've done is try to help you. I've tried to convince Imani that you're the right person for her mom. I've even given up—" He cut off. He wasn't going to say anything about giving up on his feelings for Imani.

"Nah, you say you support me, but you aren't giving me time to handle this." His dad stood up from the table.

Cyril followed suit. He wasn't going to back down on this. "You've got to handle it before the wedding. If you don't tell her then I will."

"What?"

"You heard me. You've got until the wedding. I don't want to see Ms. Kemp or Imani blindsided. You tell her before I do."

His dad's jaw dropped, and Cyril walked out before his dad could say anything else.

Cyril was so frustrated by the talk with his dad that he knew if he went to the bar, he would be no good for anyone. He changed into a pair of basketball shorts and a T-shirt and drove to the mini park near his side of town. He'd spend an hour or so running the track to get the tension and frustration out before going home to shower and get ready to work that afternoon.

He couldn't believe his dad was not only doubling down on not telling Ms. Kemp about the investigation, but that he would accuse Cyril of not supporting him. Cyril had done nothing but stand by his dad from the moment their lives were turned upside down. When everyone else doubted his dad, Cyril's trust hadn't wavered. He didn't understand why Preston refused to see that being honest would make things easier rather than make it harder. Not only that, but Imani wouldn't want anything to do with either of them. The thought of her being hurt by them caused a pressure in his chest that wasn't there before.

He didn't want to deceive Imani. He didn't want her to think less of him or his dad. In fact, he wanted her to see she could trust both of them, but more importantly that she could trust him. That he wasn't like her father, and wouldn't keep secrets. Doing that meant also going against his father's wishes. Cyril didn't agree with his dad, but he also didn't want to go against his word. He'd given his dad until the wedding before saying anything.

Several guys played basketball on the court at the park while Cyril ran laps. When he'd first started his run, he'd been too focused on his thoughts to pay much attention to them. In his last few laps, he noticed they weren't young guys like he'd assumed. After his final lap the men were walking from the court toward the picnic area. He recognized Brian along with the high school football coach, Quinton Evans, and a few other guys from around town.

Brian threw up a hand in acknowledgement as Cyril neared. He stopped running when Brian waved for Cyril to come over. Quinton waited with Brian.

"I didn't know you played out here," Cyril said.

Brian wiped sweat from his face with a towel. "Not often, but every once in a while I come out to get a little exercise. You run out here?"

Cyril placed his hands on his hips and slowed his breathing from the run. "Sometimes. I don't live too far away. I usually run on the treadmill at the house, but today I needed to get out." He looked at Quinton. "Coach Q, what are you doing out here? Isn't it a school day?"

Quinton grinned and shook his head. He was about Cyril's height, with dark skin and a muscular build. From what Cyril understood he was not only the school's football coach, but a former college and short-term professional player. "Not today. District-wide holiday. I decided to meet up with Brian instead."

"I didn't realize guys my age balled out here," Cyril said. Every time he passed by on weekends, he noticed mostly teenagers. His knees were not up to the challenge of playing basketball with boys eighteen and younger.

Brian draped the towel around his neck and held onto the ends. "We have pickup games some Sunday mornings. Today we took advantage of the school holiday and came out before the kids. You should join us some Sunday."

Quinton eyed Cyril with a half smile. "You any good?"

Cyril pressed a hand to his chest. "I'm decent. Though honestly, I haven't played ball in years. You may not want me on your team."

The guys laughed but Brian shook his head. "That's no problem. None of us out here are pros. Just a way to get out, grab some exercise and try to pretend like we still got the moves we had in our twenties."

"I get it. Maybe I will come out. I spend so much time at the bar that I need to get out and socialize more."

"Your spot is nice," Quinton said. "I was thinking of swinging through later."

"You should drop in. Both of you. Friday nights are usually busy."

Brian squinted at Cyril. "You think Imani and Tracey may come through?"

Cyril's stomach clenched. Did Brian return Imani's high school crush? He hadn't forgotten the way the two of them were laughing and smiling at each other the morning he'd found her at Tracey's bed-and-breakfast. "Not sure, why you ask?"

"I need to talk to them both about the shrubs for the wedding. If they're at the bar I can kill two birds with one stone."

Quinton frowned. "What two birds?"

"Getting answers out of Tracey and getting the drink I'm gonna need after talking to her. Tracey is always ready to go to level ten. She's been that way since high school."

"I didn't grow up here," Quinton said. "But I can't imagine her going off. She's so nice every time I see her."

Brian pursed his lips and shook his head. "That's the way she acts now. Been like that since she married Bernard. She tries to act all perfect, but she was a trip back in the day before him." He shook his head. "I still can't believe she's still with that guy."

Cyril held up a hand. "I don't know if they'll be there. I haven't talked to either of them today." He wanted to call Imani and check in on her but wasn't sure if she'd appreciate it or not. She didn't seem to like talking about her dad and he doubted she'd want to relive crying on his shoulder the night before.

Brian raised a brow. "I was surprised when I found out Imani was back in town. I haven't seen her since high school."

"Did you want to see her more?" Cyril asked quickly and

immediately realized he sounded way too invested in Brian's thoughts about Imani.

Brian shrugged. "She's cool, but I'm not checking for her like that."

Cyril tried not to let the immense relief he felt show but didn't suppress the smile on his face. "Oh, cool."

Brian cocked a brow. "Do you know someone who is?"

Cyril shook his head. "Nah, nah. You know our parents are getting married. So I'm just looking out for her."

Brian chuckled. "Okay, whatever you say."

Cyril's cheeks heated. He needed to end this conversation before he made a fool of himself. He'd already stumbled through that clumsy attempt to dig for information about Brian's interest in Imani.

"Well, I'm going to do one more lap," he said and pointed down the walking trail. "I'll see y'all later tonight."

twenty-three

Imani arrived at A Couple of Beers before Halle and Tracey. The trio decided to meet up after they all agreed they needed a break after a long week. Imani didn't ask what made their weeks particularly difficult. She decided to save getting all the information over drinks.

Cyril was behind the bar by himself while Joshua set up a microphone in the open area to the left of the bar. Cyril was the reason she'd arrived early. She wanted to clear the air between them before everyone else arrived.

He looked up and gave her a half smile as he wiped down a highball glass. Damn, he was good-looking when he smiled. He was dressed in his typical graphic T-shirt and fedora. His beard looked especially neat and trimmed which made the fullness of her lips even more noticeable. She ignored the clench of her stomach. As much as she wanted to pretend that him holding her in his arms while she cried meant nothing, she couldn't. She appreciated that he hadn't tried to force her to talk, and only gently wiped away her tears and tenderly kissed the top of her head while holding her. His actions meant a lot, and even though she was afraid to explore the deeper meaning behind what he'd done, she couldn't pretend as if the moment hadn't happened.

"How are you doing?" he asked when she reached the bar.

Heat spread in her face. She'd come to thank him. To let him know she was doing alright. To say she appreciated what he'd done. But years of suppressing her feelings and not admitting what she wanted were drowned out by the embarrassment of crying on his shoulder.

"I'm fine," she said sounding so much like her mom she wanted to cringe. She pointed to where Joshua set up the microphone. "What's going on over there?"

Cyril watched her for a few seconds, maybe judging for himself if she were good. He finally accepted her answer with a lift of his chin before glancing over at Joshua then back at her. "Setting up for the entertainment. We bring in local artists every once in a while to play."

"Oh, who's playing tonight?"

"A local cover band called Joi, with an *i* and not a *y*."

Her eyes widened. That was a name she hadn't heard or thought of in years, but which brought her immediate pleasure. "Wait, Joi is still together?"

He put down the glass in his hand. "Don't tell me you've heard of them?"

She nodded. "Yeah, they formed when I was in high school. If it's the same group I'm thinking of. Joey, Oliver, Ivan and Contessa?" The cover band used to play at parties and even during the prom her senior year.

Cyril raised his brows. "Everyone except for Contessa. The new singer's name is Octavia."

"I can't believe they're still together. Or that they still live around here. The last I heard all of them went to college in other places."

"From what I've heard they did go off but regrouped several

years ago. They all work full-time jobs but get together to play gigs in Peachtree Cove and the surrounding areas."

Imani smiled imagining seeing the group again. The members of Joi had been part of some of her good memories after what happened with her dad. Whenever she, Halle and Tracey attended a party where they played, she was able to lose herself in the music and dance for a few hours. "That's fantastic. It was their dream to keep the band going and they're still doing it. I admire people who can still live their dream."

"You're doing that. You said you always wanted to be a doctor and look at you. You're doctor of the year."

She sighed thinking about the phone call from her supervisor earlier that day. They wanted her back as soon as possible. Honestly, Imani hadn't expected to be gone this long. She thought she'd end the wedding and be back at the hospital in a week at the most. Not that she'd be conflicted about encouraging her mom to call things off. Or that she'd enjoy being in Peachtree Cove. "Yeah."

He raised a brow. "What's wrong?"

She leaned her elbows against the bar and shrugged. "You know how I feel about the doctor of the year thing. I get what you're saying about using my title to make change, which I will do, but after what happened with Kaden earlier this week, I feel like I could be doing more. That I could be making a bigger difference instead of being a box someone checked."

"Then figure out what that looks like for you and do it. I never believed I'd own my own bar, but here I am." He spread out his arms and proudly gazed around the room.

"You always make it sound so easy."

"Getting to your goals may not be easy but making the decision to chase them shouldn't be that hard. You deserve to be happy, Imani. Do what makes you happy."

Again, his words were spoken simply, but the emotion behind them pulled at her heart. She could see in his dark eyes that he meant them. That he wanted her to be happy. That he cared about her happiness. The resistance to opening herself to Cyril wavered. The need to believe in the look in his eyes called to something deep and neglected inside of her. She'd rejected affection and care from others for so long because she hadn't trusted it. Why did Cyril make her feel differently?

Joshua walked up and broke the moment. "What's up, Imani?"

Imani blinked and broke eye contact with Cyril. She smiled at Joshua, grateful for the interruption. She needed more time to process her thoughts. "Hey, Joshua. I'm meeting Tracey and Halle here. I was going to try and snatch a table before it got too crowded."

Joshua pointed to one of the tables in the back corner. "Get that one. Good view of the bar and the music but not near the line for the bathroom."

"I'm on it." She looked at Cyril. "Will you bring me that beer I liked before?"

"Most definitely."

Halle and Tracey came in the door. Imani waved at them then pointed to the table Joshua suggested. She met them at the table, and after hugging, Halle and Tracey ordered their drinks before they settled into their seats.

Joshua brought over their beers then left. Halle took a long sip then let out a sigh. "I need this and a few more."

"It must've been one hell of a day for you to meet us in your work clothes?" Imani said eyeing her friend. Halle's thick, curly hair was pulled back in a knot but several strands were loose around her face. She wore a gold polo shirt with the school district's logo on the breast pocket. When they'd met before, Halle insisted on going home to change before coming out because she never drank "in uniform," meaning when she had on something representing the school district.

Tracey raised a brow. "Didn't you have the day off today?"

Halle sighed and leaned back in her chair. "The kids didn't

have school, but I was working. District meeting with the superintendent and giving a report on our school's progress. The academics are good, but you know what he focused on?"

"What?" Tracey asked.

"The regional football match between Peachtree Cove High and Peach Valley. Like, are you serious? You're going to gloss over academics and worry about a football game with a school that isn't even in our district much less our state?"

Tracey held up a finger. "They may not be in our district, but you know how serious the rivalry goes with Peach Valley. We haven't won that game in six years. Coach Q better come with something. They didn't hire him just because he looks good."

"Who's Coach Q?" Imani asked.

"The new coach the high school brought in last year after another losing season," Tracey said. "He played defense at Georgia and even did a couple years in the pros, so that's supposed to make him fantastic."

"He also helps the middle school coaches," Halle said sighing. "Gotta get the kids ready for high school and all that. He's nice enough, but I really wish the district would focus on the work we've done increasing grades at the middle school rather than me pushing the kids to be ready for high school football."

"I guess football is still king around here," Imani said sipping her drink.

"Always," Tracey agreed with a nod. "And you better get on his good side. You know Shania wants to keep playing football in high school. Don't be mean to the coach and have him pick on her."

"I'm not worried about that," Halle said confidently. "He's going to let her play. And if he dares give her a hard time, then he'll have me to deal with."

"Would he give her a hard time?" Imani asked.

Halle's brows creased as she thought before shaking her head.

"No, he seems to be open to anyone playing. I'm just tired of sports being more important than academics."

Tracey grinned and elbowed Halle's side. "That's because you've always hated athletes."

"I don't hate athletes."

Imani raised a brow and grinned. "Yes, you do. You've hated sports since we had field day in elementary. How did you end up with a daughter who wants to play football?"

Halle sighed. "Lord knows, but I'd rather her play football than be miserable because I shoved her in a cheerleading costume. I don't hate sports. I just recognize that there are a lot of people doing more for the world and making less money than the people on a field or court."

The door opened and Brian walked in with a guy Imani didn't recognize. Tracey's eyes widened and she giggled. "Speaking of people not doing much for the world, there's Coach Q right now."

"That's him?" Imani pointed. When they both nodded, she pursed her lips. "He's cute. Where were all these cute guys when I was living here?"

Tracey gave her the side-eye. "They were cute back then, but you only had eyes for Rodney and then you were ready to leave town without a backward glance."

"I didn't leave without a backward glance. I kept in touch."

Halle wagged a finger. "Phone and video calls aren't the same thing as being here."

"Facts," Tracey agreed with a pointed stare.

"Y'all know why I left."

Halle gave her a reassuring smile. "I know and honestly, I don't blame you for leaving. That doesn't mean we didn't miss you. Things would be much better if we had you around."

"How? It's not like I'm doing anything special while I'm here."

Tracey cocked her head to the side. "Girl, don't even play

like that. What you did for Kaden this week is all over town. Don't act like we don't need a good doctor around."

Imani sighed and leaned back in her chair. "I wish I could do more for Kaden."

Halle's eyes lit up. "You can if you stay in town. Admit it, Peachtree Cove isn't as bad as it used to be."

Imani thought about the past few weeks and the changes she'd noticed and couldn't deny Halle's words. "You're right. It's not as bad. It's kind of cute. Still not the small towns you see on television. That doesn't mean I'm ready to walk away from everything I built back in Tampa."

Halle sat up straighter. "Don't forget we're growing. We've got some industry coming into the area and that's bringing people, too. Including more cute guys. So, if you ever get tired of melting in the Florida humidity, you can always come home."

"Ma'am, Georgia humidity is just as bad," Imani said with a laugh.

Tracey shook her head. "Not true. The heat in Florida is something different. I think the devil vacations there."

They all laughed, and Imani reached across the table to slap at Tracey's hand. She was going to miss hanging with them when she went back. Tracey's sense of humor and Halle's fight for what was right. She'd make a point to visit Peachtree Cove more often.

She looked at the bar where Brian and Coach Q laughed and talked with Cyril and Joshua. Cyril glanced her way, their eyes met and he lifted his chin slightly. Her stomach flipped and she returned the gesture. Yep, she could definitely see the appeal of visiting Peachtree Cove more often.

Imani couldn't believe she'd had so much fun that night. She'd laughed as she caught up with the members of Joi. Sure, all of them had fled Peachtree Cove for college after high school but returned for one reason or another. What surprised her the most was how no one regretted moving back home. Even Joey who'd worked as a lawyer at a prestigious law firm and returned home because of a sick parent. She would have expected him to somewhat regret having to be back home.

"I missed not having my family around," Joey said. "Don't get me wrong, we're the exception and not the rule. A lot of people from high school left and never came back. They still think of Peachtree Cove as the struggling place it once was. We're not Atlanta and never will be, but we've got enough going for us that living here isn't so bad."

Imani sat in the booth thinking about what he'd said as the band played their last song for the night. Tracey was already gone. Bernard called and claimed some kind of emergency with his cousin again. She'd been upset and left shortly afterward. Halle hadn't looked convinced, but as the perfect neutral party also hadn't said anything.

Now Halle glanced at her watch. "I need to get home. Shania's at a friend's house and I told their parents I'd be there by ten."

"I can't believe she's thirteen already," Imani said. "Where did the time go?"

Halle shook her head. "I don't know. It feels like I just brought her home and now she's got one year left before high school."

"Is she ready for high school?"

"She can't wait. I wish I could delay it another year or two. High school equals four short years before she graduates and moves on to the next thing. I've only got five more Christmases with her."

Imani cringed. "Oooh, don't put it like that. It sounds way too soon."

Halle put the strap of her purse on her shoulder. "Now you know how I feel. Want to walk out together?"

Imani glanced at the bar. Cyril still talked with Brian and

Quinton, but the other two men stood holding their keys. She guessed they were leaving soon.

"I need to ask Cyril something." When Halle raised a brow Imani shook her head. "About the wedding. That's all."

Halle grinned. "Whatever you say."

"Why did you say it like that?"

"I didn't say it like anything." She tilted her head and raised a brow. "You sure do look over at him a lot."

"I'm just looking around the room and taking in the atmosphere."

Halle laughed and stood. "Sure. The atmosphere. We'll talk about that later when you're ready to talk. Give me a call when you get home." Unlike Tracey, Halle wouldn't push the issue. She was always there if you needed to talk but understood keeping some things private. It's one of the reasons Imani never pushed her about Shania's dad.

"I will." Imani stood and gave Halle a hug. "Text when you're home. Drive safe."

"Always." Halle threw up a hand in a wave and then left.

Imani made her way to the bar. The crowd was still heavy, and most people didn't look like they were getting ready to leave. The place didn't close officially until midnight which meant Cyril would be there much later. She had no reason to stick around and wait for him like some groupie, yet she still wanted to wait. She'd backed out on thanking him for the previous night and she was even more embarrassed about being embarrassed to say thank you.

Brian smiled at her when she reached the bar. "I thought you were leaving with Halle."

"Not yet. Mom and Mr. Preston are back home, and I don't like to be the third wheel," she said with a wry grin.

Brian nodded. "I get that. If you want to hang out, there's the dessert bar down the corner. I think they're open if you want something sweet."

Brian tilted his head to the side and smiled. Twenty years ago, if he'd given her that same look, she would have melted into a puddle of goo right there on the floor. If he'd given her that smile when she'd first come to town and considered maybe having a quick hookup to pass the time after a dry spell, she might have gone with him. Instead, Cyril was the man whose eyes made her stomach flip on her first day back in town.

"I'm good. Plus, I need to talk to Cyril for a bit."

Quinton grinned and slapped Brian on the shoulder. "Come on, man. I've got an early morning and you're my ride." He looked at Imani. "Nice meeting you. Cyril, let's hang out again one day when you're not working."

Cyril threw up two fingers. "Let's do it."

Quinton dragged Brian from the bar and Imani slid into one of the seats they vacated. "Can I get another one of those fruity beers you gave me?"

"You've already had two."

"Okay, and I don't feel a thing."

His eyes narrowed as he studied her face. "Are you driving home tonight?"

"I planned on it."

He shook his head. "Then no, you can't have another one if you're driving."

"Well, what if you drive me home. Then can I have another one?" The words formed in her brain and flew out of her mouth before she could process their ramifications.

"I won't be getting out of here until around one," he said.

"I can wait. What I said was true. I kind of don't want to be the third wheel back home."

This wasn't flirting. She was trying to do better and properly thank him for being nice to her the other night. That was all. She wasn't just sitting at the bar, waiting for the sexy bartender to get off. She needed to talk to him, and she didn't want to do it while everyone was around or force him to take a break when he was busy working. She could wait.

He watched her for several long seconds before grabbing a glass and filling it with the strawberry ale she'd been drinking. He slid the glass in front of her. "Give me your keys."

She didn't know why she wanted to smile so much, but she suppressed the urge as she pulled her keys out of her bag and slid them across the bar. His eyes remained glued to hers as he took them and put them into his pocket.

"You leave with me tonight," he said firmly.

Imani's breathing became shallow, and her heart skipped. He was just giving her a ride. Nothing else. Still, she nodded and sipped her beer before the grin tickling her mouth burst through.

twenty-four

Cyril looked down at Imani walking next to him and raised a brow. "You good?"

They were crossing Main Street toward the public parking area behind the buildings across the street. Even if he could snag a spot on Main Street, he tended to park in the lot so customers could have easier access to the bar. It was after 1:00 a.m. and the street was nearly empty. Though there were one or two other restaurants on Main Street who closed around midnight many of them closed before ten or eleven. A Couple of Beers was one of the few open until midnight and the limited crowd who'd still been there were already in their cars and on their way home.

Just like she'd done in the bar right before she'd handed over her keys, her lips lifted in a cute little half smile. "I'm good."

"I'm just saying. You had three of those strawberry ales."

The third she'd nursed at the bar for over an hour while she'd sat and watched him work. Even though she'd handed over her keys, there were no signs of her being drunk or unable to handle herself. He'd known that even when he'd asked for her keys. When she'd actually given them to him, he'd been surprised and a small bit pleased. No, more than a small bit. When she'd turned down Brian's offer to take her to the dessert bar in town because she wanted to talk to him he'd felt like doing some type of victory dance.

A juvenile reaction? Maybe. But even though he knew he couldn't get his hopes up with Imani, the part in him that was attracted to her wouldn't let go.

"Do you want me to walk in a straight line and prove it?" she asked with a laugh.

"No need. If you say you're good, I believe you."

"You don't sound like you believe me. I think you think I'm a lightweight."

"Come on now. I never said that."

She moved until she blocked his way in the middle of the street. She pointed a finger. "But your tone implies I am one." She waved her hand for him to move back. "Watch. I can do it."

"Are you seriously about to try and walk a straight line?" He raised a brow, amused by her joking with him. He much preferred her joking with him than crying. He also liked seeing her like this. Carefree and lighthearted. He didn't know if she was like this often, but when she was occasionally like this with him, he felt good knowing she was comfortable with him.

She wagged a finger. "See, you said 'about to try.' I knew you didn't believe in me." The sparkle in her eyes and the smile on her lips made him want to reach for her and kiss her.

The streetlights played across her features. The long thin sweater she wore had an oversized neckline and constantly drooped over her shoulder, revealing a black tank top beneath. The smooth brown skin of her neck and chest had drawn his attention all night. Her pants didn't hug her full hips, but the way the soft, loose material flowed across her curves was worse. His hands itched to cup her bottom and pull her close.

"I take your silence as proof of your guilt."

Cyril blinked, her words breaking him out of the mesmerizing effect her smile had on him. "You want to prove it, fine. Although, for the record, I believe you." He took several steps back.

She pointed to the double lines in the middle of the road. "You'll believe me after I walk this line."

"*You* want to walk this line. *I* didn't tell you to do it." He crossed his arms and watched her.

Imani held out her arms as if to keep her balance and then placed her left foot straight on the line. "I have to prove my honor. Otherwise, you'll go telling my mom that I got drunk at your bar and you had to carry me home."

He laughed. "Oh, so I'm a snitch now?"

She lifted her shoulder and put her right foot in front of the other. "I don't know yet, *brother.* You might be."

The *brother* blew the wind right out of his sails. His humor faded as the realization that he was flirting, but she might not be punched the air from this lungs. This could all just be her way of getting along with him just like their parents wanted. He'd read too much into her turning down Brian and staying there with him.

Imani continued walking the line. Oblivious to his change in mood based on the smile and teasing glint that remained in her eyes. When she was a few steps in front of him, having successfully walked the line with no problem, she said, "Told you," and contined to walk toward him.

"Why didn't you leave with Brian earlier?"

"Huh?" She stumbled as if caught off guard.

Cyril shifted forward and placed a hand on her hip to keep her from falling over. He expected her to immediately pull back, but she didn't. She frowned up at him, confusion on her face. From this angle the light was behind her, and he couldn't clearly see her expression.

"Why didn't you leave with Brian?" He had to know if she'd stayed with him because she was trying to treat him like her future stepbrother, or because she'd wanted to spend time with him.

"I...wanted to talk to you."

Her soft voice scratched across the frustration growing inside him. The frustration of wondering what was going on in Imani's head. The frustration of wondering if she felt the same. The frustration of knowing that as much as he should put distance between them a part of him only wanted to draw her closer.

"You've been with me for hours and haven't said anything I'd consider a secret." In fact, she'd spent most of her time at the bar joking with him and Joshua. After they'd left the light-hearted banter continued. While he enjoyed her company, this couldn't be the only reason why she'd stayed until the bar closed, could it?

She shifted in his arms. Cyril let her go even though every part of him ached to continue holding her. He didn't step back and neither did she. That was worse, he could still feel the imprint of her body against his.

"That's because I'm not good at saying what's on my mind sometimes," she admitted. "Especially when it comes to how I'm feeling."

"Is something wrong?"

She fidgeted and looked everywhere but at him. "I want to thank you for the other night. You didn't have to hold me when I cried. You didn't push me to talk about my dad. You listened and didn't try to just fix me or the situation." She took a heavy breath and met his gaze. "I appreciate that." She said the words in a rush, then looked away again.

"I don't think I can fix that situation."

"You'd be amazed at how many people try when I tell them about my dad. It's why I don't bring it up. I don't need to hear, 'go to therapy,' 'let go and let God,' 'move on,' or 'your best revenge is living right.' I get it. I know all of that and I've tried all of that, but it still hurts and I'm still mad. I don't know why people don't want me to be mad?"

"Every single day I'm angry that my mom was taken away from me as quickly as she was. Every single day I want to scream about the events that ruined my life. I've heard everything you've heard, and I know that I should try to forgive and let go of the anger. But I'm still angry."

She stopped shuffling from foot to foot and looked up at him. Even with the shadows masking her face he felt the intensity of her stare. "And you're okay with being angry?"

"I'm okay with it because I know that anger isn't all that I have. My dad's love. My friendship with Joshua, the relationships I've made here in Peachtree Cove. The anger about what happened with my mom isn't the only part of me. I don't think your anger is the only part of you. You love your mom, or you wouldn't have rushed here to check out my dad. You're a great doctor not only because you're doctor of the year, but because of the way you jumped in to help Kaden. You're a friend who picked up right where you left off with Halle and Tracey. Your anger is just one part. You can have it, but you don't have to let it define you."

She let out an annoyed huff. "Why does your dad have to be marrying my mom?"

"That's what you say after all that?"

She shook her head. "That's not the reason I said that."

"Then what is it?"

She sighed and narrowed her eyes before meeting his gaze. "Right now, I want to kiss you, but we both agreed that isn't what we should do."

She moved to turn away. Cyril's arm shot out and wrapped around her waist. He didn't care that they were in the middle of the street, or that he'd been the one to say that they needed to move on after the kiss. The only thing he cared about were the words that had come out of her mouth. The words that soothed the frustration scratching at his insides like sandpaper.

He waited a heartbeat for her to pull away and when she didn't, he lowered his head and pressed his lips against hers. Her body relaxed and she leaned into him. She tasted sweet and her curves were soft and warm. Maybe this was a mistake, or maybe this was the best thing to ever happen to him. Her lips pressed gently against his, their breaths entwined as his tongue slid against hers and he'd swear on the mountaintop that this was the best thing to ever happen. From the second he'd met her eyes that day at the Dairy Bar he'd felt it. The electric sizzle and hum of awareness that this woman would change his life forever. He wasn't sure how they would make this work, but he'd regret never making it work more than anything else.

A horn honked. The two of them jumped apart. The streets might not be full, but they weren't exactly empty. Instead of looking at the driver who interrupted them, he put an arm around Imani's shoulder and hurried her across the road and behind the building to the parking area.

The lights in the parking area were bright enough for him to see her features. He didn't want to drop his arm from around her shoulders, so he didn't. When they got to the passenger side of his truck he placed one arm on either side of her. His gaze searched her expression for any sign of regret. There was none. Only desire reflected in her dark eyes.

"Want me to take you home?" he asked in a rough voice.

"I didn't lie about your dad being at my mom's place."

His body tightened. Need almost drove him to kiss her again, but he wouldn't assume. She could tell him to take her to Tracey's bed-and-breakfast. "Then where do you want to go?"

"To your house." Her voice was clear, steady and strong.

Cyril's heart leaped and desire roared to life. If he took her back to his place, he was going to kiss her again. With no one there, he was going to want to do a hell of lot more than kiss her.

"Are you sure?"

She nodded. "I can walk a straight line and I know what I'm doing. Take me back to your place."

twenty-five

Cyril's place wasn't what she expected. Since he and his father lived together, she expected a bachelor pad with modern leather furniture, a flat-screen television and dishes in the sink. Instead, the home was decorated in soft earth tones, with comfortable furniture and the fresh scent of lemon filled the air. Everything was spotless and organized.

"Your place is cleaner than my mom's," she said after they entered.

"My dad likes to clean. I get it from him. We both try to keep up with things before they get out of hand."

She dropped her purse on the couch and chuckled. "Your dad is kind of perfect. He cooks, cleans and dotes on my mother. You're making it hard for me to be against this wedding."

She meant the words and the three beers had nothing to do with it. After seeing how one phone call threw her mom into a tailspin, she couldn't help but appreciate that Preston did the exact opposite. He made her mom smile and spoiled her in a way her father never had.

"He was the same way with my mom. Do you want anything to drink?" He pointed over his shoulder in the direction of the kitchen.

Imani patted her stomach. "No, I'm kind of full from the beers earlier."

He nodded slowly before glancing at the television. "We can watch TV. I've got some snacks we can try out if you're hungry."

Imani took a few steps closer to Cyril. "I didn't come here for food." Her heart beat so fast and heavy in her chest her entire body vibrated.

"I don't like to assume anything." His gaze never left hers. The question in his eyes, the need to be sure this was what she wanted, was both a comfort and a turn-on.

She closed the distance between them and trailed a finger down his torso. "So, I'll be clear, I want to have sex with you."

His breathing stuttered. She would have believed she'd shocked him if it weren't for the way his eyes flashed with fire. He was holding back. Respecting the boundaries she set. Taking care of her by holding his own desire in check. She wanted him to let it all loose.

"I know we can't be together forever. I know our parents would probably be against us doing this. I realize this has the potential to be awkward in the future if we let it. But today, tonight, I don't care about all of that. I like the way I feel in your arms, and I'd like to feel that way again. That and I haven't had sex in a while."

He blinked then grinned and shook his head. "Let's get to the real reason. You need some."

She nodded. "And I wanted you from the moment I saw you at the Dairy Bar. Then the mustard mess ruined my chances."

He placed one hand on her hip. He brushed her lower lip with the thumb of the other hand. "The mustard didn't ruin your chances. I would've still given you a chance."

"You are such a liar. I saw the look in your eyes. You were pissed off at me."

"I was pissed that you ruined my shirt before I headed to meet the woman my dad wanted to marry. Other than that, I really wanted to get your number."

"Meeting my mother was that important?"

"Yes. And if I weren't in such a hurry that day, I would have laughed it off. Asked you for your name and number." His fingers trailed from her cheek, along the line of her chin to the pulse pounding at the base of her throat. "And tried to see you again."

Imani clutched the sides of his shirt, bringing him even closer until his hard body was flush against her curves. "I was just trying to figure out how to have sex with you during my stay in town."

His eyes widened. "You went straight there, huh? Only saw me as a piece of meat." The devilish smile pulling at his lips said he wasn't offended at all by the thought.

"Honestly, I wondered if it would be worth it. I have been disappointed before."

Cyril's brows drew together. "I promise you—you won't be disappointed."

She lifted onto her toes and brushed her lips over his. "Talk is cheap."

He cupped the nape of her neck. "You challenging me?"

"Just saying." She shrugged and grinned. Her pulse fluttered at the passionate look in his eyes which seemed determined to prove she would be far from disappointed.

"I love a challenge."

His head lowered and his lips covered hers. Unlike the slow, sexy kiss they'd shared in the street, this one was hot, hard and exactly what Imani needed. She wanted to let go, to forget all the other things in the world and get lost in the delicious sensations Cyril awakened in her body.

Cyril led her further into the house. They kissed and pulled at each other along the way. By the time they made it to Cyril's bedroom Imani was ready to tear his clothes off. So she did. She jerked at his shirt and pulled.

He grinned before pulling it off himself and tossing it across the room.

"Impatient much?"

"Shut up and get naked," she said, kissing him again.

He laughed while unbuttoning his pants and shoving them down. "Also bossy."

Imani didn't have a comeback. The sight of him shirtless in nothing but a pair of dark boxers had her speechless. Her breathing hitched. In a scramble, Imani jerked off her sweater and tank top before shoving down her pants.

They came back together in a rush. His mouth glided over hers, and she slid her tongue past his lips. The feel, heat and taste of him made her cling tighter. They fell onto the queen-sized bed. Imani wanted him to rush, but Cyril took his time. Kissing across her neck and shoulders, easing down the cups of her bra to kiss and lightly suck on one of the hard tips.

Imani clutched his head. "Oh my God, move faster!"

The vibration from Cyril's laugh against her breast spread from her nipples to the soles of her feet. "You know I want to enjoy this."

"Enjoy it the second time."

"I'm getting a second time?" He ran his fingertips lightly over her stomach and side. The tickling feeling sent tingles through her, which coalesced at the juncture of her thighs.

"You can have ten times," she said in a half moan.

"Hmm, but I'm enjoying this too much." His lips followed his hands as he kissed down her body. Gently sucking and flicking his tongue over her sensitive skin.

She was enjoying it, too. When his hand traced across her thighs her legs spread. Thankfully he didn't tease her further.

A deep groan rumbled through him after his hands slid up and glided across her sex. The laughter and joking left his eyes. His gaze became hotter, more focused, and he ran his fingers through the damp curls covering her mound before easing past her folds to stretch her entrance.

Imani's eyes rolled to the back of her head. She was going to lose it. The pleasure was too intense, too acute. Emotion swelled with the feelings bursting through her until her mouth fell open and she had to squeeze her eyes shut to stop the tears from flowing. The feelings, sensations and pleasure overwhelmed her. She was lost in a swell of emotions that were more than just the pleasure he brought to her body, it was the comfort she felt in his arms, the freedom to be vocal, to have fun while having sex, to feel open to everything Cyril offered her. More than that, to want everything he offered.

His lips met hers and Imani clung to him while his fingers played between her thighs. She shoved the boxers across his hips. Her hands wrapped around his length. A shudder racked his body.

"Fuck, Imani, I wanted to take this slow."

"Ten times, remember. Slow next time," she said between heavy breaths.

Cyril pulled away and reached into the drawer next to his bed. He pulled out a condom and quickly covered himself. Imani opened her arms and her legs and welcomed the heavy heat of his body over hers. Cyril grabbed her hips, pulled her forward and pushed into her with a long hard thrust. Pleasure exploded across her skin, behind her eyes, inside her heart. She was lost and all she wanted to do was ride the wave. Over and over again, regardless of the consequences.

twenty-six

Cyril woke up with Imani, soft and warm, nestled in his embrace. He waited for regret, concern or guilt to creep in and ruin the moment, but the emotions didn't come. His lips spread in a contented smile while immense satisfaction settled over him. He liked having her next to him. He didn't want to take back a moment of the night before. He understood the potential ramifications of what they'd done. He knew that if his dad found out he'd be upset, but Cyril couldn't drum up enough energy to worry about that. For now, he was going to enjoy this moment. For now, he was good with pretending he could spend as much time as he wanted wrapped in Imani's embrace without any problems. It had been so long since he'd had the chance to feel this way. He was going to savor every second.

Imani stirred. Her back was to his front. She shifted her arms from beneath the covers and stretched. "Are you awake?" she asked in a sleepy voice.

Cyril slid his hand from her stomach up to cup one of her breasts. "Just woke up."

"Mmmm, I could stay here and go back to sleep." She lowered her arms and wiggled closer causing her behind to press into his dick.

"So could I." He lightly squeezed her breast before brushing a finger across her nipple. He really could get used to waking up like this. Not just with a woman in his bed. With Imani in his bed.

"Should I ask what time it is?"

"Do we really want to know?" He kissed her shoulder. "We can pretend like it's four in the morning and we've got a few more hours together before we need to get up and face the day."

Her husky chuckle sent ripples of pleasure across his skin. "I like that because there is no way I'm getting up at four unless I'm doing rounds at the hospital."

He brushed his lips across her shoulder. "No rounds. Just a lazy day ahead. You and me, here in this bed."

"That sounds amazing."

"Yes it does."

Grinning, Cyril pushed her hair aside so he could nibble and kiss her neck. He could get down with this fantasy. She turned in his embrace and faced him. Her fingers played across the muscles of his chest. Her touch was assured and comforting, just like her.

"But we do have to face the day," she said regretfully.

The regret in her voice stirred inside him. She was right. His dad may have spent the night with Ms. Kemp, but he was an early riser and could come home at any moment.

"We do."

"And the consequences of what happened last night."

He frowned. "I don't regret what happened?" He was willing to accept whatever consequences and hoped she didn't feel sorry about what they'd done.

"I don't regret it. In fact, I want to do it again." Her smile wasn't shy or hesitant, but eager.

Cyril's heart rate sped up. This woman was everything he

could possibly want in a person. He wasn't sure how he was going to handle it when she left. "You do?"

"Yes, but can we really do this without my mom or your dad finding out?"

"I don't know. Peachtree Cove is a small town. Most people figure things out."

She grunted and frowned. "Not necessarily. We didn't figure out my dad was sleeping with the young cashier from the grocery store until it was too late."

He squeezed her hip. "Hey, we're not like that situation."

"I know." Her arms wrapped around his waist. She came forward and Cyril shifted onto his back so she could comfortably rest her head on his chest. "Plus, if we're seen together that isn't going to cause a big commotion. People expect us to be together for the wedding."

"That's true."

"Do you think you can keep the secret from your dad?"

Not for long. He didn't like keeping secrets. He hated that his dad asked him to keep the details of what happened after his mom's death from Imani and Ms. Kemp. He couldn't continue to do that. Not after he'd slept with Imani. He'd already grown to care about her and her mother. He didn't want to give them any reason to not trust him or his father.

"I'm good at keeping secrets when I have to," he said. "This one I can keep, but there are others I don't want to keep anymore."

She leaned back and looked up at him. "You're keeping a secret now?"

"Nothing about me is a secret. I just don't like diving into the past a lot. What happened with my mom. Why we ultimately moved to Peachtree Cove."

She shifted back. Her gaze dropped to the tattoo on his forearm. A cross surrounded by roses, his mom's favorite flowers, and the words *I love you* in his mother's handwriting. Taken from one of the last notes she'd written him.

Imani reached out and ran her fingers over the words. "Is this for her?" He nodded and she asked quietly, "What happened?"

"We didn't just lose her, she was murdered."

"What?" She sat up in bed and stared down at him with wide eyes. "Oh no. Cyril, I'm so sorry. I had no idea."

He shifted up and leaned against the headboard. "Most people don't know because we don't talk about what happened with her. Losing her that way was hard enough, but to deal with everything that came afterward. That's what really tore the family apart."

"What happened after?"

Concern and compassion filled her eyes. Her hand lightly rubbed his thigh as if she were trying to comfort him. He didn't want either of those emotions to go away when he told her the full story. Guilt tried to wiggle its way through his heart and shut his mouth. He'd given his dad until the wedding to tell the full story, but he couldn't do this. After everything that happened between them, he knew in his gut that not telling her the entire truth and letting her find out from someone else would be a mistake he couldn't come back from.

"I was out of town, and it was just her and my dad at the house. They were watching TV and then my dad went up to bed and my mom stayed downstairs to finish her show. She was a night owl like that. She said late at night was the best time to get her alone time." He smiled at the memory. Sometimes he would stay up late watching a movie or TV show with her long after his dad went to sleep.

"When my dad got up the next morning and she wasn't in bed he didn't think much of it. She would fall asleep on the couch sometimes, especially when she was up late watching television. When he went downstairs and she wasn't there, he first thought maybe she'd gone to the store for something, but when he found her cell phone still plugged into the wall he started to worry. The car wasn't missing, neither were her keys or wallet, just…her."

"She was just gone."

Cyril nodded, remembering the barely contained worry in his dad's voice when he'd called Cyril to find out if he'd heard from his mom. "He called the police. They came, checked the house, searched for clues and that's when they found blood." Imani gasped. Her fingers dug into his thigh, but she didn't speak. Cyril continued reciting the story. "There was blood in the kitchen, near the back door. That's around the time I got home. Just in time to overhear one of the cops say this was going from a missing person to a possible homicide investigation."

"They didn't know she was gone already. How could they say that in front of you and your dad?"

Cyril remembered the skepticism in the eyes of the cops. The way they hadn't believed from the start that his dad had no idea what happened to his wife. As soon as they'd discovered the blood, the detective made it clear he thought Preston was involved. The words stuck in his throat. Mentioning the suspicion, the original arrest and near conviction of his dad could turn the compassion in her eyes to suspicion and mistrust. That's exactly what happened with his mother's relatives. The same people who'd loved and trusted his dad during the twenty years of his parents' marriage hadn't believed he knew nothing about what happened. Even when another suspect came forward and was ultimately convicted.

He looked into Imani's eyes. He stopped himself from tightening his hold on her. He wanted to keep her close so she wouldn't pull away, but he couldn't do that. He wouldn't force her by his side to deal with this, too.

"Because they thought—"

The front door slammed. They both froze then spun toward

the closed bedroom door. Before he could get out of bed his dad was yelling down the hall.

"Cyril! You up?"

His eyes met Imani's. "He's back?" she said in a shocked whisper.

"Why is he always up at the crack of dawn?" Cyril muttered.

They scrambled out of the bed. He grabbed his pants from the floor and slid them on while Imani searched for her bra.

He scanned the floor for his discarded shirt and snatched it up. "Stay in here. I'll see what he wants and get you out of here."

"Thank you. I'm not ready to deal with this right now." She started picking up her discarded clothes.

"If we keep this up, we'll have to tell them eventually."

She frowned as she bent to look under the bed. "Yeah, but not when I'm naked and can't find my panties."

"Good point."

Cyril hurried to the door and slipped out just as his dad approached his bedroom. "Why are you yelling this early in the morning?"

Preston frowned at Cyril. "Linda is worried. Imani didn't come home again last night."

Cyril's heart jumped to his throat. Did they know she was there with him? "She was with Halle and Tracey last night."

"I know but the last time she stayed out with Tracey she texted her mom to let her know. Now she didn't call and she's not answering her phone."

He relaxed and placed a hand on his dad's shoulder. "I'm sure she's fine. Go back over to Ms. Kemp and tell her not to worry. I'll go check with Tracey and Halle." He tried to turn his dad down the hall but Preston stayed firm.

"She called Halle, but she said she wasn't there. She can't reach Tracey. What if they're in trouble together."

"Then I'll go out to the bed-and-breakfast and check."

His dad shook his head. "I don't like this. I know she's grown and all, but she can't keep making her mom worry like this. Peachtree Cove is small, but that doesn't make it perfect. Anything can happen."

Guilt squeezed his chest. He looked back at the bedroom door then at his dad. Worry filled his dad's eyes. He understood the panic of waking up and not knowing where your loved one was.

He opened his mouth to confess, consequences be damned, when Preston's cell phone rang. His dad's eyes widened. "It's Linda." He answered the phone. "You find her?" Preston nodded then he smiled. "Good. Good. Okay great. Let me tell Cyril and call you back." He hung up and grinned. "Your mom got in touch with Tracey. She stayed at the bed-and-breakfast last night. I guess they had fun hanging at the bar and decided to make it another sleepover."

Cyril blinked. Surprised and grateful that Tracey was looking out for her friend. "Yeah... I guess so."

"You want some breakfast? I'm hungry now that everything has settled down. I can make something for us," Preston said in a cheery voice.

He shook his head. "Nah, don't you think you should go back and check on Ms. Kemp?" He ushered his dad toward the front of the house.

Preston waved a hand. "No need. She's going to the bed-and-breakfast to give Imani a piece of her mind. She doesn't like her not calling like this, but I think she just wants to see her daughter."

A thump came from behind his door. Cyril coughed to try and cover it. His dad frowned at him then the door. "What was that?"

"What was what?"

"I thought I heard something in your room." Preston edged toward the door.

Cyril wrapped an arm around his dad's shoulders and ushered him down the hall. "You know I am hungry. Can you make me some pancakes? And I picked up some sausage from the Meat Market earlier this week. That would be good, too."

Preston's eyes lit up. "We do have that fresh sausage, don't we? I think I will make some."

"Good. I'll go freshen up while you do that."

"Okay." His dad nodded and headed to the kitchen.

Cyril rushed back to his room. Imani was dressed and stared at him with panic. "She's going to the bed-and-breakfast," she hissed.

Cyril rubbed his temple. "We'll get you out of here." Once he figured out how to distract his dad.

"And then how am I supposed to get there? My car is downtown. You drove me here."

He slapped a hand to his forehead. "Damn."

"What are we going to do?"

He frowned and thought of the options. "Dad's in the kitchen. We'll go out the front door. Get in my truck and then leave."

"What about your *pancakes*?"

"I'll say there's something going on at the bar. He'll understand."

twenty-seven

Imani called Tracey as Cyril drove her downtown to pick up her car. "She's coming to the bed-and-breakfast. Tell her I left already and I'm on the way back home."

"How do you know she's coming here?" The alarm in Tracey's voice took Imani back to their high school days. Tracey could stand up and cover for anyone, but she tended to buckle under Linda's gaze.

"That's what Mr. Preston told Cyril."

"Oh really? Hold up, wait! I was right. You did spend the night with Cyril." The alarm gave way to a smug *I knew it* tone.

"Why would you say that?"

"Halle told me you stayed at the bar to talk to him, and I could tell by the way you kept looking at him that you were waiting for a chance to repeat that kiss. Maybe more. So, how was it?"

Imani forced herself not to look at Cyril sitting next to her. He was focused on the road and didn't appear interested in her conversation. But still, she wasn't about to dissect what happened the night before and rave about how great it had been with him sitting beside her.

"We'll talk about that later. Thank you for covering for me."

"No problem. That's what friends do. You can give me all the juicy details later. Meet me at the bookstore this afternoon."

"That's cool. See you then." She hung up and glanced at Cyril. "Tracey's got me covered."

"Sounds like she's a good friend," he said.

"She is. We had this same system back in high school. Act like we know nothing or give an alibi when we know the other person is doing something they shouldn't be doing."

"Did you need alibis a lot?"

She shook her head. "Not hardly. I wasn't about to mess up any chances for a scholarship to get out of town as fast as I could after high school."

"Then she needed them?"

Imani laughed. "You'd think it was Tracey, but she didn't bother hiding anything she did and honestly, while she was always ready to pop off on someone she didn't really get into trouble. We had to cover for Halle a few times, though."

He turned to gape at her. "Halle? For real?" He focused back on the road.

Imani nodded and grinned. "Yep. Halle was quick to sneak out and go where she wasn't supposed to. But don't get too excited. She wasn't sneaking off to get into any trouble. If there was a rally, protest or lecture somewhere her dad would try and put her on punishment and force her to stay home. But if she was with me or Tracey, then the punishment was magically lifted. We knew if he called us asking then she'd probably used us as her excuse for why she wasn't at home studying."

"Wow," he said chuckling. "I never would have expected that of the three of you she was the sneaky one."

"That's why we got away with so much. The Get Fresh Crew was rarely suspected of getting into trouble."

"Hold up, The Get Fresh Crew?" He grinned and raised a brow.

"Yep, that's what we called ourselves."

His deep chuckle rumbled through the car. "I love it."

Despite the silliness of their current situation, him sneaking her back to her car and them using friends to find an alibi, he hadn't smiled much since earlier. She was glad she was able to make him smile and laugh. The sadness in his eyes as he talked about his mother hadn't truly lifted after his dad got home. He'd shared what had to be one of his most painful memories with her. For him to feel comfortable enough to talk to her about it meant he trusted her. She connected with his pain and the need to not let it consume you.

What he'd said the night before, about always being angry but not letting the anger guide him resonated with her. She'd lived with her anger for so long. And she'd never considered herself as an angry person and believed she'd learned to cope with what happened. But she had let the anger direct her decisions and actions for most of her life. She'd moved away from family and friends because she didn't want to be surrounded by the pain of her past. She hadn't trusted a single man she'd ever dated and broken things off whenever they asked more of her instead opening herself up to love or intimacy for fear of being betrayed. Being back home proved everyone had found a way to move on and there was a support system in Peachtree Cove she didn't have in Tampa. Then there was Cyril. She wanted to trust him. She wanted to stop letting anger guide her and finally be open with Cyril just as he'd been open with her.

They arrived downtown quickly and although she wanted to linger in his truck, kiss him goodbye and plan their next liaison, she didn't. Downtown wasn't as busy in the morning as it would be later in the day, but people were already arriving to open the stores. She couldn't risk being seen jumping out of Cyril's truck and word getting back to her mom before Imani had the chance to say anything.

"Call me later," she said as she opened the door.

"I will." He said the words as if not calling her wasn't a possibility, and her heart flipped.

Imani jumped out of the truck and held her head down as she quickly got into her car. She waved as she pulled out of the parking lot and headed home. Thankfully, Linda hadn't made it back from trekking out to the bed-and-breakfast by the time Imani arrived.

Imani called her mom's cell after realizing she wasn't there. "You're looking for me?" she said after her mom answered.

"Yes, I'm looking for you. Why are you acting like that's surprising? You didn't come home last night." Linda sounded both irritated and relieved to hear Imani's voice.

"I'm sorry. I should have texted or called."

"Yes, you should have. I know you, Tracey and Halle are back together and want to act like you can do what you want, but you can't just do stuff without thinking. I need to know you're okay."

Imani felt guilty for not checking in. She wasn't ready to tell her mom about her and Cyril, but she could have at least thought ahead and let her mom know she was okay. "I'm sorry, Mom. I got caught up having fun with them last night and didn't think. I'll do better next time."

"You better. Where are you?" The last question was asked without any lingering worry and just curiosity.

"I'm back home. Are you on the way back here?"

"I'll be there in a few. Don't go anywhere. You're helping me in the shop today."

After making her worry, she wouldn't think about saying no. "Yes, ma'am."

She hung up and got in the shower. By the time she was out her mom was sitting in the kitchen drinking coffee and scrolling through her cell phone. Imani walked over and kissed the top of her mom's head. "Sorry for making you worry." She hugged her from behind.

Linda patted her arm. "I'm just glad you're okay."

Imani gave her one last squeeze before getting coffee. She was adding cream and sugar when her mom asked, "Does having Preston here bother you that much?"

Imani turned to her mom. "Huh?"

"Don't *'huh'* me. You know what I asked and why I asked it. Now answer the question."

Imani came back to the table and sat. "No, he doesn't bother me. Not like he did at first. I'll admit getting used to him being here was hard. I'm still wrapping my mind around you wanting to get married, but I also understand. Preston is a nice guy and he obviously cares about you."

"But you're spending the night away from the house. You'd rather be somewhere else than here."

"Well, Mom, it's kind of awkward being the third wheel. Nothing against you being in love again, but that doesn't mean I want to be in the middle of your romantic interludes."

Her mom blinked and frowned. "Romantic what?"

Imani smirked. "Now you're *'huhing'* me? You heard what I said. You know you two lovebirds are syrupy sweet. It might take me a little bit to get used to that, but it doesn't mean I'm not happy to see you in love."

Linda stared back for several seconds before letting out a light laugh. "I guess it would be something to see. Me...in love again."

"I didn't believe in love for so long," Imani admitted. "After what happened with Dad, I didn't trust it. But seeing you." She shrugged. "I don't know. Maybe one day I'll feel that way."

"I hope you do fall in love one day. I never wanted you to not find someone you can care about. I want you to be happy, too." Her mom stood up and went to refill her coffee mug. "Anyone on the horizon?" she asked over her shoulder.

Imani looked away and sipped her coffee. "I've got enough

to figure out right now without worrying about my sluggish love life."

"Well, when you find someone decent let me know. I'll have to check him out of course, but don't think that I don't want you to find someone one day. Companionship is nice."

Imani shook her head. "Where is my mom and what have you done to her?" She softened the words with a laugh. "Love has done a complete one-eighty with you."

"I don't know if love did that or if I'm just getting older," Linda said with a half shrug. Her cell phone chimed before Imani could reply. Linda came to the table and picked up her phone. She looked at the screen. Her eyes bulged. "Oh, my goodness!"

Imani immediately went into panic mode. Had her dad reached back out to her somehow? "What's wrong?"

Linda's eyes scanned over the screen again before she started grinning as if she'd just discovered gold. "Sandra Brown says that Tommy Williams said that he saw Cyril kissing some woman in the middle of Main Street last night."

Imani choked on her coffee. She covered her mouth then sputtered, "He saw what?"

Her mom was busy texting back. "Sure did. They don't know who, but they said it can't be too many different people."

"How do they know he was kissing someone last night?" Had someone seen her? She didn't know Tommy Williams, but that didn't mean he didn't know her.

Her mom read the message then grinned. "Tommy almost hit them. Had to blow the horn." She shook her head and laughed. "Cyril sure likes to act like he's not interested in anyone, but we know plenty of women in town are interested. I can't wait to find out who it is."

"Shouldn't we stay out of his business? I mean, maybe he doesn't want everyone to know right now."

Linda waved away her words and scrolled through her phone.

"Well then he shouldn't have been kissing her in the middle of Main Street if he didn't want anyone to know. The Business Guild is gonna flip."

"Like be upset?"

Linda shook her head. "Oh no, everyone has been trying to set Cyril up. They're going to flip not knowing who finally caught his attention. Ooh, I can't wait to tell Preston. Though by now if I know, he knows."

"How would he know?"

"Tommy and Preston are good friends. No doubt he told Preston already. Lord, let me call him and see if he knows who this woman is. Finally, Cyril found someone. I wonder who it could be." Her cell rang and Linda grinned. "Hey, did you hear the news?…Mmm-hmm, Sandra just texted me. Did he say who it was?…Well, where is he?…Something at the bar? Goodness, tell him he's got to bring her around…We've gotta meet her." She grinned at Imani. "Isn't that right, Imani?"

Imani's stomach clenched. "Umm… I think we should stay out of Cyril's love life."

Linda waved a hand. "Girl, stop. Let me get ready so we can go to the shop." She focused on the phone as she walked out of the kitchen. "Who do you think it is? Maybe Sharonda who works at the bakery next door. She's cute and been eyeing him."

Imani watched her mom walk out of the kitchen then sank into one of the chairs. She placed her hand to her head and groaned. Just when she'd begun to think living in a small town might be okay, she was reminded that people in Peachtree Cove swarm to rumors faster than ants to an Oreo.

twenty-eight

"You know the entire town is talking about you, right?" Joshua spoke to Cyril the moment he came through the back door of A Couple of Beers. A huge grin spread across his face and his eyes were wide and curious behind his glasses.

Cyril glared at his friend. "It's not the entire town, just the nosey people who have too much time on their hands."

Cyril knew how quickly the rumor mill in Peachtree Cove worked. He'd done as much as he could to avoid ever being the topic of conversation. He'd been able to keep his name out of the mouths of the most insistent gossips by working, going home, helping the guild then repeating the process. Maybe that was why he didn't have a full appreciation of how fast news would spread of him kissing someone in the middle of Main Street.

He couldn't even claim he'd been so caught up in the moment that he hadn't considered that they weren't completely alone. He'd completely understood kissing Imani in public came with the chance of being caught. But when she'd said she wished they hadn't decided to stay apart, the excuses had overtaken common sense. It was well past midnight. No one was really out that late in Peachtree Cove. The ones who were out tended to mind their business. He hadn't considered the slim possibility that one of his dad's friends would actually be downtown that night.

"You can try to downplay this all you want, that doesn't stop you from being the talk of the town." Joshua raised his brows and lowered his voice even though no one else was in the back of the bar with them. "Who was it?"

He tried to give his friend a censuring look. "Don't tell me you're also wrapped up in this?"

"It's not about being wrapped up in this. It's about being your friend. You haven't talked about a woman in a minute. Now you're kissing one in the middle of the street? I need to know what's the deal," Joshua returned, unaffected by Cyril's look.

"Nothing's going on. I just got caught up in the moment."

Joshua cocked his head to the side. "You expect me to believe that? Out of everyone I know, you don't get caught up in stuff. Especially like this. You were kissing her in the middle of the damn street. Was it Imani?"

Cyril nearly tripped over his own foot. He settled himself and tried to casually lean against the desk. "Why would you say that?"

Joshua eyed him suspiciously. "Because she stuck around until after we closed and left with you around that same time. So, unless you ditched Imani five minutes after you left and found some other woman to kiss, then that leaves her."

Cyril groaned and rubbed his temple. "Does that mean everyone in town knows it's her?"

Joshua's eyes widened. "For real? It was her?"

"Quit playing and answer me. Has her name been brought in with the rest of these rumors?"

Joshua shook his head. "Nah, man. Our customers were gone and I'm pretty much the only person to know she left here with you."

"You said pretty much. That means others may know."

"Come on, Cyril, there's the wine bar down the street and

the people here who knew she was sitting at the end of the bar waiting to talk to you. It's not going to take long for other people to start to put two and two together. What I need to know is why were you kissing her?"

He sighed. "It just kind of happened."

"You don't just *kind of* kiss someone," Joshua said. "I thought there might be something going on with you two, but I wasn't sure. I mean, anyone around can tell there's a vibe. You two click even more than her mom and your dad."

Cyril moved to push back his fedora, but it wasn't there. He'd left the house quickly and come straight there. "Which is exactly why we shouldn't be vibing. Our parents are getting married."

Joshua shrugged. "So?"

"So? Josh, are you out of your mind? My dad has finally found happiness after everything that went down with my mom. It's his chance to start over. I never thought he'd be here, but he is. Now I'm supposed to tell him to let it all go because I want to be with Imani?"

Joshua held up a hand. "Hold up, hold up, hold up. You said a lot just now. Let me start with one thing. Why would he have to let go of what he has with Ms. Kemp just because you want Imani? And, please tell me that you don't think telling Mr. Preston that you want to be with Imani means he has to end things with her mom?"

Cyril sat down on the table and threw up his hands. That's exactly what he meant. The entire reason why he'd held back. His dad wanted them to be a family. That couldn't happen if he and Imani were together. "We can't hook up if our parents are getting married. I know all that, but when I first saw her, I was immediately attracted."

"When you met her at her mom's place?" Joshua asked frowning.

"No, before that. I first saw her at the Dairy Bar right before meeting her at her mom's. I didn't know who she was, but the second I saw her I knew I wanted to get to know this woman. Even though she squirted me with mustard." He laughed thinking about how she'd turned to face him with that sexy smile then shot the line of mustard down the front of his shirt.

"Wait, Imani is the mustard girl?"

Cyril nodded. "I kept that part out of the story when I told you because I didn't want you to know Imani was also mustard woman. What if we hook up now and it doesn't end well? Then we've made things weird for our parents."

"But you don't do hookups. You could have had plenty of hookups before her and you didn't. You 'bout to start the hit it and quit it lifestyle with her?"

"Nah." If anything, for the first time in his life Cyril was thinking about forever with a woman. He'd wondered if the feeling would ever come and had sometimes even wished that he could find someone. He never would have thought he'd find the person he could see himself spending his life with like this. "But she's not planning on staying in Peachtree Cove. She's got a life back in Florida. Hell, she's the doctor of the year. I've hinted around about her staying, but every time she pushes back. For all I know she can't wait to get through this wedding and get back to her fabulous life. No matter what I may want, this can't be more than a hookup."

"There's long distance," Joshua said. When Cyril glared, he sighed. "You're right. She lives in Florida, and she doesn't come home often."

"And I've got the bar. I can visit her, but it's not the same. Then what happens if either of us meets someone while we're separated? Then we've got a possible bad breakup but will have to see each other because our parents are married."

"If you knew all of that, then why did you kiss her?" Joshua said, clearly never having had the woman who called to every part of his body and soul in front of him and having the opportunity to kiss her. His friend dated, and had some long-term relationships, but he wasn't looking to ever settle down permanently.

"Because, again, it just happened. The talk we were having, the way she looked at me...all of that just kind of..."

He trailed off as his mind went back to that moment. The way the streetlights cast shadows on her face. The sweet smell of her perfume drifting around him like an intoxicating cloud. The barely hidden need in her voice as she'd mentioned regretting the decision to pretend their first kiss never happened. All of that led to a moment he couldn't regret despite the fallout.

"You're really into her."

He opened his mouth to deny it. He'd been trying not to be *into* Imani like that. He'd pushed the feelings to the side, tried to ignore them, came up with excuses, but at the end of the day they were still there. Refusing to go away and make his life so much simpler.

"I am."

Joshua threw up a hand in surrender. "Then quit trying to predict the future and see how things turn out."

He shook his head. "I don't need a crystal ball to know how this is going to end. It's not just our parents getting married, but it's our history."

"What do you mean?"

Cyril shook his head. He didn't want to get into the other reason why things might not work out with him and Imani. Joshua knew the entire story about his dad, but he didn't know Preston wanted to keep the entire story hidden from Ms. Kemp. He couldn't keep the truth from Imani any longer. He was going to tell her everything. The way he felt about Imani might not mean she felt the same, or that she'd want to try to make anything work, but he wasn't going to intentionally hurt her during the short time they had.

"We've both got a lot to get over considering our family history. Me and my dad, and she and her mom have been through enough. Whatever we do doesn't need to make things worse for Ms. Kemp or Imani."

Joshua nodded. "I understand where you're coming from, but if you think you're going to keep this a secret then you might need to think again. If I figured out you were kissing Imani on Main Street, then you best believe other people out there are coming to the same conclusion. Your dad isn't going to let this go, so you might as well tell him what's going on before someone else does."

twenty-nine

When Halle heard the rumor about Cyril kissing someone on Main Street, she'd guessed it might be Imani and called Tracey. Tracey spilled the beans in true girlfriend fashion, and the two of them insisted Imani meet them at their old spot on the lake to talk. If they met anywhere in town, too many people would eagerly listen in.

Halle and Imani arrived first and set up a blanket with a bottle of wine on top of the large boulder. Tracey came down the path shortly after with a basket of sweets from the bed-and-breakfast. The three of them sat on the blanket and poured wine into plastic cups.

"Well, maybe something interesting will happen at Joanne's grand opening tonight and Cyril kissing someone won't be the talk of the town anymore," Tracey said after they'd all filled their cups.

Imani frowned. "Doubtful? If Joanne is opening her salon it's going to be a classy affair. No hint of scandal."

"I don't know," Tracey said with a grin. "Maybe tonight will be the night Devante finally admits his feelings for her."

Imani gasped then laughed. "Wait, does your brother still have a thing for Joanne?"

Tracey nodded. "Yep, after all these years. He still does."

Halle smirked before sipping her drink. "Doesn't he still change girlfriends like underwear?"

"I didn't know he and Joanne were together," Imani said.

Tracey shrugged but smiled. "Sometimes feelings don't just disappear."

"Ain't that the truth," Imani said with a heavy sigh. She took a long swallow of her wine.

Halle raised a brow and eyed her. "Why you say it like that?"

"Because I wish I could make these feelings for Cyril go away."

"No, you don't," Tracey said matter of fact. "You like him, so just like him and go with it. Life is too short to deny yourself what makes you happy."

"Going for what makes me happy right now might not make my mom happy."

"How do you know that?" Tracey asked. She shook her head. "I need you to quit having this same argument with yourself over and over again. You don't know what she'll say until you tell her. Considering how happy your mom is right now I don't believe she'll go all *I forbid you two from seeing each other.* You can't help that you fell for him before you knew who he was. If y'all hook up, some people will talk about you and say it's weird, but others will accept it for what it is. So why don't you get into the real reason why you're hesitating."

Imani blinked. She'd thought she'd get to at least sulk over her impossible situation for a few more minutes before Tracey called her out. She looked from Tracey to Halle. Halle just sipped her wine and raised her brows. No help there.

"Well damn, call me out why don't you," Imani muttered.

"I already went through this with you and I meant what I said before. Life is short. You want him. He wants you. And you're both interested. So why not go for it instead of pretending as if you don't feel this way?"

"Because he might turn out to be just like my dad." She blurted out the thoughts that haunted the back of her brain.

Halle slowly put down her cup. "Yoooo. That's a lot."

Imani ran her hand over her face. "I know. It is a lot. It's the big thing that's kept me from being able to trust any guy ever. What if he's like my dad? What if he's going to lie to me? What if he's going to do something that might hurt me?"

Halle leaned forward and stared into Imani's eyes. "Everyone isn't like your dad." She spoke softly but firmly, concern etched on her features. At that moment Imani could see every bit of the concerned and caring assistant principal Halle had become.

"I know that. Logically, I understand that, but my dad was supposed to be this perfect guy, and his words led his girlfriend to come to our front door and shoot my mom. Every time I get close to a man, I worry that he's going to wake up one day and think that getting rid of me is better than just breaking up. And no, deep in my heart I don't think Cyril will try and murder me. But trusting him—trusting any man—it's hard for me. I think I can really like him, and I don't want to get in my head and mess it up later, so I'd rather not go further."

Compassion filled Halle's eyes and she reached over to rub Imani's shoulders. "Oh, sweetie, you've got to stop letting what your dad did control your life."

Usually when someone told her to stop letting her past direct her future she got irritated and pushed aside their words of comfort. With Halle, though, it was different. Her cousin had been there for her during the entire aftermath. Her compassion actually comforted Imani rather than grated on her nerves.

"I know that. I've spent countless hours telling myself the same thing. Usually, I can break things off with a guy and not think about it. I feel as if I saved myself from eventual heartache and pain, but with Cyril… I don't feel that way."

Tracey shifted closer to Imani and put her hand on her back. "How do you feel?" she asked softly.

"I feel like he's just as hurt as I am. That he understands how easily the good life you have can be snatched away. When I cried, he just held me. He didn't tell me how to feel or try to fix it, he just let me be. And he did that because he lives with his own pain. I want to trust myself with him, but there are so many other things that say I shouldn't."

Tracey frowned. "Things like what?"

"I live in Florida."

"And you hate it," Halle said with a soft laugh. "So move back here. We miss you and we need a good ob-gyn here. Dr. Baker is horrible, and Kaden wouldn't have gone to the hospital if you hadn't seen the warning signs."

"But I'm doctor of the year." She'd spent her entire career trying to be one of the best doctors out there. She'd finally achieved that with the recognition at the hospital. Moving back home meant starting over.

"And you'll be doctor of the century here," Halle said with a grin. "Plus, you can give back to a community that really appreciates you."

"I don't know if I want to do private practice. It's a lot going out on my own."

"You may not have to," Tracey said. When Imani gave her a questioning look, she shrugged. "We only have a stand-alone emergency room in Peachtree Cove, but the hospital is looking to put offices next door that specialists and general practitioners can use. It's called a timeshare or something, but you could definitely practice there. That way it's not entirely on your own."

"How did you find out about that?" Imani asked.

"The guild," Tracey said easily. "I haven't joined yet but they have damn good information at the meetings."

Imani considered what Tracey revealed. If the hospital system opened here then she wouldn't be going out on her own, but still. It wasn't a done deal or guaranteed to happen. There were other things standing in the way. "Our parents," she said, though some of the fight had left her as her friends' encouragement mingled with the interest in her brain.

"Would more than likely support you two together," Tracey said. "If anything, Mr. Dash would change everything to a double wedding if he could."

Imani laughed. "I'm not saying I want to marry Cyril."

Tracey winked at her over the rim of her cup as she took another sip. "But you can say yes to a relationship that you want. If you've never felt like trusting in someone until now, then should you give yourself a chance to experience that?"

"That's true," Halle agreed. "We all know how precious life is. If you want something, you have to go for it. Tomorrow isn't promised."

They all knew that. Halle who'd lost her parents so young. Tracey who hadn't been able to rely on her parents for anything but scandal and instability. Imani whose life was snatched away from her in a matter of seconds. They'd all experienced heartache. Heartache that had kept her from trying to find peace enough to let her heart heal. Maybe now was the time for her to be like her mom and stop living in fear and step out on faith.

Cyril sat under the umbrella at one of the picnic tables outside of the Peachtree Cove Dairy Bar. The crowd wasn't too bad and with the outdoor seating any conversation he had was less likely to be overheard. A folder stuffed with papers related to the St. Patrick's Day Festival sat in front of him in case anyone questioned why he was meeting Imani there. The hot topic in Peachtree Cove was no longer him kissing someone in the middle of Main Street. Apparently Tracey's younger brother, Devante, had been caught in a compromising position with Joanne the beautician during her grand opening. That scandal had outweighed Cyril kissing someone, but not by much.

Though after talking with Joshua earlier, he doubted he could keep the truth from getting out if anyone really tried to put two and two together.

He noticed Imani as soon as she pulled up. She got out and his breathing hitched as the afternoon sunlight glowed off her brown skin. He'd thought she'd looked irresistible under the streetlights when they'd kissed but honestly, Imani was gorgeous no matter the light. Had he really been lucky enough to have had her in his arms that morning?

She grinned when she saw him then pulled her cell phone out of her back pocket. She tapped the screen then held it up with the screen facing him as she approached. "Do you want a corn dog?" she said laughing.

He glanced at the text he'd sent her on the screen then back at her. "You like corn dogs." He pointed to the two corn dogs on the table next to his folder. He'd gone for the mustard packets instead of the larger container to avoid a possible repeat of their first encounter.

She sat across from him at the picnic table. "I thought maybe it was some new slang for hooking up or something."

Cyril chuckled. "You thought I was texting you to hook up?"

"How was I supposed to know. You might be using the word *corn dog* as a euphemism."

He raised a brow. "Please don't tell me you think I'd refer to my penis as a corn dog?"

"Hey, I've heard men refer to their penises all kinds of ways."

He cringed and shook his head. "I don't know who you dealt with before, but I can guarantee I would never call my dick a corn dog. I'm actually a little offended," he said grinning. "I mean, if I said, do you want an extralong, twelve-inch, monster dog…"

Imani held up a hand. "Okay, sir, stop it right there. Now you're doing too much."

"What? You don't think I've got an extralong—"

She reached over and tried to cover his mouth with her hand.

"How about we stop talking about that out here before someone hears us." Laughter danced in her eyes. She was so cute he wanted to kiss her.

He laughed and lightly pushed her hand away. He let his fingers glide across the soft skin of her hand before pulling back. Her breath quickened and her laughter faded as heat flared in her gaze.

He was playing with fire, and he liked it. No one appeared to be paying attention to them, but that didn't mean they weren't. He'd follow up that look later. Hopefully, if she still spoke to him after he finished telling her what he'd invited her here for.

"Fine. We'll let your dirty mind slide. I really did invite you here for a corn dog and so we could talk."

She pointed to the folder before opening a mustard packet. "What's all that?"

"Stuff about the St. Patrick's Day Festival. In case anyone wonders why we're meeting we can say that's why."

She squirted a line of mustard down the middle of her corn dog. "There are plenty of reasons for us to be together. Planning our parents wedding for one thing."

"I figured this was easier to focus on than the other." He didn't want to think about the looming wedding and how that could mean the end of what they'd just started.

"Maybe, but it's not something we can forget about."

He didn't regret kissing her or sleeping with her, but he did regret that he hadn't at least waited until they were out of the middle of Main Street to kiss her. "I'm sorry that you're having to deal with the gossip again."

"This isn't that bad. If anything, I'm kind of okay if people did know it was me."

He stiffened. Surprised by her words. "What about your mom finding out?"

"I was worried about that, but my friends forced me to face a few things."

"Things like what?"

"That I like you. I liked what we did. I've always been afraid to let go and trust a man in a relationship after what happened to my mom, but for the first time in a long time I want to try. I also think my mom will be happy for me. Your dad likes me, too. Them knowing may not be a bad thing. Maybe they'll even encourage us."

The words were spoken so easily. She picked up her corn dog and took a bite. She closed her eyes and let out a low moan of pleasure. "This is so good."

His body responded to her sexy moan, but his brain focused on what she'd said. Was she really serious about them giving this a try? "But you're moving back to Florida. You don't think they'll be upset if we're only hooking up when you come to town?"

She swallowed then licked the corner of her mouth. "I don't know if I want to move back to Florida."

The woman had to be teasing him. Tempting him with his wildest dream. If she wasn't, he was prepared to give Halle and Tracey free beers at the bar for the rest of their lives for whatever they'd said to her. "What?"

"It's true. I mean, I can't just quit. I have to at least finish up my year there, but I can make a difference here. Peachtree Cove needs a doctor who'll care about all the citizens, not just the ones they want to pick and choose."

He leaned forward and placed his hand over hers. She'd spoken with confidence, but she wouldn't quite meet his eyes. As if she were still unsure of either her decision or his reaction. He wanted her to know that his only reaction would be positive. When her eyes met his, he asked, "You're really thinking of moving back here? To make us work?"

She bit the corner of her lip before nodding slowly. "It wouldn't be because of us. Though that would be a benefit, but I miss my mom. I miss having Tracey and Halle in my life. I don't want to just be a poster child, but to make a difference. There are a lot of reasons for me to come back."

"I'd love for you to be here." He didn't hesitate to admit his feelings. He understood how difficult it had to be for her to admit that she wanted to stay, even if he was just a small part of it. If she were going to go out on the limb then he was going to dangle out there with her.

"Really? And to tell my mom and your dad?" The unsureness in her voice was also accompanied by hope.

A hope he could dash with the truth. Everything in him wanted to keep that look in her eye, but he couldn't move forward until Imani understood the entire story. "I think you're right about them, but first I need to tell you something."

"Okay, what?"

He swallowed hard and pulled back his hand. He wasn't a praying man, but he sent up a quick one that the budding emotion in her eyes didn't turn into fear, or mistrust. "It's about my mom. I told you about how she died."

She nodded. "Yes."

"There was more to the story. More that you need to know."

She frowned. "You said they caught the person who did it, right? You don't have to go through the details if it's hard to relive."

"It is hard…but you also need to know everything." He took a deep breath then opened his mouth to speak.

"Cyril! I thought that was you."

Cyril's body froze as a voice he hadn't heard in years reached him. A voice so similar to his mother's that he'd often confused them on the phone. His heart rate speed up and he jerked around to look at the older woman standing near their picnic table. The blood drained from his head so quickly he was light-headed for a moment. His aunt Gayle, his mother's younger sister, and the last person he expected to ever see in Peachtree Cove stood a few feet away.

He stood immediately. "Aunt Gayle? What are you doing here?" He took a step toward her, but she shifted back and held out a hand. Cyril froze, the spark of joy in his heart dimming from the small rejection.

Gayle crossed her arms. "I heard your dad was getting married. I couldn't believe he would have the gall to try and trick another woman the way he did my sister."

Imani sucked in a breath from behind him. Cyril's entire body went hot. *No, no, no! This was not how this was supposed to happen.* "Aunt Gayle…please don't do this."

She nodded stiffly. "I have to. I know he's your dad and you love him. I don't blame you for trying to be loyal to the one parent you have left, but I'll never forgive him for what he did."

"He didn't do anything to her."

Gayle lifted her chin. "I don't care what they say. There's no way your dad had nothing to do with it. He killed her because he wanted the insurance money."

Imani gasped. Cyril turned to face her. The horror and disbelief on her face sliced through him with the cold efficiency of a scalpel. He'd asked her here because he wanted to finish the story. To tell her about the accusations against his dad. Accusations that were proven to be wrong. He didn't want her to hear it like this.

He had to get his aunt to leave. He looked back at her and pleaded, "Aunt Gayle, please don't do this. We left. We all need to move forward and start over. This doesn't help."

"If I can prevent another family from going through what my family did then I've done enough," she said her voice rising with anger. "I'm sorry, Cyril. I do love you because you're my sister's child. But I can't keep letting you go down the wrong path of following your dad."

"It's not the wrong path. I know my dad. We all know what happened. He's heartbroken over what happened."

"Not so much if he's already marrying someone else. I won't let him hurt her, too."

"Mom!" The sound of his cousin Daryl's voice cut in.

They both turned as Daryl ran from the bathroom toward them. He threw Cyril an apologetic look before placing an arm around his mom's shoulder.

"Mom, what are you doing?"

"I saw him and I thought it best to let him know." The way she said *him*—cold and distasteful—made Cyril flinch. She'd been like a second mother to him before what happened. "We're here to stop the wedding and save another woman's life."

Cyril looked at Daryl. His cousin had once been his best friend. The closest person to him in the world, but after his mother's murder, his aunt Gayle had pulled them apart. Daryl had believed in him and Preston throughout everything, but loyalty to his mother prevented him from stepping up for them. Cyril never would have believed his cousin would bring his mom down here just to stop the wedding.

"Please don't do this," he pleaded. "Come to the house, let's talk."

Daryl nodded. "That's why we came. To talk about things. That's all."

Gayle shook her head. "There's nothing to talk about. I'm here to make sure everyone knows Preston Dash is a murderer and that no woman in her right mind should marry him."

Cyril glanced back at Imani, but she was gone. He frantically glanced around the parking lot only to see her car backing out of the lot. His stomach twisted. Everything they'd finally built up in Peachtree Cove was ruined.

thirty

Imani had no idea how she made it to her mother's shop. Her mind whirled with the accusations Cyril's aunt had thrown out like grenades.

"I won't let him hurt her, too."

"We're here to stop the wedding and save another woman's life."

"I'm here to make sure everyone knows Preston Dash is a murderer and that no woman in her right mind should marry him."

Each revelation tore a hole in Imani's heart and shattered the slim bit of confidence she'd had in her relationship with Cyril. He'd lied to her. Not just that, his father had lied to her mother. She should have gone with her initial plan and believed there was something shady about this hasty wedding. Instead, she'd been charmed by Preston and Cyril and let her own uncertainties drift away.

She couldn't believe they would keep something like this from her and her mom. Though her mind couldn't wrap itself around the idea of Mr. Preston harming anyone, she'd also never imagined her dad's actions would ultimately lead to someone trying to kill her mother. She knew better than anyone that she couldn't just trust what was in front of her.

The deeper pain was knowing Cyril had kept this from her. After they'd gotten closer, after she'd cried in his arms, after they'd made love. He hadn't said a word. Was he just as guilty as his dad?

She arrived at the flower shop and rushed inside. She had to tell her mom. There was no way she could hold on to this until later in the day. Not if Cyril's aunt was on a campaign to spread the news far and wide throughout Peachtree Cove.

Imani stopped short after crossing the threshold. Her mom and Preston stood next to each other behind the register. They laughed together while her mom playfully swatted at his arm. Preston gazed back at Linda as if she were the best thing he'd ever witnessed in his life. The contrast of seeing the way he looked at and treated her mom compared to the truth she just learned twisted her stomach into knots. The anger, hurt and betrayal bubbled inside until she thought she'd explode. There was no way she would let him hurt her mother the same way her father had.

"How could you do this?" Imani's voice, loud, angry and sharp as a whip cracked through the silence in the shop.

Her mom and Preston jumped and turned her way. Her mom scowled. "Imani, what are you yelling about?"

"I have every right to yell. I have a right to do more than that." She hurried across the room. "How could you do this? Did you think we wouldn't find out? Did you think you could lie to us forever?"

The way Preston's face went utterly still with shock only hurt her more. There was no confusion in his expression. He knew exactly what she was talking about.

"What did Cyril say to you?" he asked.

She scoffed. "Cyril? You really think he would tell the truth?"

Preston frowned. "Then how did you…"

Her mom held up her hand. "Hold up, what's going on here? The truth about what? What's going on here?"

"The truth that Preston killed his first wife," Imani snapped.

Her mom gasped. She jerked back from Preston as if he were acid. "What? No!"

Imani didn't break eye contact with Preston. "Yes. How long were you going to lie to us?"

Preston shook his head. "I didn't hurt my wife. I would never hurt her."

"If that's the case then why is your name tied up in this? Why does her family still believe you had something to do with it?"

"It's a long story." His voice, normally booming and cheerful sounded tired and shaky, but he didn't look away from her or her mom. "I was originally considered a suspect, but my name was cleared. They found the guy. Her family just won't let it go."

Linda pressed her lips together and watched him closely. "Why didn't you tell me that?"

"I was going to tell you. I just didn't want this to be the only thing you thought of when you saw me." He reached for her, but her mom took a step back.

"You know everything about my ex. If you trust me then why would you keep something like this from me?"

"I didn't want to hurt you."

"But hearing about this from my daughter makes it better?" Linda accused. "Why would you keep this from me? How can I trust that you really had nothing to do with this?"

"Because I didn't. I loved my wife. I still love and miss her every day. I would never do anything to her." He looked at Imani. "Just like I would never hurt your mother."

"We've heard that before," Imani shot back. "I knew this wedding was a bad idea. I knew it was a rush job. I was right to suspect you."

"How did you find out? If it wasn't Cyril, then who told you?" Preston asked.

"Your sister-in-law is in town and she's here to tell everyone that you killed your first wife. She's here to keep you from hurting another woman."

"I would never hurt your mom," Preston yelled and slammed his hand on the counter.

Her mom jumped and took several steps away. Preston immediately looked contrite. He reached for her. "Linda, please, I'm sorry."

She pushed his hand away and pointed toward the door. "No. Get out. Just go away right now."

"But can we talk?"

"There's nothing to talk about!" Her mom's raised voice reverberated off the walls in the store. Preston dropped his hand and took a staggering step back. "Go, Preston, before I call the cops."

Preston pressed his lips together. He gave Linda one last look before walking out of the store. Imani made sure he was gone before hurrying to her mom's side.

"Mom, are you okay?" She put her hand on her mom's shoulder.

Linda brushed aside her attempt to comfort her. "Why did you do that?"

"Do what?"

Linda turned toward Imani with a scowl. "Why did you burst in here with that news?"

Imani was momentarily speechless. Wasn't the reason obvious? "Because she's going to spread the rumor all over town. You needed to know."

"What if there had been customers in here? Then not only would the rumor spread, but you would have been the one to start it."

"You care about *how* the rumors are spread instead of the fact that Preston could have potentially killed his wife?"

She shook her head. "What I don't need is you being the reason our names are being whispered in corners. Preston told me his wife was murdered."

"You knew?"

"I did. He always said it was difficult to talk about, but I never thought…" Her voice wavered. "I never considered he would have had anything to do with it." Her mom's voice broke, and tears filled her eyes.

"Mom, I'm so sorry. We'll get through this. Whatever you need, I'm here." Imani tried to hug her.

Her mom pushed her aside. "You've done enough today, Imani. You've got what you wanted. The wedding is off."

The bell over the door chimed as a customer came in. Her mom swiped her tears. "Please handle that. I—I need a minute." She rushed toward the back of the store before Imani could say anything else.

Cyril waited at the kitchen table. He wasn't sure how long he sat there in the quiet. The silence comforted him. In the house that had provided him and his dad so much peace in the years after his mother's murder. Peachtree Cove was supposed to be their sanctuary. The place they could start over without the constant memory of the bad things that happened in the past. Had they been foolish to think that was possible?

The back door opened. He didn't turn around. He recognized the sound of his dad's footsteps as he came into the kitchen. Preston's shoulders were slumped. His brows were drawn together and the lines around his mouth were deepened by the frown on his face. He stopped in the door of the kitchen and stared at Cyril.

"Imani found out."

Cyril let out a long breath. If only he had told her before now. "I was about to tell her. Then Aunt Gayle just popped up."

Preston closed his eyes and shook his head. "Gayle…" he said in a tired voice. "Why is she here?"

"She said she heard you were getting married and came to

stop the wedding. I guess her and Daryl stopped at the Dairy Bar on their way in. Imani and I were meeting there."

Preston opened his eyes and came further into the room. "Why were you two meeting at the Dairy Bar?"

Cyril leaned his forearms on the table. "I asked her there to tell her everything. The full story about what happened to Mom."

Frustration filled his dad's face. "Why were you going to do that? I told you I would handle everything."

"I was trying to prevent what happened today," he snapped back. He didn't care about trying to remain calm or respectful. He'd known this would happen. Known it and had tried to tell his dad that they could prevent it. "I didn't want her and Ms. Kemp finding out another way and hating us."

"I don't want to keep reliving the memory of the way people looked at me. As if I would really harm my wife." The angry frustration in his dad's voice was familiar. The utter disbelief that people would think he would murder the one woman he'd loved more than anything else in this world.

Some of the anger left Cyril, but he wouldn't back down. "Don't you get it, Dad? You can't ignore what happened in the months after Mom was murdered. If you keep trying to push it aside then people will think you're guilty."

"Why did you let her listen to what Gayle had to say? Why didn't you tell her the truth?" Preston paced back and forth. He anxiously twisted the gold ring on his finger.

"I didn't get the chance to stop Aunt Gayle. I was shocked to see her there in the first place. She started throwing out her old accusations the moment I asked what she was doing in town. Imani was there and heard everything, then left before I could get the chance to explain. Now I don't know if I'll ever get the chance to explain, or if she'll even listen to me."

He lifted his hands to his face. Frustration and anger churned in his stomach. Things weren't supposed to go down like that.

He'd wanted Imani to understand he wouldn't keep secrets from her. That he was ready to face whatever came before them. He'd been ready to start a life with her. All of that had been snatched away from him before he even had the chance to say anything.

"I can't believe Gayle came down here," his dad muttered. "It's my own fault."

Cyril looked up from his hands. "It's not your fault that people won't believe the truth."

"It's my fault that she's in Peachtree Cove. I was happy about the wedding. It got me feeling nostalgic. I love the life we have here, but I miss the life we had back home. So, I called up my old buddy Clarence. I thought we could catch up and remember the good days."

"What did he say?"

"He was happy to hear from me. Said he was glad I was doing well. Then at the end of the conversation he told me that Gayle was still going around saying the police got it wrong. I got mad. All these years. All the evidence they found to show that asshole came and took my entire life from me. None of that mattered just because that sick bastard grinned and winked at me at the trial. So I called her."

Cyril groaned. "Why did you call Aunt Gayle?"

"To tell her to stop slandering my name," Preston said defensively then immediately shook his head. He rubbed the bridge of his nose. When he spoke again, the fire had left his voice and only weariness remained. "I foolishly thought I could try and convince her to see the truth now that some time has passed. As soon as I let it slip that I was starting over, I knew I messed up. I just didn't expect her to come here and try to ruin everything."

"Why didn't you tell me you'd talked to her?"

"I knew you would worry about me making things worse. Besides, you and Imani seemed to be getting along better. If I mentioned Gayle, you'd push me to say something to Linda."

"This is exactly why I pushed you. She deserved to hear

the whole story from you. If you love her, then you have to trust her with the truth. Keeping things like this hidden away doesn't make it better."

Preston hurried over to the table. He put one hand on the surface and the other clasped Cyril's shoulder. "That's why I need you to go talk to Imani. See if you can get her to calm down and talk to her mother. Maybe things will be okay?"

"Imani isn't going to talk to me. I betrayed her trust."

"Tell her I asked you not to say anything."

"That doesn't matter anymore, Dad. Not after we…" He looked away.

"You what?" Preston asked. He straightened and narrowed his eyes at Cyril. "It was her, wasn't it? The woman you were kissing on Main Street. The woman you snuck out of here the other morning."

Cyril's head snapped up. "You knew I had someone here?"

His dad cocked his head to the side. "Boy, I was born in the day, but it wasn't yesterday. Why do you think I stayed in the kitchen and didn't question when you suddenly had to rush to the bar? I figured you were sneaking someone out, but *Imani*?"

"Yes, Imani. From the moment she squirted mustard on my shirt. I couldn't get her out of my mind. I tried to ignore it because of you and Ms. Kemp, but I couldn't. That's why I was going to tell her the truth. I was in the middle of the story when you came home that day and also when Aunt Gayle showed up."

"Maybe she'll listen if you two are—"

Cyril threw up a hand. "She won't listen, Dad. Don't you get it? She doesn't even speak to her dad right now because his words convinced his mistress to try to kill her mom. That wasn't speculation or just stubborn disbelief. It's a fact. It's hard for her and her mom to trust anyone. We messed up by not giving the entire story." Cyril stared down at his hands. An emptiness he hadn't felt in years spread in his chest. He let out a shaky breath and said in a tight voice, "I don't know if we can fix this."

thirty-one

Cyril recognized the bike on the start of the trail as he left the house for work the next day. He'd considered not going into the bar to work and letting Joshua handle everything. But that's exactly what his aunt would want, for him to hide away as if guilty. Plus, he wouldn't leave Joshua to handle any fallout that might come. Nothing about Gayle had gotten back to them yet, and they didn't know where she was staying, but they'd have to deal with the rumors she planned to spread eventually. No need to delay the inevitable.

He was running late and texted Joshua, but he didn't hesitate to pull over when he saw Imani's bike at the start of the path to the lake. He got out and followed the trail through the woods to the cove. The last time he'd gone down that path they'd had a good talk, connected, he'd had to fight himself not to kiss her. Now would she even spare him a second to explain or would she immediately tell him to leave her alone?

He wanted her to hear his side of things. Needed her to know what really happened to his mom. Not the twisted tale his aunt would spread.

Imani sat on a blanket at the edge of the lake. She hugged

her knees to her chest and stared out over the flat surface of the water. The thought of her turning him away made his stomach clench, still he called her name to avoid startling her with his approach. She sat up straight and looked over her shoulder. Her body was stiff, her eyes flat and emotionless before she turned back toward the water.

He'd take her not immediately moving to get away from him as a small win. He walked over to her and then sat at the edge of her blanket. She sucked in a breath and grew more rigid, but didn't look at him.

"Can we talk?" he asked.

"It's a little too late for talking," she said in a clipped voice.

"If it were too late for talking then you would have walked away the moment you saw me coming your way."

They both kept their voices low in the quiet. She wore jeans and a thin sweater. Hair had escaped her ponytail and was frizzy around the edges. He wanted to reach out and smooth her hair back, pull her close and hold her tight. She looked like she needed a hug as much as he was dying to hug her.

"I came here to think," she said stiffly. "I shouldn't have to leave just because you came up."

"So you aren't afraid of me?"

Her head whipped around, and her eyes narrowed. "Should I be afraid of you?"

"No. I worried you'd be afraid after hearing what my aunt said."

She patted the bag sitting next to her. "I'm also protected. Do you think I'd come out here with nothing to defend myself?"

He glanced at the bag and wondered what was inside. Then hoped she didn't get the idea to use whatever defense she had in there on him. "I would never hurt you, Imani."

She snorted. "It's too late for that."

"I was never trying to hurt you. I invited you to the Dairy

Bar to tell you the entire truth. I wanted to tell you after we slept together but my dad came home."

She was silent for several seconds before letting out a long breath. "That's the other reason why I didn't leave when I saw you."

"You remembered that I wanted to tell you something." Relief fanned a small flame of hope. If she remembered that, then maybe she realized he was going to come clean. If she knew that, then maybe there was a slim chance everything wasn't gone between them.

"I did, but how can I believe this is what you wanted to tell me?"

He scooted a little closer on the blanket. Not close enough to touch her or feel the heat of her body, but shaving off any bit of distance between them was like filling in a portion of the hole inside of him.

"I care about you, Imani. From the moment I saw you, I knew I could fall hard for you. After I found out who you were I tried to ignore it but obviously couldn't. After I learned about what your dad did, I knew I had to tell you everything. After we made love, I knew I never wanted to hurt you."

She hugged her knees closer to her. "But you did hurt me. You lied to me."

"I didn't lie." She glared at him, and he sighed. "But I did keep the entire truth from you."

Her gaze sharpened as she asked, "Did your dad kill your mom?"

He didn't flinch or look away. "No. When I told you they caught the guy who killed her I was telling the entire truth."

"Then why does your aunt, her *sister*, think he had something to do with it?"

"Because no one believed my dad's story at first. I told you they were both in the house the night she disappeared. They found blood by the back door. Her body was found later. She'd been dumped in a ditch less than five miles from our house. Immediately the police suspected my dad. And when they suspected him, her family suspected him, too. I was out of town with friends and couldn't confirm that my dad had gone upstairs and fallen asleep while Mom was still downstairs watching television. Everyone believed he would have heard if something had happened to her or if she had left the house. It didn't help that they'd argued the day before."

"Was their marriage in trouble?" She frowned with her question, but she didn't look at him as if she thought he were lying. Instead, she looked at him as if she were trying to understand the entire story. That was more than some people he'd known all his life had given.

He shook his head. "My parents loved each other. I saw that every day. Look at the way my dad is with your mom, then imagine it amplified." He smiled at the memory of the good times. "They were always touching, kissing and being sweet with each other. Were they perfect, though? No. They argued and disagreed about stuff, but no more than any other couple. After the police suspected my dad, Aunt Gayle only remembered the things my mom complained about with my dad. She brought up that they'd argued about money recently. The police heard that and immediately jumped to their new insurance plan as a motive. They didn't care when I said my mom initiated the update after their previous term life policy expired. That I listened to them talk about the various options and they lectured me on why I needed life insurance when I grew up and had my own family. No one cared that they'd called me that same night she disappeared, and they were laughing and loving on each other on the phone. No one cared that my dad's voice was filled with panic and pain when he called me to say Mom was missing or how he broke down in tears and threw up after the police told him they'd found her body."

He squeezed his eyes shut and tried to block out the memory. When Imani spoke, her voice was a little closer.

"Who is the person they got?"

He opened his eyes. His hands tightened into fists on the blanket. "It was one of her co-workers. A guy who'd been obsessed with her and then got angry when she overshadowed him on a project. An offhand comment by another co-worker about him being weird at my mom's funeral got one investigator to check him out. Turns out he not only killed my mom, but three other women he felt slighted him in some way. He came by the house late that night. Knocked instead of ringing the doorbell. He attacked her right after she opened the door, dragged her out of the house. He didn't call first, so there were no records of him reaching out to her. My parents didn't have a doorbell camera to catch him. Our car never left the yard. He would have gotten away with it if it weren't for the random comment and the police discovering another woman close to him who'd gone missing. He confessed to them all."

"If they caught him then why does her family still blame your dad?"

"Because he winked at my dad in the courtroom. As if it were all a sick joke. Aunt Gayle saw it and thought that my dad must have heard something or knew the guy had done it. She blames him for her death. How could he not know that someone had kidnapped his wife when he was home with her? Rumors spread when he was originally arrested, and even though his name was cleared, we couldn't stay there anymore. We left and tried to start over."

She was silent for several moments. They both stared out at the lake. He waited for her to say something. He wouldn't push her to respond. He'd admitted to a lot.

"Why didn't you tell me or my mom this?" she asked.

"My dad worries everyone who hears the story will feel the way my aunt Gayle feels. If her family thought he would kill her then others would, too. That, and he blames himself enough for going upstairs to bed before her and hearing nothing. He carries a lot of guilt for that. He doesn't want anyone else to look at him or turn their back on him the way his in-laws did. My dad has no other family. My mom's family was his family."

"I wish you would have said something."

"I gave my dad until the wedding to tell the entire story. I told him that if he didn't say anything I would. But when you told me about your dad…and then we slept together. I knew I had to say something. I didn't want you to doubt me or how I felt." He slid closer. This time he could feel the warmth of her body and smell the sweet scent of her perfume in the breeze. "Imani, I need you to know that I care about you."

He moved his hand over until their fingers brushed. Held his breath in fear that she'd pull away. She didn't.

"I care about you, too," she said in a soft, pained voice. "Before I was ready to trust in someone. I was considering moving back to Peachtree Cove to be around my family, but also to make things work with you."

He slowly slid his fingers from her hand, up her arm. Each second his heart pounded harder as he waited for her to jerk back, but with each tentative caress she didn't move. "You can still move here." He didn't bother to hide the need in his voice. He wanted her here. He wasn't ready to let her go.

When his fingers reached the side of her face, she turned to face him, but she shook her head. "You don't understand, nothing can happen between us. My mom has called off the wedding. No matter how I may feel about you…we can never be together."

The pained expression on Cyril's face made Imani want to reach out and touch him. Instead, she tightened her hand into a fist. She couldn't reach out and touch him. Her heart wasn't supposed to ache saying the words that needed to be said. The words were true. They couldn't be together. It was hard enough before, but now... Now it was impossible. His hand dropped from her face. The cool breeze swept away the heat of his touch.

"Do you really believe my dad had something to do with my mom's murder?"

She shook her head. "No. Not anymore."

After leaving her mom's shop, she'd sat and considered everything that happened. Her mom had known about the murder, just not that Mr. Dash had been the original suspect. Being a suspect and then having someone else arrested didn't make him guilty. She wanted to hear the entire story, which is why she hadn't left when Cyril approached her. Now that she'd heard it, she was angry again. They could have made things work, but now her mom's heart was broken, the trust between them shattered. How could they come back from this?

"I know you tried to tell me what happened yesterday. I believe you called me to the Dairy Bar to finish the story. You just took too long to tell me."

"I know. Nothing I can say will make up for that. I was only trying to go with my dad's wishes. I know how much it hurt him to see friends and family turn against him. I know he didn't want the same thing to happen to him here. From the moment he told me about the engagement I let him know that he had to say something before the wedding."

"I'm glad you were willing to go against him to tell me, Cyril...but that doesn't change the fact that he still held it back. I believe he had nothing to do with it. I saw the lack of remorse in my dad's eyes after what happened with my mom. He blamed everything on the mistress and took absolutely no responsibility for her actions. Then I noticed all of the cold, calculated ways he expressed love in the form of manipulation. Your dad doesn't do any of that, but he still wasn't truthful. My mom is hurt. So hurt she called everything off. We can't be together after that."

"Maybe they'll make up."

She smiled at the hope in his voice, but she saw the look in his eyes. They both knew a reconciliation would be difficult.

"They won't," she said. "My mom is talking about closing the shop and moving back to Florida with me. She doesn't want to be the center of a scandal again."

His brows drew together. "Moving back with you. Imani... I thought you wanted to stay."

She had wanted to stay. Wanted the life she could see herself having in Peachtree Cove with her mom, Halle and Tracey, and Cyril. Saw a future that wasn't guarded and afraid of love. But if her mom didn't want to stay in Peachtree Cove there was no way Imani could come back when her mom moved somewhere else alone.

She stood before she got swept up in the emotion in Cyril's eyes and forgot that this was for the best. "I left my mom the last time she was hurt. I can't do it again."

He got up and came closer. "You don't have to leave. Neither of you do."

Imani jerked on the blanket until he stumbled back. If he touched her, pulled her into his arms, she might give in and accept his touch. "I can't stay here if she's not here. And I can't ask her to stick around and see your dad. Not after everything that happened. It's why we can't be together. It won't work." She shook out the blanket and started folding it.

Cyril came forward. He leaned down to try and meet her eyes. "For the first time I've wanted someone with every part of me. I know you feel the same."

She shook her head. She would get over this. It was just a quick fling. That was all. Getting over Cyril might take a little longer, but she would do it. He took her hands in his, stopping her from folding the blanket, and pulled her close. Imani wavered and took a half step forward. The bulk of the blanket kept their bodies from touching.

"Imani, please."

"My feelings for my mom matter more," she said forcefully. "I can't be with you. We can't do this."

"What am I supposed to do with the feelings I have for you? How am I supposed to stop loving you?"

The strain in his voice pulled at her heart until she thought it would snap. She stepped back. "You'll stop because you have to. I won't be here, so that will make it easier."

"Imani."

He reached for her, but she turned and walked away. He could catch her if he tried. Before she knew it she was on the bike. She held her breath and waited and listened, both in anticipation and fear that he would follow. She wasn't sure what she'd do if he held her, kissed her. But he didn't follow. She pedaled down the road and when she heard his truck coming behind her a few minutes later, she took the next turn in the opposite direction to avoid having to watch him drive away.

thirty-two

Cyril remained cordial and kept the conversation going with the patrons at the bar even though every time the door opened his body stiffened, and his gut clenched. He didn't know if his aunt planned to come to the bar, drop her bomb and ruin their life, but he expected it with every ring of the bell at the bar's entrance. If he knew where she was staying, he'd consider approaching her first. Even though she hated his dad, she wouldn't turn Cyril away. The problem was if he did confront her, what could he say that he hadn't already said before.

On top of the anxiety of waiting was the frustration and pain clawing at his chest every time he thought about the look in Imani's eyes when she said they couldn't be together. He got it. Everything about their situation said they just wouldn't work. He respected her and was grateful she'd even given him the time to explain everything. She didn't have to do that. She didn't owe him or his dad anything. But that didn't stop him from wishing he could still hold on to her. For years after his mom passed, he'd bottled up his feelings. He'd lived to help his dad recover, rebuild their life in Peachtree Cove, put all thoughts of what he wanted outside of the bar aside. Now, he'd finally, *finally*, felt something that wasn't related to being strong and stable for his dad and he'd lost it. He'd finally gotten a taste of the happiness he hadn't expected to find only to have it snatched away before he'd gotten the chance to savor it.

"Cyril, you good?" Joshua asked for the fortieth time in the last hour.

Cyril chuckled, not at all frustrated by his friend constantly checking on him. That was the thing about best friends. No matter how many times he said he was good, Joshua could always tell when something was up.

"I'll be fine," he said nodding at his friend.

Joshua narrowed his eyes. "You're finally going to admit that something is wrong? You gonna tell me what happened?"

"Only something I knew would eventually catch up to me finally did."

Joshua frowned then his face cleared as realization dawned in his eyes. He leaned in close so the patrons around the bar couldn't overhear. "You told her everything?"

Cyril shook his head. "I didn't get the chance to. Someone else said it before I could."

"How?"

The chime at the door rang. Cyril's body tightened. He looked toward the door hoping to see another regular and relax as he had so many other times. His gaze met his cousin's, and the air in his lungs froze. He glanced behind Daryl, but his aunt Gayle didn't follow. He only relaxed a little. Daryl had supported him and his dad, but he'd also come down here with his mom and knew the reason for her visit. He couldn't trust this wasn't the start of something bad happening.

Daryl didn't come to the bar. He lifted his chin in greeting before crossing the room and taking a seat at one of the tables in the back corner. Cyril looked at Joshua. "Can you watch the bar for a second? There's something I need to handle."

Joshua's eyes had followed Cyril's as he'd watched Daryl cross the room. "You good?" His friend's tone asked the rest of the question. *Do I need to get ready to have your back?*

Cyril slapped his friend on the shoulder. "I'm good. That's my cousin."

Joshua's eyes widened. "Ooooh. Go ahead. I got the bar."

"Thanks."

Cyril poured two drafts of the beer he'd brewed and headed over to his cousin. He set one beer in front of Daryl before sitting in the chair across from him. He cupped his hands around his own glass and waited. Daryl had come to see him, so he'd let his cousin direct this conversation.

Daryl picked up the glass and took a sip. He nodded and licked his lips. "Not bad. What is it?"

Despite himself, Cyril's chest swelled a little at the praise. There'd been many times over the years that he'd made a blend or found a new beer and wondered if Daryl would like it. "It's my blend."

Daryl's brows rose. "You make the beer here?"

"Not all of it. I typically stock from small local breweries and a few of the mainstream beers for those not into craft beer. I just make a small batch of my own brew each season. When it's gone it's gone."

"And you're wasting a glass on me?" Daryl asked with a raised brow.

Cyril shook his head. "It's not a waste. I haven't had a drink with my cousin in a while."

Daryl let out a slow breath. He took another sip before his lips twisted into his crooked smile. "Remember when we used to sit and listen to our dads talk about work, life and women."

Cyril let out a soft laugh. "Those were the best times. It's why I opened this bar. I wanted a piece of those good days."

"Did you use the insurance money to start this place?" Daryl's voice wasn't accusatory or angry, still the words put Cyril on the defensive.

Cyril met his cousin's gaze. "Some, but not all. I took out a small business loan. Got a grant to help fill the gap."

He nodded slowly. "My mom is sure you used up all of the insurance money to start over down here."

"My dad was the primary beneficiary. He gave all the money to me. What I didn't use for this—" he looked around the bar "—I put aside."

"What are you saving it for?"

Cyril shrugged. "I honestly don't know. I just know that spending it all seems like letting go of the last thing my mom gave me. Even if it's something I never wanted in the first place." He lifted the glass and took a long swallow.

Daryl cocked his head to the side. "Now you know Aunt Vera would call you out for not using it."

"I'd like to think she wouldn't encourage me on this. I think she'd understand why I held on to it."

"Probably so," Daryl said softly.

They were quiet for a several minutes. Both sipping the beer and letting the memories of the past drift around them. Cyril's impatience got the better of him. Sitting and talking with Daryl felt too much like old times. He couldn't let his guard down.

"Why are you here, Daryl?" he asked. "Is it to scope out the place before Aunt Gayle comes to make accusations in front of all my customers?"

Daryl flinched. "She's at the hotel. We're staying in the hotel near the interstate."

That answered one question. If he decided to visit her and try to talk it out, he knew where to go. That didn't answer the rest of his questions. "Why didn't she come here with you?"

Daryl leaned one elbow on the table. "When she walked around town earlier to try and get information on you and your dad, all anyone had to say was great things. It's just like back home. Everyone loves the Dash men."

"We don't try to make people love us. We're just here to

start over." Cyril was surprised he hadn't heard about someone asking about him and his dad. Even more so that she hadn't gone against the praises by accusing them of being murderers.

Daryl nodded. "I know that. I don't blame you either. I'm glad you were able to start over."

"Why didn't she use the opportunity to ruin our names?" He tried to make light of the words, but they caught in his throat. Peachtree Cove was his home. When they first moved there, he hadn't expected to care so much about the town or the people in it, but the connections they made meant almost as much as the connections he'd lost back home. His heart ached at the idea of having the people who'd welcomed him with open arms now shun him and push him away.

"She didn't. She listened and the more she heard, the more she got mad."

Cyril's spine stiffened. "What is she going to do?"

"She's trying to find the woman Uncle Preston is marrying. She says she's here to make sure she knows the kind of man she's marrying."

"They're not getting married anymore."

Daryl blinked. "Are you saying that to get rid of us?"

"Nope. The woman I was with when Aunt Gayle jumped all over me is her daughter. She told her mom, and she broke of the wedding."

Daryl cursed. "Damn, man, I'm sorry."

"For what? Isn't that what you're here for?" He didn't try to soften his words with a smile.

Daryl shifted in his chair before speaking. "I came to try and stop my mom from going completely off the rails when she got here. I tried to talk some sense into her on the ride down."

Cyril looked at his cousin and saw the truth in his eyes. "Why won't she let this go?"

"It was her only sister," Daryl explained. "She knows that

your dad didn't do it, but he didn't stop it either. He didn't protect her, and she blames him."

Cyril leaned forward and pressed his fist to the table. "And you don't think he blames himself? That he doesn't live with the torture of that every day?"

Daryl held up a hand. "Mom is lashing out. She needs someone to blame."

"Then blame the guy who did it. Better yet, be angry at my dad back home. She doesn't have to come all the way down here and try to ruin everything we've built. My dad is finally happy. He finally moved on. I finally found something for myself. Now all of that is gone."

For the first time Daryl looked sincerely remorseful for being there. "Cyril, man, I'm sorry. I couldn't just let her drive down here by herself and she wouldn't listen to me when I said she shouldn't come. I'm here now because you're my cousin. Despite everything we're still family. I want to be real with you about what's going on."

Cyril let out a breath. No matter how angry the entire situation made him, he understood why Daryl was there. Daryl was an only child. His aunt Gayle had already treated him like her little prince growing up. Her husband died years ago. Even though she had brothers and her son, her sister had been her best friend. There was no way Daryl would let his mom drive to Georgia on her own no matter what he believed. Things could have been a lot worse if Daryl hadn't come.

"Now that the wedding is off, will she stick around?"

"I hope not, but…" Daryl sighed. "I'd like to think that we could get together and talk things out. Maybe start to get things back to normal."

"Do you really think your mom is ready for that?"

Daryl opened his mouth, frowned, then closed it and shook his head. He took another sip of the beer. That was Cyril's answer. He finished his beer and stood. "Thanks for the heads-up. Enjoy your beer."

"Cyril, for real, I wish things could be different."

"So do I." He walked back to the bar. Joshua gave him another *you good?* look. Cyril gave a nod before patting his friend's shoulder. He wasn't ready to go over the conversation and would have time to do that later. After they closed up and he didn't have to worry about people overhearing.

Daryl sat at the table for another hour. When he left, he threw up a peace sign before walking out the door. Cyril had the surprising urge to go after him. A part of him wanted to ask Daryl to come back and sit at the end of the bar. Catch up with the one person who'd been as close to him as a brother. There were so many other things they could talk about. Whatever happened with the woman he'd been dating and the child they had? Was he still working for the state? When was the last time he went to a basketball game? Instead, he stood behind the bar and stared at the door. He ignored the pain as another part of his life was shut away from him for good.

thirty-three

Imani finished ringing up the bouquet of tulips for the customer in her mom's store. It was nearly six in the evening, and they were about to close up for the day. The woman had rushed in to get tulips for her best friend who'd recently gotten her dream job and was meeting her for drinks to celebrate. The smile on the woman's face when she found out they had tulips in the store made Imani's day. She needed that bit of joy after recent events.

Her mom came from the back office just as Imani waved goodbye to the customer. "Is that the last person here?"

"It is." Imani leaned her hands against the counter. "I think we're good to close up for the day."

Linda walked toward the front door. "Good, because I'm hungry. I hope Preston is making something good tonight." She stopped in her tracks. Shaking her head, Linda frowned. "Umm, never mind. What I meant to say is do you want to drive over to Augusta and eat at Applebee's?"

That wasn't the first time she'd made the mistake in the days since calling off the wedding.

Imani gave her mom a small smile. "The 2 for $20 sounds good," she replied referring to the restaurant's signature deal.

Linda nodded and turned back toward the door. It opened before she got there, and a woman walked in. Imani's stomach twisted when her gaze connected with Cyril's aunt's.

"Hey, I was just about to close up, but let me know what you're looking for and I'll be happy to help you," Linda said cheerfully.

Imani quickly came around the counter. "Mom." Her mom hadn't met Gayle and treated her like any other customer.

Gayle looked from Imani back to Linda. Her shoulders straightened and she lifted her chin. "I'm not here for flowers."

The smile on Linda's face stiffened. Her head cocked to the side and she placed a hand on her hip. "Well, this is a flower shop, so if that's not what you're here for then I can't help you."

"I came here to see you," Gayle said.

"And you are?" Linda asked. Irritation added steel to her voice.

Imani stood next to her mom. "This is Cyril's aunt Gayle. Mr. Preston's sister-in-law." She didn't need to add the sister-in-law part, her mom sucked in a breath with the first sentence.

"*Former*, sister-in-law," Gayle said. "I don't claim him after what he did to my sister."

Imani didn't know what she expected her mom to do, but it wasn't to cross her arms and raise a brow at Gayle. "And what exactly did he do to your sister?"

Gayle raised her chin. "He murdered her."

Linda didn't flinch. "From the way I understand it, the police arrested the guy responsible for the murder. He confessed to that and a few others and is now behind bars. Do you have evidence that's different?"

Imani's gaze swung from Gayle to her mom. She had not expected that response. After her mom asked for her help canceling all the contracts for the wedding, she hadn't mentioned

Preston. Only when she had a moment like before when she wondered what he was going to cook or mentioned remembering to tell him something. Then she brushed it aside and pretended as if she hadn't brought it up.

Gayle scoffed and straightened her shoulders. "That man may have killed her, but Preston is still responsible. You can't tell me he didn't hear anything."

"Preston loved his late wife. I don't believe he would have let her be taken away like that."

"How do you sleep through something like that," Gayle shot back.

"I'm sure that's a question he asks himself every day," Linda said in an even voice. "Now, if you just came here to cause problems then you've wasted your time. He's got enough to live with without you coming down here making a ruckus."

"If you trust him, then why did you call off the wedding? I heard about that today."

Linda uncrossed her arms and shrugged. "I have my reasons, but understand that they don't have a thing to do with you."

"I only came here to try and give you a warning. I'm trying to look out for you."

"Are you really trying to look out for me, or are you trying to make him suffer even more?"

Gayle pressed her lips together. Anger flashed in her eyes, but beneath that was pain. "I did what I felt I needed to do. That's all I can do. Regardless of why you called it off, I'm glad. He doesn't deserve to be happy. Not when my sister…" Her voice broke off. Gayle sniffed and blinked several times. "Either way, everything worked out for the best."

Linda took a step forward. "I pray you find peace," she said in a soft, comforting voice.

Gayle swallowed hard, before spinning on her heel and rushing out the door. Imani quickly went over and turned the lock.

She didn't want Gayle or anyone else to come in. Spinning back around, she studied her mom.

"Are you okay?"

Linda took in a shuddered breath then nodded. "I am."

"Why did you defend him?"

Linda shrugged. "Because he didn't do anything to his wife. He's suffered enough."

She turned and went back to the counter. Imani immediately followed. She had not expected her mom to defend Preston, not when she'd avoided talking about him. She'd assumed her mom was still angry or hurt by him not telling her the entire story. She expected Linda to be angry or frustrated, but instead she appeared chill.

"I thought you hated him?"

"I don't hate him." Linda went behind the counter and began shutting down the register.

"But you called off the wedding."

"Because you were right. We were rushing things. And, when you came in here the other day and told me everything, I realized that Preston didn't trust me." When Imani frowned Linda continued. "I already knew the story behind him and his wife. When he told me how she died, I looked him up. He never said anything, and I didn't say anything because I figured it was hard enough to lose your wife like that without being considered a suspect."

"Wait, you knew?"

Linda pursed her lips. "You really think I didn't look him up before I started dating him? After everything with your dad?"

"I wasn't sure. You were hesitant about the background check when I mentioned it."

"That's because I worried if you saw that you'd worry, but when you stopped talking about a background check, I did, too."

"I still don't understand why you broke things off if you already knew."

Linda pulled the cash drawer out and placed it on the counter.

She sighed before speaking. "I saw his face when you came in the other day. He wasn't keeping it back because he thought it was tough to talk about, he was keeping it back on purpose. He didn't trust me with the truth. That's when I knew that I was rushing into things. That I'd let your dad's calls about getting married stop me from looking at everything about Preston. He loved me, but if he was afraid that telling me the truth would turn me away, then I knew he didn't trust me. I wasn't going to tie myself to a man who didn't believe in me. I think I deserve a little more than that after all I've been through. Don't you?"

Imani nodded slowly. She felt foolish for not believing her mom would do her own background check. She'd rushed here thinking her mom was fragile and unable to make her own decisions, when she was far from fragile or gullible. Preston hurt her mom, but not for the reason Imani had believed. Cyril had been right, Preston should have trusted in her mom enough to tell her everything. That was what relationships were supposed to be built on, mutual trust and understanding.

"I do," she said.

Linda smiled and nodded. "Good. It's why I'm going to close the store for a while and go back to Tampa with you. I think I need a little bit of time to get my thoughts together."

"Are you sure?" Imani saw how much her mom loved working and how she had become involved in the town again. She was surprised when Linda suggested going back to Tampa with her, but she honestly didn't want to leave her alone.

"I'm more than sure. Now, let's close up and go eat. I'm hungry." Linda took the cash drawer and headed to the back of the store.

Cyril passed a beer to his dad sitting at the end of the bar. "You alright?"

His dad took the beer and nodded. He didn't bother to smile and the typical twinkle in his eyes wasn't there. "I'm alright."

Cyril sighed and leaned his hands on the bar. "Dad, just call her."

Preston shook his head. "I tried. She's not answering my calls and when I went by the house, she didn't answer the door. I'm not going to harass her and force her to talk to me."

"Then are you going to continue like this?" Cyril couldn't stand to see his dad this upset.

Preston wasn't as sad as he'd been after his wife died, but Cyril hadn't seen him this upset since they'd moved to Peachtree Cove. He still went out and helped around town, but once he finished his job he came back to their place and sat in front of the television until he fell asleep. Cyril would wake up in the middle of the night to the sound of some video playing and get up and tell his dad to go to bed. It was as if Preston didn't know what to do with himself now that he didn't have Linda in his life.

"I've done enough to Linda. I won't make her talk to me if she doesn't want to." He lifted the beer and took a sip. "Now go deal with your customers. I'll be alright."

Cyril wanted to send him home, but also worried that he didn't need to drive in that state. He wasn't drunk, he'd only had two beers, but between the alcohol and the emotional state, he preferred keeping an eye on his dad. Even if it was hanging out at the end of the bar.

"It's all good. It's Wednesday. The bar isn't that busy."

Preston nodded and took another sip. "Remember when me and the fellas used to hang out drinking beers and talking?"

"Dad, you know I remember. It's why I opened A Couple of Beers."

"I know. I know. Still, I used to really enjoy those evenings hanging with Vera's brothers. You know my brother died when I was twenty, so they became my brothers."

"I know they did."

Preston sniffed then cleared his throat. "Shame to lose them right after losing her."

"I know."

Preston nodded slowly and took another drink. "Real shame."

Cyril looked at Joshua at the other end of the bar. His friend raised a brow. Cyril shook his head. "Hey, let me go check on Joshua for a second."

Preston waved a hand. "Go work. I'm good."

Cyril walked over to Joshua who frowned at him. "Is Mr. P going to be alright?"

Cyril shrugged. "I don't know. I hope so, but this is almost as bad as losing Mom. It may take a while for him to bounce back."

"Is Ms. Kemp still not talking to him?" Joshua asked in a low voice so Preston wouldn't overhear.

"She isn't and my dad isn't going to force her to listen."

"Maybe he'll get a chance at the St. Patrick's Day Festival this weekend," Joshua said hopefully. "They're both volunteering for the guild. Maybe he'll get the chance to get back with her then."

"Maybe so, but he won't make a scene. If she refuses to be around him, he'll go the other way."

The chime above the door went off. Cyril looked up. He was no longer anxiously waiting for his aunt to come through the door. Not after talking to Daryl. Which was why he felt as if he'd been gut punched when his gaze collided with hers.

He straightened. "Aunt Gayle!"

Preston looked at Cyril before spinning around in his chair toward the door. Gayle looked from Cyril to Preston and then back.

"Hello, Cyril."

Cyril tried to remain calm while inside his emotions bounced all over the place. He'd been waiting for this confrontation, but after talking to Daryl, he'd hoped that she would drop everything and go back. He wasn't ready to talk, and honestly, he didn't want to have a confrontation with his aunt.

"What are you doing here?"

She looked at Preston. "I came to see him."

Preston stood up. He smoothed down the front of his pale yellow linen shirt before lifting his chin. "If you came here to try and make me feel bad you've wasted your time Nothing will make me feel worse than I already do."

Gayle came across the room toward him. The bar wasn't as full as it would typically be, but there were enough people for Cyril to wish they were alone. Monique, who worked with Tracey at the inn along with the owners of Books and Vibes were there. He didn't want to air out his family's dirty laundry in front of people he knew and respected.

"Aunt Gayle, now isn't the time," Cyril said.

Gayle held up a hand. "I just left your ex-fiancée," she said.

Preston's body stiffened and he scowled. "Why are you bothering her?"

"I went there to warn her about you," Gayle said. "But she already knew the entire story. Said she knew the story from the start. I don't know why she broke off your engagement, but I'm still glad she did."

Preston took a step forward. "She knew from the start?"

Gayle grunted. "You don't deserve a woman like her. After all of this, she's still defending you. You don't deserve to be happy."

Preston pressed a hand to his chest. "I know more than anyone that I don't deserve this chance to be happy."

"But you tried anyway," Gayle accused. Her eyes glinted with unshed tears. "You tried to be happy and live when my sister isn't here."

"I wish more than anything that Vera was still here. Every day, I wish she was still here." Emotion made Preston's voice thick.

Gayle pounded her fist to her chest. "Then why are you trying to start over? Why are you moving on when my sister can't?"

"I didn't look for this. I didn't try to do this," Preston said sounding frustrated. His shoulders slumped. "I just fell in love." The last point came out in a tired voice.

The fight left Gayle's eyes. "You don't deserve love after you killed my sister."

Cyril stepped forward, but before he could say anything Patricia and her husband, Van, stood up. Patricia stepped between Preston and Gayle.

"That's enough now," Patricia said. "Mr. Dash had nothing to do with that."

Van moved next to his wife and nodded. "That's right. They got the person responsible and he's behind bars."

Cyril blinked and looked between the two. "You know the story?"

Patricia nodded. "Of course we do. Do you really think no one in town looked into you all when you moved here? We understand what happened, and we know it had to have been hard. That's why we didn't pry."

Cyril looked around the bar. Other patrons nodded along with what Patricia said. His chest tightened as he realized just how nosey the people in Peachtree Cove were. And how much they cared. Of course, they would know. They'd been so afraid of being judged like they'd been back home, when, in reality, the story wasn't a secret. People knew, accepted them anyway and even stepped up for them. If he didn't love Peachtree Cove before he damn sure loved the town and its people now.

"He slept through everything," Gayle accused.

"And every day I hate myself for that," Preston said. "Every day I wonder how I missed it. How could I sleep through it. What if I had stayed downstairs with her? Every, single day. Even when I was happy with Linda, I had the same thoughts.

You may think I moved on, but I'll never truly move on from what happened. No matter what I do."

A tear trailed down Gayle's face. "I miss my sister."

"So do I, but we both know she wouldn't want to see us like this." Preston's voice was soft and careful. "She loved both of us. She wouldn't have wanted to see us fight."

Gayle's lip trembled. She glanced at Cyril. He took a step forward, but she held up her hand. "I'm going back home tomorrow. I know what my sister would want, maybe one day I can do that, but... I just can't right now."

Preston's lips lifted in a sad, knowing smile. "Take all the time you need. When you're ready, I'm ready to be your brother again."

thirty-four

No one knew how to avoid people better than Imani. In the years after the scandal with her dad, she'd learned the best times of day to go into town to avoid those most likely to pull her into an uncomfortable conversation and mastered the ability of not caring about excusing herself from a conversation, even if she appeared rude. Cutting people out of her life was a lot easier than dealing with the pain of having them there.

After her mom broke off the engagement, she'd done exactly that. She avoided any place where she might bump into Preston or Cyril. Although her mom knew the story, Imani did her own internet sleuthing into his family's case. The evidence proved his dad had nothing to do with what happened. But the hate from the people who blamed him for not knowing his wife was abducted right from their home when he was there was fierce. She understood why he would want to avoid talking about what happened.

Her heart ached for Preston and Cyril, but despite knowing that she couldn't make herself reconsider being with Cyril. Her mom's heart was broken, and Imani couldn't bring herself to acknowledge or move on from the feelings remaining in her heart. So she'd tried to avoid him completely before she left town. If she saw him, she wasn't sure if she'd be able to pretend as if she didn't want anything to do with him.

But all her efforts to avoid him couldn't prevent her from having her mom guilt-trip her into helping at the St. Patrick's Day Festival the day before leaving. She'd tried to avoid coming by convincing her mom to pack up and go back to Tampa with her instead. Linda insisted that not only had she promised to help out with the festival, but the parade had been Imani's idea and they couldn't back out. Which was how Imani ended up first helping line up the floats for the St. Patrick's Day parade before filling in for various volunteers at the festival. The parade had been a hit with multiple visitors from the region in attendance.

She'd expected to have to work hard to avoid Cyril at the festival, but as a guild board member he was kept so busy that she barely caught a glimpse of him. She told herself she was relieved, but she still scanned the crowd and searched for him.

"Imani, there you are," Carolyn Jones, the owner of Sweet Treats bakery said to Imani who was filling in for a volunteer at the tent giving out water bottles. Carolyn was one of the many local business owners who hadn't given Imani much grief when she'd called to cancel the wedding order. Imani was still surprised how supportive everyone was. They'd just taken her explanation and moved on. "Can you do me a favor?"

Imani stopped handing out bottled water. "Sure. What do you need?"

Carolyn held up a large manila envelope. "We've got to go around to the downtown businesses and make sure they have their Peachtree Cove Business Guild sticker on the door. They didn't come in until late last night so not every member has theirs. Will you help pass them out?"

"I don't know who's a guild member or not. A lot of businesses decorated their doors."

"Oh, it's fine." She looked over Imani's shoulder and her eyes lit up. She waved someone over. "I asked Cyril to help, too. He knows all our members."

The back of Imani's neck tingled a second before Cyril appeared by her side. And just like that, all her efforts to avoid Cyril were dashed. She let her guard down for a second and this was what happened.

"If you've got him then you don't need me," Carolyn said in a cheery voice. She held out the envelope toward Imani.

"Won't it go faster if you help him?" She pushed the envelope back toward Carolyn.

Carolyn pushed it back to Imani. "My daughter's tap dance class is about to perform on the stage. I've got to go see her. Thank you." She turned and hurried away before Imani could say another word.

Imani clutched the envelope to her chest. Cyril stood silently next to her, but she could feel his gaze gliding over her face. Heat filled her cheeks. "Can't you do this by yourself?" she asked in a rush.

He shifted until he stood in front of her, making Imani finally look at him. He looked good in the green Peachtree Cove St. Pats Festival T-shirt and jeans. He'd even found a green fedora to top off the outfit. His eyes studied her as if he'd been starving for the sight of her face. "I can, but I'd like to do it with you."

The whispers of her attraction fluttered in her chest. Imani let out a shuddering breath as she mentally fought the magnetic pull he had on her. "We shouldn't be together."

"Why not?"

Because when I see you, all I want is to put my arms around your neck and kiss you. She kept that confession to herself. She raised her brow and cocked her head to the side. "You know why."

"You can't blame me for wanting to enjoy any bit of time I can spend with you." He lowered his voice so that only she could hear him under the hum of the crowd. "I miss you, Imani."

I miss you, too. The words were so far on the tip of her tongue that her mouth twitched. The light in his eyes as he awaited her response made her both eager to admit the truth and frustrated with herself for being so easily pulled back to him.

"Imani—"

She turned to the other volunteers at the water stand. "I've got to help pass out stickers. I'll be right back."

The three other women and two men all nodded and waved her on. They really didn't need her there. She'd been the fill-in for the previous shift when a volunteer was gone and had stuck around afterward.

"Let's get this over with," she said to Cyril.

He smiled, despite her words, before motioning for her to walk ahead of him. They left the town square where the food vendors were set up and took the sidewalk toward Main Street.

After a few steps he asked, "Are you and your mom really leaving Peachtree Cove?"

She'd agreed to stay and help her mom cancel everything. That hadn't taken as long as expected and her plan was to go back after the festival. Her mom wanted to get someone to handle the store before following. Though she'd initially considered closing it, Linda didn't want to leave her customers with no other options.

"We are," she said. "I'm going back first. I don't think I can hold off the calls from the hospital to come back now that there isn't a wedding."

"There could still be a wedding."

She stopped and stared at him. "My mom isn't changing her mind."

"You could always marry me," he said with a straight face.

Imani's breath caught in her throat. He had to be joking. He would start laughing at any second. But he didn't start laughing. Her heart rate picked up. Nope, she would not get swept up in his silly fantasy.

"Don't play with me like that." She turned and stalked away.

Cyril caught up to her with a few quick steps. "I'm not playing. I really felt like…feel like, you're the person I could spend the rest of my life with."

She spun on him and pointed. "Stop that. We can't do this. Weren't you the one against us going there in the first place?"

He crossed his arms and nodded. "I was."

"And *now* you want to try and make things work when everything is so messed up? When it's impossible for us to make this work out?"

A group of revelers came down the street. Talking loudly with cups of green beer in their hands. Cyril took her elbow in his hand and pulled her out of the way. He didn't stop there. He pulled her into the small alley between buildings. He let her go once they were away from the crowd and stared down at her.

"Everything you said before still matters," he said. "Our parents want us to be happy."

"But they can't be near each other."

He flinched. "Does your mom hate my dad?"

Imani couldn't say that her mom hated Preston. She was angry about him not trusting her enough to tell her everything, but her mom still cared even though she'd never admit it. "She hates what he put her through. She hates that she's waiting around for your aunt to drop the bomb and put her in the middle of the gossip mill again."

"My aunt knows that my dad had nothing to do with what happened. My cousin told me. She was here for days without causing any problems."

"No problems? Do you think people haven't told my mom about the woman asking around town about him? No one will say it, but they know she has something to do with it."

"She's gone now."

"My mom and I will be, too."

She moved to go back to the main road, but he reached out and grasped her elbow. Imani froze and stared up at him.

He stepped closer to her. "You really don't want to see me again?"

Yes, she did want to see him again. She still regretted not being able to follow through with her feelings for him, but she wouldn't do that at the expense of her mom's feelings. Not after what happened with her dad. "Cyril…"

He turned her to face him and pulled her forward until her breasts brushed his chest. "You really want to give up on us?"

Memories flooded her brain. Memories of his body against hers. The way he'd kissed and touched her. The way he'd made her feel. How he'd held her and comforted her. She should pull back, but her body refused to follow her brain's instructions.

"We have to. This won't work," she said to herself as much as she spoke to him. She was wavering and they both needed the reminder of why they couldn't be foolish in the face of their parents' imploding relationship. "I can't hurt my mom and you don't want to torture your dad by having me around to remind him of everything he lost."

He leaned forward. She took a step back but bumped into the wall. "They'll understand," he said.

"Or they won't, and we'll be selfish."

"Don't you want to be selfish." His voice lowered, and he leaned in close. "Haven't we both held back for our parents enough?"

Imani's heart pounded and she sucked in a breath. She was doing what was right. Continuing to see Cyril wasn't going to help anything. But what if she just indulged before she went back? Would she really be wrong to have one more taste of him?

She shook her head. "We can't."

He closed his eyes and pressed his forehead against hers. "I know, but for once in my life I really want to be selfish."

So did she. She lifted her head. Their lips brushed. Cyril's shuddering breath caressed her lips. She let go and leaned in. Their lips met in a kiss that started hesitantly then quickly turned passionate. Cyril clutched her against him as if he couldn't bear to let her go. She submitted herself to his kiss. Opening her lips and letting him in. Letting go, for the moment, the reasons why she shouldn't be doing this and reveling in the feelings she'd suppressed.

He pressed her back against the rough bricks of the building. Her breasts cushioned the solid weight of his chest. The sounds of voices of the people at the festival trailed into the alleyway. They hadn't gone very far. Anyone could see them if they bothered to look into the shadows. Knowing that only made her cling tighter to him. The rush of doing what she wanted mingled with the fear of someone seeing and snatching the moment away.

Her hands roamed over his back, up to his shoulders and cupped the sides of his face. Cyril broke the kiss. His breath was ragged, and he pressed his forehead against hers.

"Meet me later tonight," he said in a rough voice.

"Meet you? Where?" There weren't many places where they could meet. She was with her mom, and he lived with his dad.

"At Tracey's bed-and-breakfast."

"Why?"

"Because I want to see you again. I need to see you again."

The longing in his voice tugged and pulled at her heart. "I'm leaving tomorrow."

He lifted his head and stared down into her eyes. "Please, come see me before you go."

Imani held his gaze. She couldn't say the words she should say. All she could do was push aside all the reasons why she shouldn't. Once she went back home, they would never get another chance. She wouldn't return to Peachtree Cove for at least another year, maybe two. If she did return to Peachtree

Cove, he might have moved on and found someone else. If her mom decided to stay in Florida, the next time she was in town would be even longer. She might never get the chance back to be with him.

Swallowing hard, she nodded.

thirty-five

Cyril begged Joshua to watch the bar with a few of their part-timers so he could leave early. Despite the huge crowd in there from the festival, Joshua was a true friend and told Cyril to dip out before ten. He texted Imani to see if she was still willing to see him and his knees nearly buckled with joy when she texted back that she was in the carriage house behind Tracey's bed-and-breakfast.

He drove straight there. Lights reflected behind the lacy curtains in the window of the small yellow house. His heart hammered and his palms sweated despite the cool night air as he made his way to the door. He was asking for too much. Wanting too much, but he couldn't help it. Seeing and kissing her earlier that day had scrambled his brain. She was leaving the next day. Who knew when he'd get the chance to see her again? He couldn't let her go without at least trying to convince her to give him a chance.

Imani answered quickly after he knocked. She'd changed out of the volunteer T-shirt from earlier and put on a light sweater with leggings. Her hair looked messy, as if she'd run her fingers through it several times and her face was clear of makeup. She was beautiful.

Imani reached for his arm and pulled him inside. "Hurry up before someone sees you."

"There's no one out there."

"Well, there was no one on Main Street that night either until there was."

He nodded. "I can't argue with that."

She closed the door behind him. The space was split in two and separated by a wall with a fireplace. To the right was a bed, two accent chairs and a television, and to the left was a large soaking tub and bathroom. He turned and faced Imani and was very aware they were alone in a bedroom.

She cleared her throat and pointed to the bag in his hand. "What's that?"

"Oh, it's for you." He held out the small brown gift bag.

"What is it?"

He shrugged. "Nothing too big. Open it up and see."

She took the bag from him. She bit the corner of her lip, but it didn't hide her smile. "You got me something?"

"Just open the bag."

Imani nodded before opening the bag. Frowning, she reached inside and pulled out her gift, a rectangular acrylic nameplate. "'Doctor Imani Kemp. Doctor of the Year.'" She looked up at him.

"It's for your desk. It's a reminder that regardless of the reason, you are the doctor of the year and you deserve it."

"You didn't have to get me anything."

"I *wanted* to get you something." His lips lifted in a sad smile before he spoke again. "Honestly, when I ordered it I hoped you would be staying in town. I thought you could put it on your desk when you started working here in Peachtree Cove."

Sadness clouded her eyes as she ran her fingers over her name. "I would have liked to stay."

He took a step toward her. "You can stay."

She lifted her chin and raised her brow. "Did you ask me here to rehash what we already know?"

He shook his head but stepped closer. "A man can try."

She put the nameplate back in the bag. "And a woman can be tempted."

He took the bag from her and put it on the small table next to the door. "Things could be different."

She looked up into his eyes. "Do you really believe they will be?"

He didn't. Even though he wanted Imani and wanted his dad to be happy for them, he also knew he couldn't imagine having his dad around Ms. Kemp knowing the way things ended with them. He couldn't be selfish and flaunt having the woman he wanted in front of his father. Especially when that woman was the daughter of the woman Preston lost.

"I don't know if I can forget you, Imani." He ran his fingers across her cheek.

"I don't want you to forget me. I want you to think about me every day. Just like I'll be thinking about you."

The soft admission seeped into his soul. He cupped the back of her head and wrapped his other arm around her waist. "Tell me now if you don't want this."

"What if I change my mind later?"

"It'll hurt, but I'll still let you go."

Her full lips lifted before her hands splayed across his chest. "I know why you asked me here, and I want to be here. I want this last time, with you."

The words *last time* ripped through him like a chainsaw. Painful, ragged and chaotic, but that didn't make them any less true. He lowered his head and kissed her. He didn't want tonight to be just regrets and sadness. Tonight he was being selfish, and from the way Imani's lips spread and she passionately deepened the kiss, she wanted to be selfish, too.

He pulled on the edge of her sweater. She lifted her arms and he quickly jerked it off and tossed it aside. He wanted her so badly his hands shook. His entire body vibrated with the need to feel her skin, caress her curves and kiss every inch of her. If this was all he was going to have of her then he wanted to make it last.

All of his noble intentions of taking things slow and savoring her flew out the window when she unfastened his jeans and her hands slipped into the front of his boxers. She took him in her hand and stroked all thoughts from his head except to get inside of her immediately.

"I'm trying to make this last." His voice was raspy, need-soaked and he wasn't the least bit embarrassed.

Imani gently squeezed him before sliding her thumb across the tip. "Round two can be slower."

He didn't think he could get harder, but he almost lost himself at those words. He lifted her by the waist and put her on the small table by the door. The bag fell onto the floor with a thud.

"My nameplate," Imani said trying to look down.

He kissed her neck and sucked softly. "Did not break and I'll buy you a hundred more if it's damaged."

Her sexy chuckle was like accelerant to the fire burning in him. He kissed her fiercely. With all the pent-up frustration, need and longing surging through his veins. Imani met his kiss with just as much passion. She shoved down the waistband of his jeans and underwear. Not breaking the kiss, Cyril awkwardly shook them off his legs and kicked them to the side. The table wobbled as they pulled off Imani's leggings and underwear.

"Tracey is going to kill me if I break her table," Imani said giggling after they got them off.

He lifted her into his arms and her legs wrapped around his waist. The sweet heat of her sex on his stomach made him bite his lip. "We're not risking your life over a table."

He took her to the bed. Imani smiled up at him. She was so

sexy and beautiful and once again he was struck with that same amazement that he'd felt when he'd first seen her at the Dairy Bar. She was the one for him. The one person he wanted to learn everything about. The woman he could envision spending his life with. And after tonight he wouldn't have her.

Her hand cupped his chin. "Don't do that. Don't look at me like that. We aren't going to think about tomorrow. Just love me tonight."

Emotion wrapped round his chest like a vice. He couldn't speak. If he did, he'd beg her to stay. Instead, he shifted so her legs would spread wider. Lowered his head and kissed just as he adjusted his hips so he could push deep into her.

thirty-six

Imani sat and waited for an opportunity to jump into the conversation at the hospital board meeting. She'd been trying to jump in for several minutes, but every time she opened her mouth, she was either talked over or asked to hold on a second for the person to finish their thought. Unfortunately, the person's thought tended to end with a question for someone else. She was getting sick and tired of waiting her turn.

When she'd participated in the previous board meeting via video conference she hadn't bothered to talk much. She listened to the discussion and honestly showed up because she was expected to be there. Now she couldn't get Cyril's words out of her head. She wanted to use her time as doctor of the year to her best advantage.

And just like that, thoughts of Cyril came back to her. Honestly, it didn't take much for thoughts of him to take over her mind. From the moment she'd left him sleeping in bed after spending the night with him until she arrived back in Florida, she thought about him constantly. The man was like a television jingle playing over and over in her head. He wouldn't go away. She'd known spending the night with him ran the risk of having that happen. But like any person addicted to something, she couldn't deny herself one more hit.

The way they spent that night together made things worse. They hadn't just spent time making love. Afterward they talked. He'd asked her about her childhood; she told him about the good days before her father's mistress ruined their life. He talked about the summer beer blend he was concocting for the bar and his dreams for the town to win Best Small Town and how he was excited about all the attention the label would bring to Peachtree Cove. She'd even admitted that she was nervous about coming back to the board, expressing her thoughts and trying to be the doctor of the year they claimed she was. Of course he told her she would do great and supported her even though he wished she would be doctor of the year in Peachtree Cove.

That last night had been more than just a night of "getting each other out of their system." It was as if they tried to pretend they really were a couple who could still be together when the sun rose. Which made being together even more sweet and painful because the sun had risen, and she had to leave and come back to Florida. Now she was here in the board meeting listening as the other members went on and on about all the things they needed to do to improve the hospital's image without really naming how all of this could really improve patient experiences.

There was a lull in the conversation which drew Imani from her thoughts of Cyril and their last night together. This was her best chance to jump in.

Imani raised a hand. "Excuse me, but I have a point I'd like to make."

Bill Robinson, the board chair, was a middle-aged white guy with wire-frame glasses and an expression that was pleasant on all of his company photos but seemed to pull tight every time Imani tried to jump in.

"Yes, Doctor Kemp, what would you like to add?" Bill asked trying and failing to sound as if he welcomed her input.

Imani didn't care if he didn't want to hear what she had to say, this was why she was here. They'd made her doctor of the year, which meant she was supposed to be here and could speak up. "While we're talking about things that can help the hospital look better, it would also be beneficial to consider ideas about ways to make our patient experiences better."

Bill raised his brow. "Really? You know Mid-State Health has a pretty good rating with our customers."

"True, but pretty good isn't great. We've also received some very valid complaints. Just because the majority of our customer base is content doesn't mean we should underestimate the experiences of others."

"And what do you think we should do? We all realize that there will be outliers. Patients won't be happy even if we give outstanding service all the time. It's human nature for some to complain."

There was a round of head nods and agreement with Bill's comment. Imani straightened her shoulders. "I believe we should include training programs for the staff, doctors, nurses, technicians and others on ways to recognize warning signs and high-risk patients. Some of our complaints come from minority patients or members of the LGBTQ community about feeling as if their needs are overlooked. It may not be the case with each example, but training to identify ways to recognize bias may help some employees pay more attention to patients when they complain about pain and other symptoms. There haven't been any training programs here that can help employees recognize these kinds of underlying biases so that they can overcome them and be sure their patients get the best care."

"How will a training program make the hospital look better?" Bill asked in a tone that said unless it helped the hospital's image the betterment of the staff didn't matter.

Imani had to fight not to roll her eyes. She'd started the conversation by saying her idea would make patients feel more comfortable. She took a deep breath and tried to smile. "Well, again, I was focusing more on the patients. This training program targets all levels of staff who encounter patients and can help improve patient experiences here at the hospital. Improved patient experiences mean they'll say good things about the hospital when they go out in public. If they say good things about us in the public that in turn improves the hospital's image."

He squinted his eyes as if considering before nodding. "I can kind of see what you're talking about. It may be something that the board can consider in the next budget cycle."

Imani raised a brow. "Are you trying to say there's not enough money in this current budget cycle? I was under the impression that the budget for training was large. I don't understand why this type of training can't be included with some of the other trainings that we have."

"The training budget is designed to ensure we don't have any increased liability and to keep everyone up-to-date with any professional development hours they need."

"Recognizing how underlying biases may affect your reactions to patients and keep the hospital out of trouble reduces liability. I don't understand how this doesn't tie directly into what you're trying to do?" she countered.

Bill waved a hand. "Now, now, there's no need for you to get upset. I understand what you're trying to do. I'm just making the point that we'll look at the hospital budget next year and see if we can tie in some type of... I don't know, diversity and inclusion type of training in the future."

She wasn't upset. She was being direct and straightforward. Why did that have to be interpreted as being upset? "But—"

Bill cut her off. "Very good points, Imani, but we're getting close to the end of the meeting." He glanced at his watch. "We all have a lot of other things that we need to do. I try to be respectful of all members' time and not keep them longer than necessary. If you'll just write up your ideas and send them to my admin assistant, I'll be sure to have her check with finance and see what the current training schedule is. We'll see if we can have something added in." He gave her a patronizing smile and spoke in a tone that didn't give her much confidence that he'd look into her training suggestion.

"Okay, folks," Bill said. "If that's all then we'll wrap up today's meeting. Do I have a motion to adjourn?"

Imani stared, dumbfounded. Had he really just cut her off? Not only that, he'd implied that she was upset when she'd just been direct and blown off her idea as if she'd suggested weekly pool parties or something. The meeting adjourned and then the rest of the board members began to leave the room. Imani walked over to Bill.

"Dr. Robinson, I just want to let you know why I recommended the training. I've noticed this is a problem in our practice."

"How so?" he asked, reminding her of an annoyed school principal by the way he looked over the tops of his glasses at her. She'd have to remind Halle to never look at students like that.

"I tend to get more of the patients that are considered difficult when it's mostly that the other doctors don't want to deal with them. Whether it's a Black woman they say has too much attitude or a trans patient that makes the staff member feel *uncomfortable* because their preferred pronoun isn't one they agree with."

His eyes widened and he nodded. "Ahh, this is about you not wanting to handle the workload."

Imani frowned. "What? No, I'm trying to relay a legitimate issue."

"Dr. Kemp, all doctors have to deal with difficult patients. A training class won't relieve you of your duties. You're the hospital's doctor of the year. That title comes because you are good at what you do and not because you bring up erroneous ideas. I'd recommend you attend a few more meetings and get a better feel of the board."

He nodded at her as if she were a child who didn't understand before turning and walking away. Imani stared at his retreating back. She'd assumed she was only on the board to be a figurehead. That being named doctor of the year meant she was just a poster child for everything the hospital said it wanted to be. She hadn't expected them to be so blatant about it.

Sighing, Imani left the boardroom. Her friend Towanda was outside the waiting room. Imani smiled and went over to her friend. "What are you doing here?"

"I had a moment between patients, so I came to see how it went. Did they listen to your idea?"

Imani sighed. "No, I was accused of not wanting to deal with difficult patients."

Towanda's head jerked back and she scowled. "What? Doesn't that go against you being the doctor of the year? You got the title because you're so good with all patients, difficult or not."

"That's what they say. Not exactly what they mean." She rubbed her temple as they went down the hall. "I wonder if I should've just stayed in Peachtree Cove."

Towanda bumped her with her elbow. "That's the third or fourth time you've said that since you came back."

Imani frowned. "No, I haven't."

Towanda nodded. "Yes, you have. Admit it, you want to go back to your hometown. You miss small-town life."

She missed Cyril. She also missed Halle and Tracey. She missed helping her mom at the flower shop. She missed running into old friends and seeing the things they were up to. She missed people who appreciated her work as a doctor like Kaden.

"Maybe I do, but my mom hasn't made any mention of going back. She's been through enough calling off the wedding. Whatever she wants, I'll give."

Her cell phone rang. Imani pulled it out of her jacket pocket and smiled. "Speak of the devil."

Towanda grinned. "Tell your mom I said hey. I've got to get

back to my floor. Call me later and we can curse the hospital administration together."

Imani laughed. "Sounds like a plan." She waved at Towanda as she got on the elevator and answered her mom's call. "Hello."

"Imani! I need to go back to Peachtree Cove."

The panic in her mom's voice erased the smile from her face. Had something happened to Preston? Or worse, was Cyril hurt? "Why? What's going on?"

"It's Halle. She was in an accident. Shania called me all shaken up. I've got to go back and check on her."

The panic she felt didn't ease. Instead worry jumped in with it. She didn't even think twice before saying, "I'll go with you."

thirty-seven

Imani handed Halle a glass of orange juice before fluffing the pillow behind her cousin. They'd arrived in Peachtree Cove the day before. Her mom had insisted on going straight to Halle to make sure she was okay, and Imani readily agreed. Unfortunately, Halle wasn't one to enjoy being waited on hand and foot.

She took the orange juice with her good hand and awkwardly swatted Imani away with the arm in a cast. "Will you stop treating me like I'm on my deathbed? I just have a broken arm." Halle grinned as she pushed Imani away.

"I can't help it. You look like you're in pain." Imani moved away and sat on the love seat opposite Halle resting on the couch in her living room.

"I don't look like I'm in pain. I look pitiful," Halle said with an eye roll before taking a sip of juice.

Imani shrugged. "Pitiful, in pain, what's the difference?"

Halle flipped Imani the bird and they both laughed. "I can't believe I fell down the damn stairs."

When Imani's mom said Halle was in an accident she'd automatically assumed it was a car accident. Instead, Halle had fallen down the stairs at the middle school and broken her arm.

Though she was bruised in other places and taking some leave time, the damage to her ego seemed to be worse than the broken arm.

"I can believe it," Imani said grinning. "You were always so clumsy."

"Everyone is clumsy as a teen. I can't believe I'm clumsy as a thirty-five-year-old."

Shania skipped into the room. "All teenagers aren't as clumsy as you," the girl said grinning at her mom.

Halle cut her eyes at her daughter. "Didn't you want to go to your friend's house later?"

"I do." Shania held out a small plastic container. "Spit in this."

Halle cringed. "What? I'm not spitting in that."

Shania pouted and continued to hold out the container. "I need a DNA sample."

The humor in Halle's eyes evaporated and she sat up straighter. "For what?"

"We're doing an ancestry project in social studies. I have the family tree from Grandma's Bible, but I wanted to see what I could find with DNA. So…" She waved the small container.

Halle shook her head. "Nope. Not doing it. You've got the family tree and that's enough. No DNA samples here."

"But what if I—"

"Shania, I mean what I said. Go throw that away. We aren't doing that."

Shania's shoulders slumped before she grunted, spun on her heels and rushed out of the room. Imani looked in the direction she'd gone before turning to Halle. "Why not do the DNA sample?"

"Because," Halle said stiffly.

"Because why? It's pretty harmless."

Halle stretched her neck and looked in the direction Shania had gone before looking back at Imani. "Because I don't need her finding stuff she doesn't need to know."

Imani frowned. "You've got to tell her about her dad one day."

"Today isn't the day."

Imani raised a brow and leaned forward. "Are you going to tell me?"

Halle pursed her lips and shook her head. "It's not the day for you either."

Imani sighed but didn't push. Whatever reasons Halle had for keeping Shania's dad a secret were her own. She wished her cousin would be open with them, but figured the memory must be painful for her to keep things to herself. Still, she didn't want her cousin to think she would judge her for the situation.

"You know you can tell me anything and we'd be good."

The stiffness in Halle's shoulders disappeared and she smiled. "I know and I appreciate that. I'm not afraid of judgment. I just don't want Shania to change...that's all."

"Change how?"

"Are you going to see Cyril?"

They spoke at the same time. The sudden change of subject did what it was supposed to do. It quickly distracted Imani from the original point of the conversation.

"What? No! Why would I go see him?" she scoffed and shrugged.

Halle's smile widened. "Because you miss him, and you want to see him."

That was true. She did miss him. Had missed him from the moment she left him. But she couldn't go see him. Not when her mom was still hurting from the breakup with Preston.

"It doesn't matter if I want to see him. My mom doesn't want to see him or his dad."

"Your mom doesn't have to see him," Halle replied dryly.

"You always were the instigator in the group," Imani said giving her friend a narrow-eyed look.

Halle only shrugged. "I'm just saying. You're in town, you might as well see him."

"What if he doesn't want to see me."

Halle rolled her eyes. "Girl, I should throw this pillow at you. Of course, the man wants to see you. He asks about you every time he sees me or Tracey."

"He does?" Imani perked up.

Halle raised a brow. "And since you're lighting up like a Christmas tree, that proves you want to see him."

"I'm not lighting up."

"Chile, please! Don't even sit there and lie. Go see that man."

"Can I take care of you first?" Imani protested.

"My arm is broken. My legs, feet and everything else works just fine. And since your mom is not here hovering, now is the perfect time for you to sneak away and see him."

Imani considered the words. She couldn't deny that she wanted to see Cyril. He'd been in her thoughts constantly and the moment she'd gotten into town and confirmed Halle wasn't in any imminent danger she'd obsessed about seeing him even more.

"But what—"

"But nothing. I'll tell Aunt Linda that you went to get me something from the store and Tracey will cover for you if you take a long time. Just go see that man."

As much as good sense said not to, Imani couldn't ignore the quickening of her heart. She wanted to see him. That didn't mean anything would happen. She'd just make sure he was okay. Doing that didn't mean she was betraying her mom.

She stood. "I'll only be gone for a minute."

Halle shook her head. "If you're only gone for a minute then Cyril isn't the man I thought he was."

Imani didn't find Cyril at the bar. Joshua said he left to check on Mr. Preston, who hadn't shown up to help cut the middle school football field and wasn't answering his phone. Worried, Imani went to their home, but no one was there either. She decided to go home and see if her mom had heard from him or had any idea of where he might be. She'd considered calling Cyril, but felt her call would just be a distraction if he was worried about his dad.

To her surprise, Cyril's truck pulled up to the front of her mom's house at the same time she arrived. She quickly got out of the car and walked to the end of the driveway. Cyril got out of the truck and she had to bite her lip to stop herself from sighing. He wore a tan T-shirt that fit his broad shoulders and dark pants. A brown fedora shaded his face from the midafternoon sun, but that didn't block the way his eyes lit up after he saw her.

"What are you doing here?" she asked.

Cyril walked up to her. He was so close she wanted to reach out and hug him. She'd missed him so much.

"Looking for my dad," he said. His gaze scanned her face as if searching for something.

"You think he's here?"

Cyril shrugged. "I don't know. I heard you and your mom were back in town and wondered if maybe he would come see her."

"I was here to see if she might know where he would go."

Cyril frowned and looked confused. "You're looking for my dad?"

"I went by the bar to see you and Joshua told me that he didn't show up for work. I also went by your house."

He shifted even closer. The heat of him drawing her in and melting the flimsy walls she'd put up around her heart. "You came looking for me?"

She cleared her throat and glanced away. "I wanted to see how you were doing."

His hand traced down her arm before entwining his fingers with hers and squeezing. "I was going to find you today, too."

Imani looked back at him. The emotion in his eyes pushed

past any lingering doubts about how she felt. She wasn't sure how to make this work, or even if she could make this work, but she couldn't pretend as if she didn't care about Cyril.

"Let's find your dad first and then deal with us."

He nodded. "Deal."

Imani didn't let go of his hand as they went to the front of the house. When she had to break the contact to unlock the front door, he placed a hand on her hip. Imani's lips twitched as she tried to fight back a grin. She wanted him to touch her and loved the fact that he wasn't ready to break contact with her.

The house was quiet when they entered. "Mom?" Imani called out. There wasn't an answer.

She frowned at Cyril. "Her car is here."

"Maybe she's taking a nap or something," he offered.

"Let me go check."

Imani left him and went down the hall. Her mom's door was closed. She knocked and opened before waiting on an answer. When she opened the door, she realized she should have waited for the answer.

"Mom!" she yelled.

Her mom jumped up in the bed and snatched the sheet to just under her chin, covering her naked body. Mr. Preston also sat up and held the sheet to his chin. Imani closed her eyes, shook her head, but they were still there when she opened them.

Cyril's footsteps pounded down the hall to her side. "What's wrong? Is she okay?" He was out of breath when he got to her side and put his hand on the small of her back.

Imani pointed in the room. He looked that way then screamed. "Dad!"

Her mom waved her hand. "You two get out right now."

"But… Mom—"

"Don't *but Mom* me. Get out and let us get dressed. Unless you want to get an eyeful." Her mom moved to get out of the bed. Imani quickly reached for the doorknob and slammed the door shut.

Half an hour later the four sat around the living room. Imani and Cyril on the love seat while Preston and Linda sat close to each other on the couch. Dozens of questions bounced around in Imani's head like bees. She wasn't sure which one to blurt out first.

"I thought you never wanted to see my dad again," Cyril said breaking the awkward silence.

Imani nodded and looked at her mom. "You said you couldn't be with a man who didn't trust you."

Preston flinched and Linda gave him a small smile before looking back at Imani. "We aren't back together."

Preston's chest puffed up. "We aren't?"

Linda lifted a finger. "Not officially anyway."

Imani cleared her throat and shifted on the couch. If they weren't officially together then what exactly were they doing?

"But you two…" Unable to finish the words Imani gestured between them and then to the bedroom.

Her mom shrugged. "We're two consenting adults who missed each other's company."

"Linda, you know that's not all that was," Preston said gently before reaching over and taking her hand.

Linda relaxed a little before pulling her hand away and meeting Imani's eyes. "I've decided to take things slowly this time."

"We may have rushed into the wedding," Preston said with a shrug.

Imani cocked her head to the side. "You think."

Cyril bumped her knee with his. When she looked at him, he shook his head. Sighing, Imani decided that just because the sudden switch in the situation had her brain scrambled, she didn't have to make the situation more uncomfortable.

"Is this what you really want?" she asked her mom.

Linda nodded before patting Preston's leg. "I do. I'll admit when we first jumped into the idea of a wedding that I may have been influenced by your dad calling and saying he was marrying someone else. But what I feel when I'm with Preston has nothing to do with any of that."

"And I know I was pushing to try and get back the family feeling I had before your mom died," Preston said to Cyril. "Instead of recreating something old, we're both going to take the time to find out what us being together should look like."

"And that may or may not mean marriage," Linda said. "But for now it means we enjoy each other's company and will continue to do so."

"Does this mean you're not going back to Tampa with me?"

Linda shook her head. "I'm not. I love being here in Peachtree Cove. And if you're honest with yourself, you do, too." She held up a hand before Imani could protest. "You don't have to decide now. But you've got a lot of good reasons to stay." She grinned and looked pointedly at Cyril.

Imani sat up straighter. "What are you trying to say?"

Her mom gave her a *don't be silly* look. "Do you really think we don't know about you two?"

Preston nodded. "I knew it the moment they said Cyril was kissing some woman on Main Street. Heck, half the town probably figured it out by now."

Imani's jaw dropped. Heat spread up her neck to her cheeks. She didn't know what to say. She'd thought they'd been discreet, but what secrets could be kept in Peachtree Cove?

If Cyril was shocked, he didn't show it. Instead, he reached over and rubbed Imani's back before grinning at their parents like a kid who'd been given free rein at a candy store. "So you don't have a problem with us being together?"

His dad looked confused. "Why would we have a problem?"

"You said you wanted us to be a family."

Preston nodded. "I do, but there are all types of families out there. You two being together and me and Linda being together may not be what people are used to, but who cares as long as everyone here is happy."

Imani looked at her mom. "You feel the same."

"I do. Don't keep holding back, Imani. If you want something, whether it's to speak up at the hospital, strike out on your own or finally trust yourself in a relationship, go for it. Don't be like me and wait so long to finally find joy despite the pain of the past."

thirty-eight

Six months later, Imani walked into A Couple of Beers. The Friday night crowd hadn't thickened yet but would soon. She waved at Joshua setting up the area for Joi to perform later.

"Where's Cyril?" she asked.

"In the back. You can go on back and see him. How did things go today with the hospital?"

Imani grinned. "Better than expected. Looks like I might be able to set up here soon. Keep your fingers crossed."

Joshua raised his hand and crossed his fingers. "I will."

She kept smiling as she headed to the back of the bar. When she'd turned in her resignation in Tampa the hospital administration had seemed more concerned about how to handle the publicity of losing the doctor of the year than they seemed concerned about losing her. The other doctors in her practice were sincerely sad to see her go, and Towanda threatened to follow her to Peachtree Cove.

"If you don't keep in touch I'm coming after you. You're my best friend and I'm going to miss you."

Imani would miss her, too, but there was so much more for her in Peachtree Cove. Not just her family, Tracey and Halle, and Cyril, but the community that continued to embrace her. The hospital was hoping to open a doctors' office next to the ER; sure enough, once the mayor learned Imani was moving back, she'd immediately put in a good word for her. Imani met with those hospital executives today about coming to work for them.

She found Cyril in the back, sampling the fall blend he'd finally finished. He took one look at her, grinned and waved her over. "Try this?"

Imani cringed and shook her head. "I tried it. I like the fruity beers, but not regular-tasting beer."

Cyril rolled his eyes in mock annoyance before leaning down to kiss her cheek. "I'll turn you into a real beer drinker one day."

She patted his back before sitting on the stool next to him. "Not gonna happen."

He finished the sample before letting out a satisfied sigh. "How'd it go at the hospital?"

"Really well. I'll have to share the space with the other doctors who'll be using the office. We'll switch out days to provide a multitude of services, but it'll really help me build up my patients."

He held up his hand for a high five. "You got this."

Imani slapped his hand. "I know it. I'm excited. Not just about the job, but because they actually listened. When I brought up training about biases and making sure patients' needs are heard, they agreed. They acknowledged that just because they are a small-town hospital system doesn't mean they can't provide a large range of services. Plus, they agreed with my ideas about making sure all patients feel welcome. I was impressed."

"See, what did I tell you. Doing doctor of the year stuff already." He bent to write something down in a notebook on the table.

She waved away his words and laughed, but inside her heart

swelled. She loved the way he supported her. It wasn't an after-thought or something that felt fake. She liked that all he wanted was to support her and see her happy.

"Hey," she said.

Cyril looked up from writing. "What's up?"

Her heart fluttered and her palms dampened. She licked her lips, suddenly shy and anxious about the words bubbling up. Words she'd never thought she'd say, but right now, in this mundane moment of talking about work and watching him take notes on something he loved doing the feeling struck her.

"I love you," she blurted out.

Cyril dropped his pencil. A bright smile covered his face and he stood. He pushed back the black fedora on his head before cupping her face and kissing her. The kiss was deep, and pas-sionate, and Imani clung to the sides of his shirt as liquid heat spread through her midsection.

When he pulled back, he grinned down at her. "I love you, too."

"You sure?"

"Completely, sure." He raised a brow. "So will you marry me now?"

She sucked in a breath and pushed on him, but he didn't budge. "Quit teasing me."

"I'm not teasing. I meant it when I asked you months ago and I mean it now. When I saw you at the Dairy Bar bounc-ing all happy because of a corn dog I knew you were the one."

"No, you didn't," she said pursing her lips.

He kissed her quickly and nodded. "Yes, I did. I don't want to waste time or delay happiness. I mean it, Imani. I want to marry you."

Her heart squeezed. She couldn't believe it, but she wanted to marry him, too. She wanted to sleep next to him, wake up beside him, spend her life being loved by him.

"You and your dad. Y'all love a hasty wedding, huh."

He shrugged but the smile never left his eyes. "I guess that's the secret. Move to Georgia, find a sweet Southern belle and marry her quick."

Imani raised her brow but wrapped her arms around his shoulders. "The secret to a Southern wedding, huh."

He pressed his forehead to hers. "The secret to a lifetime of happiness. I love you, Imani. Will you give this guy a chance to make you happy for the rest of your life?"

Imani searched her heart and waited for the doubt, insecurities or hesitancy to enter. They didn't show up. The only thing she felt was safe, loved and finally content. "Yes, I will."

★ ★ ★ ★ ★

About
Last Night

one

"What do you mean you're not coming?"

Joanne Wilson placed one hand on her hip while the other gripped the cell phone against her ear. She looked around at the multiple boxes filling what would be the lobby of her new beauty salon. A beauty salon she'd waited two decades to finally turn from previously failed dream into reality. The boxes contained the decorative tables and accent chairs she'd ordered online with the hope of giving the place a polished, sophisticated look. Stacks of framed prints by Black artists leaned against one wall waiting to be hung, along with the strings of lights she'd gotten to add just a small touch of whimsicality to the space. Her brother had agreed to meet her bright and early to help put together the furniture, hang the pictures and the lights. Now he was giving her some excuse about another job.

She wanted to scream. Or cry. Maybe both.

"Kalen, you know my grand-opening party is next Saturday before I officially open for clients on Tuesday. I need to get this stuff together today." Which meant she had a week to get the space cleaned up and ready before the party that weekend.

"I know, I know," he said, not sounding the least bit repentant about bailing on her.

"Then why are you on my phone telling me that you can't come?" She tried and failed to keep her voice even. Snapping at her younger brother typically got her the opposite of what her goal was, but today she didn't care about sweet-talking to get what she wanted. "I've got to help Mom with Bible study at her church tomorrow night and if we wait until Thursday or Friday there's a chance we won't get everything done before Saturday. I need all day Friday to finalize any last-minute details."

"Jo, chill, all right—I've got you." She could hear the smile in Kalen's voice. How dare he smile right now? This was serious.

"How do you have me? Because you just said you're driving to Augusta for a job. Is it money? Okay, I'll pay you to help me."

"It's not about the money. This is about my reputation. I promised to do this job but forgot to put it on my schedule." Kalen did home inspections for new home buyers and was constantly forgetting to add an inspection to his calendar, despite the hundreds of times Joanne reminded him to use an actual scheduler instead of sticky notes and napkins.

"So I've got to suffer? Seriously, Kalen, how could you leave me hanging like this?" she snapped, no longer caring about irritating him as panic twisted her stomach. She needed this grand opening to be perfect. She didn't want to wait until the last minute only to have something go wrong.

Joanne paced back and forth in the small area between the boxes and other decorations waiting to fill her space. The space she'd saved up for so she could finally afford a prime spot in the revitalized downtown commercial district of her hometown of Peachtree Cove, Georgia. The storefront in the refurbished building had been coveted by other business owners in the area, but Joanne had managed to snatch it up before anyone else, thanks to a client casually mentioning the property would be listed the next morning.

About Last Night

A few people around town doubted she'd be able to afford the rent, much less keep her business open. After giving birth to her son when she was eighteen, she'd spent years doing hair in her mother's kitchen. When she'd first tried opening her own salon at twenty-five, she'd had to quickly scale back to doing hair in her home. The same people she knew doubted her now had received invitations to her opening celebration on Saturday, but thanks to Kalen and his inability to use a calendar correctly, there might not be any furniture to sit on if she couldn't get everything assembled that day.

"If you'll let me talk, you'll understand I didn't leave you hanging. I got you some help."

Joanne rolled her eyes. She turned away from the boxes to look at the large pane windows that would provide a view of Main Street. Brown paper covered them from the inside to prevent people from looking in. The sign that read Joanne's Day Spa and Salon would be installed the next morning. She walked to the door, which wasn't covered, and looked out. Only a few people were downtown at 7:00 a.m. on a Saturday. The boutiques and restaurants that had returned to downtown as part of Peachtree Cove's revitalization effort wouldn't open for a few more hours. The streets would be bustling with activity then.

A dark burgundy pickup truck pulled into the space next to her small SUV. Joanne sucked in a breath. She recognized that truck.

"Who did you get to help me, Kalen?" she asked in a low voice.

The driver's-side door opened right as she asked the question. She spun away, hoping her hunch was wrong. That maybe someone else with a similar pickup had parked next to her. That she wasn't about to come face-to-face with a temptation she had no business feeling.

"Devante should be there by now." Her brother dashed her hopes with one sentence spoken in a look-at-me-saving-the-day tone of voice.

"Why did you call Devante?" Joanne asked, trying not to reveal the wild emotions bouncing through her.

She spun back toward the door and looked out. Sure enough, the tall, dark-skinned man getting out of the truck was Devante Thompson. Instead of heading her way, he rummaged through the storage container in the bed of his truck.

"Because he's my boy and he's better than me at this stuff. We were out last night and when I realized I mixed up the dates, he offered to help you out. Why you acting all irritated? Devante is like family. I thought you'd be happier having him there than me."

Joanne suppressed a sigh. Of course, he would think that. Everyone would think that. Devante and her brother were best friends. They'd bonded over a mutual love of anime and comic books when they were in middle school and the bond had grown ever since. Devante had just been another kid in the house full of family and friends at every cookout, holiday and birthday party. He was like family.

Her problem was that in the last year or so, she'd had a hard time viewing him as her kid brother's homeboy and could only see him as the very handsome, very sexy man he'd grown to become. Had to be the post-forty hormone fluctuation. At least that was what she tried to tell herself.

"Nothing's wrong," she said to her brother. If she continued to panic, he'd get suspicious. Then she'd have to try and find an excuse to explain why she didn't want Devante's help. Something other than spending the day in her new salon with him was going to be difficult because his smile made her heart race and anytime they accidentally touched, her body went into a lay-me-down-and-make-sweet-love-to-me tailspin. She was not going to admit to that.

"As a matter of fact, he just pulled up," she said. "Go do your inspection and I'll talk with him."

"Good," he said, sounding relieved. "You're welcome."

About Last Night

"Mmm-hmm...thanks." She ended the call before he could complain about her lukewarm thanks.

She turned back to the door. Her eyes met Devante's. On cue, her stomach did a little clench. Full, thick lips creased up in a heart-stopping grin as he raised a big hand to wave. Joanne pressed one hand to her heart, which was currently doing backflips, and waved the other.

Down, girl! He probably sees you as a big sister. Or worse...an auntie. She fought not to cringe with the idea of that moniker and unlocked the door.

She forced her gaze not to linger on his broad shoulders, or the gray joggers clinging to his butt and thighs as he walked toward her. She didn't know when Devante had grown into his looks. She'd been so busy trying to get her son through college and saving enough to open her own salon, that one day she'd looked up and the scrawny kid who also liked building things was a successful contractor with half the women in town fawning over him. Some of whom had once rejected him.

She used to just wave a hand and laugh when ladies in the salon gossiped about how fine he was, or wondered whom he might be sleeping with, because like her brother he got around. Now she fought not to join in to get more information, and in the last few years, there had been a lot of information about the various women Devante was with. He wasn't considered a playboy because there were never rumors of him treating anyone badly, but no one doubted he enjoyed the single life. Last she heard, he was fooling around with some woman named Mandy from the other side of town.

She pushed open the door as he neared. He stopped at the threshold and grinned down at her. "Hey, Jo, did Kalen tell you I was coming?"

She met dark, cocoa-brown eyes set in a chocolate-brown face. He didn't have facial hair, like many guys wore today, but the dark shadow of a beard and mustache on his chin and cheeks made her wonder if he hadn't shaved this morning. He was several inches taller than her, with a compact, muscled body that even the plainest of outfits, like he was wearing today, couldn't hide the strength beneath. Back when she'd had to babysit him and her brother, he'd been awkward and intelligent. That awkwardness had smoothed out into a comfortable sex appeal and the intelligence still lingered beneath his confident smile.

"Yeah… I just got off the phone with him. You sure you want to help me? I know you've got to be busy."

Devante lifted a shoulder. "For you? Of course. You know I'll do anything for you, Jo." He cocked his chin slightly with the words. His eyes narrowed slightly as he looked at her as if he really would do anything she asked.

Jo sucked in a breath and pressed a hand to her head. She fought the urge to tug on her microlocs in embarrassment. Oh, no, what she wouldn't—couldn't—do was spend today hearing innuendos in every damn word he said. Otherwise, this was going to be a long, frustrating day.

His smile deepened and he bit the corner of his lip. Joanne swallowed hard. Jesus be a fence! This young man was going to make her embarrass herself today.

two

Devante tightened the last screw in a small, round accent table Joanne had taken out of one of the many boxes in her new salon. He liked putting things together, so helping her wasn't a problem and he'd finish up in no time. He completed the last turn just as she came back through the door carrying a tray with two cups of coffee and a bag.

"Breakfast is ready," she said. She smiled as she crossed the room to him.

Devante dropped the Allen wrench. It clattered against the underside of the table. Heat filled his cheeks, and he ran sweaty palms across his sweats. Damn, he was pitiful. It was as if he was still the teenager struck speechless whenever she walked into a room. He'd had a crush on Joanne since he was thirteen. A crush that had waned as he'd gotten older and accepted that she had absolutely no interest in him, but had never completely gone away.

Not crushing on Joanne was next to impossible. Not just because she was beautiful. Her caramel skin, thick hips and ass, bright smile and small, shoulder-length, blond locs typically got attention, but it was her never-give-up attitude encased in a giving heart that made him want to stick around for a while.

She put down the bag with the Books and Vibes logo on the side. Joanne slid out one of the cups of coffee. "Sumatra blend, black." She held out the coffee to him. "Here you go, young man."

Devante scowled as he took the coffee from her. In the last year she'd taken to calling him "young man." He didn't know why, and the words weren't really an insult, but every time they spilled from her lips his neck and shoulders tightened. He was thirty-five. Ten years younger than her. He wasn't that damn young.

She responded with a cute smile that made his insides twist, then she pulled out the second cup. "And a caramel latte for me. I'm so glad Patricia and Van opened the bookstore and coffee shop around the corner. It'll be nice having quality caffeine nearby."

"Yeah, they're cool. They've even got a small manga section. Peachtree Cove is really coming up."

"And my day spa is going to be a big part of that come up." Confidence filled her voice. Her eyes left his and looked over the table. "You're done with that already?"

Devante nodded. He set down the coffee, then flipped over the table. "Yep. I told you it wouldn't take long."

She had five chairs for her waiting area and four of the round accent tables. They only required attaching the legs and tightening a few screws to make it work. He'd hoped she'd have more stuff so he could extend his time with her.

"I was upset when Kalen bailed on me, but maybe sending you was a good idea. You've already got the tables and chairs put together." She took a tentative sip of her latte then licked her lips.

He licked his own in response, then looked away before she noticed his longing. He remained seated on the floor and bent one knee to rest his arm on. "All you needed was to add the legs to the chairs. It really wasn't that hard."

She sighed and sat in one of the chairs he'd just put together that had a dark blue plush seat with silver buttons along the arms and back. "I was so worried it would take a long time. When Kalen called, all I could think of was a terrible opening next Saturday."

"Terrible opening? Woman, don't you know everyone in Peachtree Cove is waiting for your grand-opening party? This space could be empty, and it would still be a hit."

He wasn't lying. Joanne had been doing hair in Peachtree Cove since high school. He remembered her styling her friends' hair in her parents' kitchen back when he'd be over playing video games with Kalen. Later, she'd done hair at her apartment and eventually in her own home, not missing a beat when she'd become a single mom at eighteen. Everybody in town knew Joanne was the best stylist in Peachtree Cove and only haters wouldn't be happy for her new success.

"Maybe so, but I want it to be perfect." The conviction in her voice mingled with doubt. "You know how many people in this town didn't think I would be able to do this after I failed the first time. They'll show up, too. I don't want to give anyone a reason to talk badly about my new shop."

"That first time was a learning experience. Owning a business is difficult and now you know what to expect. You're more prepared now."

"I wasn't at all prepared before. I really didn't have a clue about what I was doing. I just wanted to make money and get out of my mom's house."

He remembered the arguments she used to have with her mom about finding a stable job and doing more for her son. One day Joanne was there and the next day she'd moved out and was opening a business. When things hadn't worked out, her family expected her to move back in with her mom, but instead, she'd gotten a job, kept her place and styled hair on the side. Giving up wasn't in Joanne's vocabulary and it was one of the reasons why he admired her.

"I want everyone to see my place as *the* place to get your hair done in town," she said.

"You're already *the* place. Even in high school you had a list of people waiting for you to style their hair. That hasn't changed no matter where you set up shop."

She laughed and raised her brows. "You remember that?"

He grinned and leaned back against the wall. "Yeah, I remember. I used to watch you and be in awe at the way you would whip up those styles in no time. All you'd talk about is how you were going to have your own shop one day and how it would be the fanciest place this town ever saw."

She placed a hand to her cheek and shook her head. "Wow! I can't believe you remember the way I'd brag to anyone who'd listen. I was full of so many dreams."

"And, despite some bumps on the road, you made those dreams come true. You know, you are part of the reason why I became a contractor."

Her brows drew together. "Now you're messing with me."

"I'm serious."

"How in the world did me doing hair make you want to be a contractor?" She leaned against the armrest and smirked. Despite the skeptical look in her eyes, his body heated from the cute way her lips pursed with the movement.

He took another sip of the coffee. The burn of the liquid was a welcome distraction from the other burn growing in his midsection. "Everyone said I needed to go into gaming or computers or something just because I liked comic books and anime, but I always wanted to do stuff with my hands. I liked building things, taking stuff apart and putting it back together. You know my dad was a handyman…if you could catch him sober."

Joanne's smirk dissolved and compassion filled her face. Part of the reason he spent so much time at her place was because whenever his dad came home drunk, his mom yelled and fussed about him being no good and then turned that same anger on her kids. She'd dump her disappointment on them right before she'd storm out of the house to spend time with her married boyfriend. He and his sister, Tracey, took every opportunity to escape their house. Tracey escaped to hang out with her two best friends, Imani and Halle. Devante found the stability of Kalen's home as his place of solace. Kalen's family became his second family, and his friendship with Kalen was something he'd always appreciate.

Pushing aside the old memories, he continued, "When I helped him fix stuff, I enjoyed it. My mom didn't think there was any money in being a handyman. I didn't, either, until one day Dad brought me with him to help fix the cabinet at Ms. Baker's house. You remember Ms. Baker?" Joanne nodded and he continued. "Well, Dad wasn't sober that day and hadn't been the day before when he'd messed up her cabinet. When we got there, she'd hired a contractor. This white guy with the name Richards Contracting on the side of a fancy black truck. He was nice and all, but Dad was pissed about losing another job. I asked what a contractor was, and he said nothing but a fancy handyman."

Joanne cocked her head to the side. "It's a little more than that."

He chuckled. "I had that same look. I looked up his business, then learned about what contractors did, and made up my mind that I'd be a fancy handyman. Make real money fixing things and not be like my dad."

Confusion remained in her eyes. "That sounds like you were inspired by something other than me."

He leaned forward. "You probably don't remember, but one day when you were talking about your dream, I said I would own a fancy truck with Thompson Contracting on the side.

You gave me a high five, and the biggest smile, before looking me in the eye and saying 'hell yes, you will.'"

She stared at him for several long seconds before blinking. "Really? I'd forgotten all about that," she said with a slight laugh. "I didn't know that inspired you. I meant what I said, but you were always so smart and determined. You kept Kalen in line half the time. When you started a business I just assumed it was because that's what you wanted to do."

He wasn't surprised she didn't know. He'd never told anyone how much Joanne's words affected him. Admitting that meant also admitting the reason why. His crush was obvious when he was younger, but most assumed it had gone away with time. Despite how Joanne might view her failures, he'd always considered her out of his league. Older, wiser and interested in men who seemed completely the opposite of him. He'd never believed he'd have a chance.

"I never forgot," he said. "I watched you never give up on your dream even after your first try didn't work out. That inspired me to never give up on mine."

She took another sip of her coffee. Her brows knitted as his words sunk in. "I mean… I never thought you, much less anyone, would look at me as any type of inspiration or role model."

"Why not?"

She shrugged before waving a hand. "I don't know." She stood and pointed at the pictures propped against the wall next to him. "Help me hang these."

He got up from the floor and stretched. "Nah, tell me. Why didn't you think you'd be considered a role model?"

He wasn't the only one who looked up to Joanne. Kalen was proud of her. He'd begged Devante to help because he didn't want his sister's grand opening to be ruined. Everyone Devante knew who got their hair styled by Joanne sang her praises. Not only did people love her styling abilities, but they also talked about feeling comfortable in her chair. She didn't judge, spread anyone's business to other clients, or give unsolicited advice. Her time with a client was about relaxation. After failing to open a successful salon, she'd joined the town's business guild and became an active member in the organization. Joanne was a part of the Peachtree Cove community. So many people in town liked and respected her.

"A lot of folks supported me before and I failed," she admitted. "After I had Julian, my family and some friends really thought I wouldn't be able to start my own business. That first shop was a way to prove them wrong. When I had to close down, everyone I cared about was supportive, but I remember the comments about all the things I should have done differently to make it work, or that I was trying to do too much and should focus on raising Julian. Then there were the few people who outright said they knew I wouldn't amount to much after having Julian."

"People brought that back up?"

She scoffed and cocked a brow. "You were a kid when I had Julian, so you don't remember the things people said."

He hated that she said it as if he'd been absolutely clueless about her situation. "Because of his father?"

She cleared her throat. "Mmm-hmm." She sipped from her cup and avoided his eyes.

"Well, despite being a kid, I remembered the way you cried. He lied to you and then didn't treat you right. I never did like that guy."

Joanne's eyes widened. "Excuse me? You were too young to be judging who I dated."

He stared her dead in the eye. "I was right not to like him."

He remembered the guy. Flashy college student from Atlanta, in designer clothes and driving an expensive car. Joanne's family hadn't struggled as much as Devante's, but they'd struggled enough for her to also talk about wanting to one day meet and marry a rich man who could give her a fancy life. He remembered how much Joanne had liked that guy because his name brands and slick style had shown Devante just how far he was from being on Joanne's radar. So, yeah, a part of him had hated the guy just on principle, but he and her brother had thought he was shady.

Turns out they were right. He'd also gotten someone else pregnant while dating Jo. After Joanne got pregnant, they'd never seen him in Peachtree Cove again.

Joanne sighed and nodded. "You were right not to like him. The only good thing I got from him was Julian."

"And look how you raised him. He graduated, right?"

The smile that spread across her face was like sunshine on a Sunday morning. "Yes, he did. Dean's list and summa cum laude. He got a job with the engineering firm he had the internship with last year."

The pride in her voice rang clear and strong. The radiant smile on her face drew him to her side. Her eyes, a clear espresso-brown, sparkled with the joy of talking about her son.

"That's why people look up to you. Why I look up to you. You worked hard to get Julian through college and graduate school and to grow your business. You're awesome and you know it."

"Hell yes, I am." She snapped her finger and did a quick shimmy of her hips. "Sometimes I have to remind myself of that." She put her latte on one of the tables then flipped through the framed art. "Now, Momma plans to enjoy her life. Julian's settled and able to support himself. I'm ready to figure out how to start living again."

He froze. "What do you mean?"

"My life has been work and Julian. After my grand opening, I'll have achieved the work goal. Figuring out the personal goals…well, that's a little bit harder."

"What kind of personal goals?"

Devante's heart thumped heavily. This was what he'd wanted

to confirm. A few weeks ago, Kalen mentioned Joanne wanted to start dating again. Devante had less than a tenth of a chance, but he damn sure was going to try. He was sure there'd be competition. She'd had no problem with boyfriends and admirers over the years. Her personality and charm was a natural draw. After she'd had Julian, she'd only openly dated a few people. He only knew that because of his friendship with Kalen.

"Just personal." Her smile was sly and secretive as she glanced at him out of the corner of her eye.

His heart pounded. No way in hell was she going to look at him like that and he wouldn't shoot his shot. "If you're looking for a man you shouldn't have any problem with that." His eyes dipped, traced over her ample curves, jumped back to her face. "Any man would jump at the chance."

Her lips parted as she sucked in a breath. In an instant, the comfortable, easy atmosphere between them shifted. An electric current that he'd felt plenty of times in her presence kicked to life. He was used to feeling this way around her only for her to look back at him with no hint of attraction or interest. This time was different. This time, her eyes widened ever so slightly. She quickly licked her lips and glanced away.

She lifted a hand and lightly pushed his shoulder. "Stop before you make an old woman feel good."

Devante took a step closer. Their bodies didn't touch, but the heat of her, tempting and reassuring, pressed against him. She smelled like coconut and lemongrass, a body butter mixture she'd used before. A smell that automatically sent his body on alert, made him want to pull her close, lose himself in her.

"I don't see an old woman." His voice came out lower than he'd planned.

She swallowed and stared down at the pictures, though her fingers were no longer flipping through them. "What do you see?"

The rasp in her voice was as tantalizing as the scratch of nails across his back, igniting a primal response in him he wasn't ready to control.

"I see," he said slowly and took a half step closer, as his chest brushed her arm and her body shivered, "a smart, capable and sexy woman."

For several agonizing seconds the only sound in the space was of her choppy breaths. Had he gone too far? Said too much? She'd only looked at him as her kid brother's friend. Hell, she'd once wiped his tears when he'd broken his arm on the swing set in their backyard. He never would have dreamed she'd feel a fraction of what he felt, but if she did, he damn sure wouldn't let the opportunity pass him by.

Slowly, she turned and faced him. Her eyes were lowered, and she ran her tongue over her bottom lip. Rejoicing that she hadn't scolded him, stepped away, or worse, broke out in laughter, he followed his instincts. He brushed a hand over her arm. Her skin was soft and smooth. He wanted to touch more.

His fingers trailed up her arm then back down. Her eyes raised to his and his heart slammed against his rib cage. Desire simmered in the depths of her gaze. He leaned in, ready to kiss her.

The door to the shop opened. "Hello!"

Devante and Joanne both jumped back. Disappointment rushed through him. He looked up and spotted Joanne's best friend, Kayce.

"Oh, my God, Jo, this place looks great!" Kayce exclaimed, oblivious to the scene she'd interrupted. "I knew you were working and decided to come over and help."

Joanne hurried over to her friend. "Great, I'm glad you came. Kalen couldn't make it, so Devante agreed to help out. Isn't he great? Such a nice young man." She glanced at him then looked away quickly.

Devante gritted his teeth as the words *young man* punched him in the jaw. The urge to cross the room, pull her into his arms and show her exactly what this *young man* could do made his feet twitch. Somehow, he managed to raise a hand and give Kayce a semblance of a smile. There was plenty of time for that later.

Joanne glanced at him, then away. She quickly went into details with Kayce about how she wanted the room set up.

That's all right, Jo, he thought as he tried to cool the adrenaline and desire pumping through his veins at a hundred beats per minute. *I've got your young man.*

three

"Joanne, this place is amazing!"

Joanne grinned and accepted the hug from Octavia, one of Joanne's teammates on the recreational tennis team. She'd decided to join after one of her clients mentioned needing a new player for their beginners' team. Joanne needed exercise and a way to socialize with other adults, so she'd joined. Two years later and she now was a member of two teams.

Octavia and many of her other teammates had shown up for the grand-opening celebration, which, thanks to Devante's help, had arrived with everything in place. Tonight was about showing off her new space, giving information on the services that would be offered besides just hairstyling and thanking the clients and friends who'd supported her over the years. She wanted—needed—everything to be perfect. Tonight was her night to prove she belonged with the other respected members of Peachtree Cove's business owners.

"Thank you so much, Octavia," Joanne said after pulling back. "I'm glad you were able to make it out."

"I wouldn't miss it for the world." Octavia's broad smile revealed her dimples and her short, natural hair was cut so low to her scalp that if Joanne hadn't bleached it platinum-blond, people might've thought she'd shaved it all off. "Nobody does hair like you and I'm so glad that you were finally able to open your own place."

"It's been a lifelong dream." That was the only response she had. She'd received so many congratulations in the first hour of the grand opening that she was overwhelmed with the outpouring of support for her second chance at being a business owner.

Someone called her name and Joanne turned to see Kayce waving her over. She nodded and turned back to Octavia. "Be sure to get a chair massage and sign up for the drawing for a free facial."

Octavia's eyes lit up. "I will."

Joanne urged her in the direction of the room where the masseuse was set up. Massages weren't going to be a staple at her salon, but for her grand opening she decided to offer free chair massages. Tonight was going to be a night people would remember as celebrating the opening of more than a traditional beauty salon. That's one of the reasons it had taken her so long to save up and finally get to this point. She'd hired colleagues she'd known from beauty school, a nail technician to offer manicures and pedicures and an esthetician for facials. There were also three other stylists in her salon. Each one was there tonight discussing their services and giving mini-tutorials on hair, skin and nail care. The sound of smooth jazz played over the speakers inserted in the ceiling and she'd gotten a local restaurant to cater the appetizers.

She'd worried things wouldn't go well, but it had all been for nothing. The grand opening was going much better than she'd planned and the people who'd come out to celebrate with her filled the space.

When she reached Kayce, she asked, "Is everything okay?"

Her best friend since high school was tall and wore six-inch heels that added to her height. Her braids were pulled back and a simple black wrap dress hugged her slim frame. "It is. I just wanted you to meet Jackson Cooper." Kayce indicated the man standing next to her. "He's rented the space next to yours and will be opening an art studio."

Kayce wiggled her brows as she looked at Joanne and she immediately understood the real reason she'd been summoned. Jackson was a handsome white guy who looked to be around the same age as Joanne. A dusting of white at his temples and glasses gave him the air of a sexy professor and his gray eyes were kind as they met hers.

"Hello, Jackson. I think I've seen you around. You've been renovating your space as well."

Jackson nodded. "I have. I hope you don't mind that I've joined your grand opening. When I heard about it, I was curious to see how you'd set up the place. That and I was hoping for a reason to introduce myself. Since we're neighbors."

Kayce grinned and bumped her elbow to Joanne's. Joanne smiled and tried not to bump her friend back. Kayce was on a mission to hook up Joanne with an eligible guy. She'd gotten married the year before and because she was blissfully wed, she wanted her best friend to join her.

For years, Joanne had given up hopes of joining the married squad. At one point she thought she was too set in her ways to change for any man. Now that her son was officially out of her pocket and she'd reached her professional goal, the spark of hope that maybe she'd also find someone to spend her life with had reignited.

The memory of Devante looking into her eyes filled her mind. *I see a smart, capable and sexy woman.* Those words in his rumbling voice made her suck in a breath. She pushed them aside for the hundredth time since that day. She reminded herself that Devante was supposedly dating a girl named Mandy. If he wasn't dating, then she was pretty sure he was sleeping with her. He was just being nice, not insinuating that he wanted anything to do with her romantically.

"Well, neighbor, I don't mind at all," she said, focusing on the man in front of her. "Just know I'll be coming to your grand opening as well."

Jackson leaned forward and winked. "You'll get a special invitation."

The back of Joanne's neck tingled a second before Devante's broad shoulders butted into the small space separating Joanne and Jackson. "Special invitation to what?"

Joanne's face heated as Devante stared down at her. She didn't know why she felt guilty—she hadn't done anything, and Devante wasn't her man. She had to be projecting again. One compliment when he'd helped her with the furniture had her spending too much time dissecting every word, facial expression and nuance since that day. She was overreacting, and he had not been seriously flirting. The fact that a few words from Devante had her fantasizing about a guy who was not thinking of her in that way proved she needed to start dating again and quick.

She pushed aside the feelings of guilt. "Devante, this is Jackson. He's opening the art gallery in the space next to me. We were talking about his grand opening. Jackson, this is Devante. This young man is my little brother's best friend."

She added the "young man" and "little brother" after she noticed the curiosity in Jackson's eyes as he'd looked between her and Devante. As much as her body may react to Devante, it didn't mean she would ruin the possibility of starting something with a nice guy. Jackson was new in town, but the rumor mill had already supplied that he was a nice, single and not screwing around with the women in town.

Jackson's eyes lit up. "Ah, nice to meet you, Devante. I saw you helping the other day." He held out his hand.

Devante took his hand. "Jo knows I'm willing to help her. Anytime and with anything she needs." He stared back at Jackson.

Jackson's smile wavered and he pulled back on his hand.

Devante let him go and Jackson flexed his fingers. "Umm… good to know. I guess you would look out for a friend of the family."

Joanne nodded. "He does. He's like a part of the family. My son looks up to him almost as if he's another uncle."

Devante narrowed his eyes at her. "He doesn't view me as an uncle."

She tried to laugh but Devante's frown made her feel awkward. She looked from Devante back to Jackson. "Yes, he does. I always tell him that he should model himself to be like Kalen. You both are young men who serve as good role models."

Devante's nostrils flared. He rubbed the back of his neck. "Oh, really."

His jaw and shoulders were tense and there was a glint in his eye. He couldn't possibly be mad? She'd complimented him. "Really. You are a very nice young man."

"Can I talk to you somewhere for a second," he said quickly.

Joanne blinked. She looked at Kayce, who appeared just as confused as she felt. "Sure."

"In private," he said.

Nodding, she pointed to the storage room in the back. "We can go over there."

"Aight, let's go." He put his hand on her elbow and led her toward the storage area.

Joanne smiled and nodded at the patrons as Devante pushed through the crowd. She had no idea why he seemed angry, but whatever the reason was, it didn't give him the right to be rude to her guests. She frowned after they were in the storage room. "What is wrong with you?"

He let her go and placed his hands on his waist. "What's wrong with you?"

Joanne's head snapped back. Oh, he was angry. Her own frustration jumped up in response. She'd done nothing wrong. He was acting foolish. "What are you talking about?"

"This *young-man* mess. Why do you keep calling me that?"

Joanne blinked, surprised and embarrassed that he'd called her out. "Because you are a young man… I mean…what do you want me to call you?"

"You say it like I'm some kid. I'm not a kid, Jo."

"Nobody said you were a kid. I didn't mean anything by it."

"I think you do mean something." He took a step closer. "I think you're trying to make it seem like I'm too young."

"Too young for what?" Damn, she sounded breathless. She tried to focus on slowing her breathing, but he stood too close. His cologne was too intoxicating. The fire in his eyes too intense.

"Too young for you. I'm not a young man. I'm a grown man. A grown man who wants to be your man."

Joanne's jaw dropped. Her heart stuttered before beating frantically. She tried to come up with words. To formulate an appropriate response, but she had nothing. She'd never really prepared to have a fantasy come to life. Unease crept up her spine. Fantasies too often turned into heartbreak.

Devante closed the distance between them and cupped the back of her neck. Joanne leaned into him, stunned but automatically reacting to his embrace. "If you'll let me." Seconds ticked by like hours as he lowered his head and brushed his lips across hers. "Will you let me be your man, Jo?"

four

She couldn't believe he kissed her. The brush of his lips over hers and the whispered "Will you let me be your man, Jo?" was so surreal she wondered if she was daydreaming. This wouldn't be the first time she'd pictured Devante's lips on her, his hands pulling her tight against his body or his arms embracing her. This wasn't a daydream, this was very real.

The heat of his body ignited her desire. The feel of his lips, soft but confident, turned her thoughts into bubbles. This was no dream. The first brush of his lips gave way to a full-on press of his mouth against hers. Shock held her still momentarily. Desire shoved shock out of the way. Before she could overthink what was happening, and why, her hands clutched his wide shoulders and her lips parted.

Devante kissed her deeply. His tongue slipped past her lips and boldly explored her mouth. There was no hesitancy, no timidness, no testing the waters. He kissed her as if he was her man, and he finally had her in his arms after a long separation. The last time she'd been held like this, kissed this thoroughly, was longer ago than she cared to remember. The passage of time didn't matter, because her body responded as if she always belonged in Devante's embrace.

His strong hands roamed over her back, down to her ass, which he palmed and kneaded. He squeezed her curves and tugged her forward until the hard press of his growing erection dug into her lower abdomen. A delicious shiver went through her body. Her mind filled with images of everything she'd ever imagined him doing to her. She wanted him to back her against the wall, craved for him to tug up her shirt, to kiss and caress her all over, jerk up her skirt, rip off her panties and touch her there.

The mental playlist shot fire through her veins. She squirmed against him, wanting more but knowing just kissing him wouldn't put out this fire. He gripped a handful of her skirt in his hands and pulled it up until the hem brushed the top of her thighs. In the back of her mind, she remembered they were in the storage room. That multiple people had watched them enter together, and that if Devante did all the things running through her mind, everyone out there would know because she wouldn't be able to suppress any cries of ecstasy. She started to pull back, but his hand slid under her hemline and the heat of his palm against her thigh seared away all worries about being caught in a compromising position.

"Devante," she breathed out shakily when he quickly broke the kiss.

"Damn, I love the way you say my name." His low voice rumbled through her body. He kissed her again.

"We should..." His fingers dug into the tender flesh of her behind and her voice trailed off.

"Should what?" he murmured against her mouth.

His voice, so daring and delicious. Why in the world would she break this magical spell? "Keep going." She lifted her chin and kissed him deeper.

He took a step forward and she moved with him. They didn't

break the kiss as he guided her farther into the storage room. With ease, he lifted then sat her down on top of the plastic storage bins stacked against the wall. Her legs spread and his hips fit right in the junction of her thighs. His hands gripped her thighs before easing up her skirt until the tips of his fingers traced the seam of her panties. Joanne's soft moan echoed with his in the small space.

"Joanne?" The question in his gruff voice was one she didn't hesitate to answer.

"Keep going." No part of her wanted to stop now. Now when they were so close, and she'd fantasized about this for so long.

Devante quickly pulled aside her panties and touched her. The soft brush across her sex sent waves of pleasure through her body.

She felt his lips rise with a smile. "You're wet for me."

The fire in her veins combusted into a full-body inferno as his fingers dipped into her folds. Her head fell back, but he cupped the back of her head and pulled her forward, their lips and tongues once again coming together in a wave of passion. His other hand glided across her sex casually, back and forth in a rhythm that had her hips gyrating and pressing forward for more.

The door to the storage room flew open. "I'll get more from back here. Oh, my God!"

Joanne pushed against Devante's chest. He jerked back. They both looked over his shoulder into the shocked eyes of Robin, the nail technician. Behind her stood Octavia. Behind Octavia stood Kayce, and behind Kayce, every other guest in the party stared at the open doors of the storage room to see the cause of the exclamation.

Kayce moved first. She hurried forward, jerked back Octavia and the other guest, then threw Joanne a what-the-hell look and slammed the door shut.

About Last Night

"What the hell were you thinking? And with Devante, of all people? You ain't got no business fooling around with that boy!"

Joanne leaned against the counter in her mom's kitchen and pinched the bridge of her nose. She shouldn't have come over here. She should have stayed home, in bed, hiding from the embarrassment of getting caught with Devante's hand up her skirt by practically everyone in town. But, no, she had to be a "good daughter" and come over when her mom said she needed Joanne to take her to the pharmacy because her car was in the shop and none of her other kids could make it.

Joanne had hoped word hadn't gotten back to her mom yet. Had almost believed she'd been lucky when they'd gotten through Joanne's arrival and the trip to the pharmacy with no mention of what happened. She should have known her mom would blindside her and bring it up as soon as Joanne's guard was down. Right as Joanne was heading to the door and trying to escape to the safety of her home.

She dropped her hand from her face and looked at her mom. Doris Wilson was an older version of Joanne. Her golden-brown skin was now lined with age and her short, styled hair was fully gray. Her mom had never been short of opinions. Opinions she loved to share whether her kids wanted to hear it or not.

"Momma, I'm not fooling around with Devante and he's a man, not a boy." She didn't even ask how word had gotten back to her mom. There were very few secrets in Peachtree Cove. Not to mention everyone loved to mind other people's business.

Doris crossed her arms and legs from where she sat at the table, watching Joanne. Her brows drawn together. A mask of frustration on her face. Joanne was used to that look of frustration. She'd received that same look when she'd come home from work only to find Joanne styling someone's hair at her kitchen table. Then again, when Joanne said she was keeping the baby after the guy she thought loved her said he didn't want anything to do with either of them. And the look resurfaced later when Joanne had announced she was moving out and starting her own business because she wouldn't raise Julian under her mom's thumb. Almost every move Joanne made resulted in frustration from her mom.

"What do you call it then? Is it true you two were doing it in the storage room?"

"No! We weren't doing anything. He kissed me. That's all." At least, that was all she was going to admit to with her mom.

"Why are you *kissing* that boy?" Doris said *kissing* as if kissing was just as bad as being caught *doing it*. "He's way too young for you."

"He's thirty-five, Momma. Please stop calling him a boy," Joanne said, exasperated.

"He's the same age as Kalen, who will always be my baby, which makes him a baby to me. I thought you got all that foolishness out of your system. First you come home pregnant by that stuck-up college boy and then a few years ago you go and date that married guy, and now this."

Her mom never called Julian's father by his real name. He was always "that stuck-up college boy." Joanne agreed—Orlando had been stuck-up. Her impressionable heart had viewed his personality as sophisticated at the time. She'd realized just how wrong she'd been after he told her to get rid of the baby. That he was having a baby with someone else, a law student who would be accustomed to the lifestyle he planned to live. He never said the words "you aren't good enough" but his actions more than implied his true feelings.

Believing Orlando loved her had been all her mistake. The lies told to her by the men she'd dated after him, however, were not her fault. She'd learned to forgive herself for the mistakes she made in the past. She'd entered each relationship with honesty and an open heart. Which is why she wouldn't stand here and let her mother make her feel bad, or accuse her of being the deceptive one in those relationships.

"I came home pregnant over twenty-five years ago," she said. "And you know Douglas was not married but lied to me about being engaged. Why you gotta bring up those situations now?"

Doris looked at Joanne as if her question was out of line. "Because apparently I need to remind you how the last time you were acting fast you derailed your life. Here you are, opening your own business again and finally getting your life together, and now you want to throw it all away messing with some young man. And not just any young man, but Devante Thompson, of all people?"

Joanne's shoulders tensed. "How am I throwing anything away? And what's wrong with Devante? You like him."

Her mom threw up a hand and shrugged. "Devante's nice and all, but you don't need to be messing around with someone who can't lift you up. He's too young and you know he's still out there acting wild. Just like his mom. Always out in the street. You know he was screwing Gwendolyn's granddaughter, Mandy, just last month. Now he's trying to add you as a notch on his bedpost."

"I'm not a notch," she said with conviction. In her heart, she wavered. She'd known about the rumors surrounding Devante and Mandy. Rumors she'd completely forgotten about the moment he kissed her. Was she really just lining up to be another name in a string of names of people he'd slept with? That had been the main reason why she'd talked herself out of ever acting on the attraction she'd developed for Devante. He was single and was obviously enjoying being single. She, on the other hand, wanted to be special to someone. She hadn't been special to Julian's father. Hadn't been worth commitment from the men she'd dated after. She'd always refused to settle for anything less in a relationship and she wouldn't start now.

"You don't have the best track record with men," her mom

said, as if she could read the direction of Joanne's thoughts. "Devante's been drooling over you since he was a boy. Now he's getting to live out a fantasy. Don't go messing up your life because some young man got you thinking you can play a cougar. You ain't built for that."

"I'm not playing cougar. Ten years isn't that big of an age difference. Daddy was eight years older than you."

Her mom grunted before waving a hand. "Then are you playing dumb? Because you ruined your grand-opening celebration following behind that boy. You ought to know better than that, Jo. I helped you out as much as I could when you got pregnant with Julian. I let you live here and do hair out of my kitchen. I helped you out when the first store didn't work out because I understood you were trying to do better. I'm old now. If your business tanks because of this thing I can't help you out of this hole. Find you a nice man. I don't care if he's your age, older or younger, but he needs to be about the same things you're about. Quit being stupid behind some guy. You know better than that."

Her mother's phone rang before Joanne could reply. She didn't need to hear any more. As much as she hated the lecture, she also couldn't deny the truth and good intentions behind her mom's words. Joanne was a romantic. Had believed in love and happily-ever-afters and that the sweet words men whispered during lovemaking were true. She'd learned the hard way they weren't. She'd been tossed aside enough when she was younger to finally stop dating and focus on raising her son and saving to open a salon ten times better than the one she first tried. Now that she was ready to start dating again, was she just falling into the same habits that had hurt her in the past?

Despite years of being a stylist and having a business, she never felt she belonged in the circles of other business owners working to make Peachtree Cove thrive again. She'd struggled to make a dream that seemed as reachable as the moon a reality.

About Last Night

It had taken this long to get her life on track. Her grand opening had been a success until that embarrassing moment. She wasn't sure if clients would show up on Tuesday and, if they did, she'd lost any respect or semblance of class she'd wanted her place to have the second she'd followed Devante into that storage room. She had to think carefully about what she was doing before she let Devante, and the possibility of being a fantasy notch on his bedpost, upset and ruin everything she'd worked for.

five

"Yo, man, my sister?"

Devante froze in the middle of adding a twenty-five-pound weight to the bar on the weight bench in his garage. Suppressing a sigh, he turned and faced his friend. Kalen stood at the garage's entrance. He was a few inches shorter than Devante with a low-cut fade and an athletic build that came from continuing to play recreational flag football. He stood with his legs spread, and hands planted firmly on his hips. Disbelief filled his dark eyes as he stared at Devante like a stranger. Devante slid the twenty-five-pound weight on the bar before facing what he'd known was coming.

"It's not what you think," Devante said.

Kalen raised his brows. "Then you better get to talking because what I'm thinking is not what I want for my sister."

The words stopped Devante in his tracks. He could understand Kalen being surprised even though he knew about Devante's crush on Joanne. He hadn't expected his friend to take Devante being in a relationship with Joanne as something he wouldn't want for his sister.

Devante pressed a hand to his chest. "Come on, Kalen, you know me. I wouldn't treat your sister wrong."

Kalen wagged a finger at Devante. "You say that, but I also don't know what's going on in your head. You aren't looking for anything serious. Jo may talk a lot of junk about being ready to be out there and start dating again, but she's not looking for one-night stands and hookups. She's not like that despite what people say about her after that mess with Douglas Stone."

"You think I listen to what people say about her?" Devante replied, annoyed. "I know Jo better than that. I know what she's really looking for."

Devante knew about the rumors, but that situation with Douglas lying about being engaged was over two years ago. He knew better than most that rumors were spread by simpleminded people who only found happiness in spreading the misery of others. His family had been the source of much of the gossip and rumors in town back when his parents were still together. Kalen was the very one who'd talked him down whenever he'd wanted to blow up and get into a fight after someone called his mom a whore, his dad a drunk, or claimed he and his sister, Tracey, would be just like them. Kalen, more than anyone, should know Devante didn't judge people based on the town gossips.

"After the way people talked about me and my family, you actually think I believe what people say about her?"

Some of the fight in Kalen's eyes evaporated. He ran a hand over his face. "But what are you looking for? 'Cause if it's just another hookup I can't be cool with that. Not for Jo. She's been through a lot and worked hard to get where she is. I don't want you messing around or playing around with her just as she's finally getting what she wants."

He wished he could fault Kalen for thinking Devante would only want to sleep with his sister. He hadn't been interested in much more than hookups and superficial dating. He'd been more focused on building his contracting company than settling down. But to think he'd play around with Joanne, his best friend's sister and someone he'd not only liked for years, but also respected, made him want to defend himself.

"Playing around…really, Kalen? You think I would do that to your sister? Forget you kicking my ass, I know she wouldn't stand for it."

Kalen cocked his head to the side. "So you're not fucking Mandy right now?"

Leave it to Kalen to be blunt. "I'm not. I cut things off with Mandy the day you told me Jo was ready to date again and asked you to hook her up."

He and Mandy had been hooking up, but neither had been interested in making the move to turn their fling into a full-fledged relationship. He always held out on getting serious. The moment Kalen said his sister wanted to start dating again he'd immediately known that he hadn't held out on relationships because he wanted to grow his business. A part of him had always been waiting for a chance with Jo.

Kalen narrowed his eyes. "For real?"

Devante raised a brow. "Have you seen me with anyone since that day? Have I mentioned Mandy or anyone else since then?" When Kalen frowned and his gaze drifted away, Devante waited.

Kalen's eyes focused back on him with a look of shock. He waved a hand. "Hold up, hold up, hold up…is that really why you broke things off with Mandy?"

Devante nodded. "Pretty much."

"Wait…you're for real?" This time only shock coated Kalen's voice. No hints of disapproval or an underlying threat of bodily harm to anyone who dared to break his sister's heart.

"Yes. I'm for real. I want to be with Jo. You know I like her."

Kalen came farther into the garage. "I know you've crushed on her since we were teens, but… I mean I never thought you were holding on to it this long. Or that you were serious."

"Well, I did and I am."

About Last Night

"You know people are gonna talk if ya'll hook up. They're going to think that you're just playing around with her."

Devante shrugged. He didn't give a damn about what anyone would have to say. He doubted anyone would doubt the reasons why he was interested in her. More people respected and appreciated her in the community than didn't. He, on the other hand, still walked in the shadow of his family being social pariahs in their town. More people would probably talk about Joanne lowering her standards to date him. Despite the small group of people who might hate on anything he started with Joanne, all that mattered was what she thought.

"It took this long for her to finally see me as a real option. I don't care what other people say—as long as she's okay with this then I'm okay."

He meant that. Joanne never cared about his screwed-up family dynamics. She always judged him for himself. Her willingness to give them a try was all that mattered.

"Oh, really?"

"Really. I'm going to marry your sister." He knew the words as surely as he knew he could bench the two hundred and fifty pounds on his weight bench. Joanne was the woman he wanted to spend the rest of his life with. If she would have him.

Kalen leaned back and grinned. "Oh, it's like that?"

"Yes. It's been like that. I was just waiting on my time."

Kalen studied him for several long seconds before grinning and holding out his hand. Devante slapped hands with his friend and didn't resist when Kalen pulled him in for a hug.

"You trying to be my brother for real, huh," Kalen said with a half grin.

"God willing and the creek don't rise," Devante said, grinning back. That's one of the things he appreciated about Kalen. When he was convinced, he was all in. His best friend readily accepting him as his brother spread warmth through his chest.

"Then as my potential brother, let me give you some advice," Kalen said, looking serious again.

"What advice?"

"Joanne wants her new salon to be successful. She planned for the grand opening forever and what happened? You two are caught in her storage room. Now people are talking, and my mom is going to give her a hard time about ruining her life over a man again. I don't know why you decided to finally make a play for her at the party, but that's also going to make people talk about her and her business."

Devante stepped back. Guilt twisted his insides. He'd overheard Kayce mention introducing Joanne to that guy Jackson and he'd felt his chance at being with her slipping away with each passing second. He hadn't thought about ruining her big night, but in the end he had.

Devante pinched the bridge of his nose. "Shit. I ruined everything."

Kalen put a hand on Devante's shoulder. "I wouldn't say you ruined everything. Joanne's too good at her job and people like her too much for me to say her business is ruined. This is me throwing you a lifeline. Jo's also looking for someone who can support her as she grows her dream. The next time you want to show her how you feel…maybe don't do it at her shop."

Devante sighed and nodded. "I'll apologize to Jo."

Kalen chuckled and shook his head. "You don't have to look so dejected. I just had to say something."

"I understand. Believe me when I say this, I only want what's best for her. I'll do better the next time."

"I can't believe you waited this long to make a move, but if you're serious and you really want to make my sister happy then I'm all for it. She deserves to be happy."

"She does, and if she believes me when I say I only want to make her happy, being with her will have been worth waiting for."

After leaving her mom's house, Joanne settled on the couch in her bathrobe for an afternoon of watching Lifetime. There had to be someone whose day was going worse than hers, even if it was a fictional character. Her mother's warnings stuck to her like glue. Even though she wanted to reach out to Devante and ask what their moment in her storage room meant, she also wasn't going to be clingy with a guy she wasn't dating. She didn't know if he was still seeing Mandy or anyone else. He could've just kissed her because she'd called him young man and he wanted to prove a point.

He didn't have to kiss you to prove that particular point. Her hopeful thoughts cut through the doubt. She wanted to cling to that, but hopeful thoughts had led her astray in the past.

Julian called her halfway through a movie about a woman discovering her landlord was a serial killer. Definitely a worse day than hers. Joanne happily accepted his call. She listened as Julian updated her on his new job and how he was getting acclimated to living in his new apartment.

"Let me know if you need anything," she said. "I'll be sure to send it to you."

Julian groaned then laughed. "Mom, seriously, you don't have to send me anything. I'm making good money now and it's my time to help you out."

"You don't have to help me with anything. I've got me. I just need to make sure my baby is doing well and is comfortable."

Even though she'd counted down the days until he graduated high school, then college and finally graduate school, she still missed having her only child close by. Now that he was truly out of the nest and living life as a responsible adult, she still wanted to take care of him in some way. To know that despite him being a grown man, a part of him still needed her. Maybe this was what most empty nesters felt.

"I'm doing well. You did a good job with me." Pride filled his voice, and she could imagine his handsome face smiling the same way he used to whenever he brought home a good grade on a test in elementary school. "I hope to be settled enough to have you come and stay with me this summer."

"I'd love to come visit you. Just say when and I'll buy the ticket."

"I'll buy your ticket." She didn't have to see him to know he was shaking his head. She didn't care. After sacrificing so much for him for the last twenty-five years she was also having a hard time imagining him being able to take care of her.

"We'll see when you're settled," she offered as a truce.

"Good." There was a brief pause before he spoke again. This time his voice hesitant. "So, Mom... I've got a question."

"What is it, baby?" Joanne asked, distracted by the woman on screen fighting off her serial-killer landlord with a baseball bat. She'd have to remember to buy a bat to put beside her front door.

"Um...you and Devante."

All thoughts of bats and the TV movie flew out of her head with those simple words. She knew the Peachtree Cove gossip mill was fast, but not fast enough to reach Julian in Chicago in less than twenty-four hours. He did keep up with his high-school friends, some of whom had returned to town after college and would have heard what happened. Which meant she was even a hot topic with Peachtree Cove's young crowd. Julian kept talking before she could reply.

"I mean, I don't typically get in your business, but when one of my old friends called and said you and Devante were...you know. Well, I decided to check for myself."

She'd hoped word about what had happened wouldn't have ever gotten to Julian. She should have known better than to underestimate the Peachtree Cove gossips.

Her immediate urge was to tell Julian to mind his business. She didn't talk about her dating life with her son, but she also didn't want lies or exaggerations about what happened to reach him and make him worry. "What did you hear?"

"Just that you two were kissing at your grand opening. Is it true? Are you and he...?"

She looked skyward and pressed a hand to her temple. Thank

goodness, he'd only heard they were kissing. If he'd heard more, she doubted he'd tell her, and she wasn't about to push to hear any additional details he may have gotten.

"Do you have a problem with Devante?" She cared about that more than him hearing the gossip. Did he disapprove just like her mom? She had no clue what was going on with her and Devante, or if it would amount to anything, but whatever happened she didn't want Julian to worry about her.

"Nah, in fact, I'm not really surprised. I've always known he had a crush on you. I just never thought you'd go for him."

"You knew he had a crush on me?"

"Yeah, me and Uncle Kalen tease him about it sometimes."

"Say what?" she said louder than she'd intended.

Julian laughed. "We tease him about it. I thought you knew he had a crush on you?"

She'd known he'd had a crush when he was a teenager, because Kalen would sometimes tease him in front of her. She'd thought it was cute and hadn't given it much thought. Her life was on another path with working and raising Julian. As she'd gotten older, she'd hadn't considered Devante as anything other than Kalen's friend until the last year or so, when her body and brain registered an attraction for him.

"And you're okay if I date him?"

"I am. I like Devante. He's got his own business and I think he's a good guy. Besides, I don't want you to be lonely."

"Who says I'm lonely," she said defensively.

"I didn't say you were lonely. I'm saying I don't want you to *get* lonely. I worry about you, Mom. I know you did a lot for me while I was growing up. I appreciate all that you did, and I want you to finally find someone who can do that for you. Be happy. You deserve it."

The doorbell rang and Joanne got up from the couch. "You don't think he's not right for me?"

"Ma, Devante would do anything for you. I can't believe you didn't realize he's been crushing on you this long," Julian said, as if Devante's feelings had been stitched across his forehead for years.

Joanne shook her head as she walked to the front door. Maybe they had been and she'd been too oblivious to notice. Her track record with men hadn't allowed her to think of Devante's actions as anything but him being nice. "He's ten years younger than me."

"As if that matters. You're forty-five. That's not that old," he replied.

"Who said forty-five is any kind of old?"

"That's not what I meant. I'm messing this up. What I'm trying to say is you're still good-looking and I've got friends from college who thought you were fine. I'm not surprised that guys your age and younger are interested. So go for who you like."

"You never stop finding ways to make your momma feel special," she said. She looked out the window next to her front door and gulped in air. "Devante!"

"What?" Julian asked. "Are you saying that you like him, too?"

"No, he's at the door. Um… I've got to call you back."

"Good luck!" he said with a laugh.

Joanne ended the call then quickly unlocked the door. After she opened the door, she remembered she was in her lounging-at-home attire: a fluffy bathrobe with nothing but a tank top and underwear underneath and a satin bonnet over her locs. Changing wasn't an option since she'd been too shocked to think before answering.

"Devante? Why are you here?"

She tried to sound casual despite her heart impersonating a jackrabbit in her chest. He would show up looking absolutely divine in a long-sleeved, dark T-shirt and gray sweats that paid homage to every line and curve of his strong body. How was she supposed to behave and think rationally when she wanted to toss off her robe and let him prop her up on a table and pick up where they'd left off the night before?

"We need to talk," he said. "Can I come in?"

She stepped back and waved him in. "Sure."

He crossed the threshold and followed her from the foyer to the living area. The sound of gunshots followed by a man's scream came from the television. Guessing the woman in the movie finally eliminated her landlord, Joanne picked up the remote and muted the television.

"About last night," Devante said.

She met his gaze. "Did you mean what you said?"

His brows drew together. "What I said?"

"When you asked if you could be my man. Did you mean it?"

The confusion on his face cleared up. He took two steps toward her. His face was serious as he stared into her eyes. "I meant it."

"But what does that mean? What's your definition of being my man? Does that mean you want to sleep with me for a little bit? That you want to date exclusively? That you want to date me and other people like Mandy? I need to know because I'm not making assumptions only to end up hurt later."

Maybe tossing out all these questions up front was too much, but she didn't have the patience or the energy for a wait-and-see situation. She needed to know where they stood. She needed to know if she was heading toward a mistake or if this was a chance she needed to take.

"It means I want to date you. Exclusively you. Mandy and I are through. It also means I want to be there to support you. That I laugh with you on good days and hold you on bad days. That I stand next to you as you continue to grow and become even more amazing. That I can take care of you without smothering you. That I hold you in my arms and make love to you. That's what I mean when I say I want to be your man." He stepped close enough for the smell of his cologne to swirl around her. "Is that okay with you?"

six

Devante held his breath as he watched Joanne. A multitude of emotions skittered across her face. He'd surprised her, that was clear by the widening of her eyes as he spoke. Skepticism made her lips purse and one brow raise. Then there was the wary hope in her expression. A hesitancy in her gaze that spoke to the previous hurts that pushed her to question if he meant what he said. He hated the hesitancy. Not because he wanted her immediate answer. He hated it because lies from others caused her to doubt his word. All he wanted to do was prove to her that she could put her trust in him.

"I'm okay with that," she finally said in a soft, but firm, voice.

Devante exhaled and grinned. The relief that hit him was so satisfying and exhilarating that he couldn't stop himself from placing a hand on her hip and pulling her forward until the soft material of her robe rested against his chest.

He wondered what was beneath the robe, then tried to push aside the thought. He hadn't come over here for sex. He'd come to clear the air. To let her know how he felt, but when she put her hands on his shoulders and leaned into him, not thinking about what was beneath the robe was nearly impossible.

"Are you sure?" he asked.

She cocked her head to the side "Are you sure?"

"You're still asking after everything I just said?" Couldn't she see how much he wanted her?

Her eyes were serious as they stared back into his. "History has taught me to check and double-check. I don't want to be surprised later because I didn't ask."

He gently tugged her hips. "Jo, can you remember one thing for me?"

"What?"

"I'm not like those other brothas."

He lowered his head and kissed her. She gasped and for a half a second, he worried she'd pull back. That maybe she wanted to talk more instead of kiss, but a moment later her body relaxed, and she softened into his embrace. Devante didn't need any other encouragement. His tongue slipped between her sweet lips and deepened the kiss.

Joanne let out the softest of whimpers and his heart rate jumped up a thousandfold. His hand moved from her hip to grip the fullness of her ass. He squeezed and pressed her forward. She was so soft, but the thick material of her robe was in the way. He jerked the loose knot free and pushed back the sides of the robe. His hands slid beneath the material to the warmth beneath, where his fingertips brushed over soft curves. His hand explored, only encountering a thin shirt and underwear blocking his fingers from her naked body. His breathing stuttered as desire swelled within him.

"Where are your clothes, Jo?" he said in a low, gruff voice as he brushed his lips over her cheeks.

"Do I need clothes for what we're doing?" Her snarky reply set his body on fire.

"No, the hell we don't."

Need drove him and he pushed his hands beneath her shirt and cupped the heavy weight of her breasts. Her nipples were so damn hard his mouth watered the second his fingers brushed over them. He wanted to taste them, roll them over his tongue and pull them deep into his mouth, hear every damn moan and catch of her breath as he sucked to his heart's content.

Devante's entire body shook. If he didn't calm down, he'd barely make it to the bedroom. All his fantasies of having Joanne in his arms were coming true and they were better than he imagined. Her softness, her scent and her sighs all invaded his senses and would be forever imprinted into his memory. He didn't know how to process or handle all the feelings bouncing through him.

He shoved the robe off her shoulders. It pooled in a heap at her feet. Joanne's hands jerked on the edge of his shirt. He stepped back long enough to pull it over his head and toss it to the side. Her eyes widened appreciatively as she took in his bare chest. They both rushed forward, and their mouths met in an urgent, hungry kiss.

He didn't know how they got to the bedroom without breaking something. Their lips barely left each other. Their clothes created a messy trail behind them. Their hands explored every inch of skin exposed to the other.

When they finally made their way to her queen-size bed, they were both naked except for his socks and the bonnet on Joanne's head. She sat on the edge of the bed, legs spread, and more tempting than anything he'd ever experienced in life. Devante stood between her legs. He leaned forward and kissed her. His hands gripped the soft skin of her thighs. Joanne gasped and her hips pushed forward. He ran his hands to where her hips and thighs met. Pushing her legs wider, he brushed his thumbs over the damp curls covering her sex. She was so soft and warm that he worried he'd lose control in that moment.

Joanne stared at him between lowered lids. "What's that smile for?"

Devante's grin grew hearing the desire thick in her voice.

He ran his fingers over her sweet heat. "Because I can't wait to feel you against my tongue."

Joanne thought her body would erupt in flames after Devante's words. She was so close to the edge. No one had touched her like this in so long she was afraid she'd shatter just from imagining his tongue against her most sensitive spot. She didn't want to shatter. She wanted to savor.

Her hand wrapped around the hard length of his erection. Devante shuddered and when he straightened, she didn't hesitate to take him deep into her mouth.

He gasped. "Jo...damn, Jo."

The way he said her name, his tone reverent and throaty, sent a thrill down her spine. She relished in every tremble of his body. The way he snatched the bonnet off her head to bury his fingers into her hair and pull. The erratic tensing of his muscles. How he sucked air through his teeth and his head fell back, then forward.

When his eyes opened and met hers, the raw desire there made her sex clench. And the tender emotion she saw reflected also made her heart ache. She wanted to believe every word he said.

He pulled back quickly. "Not yet, Jo."

She bit her lips to try and suppress her cocky grin. "Are you that close?"

The lift of his lips made her heart flip. "Don't get it twisted. No matter how close I am, you come before me. And best believe, we're going multiple rounds."

Her eyes widened. The promise in his voice made her want to clap in delight. A delighted smile brushed her lips just as he dropped to his knees. She barely registered his intention before his mouth was there, and pleasure became her best friend.

Joanne cried out. The delicious feelings acute and wonderful. She leaned back on the bed, using her forearms for support.

Her hands clutched the sheets in fists and she was gone, so lost in a whirlwind of pleasure that when his long fingers joined his mouth, she exploded. Devante rode the wave with her, slowly easing her back down with soft kisses and until she was lying sated and spent on the bed.

Joanne pointed to the nightstand. "Condoms are there." He reached for the drawer. "And lube." If he really was going to give her the multiple rounds he promised then they were going to need it.

He grinned as he pulled them both out. "My girl."

He quickly slid on the condom and added the extra lube before pulling her into his embrace and filling her completely. Afterward, he pulled her against his chest and kissed her softly. The delicious ache in her body from their lovemaking told her one very important thing. If this was what a relationship with Devante was like she was going to be a very happy woman.

seven

Later that night, Devante leaned against Jo's headboard. She sat between his legs, her back against his chest. He lazily ran his hands up and down her arms as they listened to the jazz playing through the Bluetooth speaker on her nightstand. They'd spent the time between lovemaking talking, and when she mentioned Gregory Porter was one of her favorite musicians, he'd pulled up the latest album on his streaming service so they could listen together.

That moment, the entire afternoon, was surreal. He'd fantasized and dreamed about spending a day with Joanne in his arms, but never really thought it would happen. They were really together. His lips lifted and he grinned.

"You know what surprised me?" Joanne said quietly.

He stopped trailing his fingers over her stomach. "What surprised you?"

Her head tilted to the side. "All of the people saying you had a crush on me. My mom, Kayce, even Julian. They all said the same thing."

Devante wrapped his arms around her and gently squeezed her soft curves close. "I'm surprised you couldn't tell. I've had a crush on you since I was a teenager. I thought you were the finest, coolest girl out there."

Joanne chuckled and shook her head. "I mean… I noticed a little when you were younger, but I always viewed your crush as puppy love or something. After I got pregnant and had Julian, I focused so much on taking care of him while also trying to make money that I forgot all about your crush." She sighed and stared at the wall. "Not to mention, I haven't been really good at reading signals from men."

"What I said at your shop the other day is true. I've not only liked you, but respected and admired your drive. You never gave up on your dream and you supported Julian's dreams. Of course, I still crushed on you." He leaned down and kissed her cheek.

Her resulting smile was what he wanted. He didn't like the self-doubt in her eyes or the worry about how her past relationships played out when they were together. He only wanted her to look forward to the bright future he would work hard as hell to give her.

"I'm sorry about your grand opening."

She twisted in his arms so she could frown at him over her shoulder. "Sorry for what?"

"For what happened. I didn't mean to ruin your night. I knew you wanted everything to be perfect. I swear I didn't come with the intention of trying to have sex with you in the storage room."

"Then why did you take me in the storage room?"

"When I saw you and that guy…what was his name?"

"Jackson?" The pitch of her voice and her brows both rose.

"Yeah, Jackson. It wasn't just seeing you flirt with him. It was you calling me *young man*. All I knew was that I didn't want you to think of me like that anymore. I wanted you to know how I felt. I don't regret letting you know my feelings, but I do regret that it ruined your night. I'm sorry."

Joanne took a long breath before settling back into her original position. "Thank you for saying that, but I played a part in what happened, too."

"Do you regret it?"

She placed her arms over his, which were encircling her waist, and squeezed. "No. Not really. Do I regret getting caught? Yes. Do I regret kissing you back? No. I am nervous about Tuesday. I was worried about clients canceling on me, but honestly, I've been caught up in worse scandals than this and people still came to me and that was when I was doing hair at home. This won't be the first time people talk about me and it won't be the last. Whatever happens on Tuesday, I'll deal with it."

"But that's the thing. I don't want you to have to deal with gossip because you're with me. I don't want to make your life harder."

Joanne chuckled. "Devante, people are going to talk about us regardless."

He stiffened, expecting her to say because of his family's reputation. That she was dating a guy from a less-than-stellar family who could do nothing for her.

"Until you kissed me, I would've kept thinking of you as off-limits. Why do you think I called you 'young man' so much? So I could remind myself that my little brother's best friend who was out here, let's be honest, hooking up with different people, wasn't seriously interested in me."

Devante only slightly relaxed. "I wasn't out here hooking up with different people. I've dated, but I haven't been with anyone I wanted to start anything long-term or serious with."

"What makes this different?" The unsureness in her voice made him wish he could chase away all her doubts. That would come with time. When he consistently showed her his feelings were real, then she'd never doubt his feelings, and he planned to be consistent.

"Because you're the only person I've liked and wanted to be

with for most of my life. You're the woman I compare other women to. You're the woman whose smile makes me smile. You're the woman I not only desire, but admire. The way I feel about you isn't how I feel about other people."

She smiled at him over her shoulder. "You are really good with the words."

"They're nothing but the truth." He leaned down and kissed her. "I know it'll take time for you to believe everything I say. I'm not going to rush you. I'm going to show you. Every day we're together."

She was quiet for a few seconds, then asked in a hesitant voice, "Does my age bother you at all? It may not seem like much now, but I am ten years older. I can have kids but I'm not really in the mood to start over after getting Julian through college."

Devante considered her words before answering. "I haven't thought a lot about having kids. I'm not in a big rush. There's also adoption or being a foster parent if that particular urge ever comes up."

She pursed her lips as if considering before nodding slowly and smiling. "I might be okay with being a foster parent. Believe it or not, I considered that when Julian first went to college. The house was so quiet, and I wanted someone to take care of, but was struggling so hard just to save up and cover his expenses that I let the idea go."

"Well, then we'll think about that later. I want to be with you. Let's figure this out one day at a time. Can we do that?"

She sat up and shifted until she faced him. "What if you change your mind?"

Her blond locs hung loose around her shoulders. She looked beautiful, and vulnerable, and all he wanted to do was pull her back into his arms and make love to her until she never questioned his feelings. He'd do that, but first he needed her to understand that the way he felt about her went deeper than just sexual attraction.

About Last Night

Devante took her hands in his and pulled. She repositioned her legs until they were on either side of his waist. He wrapped his arms around her waist, and she put hers loosely around his neck. He stared deep into her eyes when he spoke.

"Jo, I won't change my mind anytime soon, if ever. What if you change your mind?"

She laughed. "Sir, we've officially been together for a few hours, and you've already made me happier than I've been in any other relationship. If you keep this up, you might be stuck with me."

He hoped that was the case. Joanne was a smart, hardworking woman who wanted a bit of glamour in her life. While he was trying to get to a point where he could give her all of that, he wasn't there yet. His earnest feelings might have gotten him here, but would they keep him by her side?

He wouldn't bring up his insecurities today. Today was too great to cast a shadow over. He only wanted to show her confidence. Confidence and assurance of his commitment to making this work.

Grinning, he leaned forward and kissed her. "Oh, really? I kind of like the idea of you being stuck to me." He moved his hands to squeeze her hips and tugged her forward until the softness between her thighs brushed against his thickening erection.

Joanne gasped and her eyes widened. "Are you seriously ready to go again? Are you trying to wear me out?"

Honestly, he couldn't get enough of her. "I asked you before if you could hang. But if you'd rather do something else, I'm down for whatever you want."

The warmth of her body seeped into his as she tightened her arms around his neck and pressed her forehead against his. "Oh, I can hang. I'm just making sure you can keep up with me."

Devante grabbed a handful of her locs and lightly pulled. "Don't doubt that I can keep up. I'll follow you to the ends of the earth, Jo." Emotion filled his voice. An emotion he hadn't planned to let slip through so soon. He was afraid to let her know how much he cared, because he didn't want to scare her off. Maybe he was offering too much too soon.

For a second, she seemed unsure, doubtful. Devante kissed her before those thoughts could take root. He may not be the best match for her, but he'd use every weapon in his arsenal to keep her until he was the perfect man for her. Her body softened and a moment later they were both lost in the kiss. Devante's insecurities drifted away. Right now, they were together and that's all that mattered.

eight

Despite being caught nearly making love to Devante in her storage room during her grand-opening celebration, Joanne's first day officially open was going extremely well. She'd been worried no one would show up, or worse, everyone who did show up would only come to shame her for what happened. Her clients hadn't canceled, and even though there were the occasional smirks or questions about if it was true that she and Devante were dating, no one threw shade or gave her a hard time about her new relationship.

Emily Coleman, president of the business guild, and its secretary, Cyril Dash, who also owned a brewery downtown, came by to wish Joanne well on her opening day. Jackson smiled and waved as he passed by to go to his studio next door. Her mom and brother came through to drop off lunch because they knew she would be busy and not have time to go eat anything. And several of the other business owners in the downtown area dropped by to wish her luck while many residents shopping in the area waved or gave a thumbs-up as they passed by.

If anyone did try to bring up her relationship with Devante, she was quick to say yes they were dating and deflect. As she worked with her various clients, she deftly changed the conversation to her clients' children, what was happening with their jobs, the upcoming St. Patrick's Day Festival, or the latest antics on the soaps that Joanne had playing in the background. She diverted the conversation from other town gossip. All in all, her first day was going perfectly. The two nail technicians kept busy, and Joanne and the three other stylists managed to convince a few clients to fill in the two open spots on the esthetician's schedule for a facial.

"Joanne, this place is fantastic. I am so proud of you," Latasha Baker, Joanne's latest client, said as Joanne removed the plastic cape around her neck. Latasha looked in the mirror and did one last pat of her hair, a braided updo, before following Joanne to the front desk.

There wasn't a receptionist there yet, but Joanne planned to eventually have someone sitting at the front desk to greet clients as they walked in the door. Latasha stopped before the desk and grinned at Joanne. "Who would have thought you'd have all this when you were doing hair out of your kitchen?"

"I imagined all of this back when I was doing hair in my momma's kitchen. I'm just blessed to finally get here." Joanne handed Latasha a brochure with the various services now offered at her salon. She made sure to give one to every client she'd worked with today.

Latasha pursed her lips then wagged a finger. "You did imagine all this and made it a reality. Good for you."

"Nothing wrong with going after big dreams," Joanne replied confidently.

The door to the salon opened. Joanne looked up, prepared to greet the next customer. "Hey, how can I help—" Her eyes met those of the woman who entered, and her smile hardened around the edges. "Mattie? I didn't know you had an appointment today?"

Mattie Bryant was the sister of Peachtree Cove's mayor, Miriam Parker. While most people in town adored and got along well with Miriam, Mattie was an entirely different story. *Bougie* was the nicest word Joanne could use to describe her, because Mattie didn't mind letting everyone in town know that she had the best taste and the most class of any of them around there.

She was of average height and wore a curly, auburn-colored wig that flattered her sienna complexion and round face. She tugged on the stylish houndstooth blazer she'd matched with a denim shirt and tan pants as she glanced round the entry-way with a critical eye. Her inspection ended with a sniff after she scanned the back of the salon, where the stylists and their customers were chatting and laughing. She crinkled her nose before giving Joanne a fake smile. "Well, I heard today was opening day for your little salon and as a board member for the downtown revitalization committee I had to come by and show my support. I have a brow-waxing appointment with Keisha."

Joanne ignored the "little salon" comment. Mattie loved getting a rise out of people and Joanne wasn't about to give her the satisfaction. Instead, she glanced back at Keisha, who'd just finished a silk press for the client in her seat. "She'll be with you in a moment. Please have a seat." Joanne pointed to one of the plush blue chairs in the waiting area.

"I see timeliness isn't at the forefront here," Mattie mumbled before sitting on the edge of the chair.

Joanne stopped herself from rolling her eyes and looked back at Latasha. "Have a good day, Latasha. I'll see you at your next appointment."

Latasha glanced over at Mattie, then back at Joanne. She looked as if she wanted to hover. Not surprising—when Mattie showed up there was usually drama and Latasha, who was also the editor of the *Peachtree Cove Gazette*, enjoyed drama.

"Um…okay. Thanks, Joanne," she murmured, then was off with a wiggle of her fingers.

Thankfully, Keisha came to the front with her client just as

Latasha walked out. She turned a pleasant smile Mattie's way, but Joanne knew the young stylist well enough to recognize a fake smile from a sincere one.

"I'm ready for you, Ms. Bryant," Keisha said.

Mattie stood slowly and sniffed. "I'm glad I didn't have to wait too long."

Keisha's smile didn't waver. "You're actually here early. But I'm ready for you now. You can come on back."

Keisha headed toward her chair. Mattie followed and Joanne took up the rear. Since Mattie was only there for a brow waxing, Joanne hoped she would be in and out with no problem. Joanne had thirty minutes before her next client, so she swept up the hair around her chair.

"So, Joanne, I hear you're sleeping around with Devante Thompson," Mattie said loudly, not two seconds after she was settled back in the chair and Keisha had slathered wax on her right brow.

A hush fell over the salon as everyone turned to eye Mattie with varying levels of curiosity and disbelief. Not surprising, since that was what Mattie hoped for. Publicly calling out other people had to be one of her kinks.

Taking a calming breath, Joanne stopped sweeping and turned toward Mattie. She gave the woman a pointed stare. "Not that it's any of your business, but yes, we are dating. If that's what you're getting at."

Mattie laughed as if she'd made some great joke. "I never expected you to be the next notch on his bedpost. Really, Joanne, I'm surprised," she said as if she was lecturing a misbehaving child. She tilted her head to the side and pressed a finger to the corner of her mouth. "Though honestly, you were always one to walk on the wild side. Remember when you were messing around with Douglas Stone. Wasn't he married to someone one town over?"

Keisha ripped off the paper on Mattie's brow. Her gasp matched the ones from the other women in the salon. Joanne gripped the broom. Douglas was the last guy she'd openly dated. He hadn't been married, but he'd apparently been hiding a fiancée in Augusta. Mattie knew the other woman and had happily spread the word far and wide. When the other woman found out about Joanne, she'd publicly confronted Joanne when she was out with Julian at the town's Peach Festival and accused her of intentionally going after Douglas. One thing Joanne didn't do was fight over a man. She'd told the woman Douglas was all hers and she wouldn't have to worry about Joanne knocking on his door ever again. Everyone heard and talked about the scene for weeks.

That had been years ago. And while Joanne had never forgotten that Mattie was the one who'd initiated the embarrassing scene, she'd been glad to discover Douglas's true colors before she'd gotten further involved. She'd long since moved on, but, of course, today would be the day Mattie decided to remind everyone in town.

"Do you have a point, Mattie? Or do you get off coming into someone's place of business to spread negativity and lies."

There was no way she was about to show how much Mattie's petty dig had gotten to her. If she let the memory take hold, she would begin to question her decision to date Devante. She wouldn't let the pain of her past relationships have a seat at the table now and ruin her happiness.

Mattie blinked, but her coy smile didn't go away. The door to the salon opened, but Joanne was too focused on the rattlesnake in Keisha's chair to greet the newcomer.

"I'm just saying you have a history. Now you're trying to get your groove back or something. Not that I blame you, but with Devante Thompson, of all people?"

Joanne placed a hand on her hip and glared. "What are you trying to say about Devante?"

Mattie shrugged. "I mean… I give it to him and his sister for trying to dig themselves out of the gutter by starting businesses, but everyone knows their entire family is ghetto." Mattie chuckled as if she'd made a joke, ignoring the fact that no one joined in her laughter. "I wonder what his sister thinks. Knowing a woman older than her is messing with her baby brother."

A woman's angry voice came from the front of the salon. "How about you keep my name and my brother's name out your mouth before you catch these hands. That's what you can wonder about."

A collective gasp went through the room. Joanne spun around and froze. Devante's older sister, Tracey, was standing there, legs spread, hands on her full hips and her normally thick wavy hair braided back. She wore a navy blue polo shirt with the logo of the bed-and-breakfast she'd opened three years before, and she was glaring like a prizefighter. She was flanked by two other women: one tall and curvy, wearing black slacks and a green button-up blouse, and the other of average height and thinner, wearing jeans and a T-shirt with her hair in a messy ponytail. Tracey's two best friends, Halle and Imani.

Joanne's surprise at seeing the trio lasted a second before she focused on the rage simmering in Tracey's eyes. She'd seen that look before. The last thing she needed on her first day open was a fight.

She spun back toward Mattie. "I think it's time for you to go."

Mattie's shock morphed into disbelief. "But she only finished one brow."

Joanne waved off her words. She did not care about Mattie's half-done wax job. "And you started something knowing you were in the middle of a service. You should have saved your comments until after you were done."

Keisha smirked as she put down the waxing stick and stepped back. She crossed her arms and leaned against the counter. Joanne cocked her head to the side and gave Mattie a hurry-up look.

"What? I can't believe you would do this. Kicking out a client without even finishing the work. All I'm trying to do is look out and give a fellow business owner some advice. Do you really think your little shop is going to make it if you don't try to clean up appearances?"

Tracey spoke up again. "My brother is happy. Joanne is happy. Everyone in here is happy except for your hateful ass. Maybe if you met a guy who could give it to you on the regular you wouldn't be here minding other people's business."

Mattie scoffed and jumped up from her seat. Tracey took a step forward. Joanne moved between them. She turned to Mattie. "You really don't want to go there. You've done what you came to do. Stir up trouble. Get out now before you make things worse."

Sputtering, Mattie jerked off the cape and threw it on the floor. "I didn't want anything from your silly little shop, anyway." She raised her chin and stormed out.

The women in the shop burst out laughing and clapped as she left. Joanne's relief at her being gone was palpable, but other concerns wouldn't let her celebrate. More drama, and more stuff for people to talk about. Her perfect opening day would forever be tainted by Mattie's hatefulness.

She met Tracey's eyes, which still simmered from the encounter. Joanne wondered if any of the lingering anger was directed at her. Though Tracey was older than Devante, she was still several years younger than Joanne. She was also fiercely loyal and ready to fight anyone who did her family wrong. And she'd shown up with her friends.

"Can we talk?" Tracey asked.

Joanne nodded. "Sure. We can go outside."

Tracey nodded and turned to walk out. Imani and Halle gave Joanne small, reassuring smiles before they followed. Outside they moved away from the door to stand by Tracey's burgundy minivan. Despite her ride-or-die personality, Tracey had done a good job of separating herself from the wild child she'd once been. Occasional appearances from her fiery temper wouldn't let her completely live it down.

"Is this about Devante?" Joanne asked.

Tracey shook her head. "Not really, but kinda. I was over at the bookstore when I heard Mattie talking on her cell to a friend about coming by your shop. She was saying it was probably a crappy hole-in-the-wall and that she was going to give you a hard time. Especially since you're screwing around with my brother. Well, that made me mad."

Imani nodded and chuckled. "So she called us."

Halle looked at her friends with affection. "And we came to make sure she didn't start any trouble."

Joanne stared at the three women and then shook her head. "Don't tell me The Get Fresh Crew showed up to help me out?" Joanne said, using the nickname the women had used to describe their group when they were teens who picked peaches around town during the summers.

The three friends laughed. "I haven't heard that in forever," Imani said.

"That's because you don't come to town enough," Tracey replied. "They still talk about us."

The three had been best friends growing up. Seeing one usually meant the other two weren't far behind and they always had each other's backs. Imani worked as a doctor in Florida, but was in town for her mother's upcoming wedding, which had been the talk of the town pre-Joanne's scene with Devante. Halle was Peachtree Cove Middle School's vice principal.

"I appreciate you all rolling up," Joanne said. "But I could handle Mattie."

Tracey shrugged again. "I know that, but you're dating Devante. He's been in love with you since forever. Now that you're together, you're family. No one talks about or messes with my family."

Joanne grinned, touched by Tracey's words and the emotions they swirled in her. She'd been prepared to face all of the claims that she was being a fool in love again, or that maybe she was just another notch on Devante's bedpost, because she believed in the emotion in Devante's voice when he spoke to her, and the trust in his eyes when they stared into hers. But having the support of his sister, though—that unexpected action made her throat tighten.

Joanne stepped forward and hugged Tracey. "I'm more than happy to be a part of the family."

nine

Devante took one last look at the setup in the living area of his two-bedroom apartment and wondered if it was too much or not enough. He'd seen a picture online of someone who'd turned their living room into a home theater for a romantic date night and decided to give it a try. He'd blown up an air mattress and laid it before his sofa for plenty of lounging space, hooked up a projector that would display the movie on a screen he'd set up in front of the television and decorated the screen with Christmas lights he'd gotten from his sister. Bowls of popcorn, candy and a meat-and-cheese tray he'd put together himself sat waiting on a platter next to the air mattress.

He thought the setup was nice, but he couldn't get some of the comments on the picture out of his mind. He shouldn't have read the comments. That was his first mistake. There'd been a lot of people who called the idea cheap and stupid. Others said if your partner couldn't afford movie tickets then why date them in the first place. Those comments made him doubt if his idea was a romantic as he'd originally thought, or just tacky.

All he could do now was hope Joanne liked the idea. He'd already invited her to his place to celebrate ending her first full week open, and he didn't want to change their plans. The men she'd dated before him might have turned out to be jerks, but they'd all had one thing in common: class. They'd been college guys or professionals. The type of guys Joanne used to say she wanted to be with. He was proud of being a contractor, but no one would say he was classy. His contracting business was successful, but small. The call for bids on a new state project he'd gone after would help him grow. It was the biggest contract he'd ever sought, but even if he was selected, that wouldn't take away his past or the way people in town, like Mattie, might view him.

A knock on the door broke him from his thoughts. He took a deep breath. The time to change was too late. If she didn't like it, then he'd do what he could to impress her the next time.

He opened the door and Joanne greeted him on the other side with a big smile. "I hope I'm not too early." Her locs were twisted up into a cute style and she was dressed casually in a pair of jeans and a red sweater.

Devante grinned and pulled her into his arms for a huge hug. "You're never too early." He breathed in the lemongrass-and-coconut scent of her lotion and kissed her. He still couldn't believe she was dating him, but he damn sure wouldn't take their time for granted.

"Good, because I was getting ready and could have hung around the house longer, but I was ready to see you."

Her words warmed him faster than a blazing fire. "Same for me. I hope you're ready for a fun night."

"What do you have planned?"

He pulled her in and waved his hand toward the living room. "Ta da! A romantic indoor movie experience."

Joanne's eyes widened and she took in the space. Devante held his breath as she looked over his attempt to be romantic. His anxiety rose with each second she examined the room. Now he couldn't overlook how the Christmas lights drooped a little on one side. The crackers he'd put on the plate weren't arranged perfectly, and he'd gotten the first box of butter crackers he'd seen. Maybe he should have gone for the fancier brand. In fact, maybe he should have ordered a tray from the natural-foods store. Didn't she enjoy natural foods?

"I love this!" Joanne clamped a hand to her heart.

Devante let out a breath. He worried his knees would buckle from his relief. "Really?"

She beamed up at him. "Yes. I saw something like this online a while back. I thought it would be fun to do, but I never got around to setting it up. I wasn't sure if my girlfriends were interested, and well… Julian isn't coming home just to watch movies on an air mattress with his momma."

"Anything you see that you want to try, let me know. I'm always willing to do something new."

Her eyes sparkled. "Don't tease me, because I see a lot of stuff I want to try." She left him to settle onto the air mattress. He'd set it up so they could lean against the couch for support, and he'd put several pillows out to also make the space more comfortable. "What are we watching?"

"*The Photograph*. I heard it was a good romantic movie. Have you seen it?"

She nodded but frowned. "I went to the theater to see it but didn't get to finish."

"Why not?"

She sighed and shrugged. "The person I was with said it was boring and wanted to go. I just never got back to watching it."

"Did you think it was boring?" He grabbed the wine chilling in a bucket off the dinette table that separated the kitchen from the living area and came back to her.

"Nope. I was enjoying the story."

"And they wanted to leave even though you liked it?"

She rolled her eyes and reached for the popcorn. "He was like that. I didn't see him anymore after that."

About Last Night

Devante frowned as he poured wine into the glasses already on the tray table on the air mattress. "Was that that investment guy?"

"You remember him?"

He handed her a glass and met her eye. "Yeah. I remember most of the guys you dated."

She blinked then lowered her eyes. "Keeping a tally?"

He placed a finger under her chin, so she'd meet his eyes again. "Nah, checking out the competition."

That made her smile, and she shook her head. "There is no competition."

"It felt a little like that to me. On the real, the types of guys you dated is one of the reasons I didn't think I stood a chance with you."

"Why? Those guys weren't great. You, on the other hand, are pretty amazing." She leaned forward and kissed him.

Devante wanted to follow her when she pulled back, but instead he sipped his wine. There would be plenty of time to kiss and do all the things he wanted to do with Joanne. He hadn't brought the air mattress out just for lounging.

"Yeah, but those guys were professional, suit-and-tie guys," he said. "I knew you wanted someone who could help take care of you and Julian. You wanted someone stable who would lift you up, not hold you back. I never knew if I'd live up to that."

She scrunched up her nose. "You make me sound a little stuck-up."

He shook his head. "I always understood what you meant. You had enough on your plate taking care of Julian. I knew you didn't want a man who was just going to be like another person to raise."

She sighed and leaned back against his sofa. "I did think I could only get support from a certain type of guy," she said in a considering tone. "I know all successful men aren't jerks. I just happened to end up with a few who were. They thought

I should be thankful if they showed me the slightest bit of interest because I wouldn't be able to do better. Those guys, I quickly tossed aside."

Devante sat next to her on the mattress. He rested an arm on the seat of the sofa and met her eyes. "I want to be a partner to you. I don't want to hold you back. I'm going after this new contract in Augusta. If I get it, I'll finally be the lead contractor on a project and not just a sub. Which means, this will be the most money my business has made. It'll help me be able to give you nice things."

Joanne placed a hand on his cheek. "Devante, I'll be the first one to celebrate if you get the new contract. But only because I'd be proud of you. I'm not looking for someone who can give me nice things. I'm looking for someone who treats me well and who's kind. You've already proven to be both."

Tracey and Joanne had told him about what happened on her opening day. The way Mattie had talked about their family. He didn't expect anything less of Joanne or his sister than for them to stand up for him. But, once again, he'd caused a scene at her shop.

"You mean that?" he asked, hating the uncertainty in his voice.

"More than anything. I'm not chasing money or status. The other day you said you want to be my partner as I grow. Let's be partners as we grow together."

The sincerity in her voice and the affection in her eyes calmed the worry in his heart. "I can't help but think about what Mattie Bryant said at your shop."

She sighed and rolled her eyes. "Mattie's got her own problems and everyone in town knows she's hateful."

"She is, but Mattie isn't the only one in town who still thinks of us as nobodies. That we're pretending to be something we're not."

"Mattie and the people like her are unhappy with their own

lives for whatever reason and try to make other people unhappy. I've never judged you or your family. Lord knows I am not a model of virtuous behavior."

"Hearing people still think like that…it makes me mad that people only see me for where I started and not what I've accomplished. My parents didn't have it easy, and they didn't always know how to make things better, but they loved us…in their own way. I guess those feelings of not being good enough still sit with me sometimes. Makes me want to be more, do more. Makes me want to become so successful they can't say a damn thing about me or my past."

"I get it. I felt that way at first about my new salon. I wanted to be a success with no drama. I worried that people would only see the bad and not my hard work. But guess what, opening day was great, despite Mattie. Everyone who matters supports me. And my work speaks for itself. It did when I was doing hair at a kitchen table, and it matters now. I do what makes me happy. Always have and always will. What makes you happy? Are you only going to be happy if you get this contract and can show people you're worthy? Or will you go after the next contract and the next one?"

He shook his head. "Even if I don't get it, I won't give up. Worked my butt off to one day become the lead contractor. I'm proud of my business."

She patted his chest. "Then that's what matters. Not Mattie, or even me if I were looking for someone to buy me stuff. I like you, Devante. Your kindness, your drive and your determination. Let's do what we both want and grow together."

Devante stared down into Joanne's dark eyes and emotion swelled in his chest. He loved her. Not just the puppy love from before, not the infatuation he'd carried for years. He was in love with this strong, supportive, amazing woman. He wanted to tell her, but knew the time wasn't right. They were just getting started, and she was still learning to trust what they had.

Instead of saying what he felt, he kissed her. The kiss was deep, and before long they were both lost.

When he finally pulled back, her moan made him want to forget the romantic evening he planned and spend the rest of the night making love to her. "The movie," he said in a rumbling voice.

Joanne's wicked smile made his body burn. "Can wait," she whispered against his lips.

That's all he needed to hear.

ten

Joanne swayed to the sounds of the Gregory Porter album as part of her last round of cleaning the shop when someone knocked on the glass door. Although the other stylists and technicians did a good job keeping their areas clean, she always did one final walk-through to check everything and make sure the shop was in top shape before opening the next day. In the month since she'd opened, business had been great. So great she might even be able to reduce the number of heads she styled a day and rent out her booth space to another stylist. Then she could focus solely on running the business, but that was a dream and a thought for another day.

She leaned the broom against her styling chair and sashayed to the door. As expected, Devante stood on the other side of the glass on the sidewalk. It was dark outside, and the streetlights along Main Street, along with the lights from the other shops, cast a golden glow against his skin. She quickly unlocked the door and let him in.

A burst of cool spring air accompanied him as he hurried inside. "Ready to leave?"

She nodded but didn't move to get her stuff. "I am." She

raised her brows and excitedly patted his chest. "So…what happened at the bid opening?"

She was anxious to know the answer. For the last few days he'd been nervous about the bid he submitted. She'd overheard him talking to the people he worked with about their capacity to take on the project. Watched as he'd gone over the list of his equipment and the quantities of materials needed to do the job. He'd put together a competitive bid that wouldn't stretch him and would allow him to do a good job.

He took in a deep breath before placing his hands on her shoulders. "Well, it looks like I'm…"

Joanne raised her brows and waited. When he continued to stare at her without revealing if the news was good or bad, she thought she would burst with anticipation. She gripped his shirt and tried to shake him.

"Looks like you're what? Quit playing with me?"

He laughed and pulled her into his arms for a tight hug. "It looks like I'm the low bidder."

Joanne screamed in excitement and jumped up and down. "See, I told you that you'd get it. I knew you didn't have anything to worry about."

His hands looped around her waist and stopped her celebratory hopping. "I know, but they still have to do a full review of the bids. Make sure I didn't miss anything."

"You didn't. You spent so much time making sure you met all the requirements for the project. I'm not surprised at all."

"It's amazing and kind of unbelievable. I always dreamed of this, but it's still kind of hard to believe, if that makes sense."

"It makes sense. I still have to look around my shop and pinch myself to believe it's real. That something I've dreamed of for so long is actually real."

She pulled away from him and went back to her station. Devante followed her as she took the broom and put it in the storage room.

"You know you don't have to stay here after everyone else leaves and clean up," he said evenly.

Joanne suppressed a chuckle. He didn't like her staying later than everyone else and often came to walk her out whenever he didn't have another job. "I know, but I still like doing it. Cleaning up after the last client was one of my favorite things to do when I was doing hair out of my kitchen."

"Why?" There wasn't any judgment in his voice, just curiosity.

"One, I don't mind cleaning. I enjoy putting things back in order. Two, because when I cleaned up by myself, I could think back on the day and my accomplishments. Back then that was the only way I could make myself feel as if I'd done something worthwhile."

"Do you still need to feel that way?"

She looked around her salon. Clean and ready for the next day. Thought about earlier, with all of the seats filled with clients, the nail technicians busy with manicures and pedicures all day, and the esthetician working on facials and making product recommendations. Her dream was a reality and she'd done that. Something she never thought she'd accomplish back when she was struggling to buy formula and diapers for Julian. When she had to fight his father in court for child-support payments. When people who were supposed to be close to her said her dream was cool and all, but didn't look at her as if she'd really accomplish it.

She looked back at Devante and smiled. "No. Now I like to stick around and just bask in what I've built. I'm so damn proud of this shop. So humbled to see it be successful. I just like being here."

He stood, crossed over to her and wrapped her in his embrace. "Then I won't bother you about sticking around after everyone leaves. You should enjoy and bask in what you've accomplished."

"I'm not just happy about what I did here with the salon. I'm also happy when I'm with you."

"You are?" The way he asked, as if he still couldn't believe she was excited about being with him, was another humbling thing. She never would have believed a man would feel blessed to be with her. She'd internalized the rejections so much she'd lost sight of just how precious she was. That's why it had taken her so long to admit that she wanted to start dating again. She'd been afraid of being rejected and once again shown she wasn't enough. She was deserving of love and affection. She wasn't afraid to admit that anymore, and she wasn't going to let the past stop her from accepting every bit of affection Devante was willing to give.

"I am. I know it's early and we're just starting…but I think I love you." She said the words she'd promised never to say to another man. Every time she said the words, disaster struck. A small part of her heart worried that this would be the breaking point. That Devante would look at her and realize he could find someone younger, prettier, sexier.

Instead, Devante's face filled with such joy it made her heart ache. "I know I love you, Joanne. It started with puppy love, turned into something else. Something I never thought I'd see returned by you, and it's grown into a feeling I can't call anything but love. I love you and I can't believe someone as amazing as you loves me, too."

She lifted on her toes and pressed her lips to his. "Believe it. Otherwise, I'll have to find ways to constantly show you."

"Ways like what?"

She looked at him and grinned. Slipping out of his arms, she went to the front door and flipped the lock. His brows raised as she came back to him and took his hand in hers.

"What are you doing?"

She gave him a wicked smile. "Taking you to the storage room. I'm going to show you just how much I love you as we finish what we started the night of my grand opening."

★ ★ ★ ★ ★

acknowledgments

Thank you to all the family and friends who encouraged me, supported me, and put up with me as I worked on this book during ladies' trips, family trips, and coffee meet ups. Thank you to Ashley, Toya, Tori, KD, Dren, Cheris, Yasmin, Eric, EJ, Sam, Mom, Dad, James, Jayden, Jacob and Timmy. I appreciate each and every one of you.